MAUGHAM'S CHOICE OF KIPLING'S BEST

MAUGHAM'S CHOICE OF KIPLING'S BEST

Sixteen Stories Selected and with an Introductory Essay

by

W. SOMERSET MAUGHAM

Garden City, New York

DOUBLEDAY & COMPANY, INC.

Library of Congress Catalog Card Number 53–7988

First published, 1953, in the United States

PRINTED IN THE UNITED STATES

CONTENTS

INTRODUCTION

In this essay it is my business to deal only with Rudyard Kipling's short stories. I am not concerned with his verse nor, except in so far as they sometimes directly affected his stories, with his political opinions.

In making a selection of them I have had to decide whether I should choose only those I most liked. In that case I should have chosen nearly all the Indian stories. For in them to my mind he was at his best. When he wrote stories about Indians and about the British in India he felt himself at home and he wrote with an ease, a freedom, a variety of invention which gave them a quality which in stories in which the subject matter was different he did not always attain. Even the slightest of them are readable. They give you the tang of the East, the smell of the bazaars, the torpor of the rains, the heat of the sun-scorched earth, the rough life of the barracks in which the occupying troops were quartered, and the other life, so English and yet so alien to the English way, led by the officers, the Indian Civilians and the swarm of minor officials who combined to administer that vast territory.

A great many years ago, when Kipling was still at the height of his popularity, I used sometimes to meet Indian Civilians and professors at Indian universities who spoke of him with something very like contempt. That was partly due to an ignoble but natural jealousy. They resented it that this obscure journalist, of no social consequence, should have achieved world-wide renown. They protested that he did not know India. Which of them did? India is not a country, it is a continent. It is true that Kipling seems to have been intimately acquainted only with the North-West. Like any other sensible writer he placed the scene of his stories in the region he knew best. His Anglo-Indian critics blamed him because he had not dealt with this and that subject which they thought important. His sympathies lay with the Muslims rather than with the Hindus. He took but a very casual interest in Hinduism and the religion which has so deep-rooted an influence on the great mass of the teeming populations of India. There were qualities in the Muslims that aroused his admiration: he seldom spoke of the Hindus with appreciation. It never seems to have occurred to him that there were among them men of erudition, distinguished scientists and able philosophers. The Bengali, for instance, to him was a coward, a muddler, a braggart, who lost his head in an emergency and shirked responsibility. This is a pity, but it was Kipling's right, as it is of every author, to deal with the subjects that appealed to him.

But I felt that if in this volume I confined myself to Kipling's Indian stories I should not give the reader a fair impression of his varied talent. I have therefore included a few stories with an English setting which have been very widely admired.

It is not to my purpose to give more biographical details of Kipling's life than seem to me useful in my consideration of his short stories. He was born in 1865 at Bombay, where his father was Professor of Architectural Sculpture. When a little more than five his parents took him with his younger sister back to England and placed the two of them in a family where, owing to the unkindness and stupidity of the woman who looked after them, they were miserably unhappy. The wretched little boy was nagged, bullied and beaten. When his mother, after some years, once more came home she was deeply shocked by what she discovered and took the two children away. At the age of twelve Kipling was sent to a school at Westward Ho! It was called the United Services College and had been recently founded to provide education at a small cost for the sons of officers who were to be prepared to go into the army. There were about two hundred boys and they were herded together in a row of lodging-houses. Now, what the school was really like has nothing to do with me; I am only concerned with the picture Kipling has drawn of it in the work of fiction to which he gave the title *Stalky & Co.* A more odious picture of school life can seldom have been drawn. With the exception of the headmaster and the chaplain the masters are represented as savage, brutal, narrow-minded and incompetent. The boys, supposedly the sons of gentlemen, were devoid of any decent instincts. To the three lads with whom these stories deal Kipling gave the names of Stalky, Turkey and Beetle. Stalky was the ringleader. He remained Kipling's ideal of the gallant, resourceful, adventurous, high-spirited soldier and gentleman. Beetle was Kipling's portrait of himself. The three of them exercised their humour in practical jokes of a singular nastiness. Kipling has narrated them with immense gusto and it is only just to say that the stories are so brilliantly told that though it may give you gooseflesh to read them, when you have once begun you will read them to the end. I should not have dwelt on them at all if it were not plain to me that the influences Kipling was exposed to during the four years he spent at what he called 'the Coll' gained a hold on him which throughout his career he never outgrew. He was never quite able to rid himself of the impressions, the prejudices, the spiritual posture he then acquired. Indeed there is no sign that he wanted to. He retained to the end his relish for the rough and tumble, the ragging, the brutal horseplay of fourth-form schoolboys and their delight in practical jokes. It never seems to have occurred to him that the school was third-rate and the boys a rotten lot. In fact after visiting it many years later he wrote a charming account of it, in which he paid a glowing tribute to that harsh disciplinarian, his old headmaster, and expressed his gratitude for the great benefits he had received during the period he had spent under his care.

When Kipling was a little less than seventeen, his father, who was then curator of the museum at Lahore, got him a job as assistant editor of the English paper, *The Civil and Military Gazette,* which was published in that city, and he left school to return to India. This was in 1882. The world he entered was very different from the world we live in now. Great Britain was at the height of her power. A map showed in pink vast stretches of the earth's surface under the sovereignty of Queen Victoria. The mother country was immensely rich. The British were the world's bankers. British commerce sent its products to the uttermost parts of the earth, and their quality was generally acknowledged to be higher than those manufactured by any other nation. Peace reigned except for small punitive expeditions here and there. The army, though small, was confident (notwithstanding the reverse on Majuba Hill) that it could hold its own against any force that was likely to be brought against it. The British navy was the greatest in the world. In sport the British were supreme. None could compete with them in the games they played, and in the classic races it was almost unheard-of that a horse from abroad should win. It looked as though nothing could ever change this happy state of things. The inhabitants of these islands of ours trusted in God, and God, they were assured, had taken the British Empire under his particular protection. It is true that the Irish were making a nuisance of themselves. It is true that the factory workers were underpaid and overworked. But that seemed an inevitable consequence of the industrialisation of the country and there was nothing to do about it. The reformers who tried to improve their lot were regarded as mischievous troublemakers. It is true that the agricultural labourers lived in miserable hovels and earned a pitiful wage, but the Ladies Bountiful of the landowners were kind to them. Many of them occupied themselves with their moral welfare, sent them beef tea and calves-foot jelly when they were ill and often clothes for their children. People said there always had been rich and poor in the world and always would be, and that seemed to settle the matter.

The British travelled a great deal on the Continent. They crowded the health resorts, Spa, Vichy, Homburg, Aix-les-Bains and Baden-Baden. In winter they went to the Riviera. They built themselves sumptuous villas at Cannes and Monte Carlo. Vast hotels were erected to accommodate them. They had plenty of money and they spent it freely. They felt that they were a race apart and no sooner had they landed at Calais than it was borne in upon them that they were now among natives, not of course natives as were the Indians or the Chinese, but—natives. They alone washed, and the baths that they frequently travelled with were a tangible proof that they were not as others. They were healthy, athletic, sensible, and in every way superior. Because they enjoyed their sojourn among the natives whose habits were so curiously un-English, because, though they thought them frivolous (the French), lazy (the Italians), stupid but funny (the Germans), with the kindness of heart natural to them, they liked them. And they in turn thought that these foreigners liked them. It never entered their heads that the courtesy which they received, the bows, the smiles, the desire to please were owing to their lavish spending, and that behind their backs the 'natives' mocked them for their uncouth dress, their gawkiness, their bad manners, their insolence, their silliness in letting themselves be consistently overcharged, their patronising tolerance; and it required disastrous wars for it to dawn upon them how greatly they had been mistaken. The Anglo-Indian society into which Kipling was introduced when he joined his parents at Lahore shared to the full the prepossessions and the self-complacency of their fellow-subjects in Britain.

Since his short sight prevented him from playing games, Kipling had had the leisure at school to read a great deal and to write. The headmaster seems to have been impressed by the promise he showed and had the good sense to give him the run of his own library. He wrote the stories which he afterwards published in book form as *Plain Tales from the Hills* during such leisure as his duties as sub-editor of *The Civil and Military Gazette* allowed him. To me their chief interest is in the picture they give of the society with which he was dealing. It is a devastating one. There is no sign that any of the persons he wrote about took any interest in art, literature or music.

The notion seems to have been prevalent that there was something fishy about a man who took pains to learn about things Indian. Of one character Kipling wrote: 'he knew as much about Indians as it is good for a man to know.' A man who was absorbed in his work appears to have been regarded with misgiving; at best he was eccentric, at worst a bore. The life described was empty and frivolous. The self-sufficiency of these people is fearful to contemplate. And what sort of people were they? They were ordinary middle-class people, who came from modest homes in England, sons and daughters of retired government servants and of parsons, doctors and lawyers. The men were empty-headed; such of them as were in the army or had been to universities had acquired a certain polish; but the women were shallow, provincial and genteel. They spent their time in idle flirtation and their chief amusement seems to have been to get some man away from another woman. Perhaps because Kipling wrote in a prudish period which made him afraid of shocking his readers, perhaps from an innate disinclination to treat of sex, though in these stories there is a great deal of philandering, it very rarely led to sexual intercouse. Whatever encouragement these women gave the men whom they attracted, when it came to a showdown they drew back. They were, in short, what is described in English by a coarse hyphenated word, and in France, more elegantly, by *allumeuses.*

It is surprising that Kipling, with his quick mind and wonderful power of observation, with his wide reading, should have taken these people at their face value. He was, of course, very young. *Plain Tales from the Hills* was published when he was only twenty-two. It is perhaps natural that, coming straight from the brutalities of Westward Ho! to the unpretentious establishment of the curator of the Lahore museum, he should have been dazzled on his first acquaintance with a society that to his inexperienced eyes had glamour. So was the little bourgeois Marcel dazzled when he first gained admittance to the exclusive circle of Madame de Guermantes. Mrs. Hauksbee was neither so brilliant nor so witty as Kipling would have us think. He reveals her essential drabness when he makes her compare a woman's voice to the grinding brakes of an underground train coming into Earl's Court station. We are asked to believe that she was a woman of fashion. If she had been she would never have gone to Earl's Court except to see an old nurse and then not by underground, but in a hansom cab.

But *Plain Tales from the Hills* is not only concerned with Anglo-Indian society. The volume contains stories of Indian life and stories of the soldiery. When you consider that they were written when their author was still in his teens or only just out of them they show an astonishing competence. Kipling said that the best of them were provided for him by his father. I think we may ascribe this statement to filial piety. I believe it to be very seldom that an author can make use of a story given to him ready made, as seldom indeed as a person in real life can be transferred to fiction just as he is and maintain an air of verisimilitude. Of course the author gets his ideas from somewhere, they don't spring out of his head like Pallas-Athene from the head of her sire in perfect panoply, ready to be written down. But it is curious how small a hint, how vague a suggestion, will be enough to give the author's invention the material to work upon and enable him in due course to construct a properly disposed story. Take, for instance, the later story, *The Tomb of his Ancestors*. It may very well have needed no more than such a casual remark from one of the officers Kipling had known at Lahore as: 'Funny chaps these natives are. There was a feller called So-and-So who was stationed up country among the Bhils, whose grandfather had kept them in order for donkeys' years and was buried there, and they got it into their thick heads that he was a reincarnation of the old man, and he could do anything he liked with them.' That would have been quite enough to set Kipling's vivid imagination to work upon what turned out to be an amusing and delightful tale. *Plain Tales from the Hills* is very uneven, as indeed Kipling's work always was. That I believe to be inevitable in a writer of short stories. It is a ticklish thing to write a short story and whether it is good or bad depends on more than the author's conception, power of expression, skill in construction, invention and imagination: it depends also on luck. So the clever Japanese, taking from his little pile of seed pearls, all to his eyes indistinguishable from one another, the first that comes to hand and inserting it into the oyster, cannot tell whether it will turn into a perfect, rounded pearl or a misshapen object neither of beauty nor of value. Nor is the author a good judge of his own work. Kipling had a high opinion of *The Phantom 'Rickshaw*. I think if he had been more sophisticated when he wrote it, it might have occurred to him that there was more to be said in extenuation of the man's behaviour than he apprehended. It is very unfortunate that you should fall out of love with a married woman with whom you have had an affair and fall in love with someone else and want to marry her. But such things happen. And when the woman won't accept the situation, but pursues you and waylays you and pesters you with tears and supplications it is not unnatural that at last you should grow impatient and lose your temper. Mrs.

Keith-Wessington is the most persistent *crampon* in fiction, for even after her death she continued to harry the wretched man in her phantom 'rickshaw. Jack Pansay deserves our sympathy rather than our censure. Because a story has been difficult to write an author may well think better of it than of a story that has seemed to write itself, sometimes there is a psychological error at the basis of it which he has not noticed, and sometimes he sees in the finished story what he saw in his mind's eye when he conceived it rather than what he has presented to the reader. But we should not be surprised that Kipling sometimes wrote stories which were poor, unconvincing or trivial; we should wonder rather that he wrote so many of such excellence. He was wonderfully various.

In the essay Mr. T. S. Eliot wrote to preface his selection of Kipling's verse he seems to suggest that variety is not a laudable quality in a poet. I would not venture to dispute any opinion of Mr. Eliot's on a question in which poetry is concerned, but though variety may not be a merit in a poet, it surely is in a writer of fiction. The good writer of fiction has the peculiarity, shared to a degree by all men, but in him more abundant, that he has not only one self, but is a queer mixture of several, or, if that seems an extravagant way of putting it, that there are several, often discordant aspects of his personality. The critics could not understand how the same man could write '*Brugglesmith*' and *Recessional,* and so accused him of insincerity. They were unjust. It was the self called Beetle who wrote '*Brugglesmith*' and the self called Yardley-Orde who wrote *Recessional.* When most of us look back on ourselves we can sometimes find consolation in believing that a self in us which we can only deplore has, generally through no merit of ours, perished. The strange thing about Kipling is that the self called Beetle which one would have thought increasing age and the experience of life would have caused to disintegrate, remained alive in all its strength almost to his dying day.

As a child at Bombay Kipling had spoken Hindustani with his ayah and the servants as his native language and in *Something of Myself* he has told that when he was taken to see his parents he translated what he had to say into broken English. It may be supposed that on his return to India he quickly recovered his old knowledge of the language. In the same book he has related in terms that couldn't be bettered how at Lahore he got the material which so soon afterwards he was to make effective use of. As a reporter 'I described openings of big bridges and such-like, which meant a night or two with the engineers; floods on railways—more nights in the wet with wretched heads of repair gangs; village festivals and consequent outbreaks of cholera or small-pox; communal riots under the shadow of the Mosque of Wazir Khan, where the patient waiting troops lay in timber-yards or side-alleys till the order came to go in and hit the crowds on the feet with the gun-butt, and the growling, flaring, creed-drunk city would be brought to hand without effusion of blood' . . . Often at night 'I would wander till dawn in all manner of odd places—liquor-shops, gambling- and opium-dens, which are not a bit mysterious, wayside entertainments such as puppet-shows, native dances; or in and about the narrow gullies under the Mosque of Wazir Khan for the sheer sake of looking . . . And there were "wet" nights too at the Club or one Mess, when a tableful of boys, half crazed with discomfort, but with just sense enough to stick to beer and bones which seldom betray, tried to rejoice and somehow succeeded . . . I got to meet the soldiery of those days in visits to Fort Lahore and, in a less degree, at Mian Mir Cantonments. . . . Having no position to consider, and my trade enforcing it, I could move at will in the fourth dimension. I came to realize the bare horrors of the private's life, and the unnecessary torments he endured on account of the Christian doctrine that lays it down that "the wages of sin is death." '

I have included in this selection two stories in which figure the three privates, Mulvaney, Learoyd and Ortheris. They have been immensely popular. I think they have the disadvantage for most readers that they are written in the peculiar dialect of the speakers. It is no easy matter to decide how far an author should go in this direction. Manifestly it would be absurd to make men like Mulvaney and Ortheris deliver themselves in the cultured language of a don at King's, but to make them speak consistently in dialect may well make a narrative tedious. Perhaps the best plan is to use the turns of phase, the grammar and the vocabulary of the persons concerned, but to reproduce peculiarities of pronunciation so sparingly as not to incommode the reader. That was not, however, Kipling's way. He reproduced the accents of his three soldiers phonetically. No one has found fault with Learoyd's Yorkshire, which was corrected by Kipling's father, himself a Yorkshireman; but critics have claimed that neither Mulvaney's Irish nor Ortheris's cockney was real. Kipling was a master of description and could relate incident brilliantly, but it does not seem to me that his dialogue was always plausible. He put into the mouth of Ortheris expressions he could never have used and one may well ask oneself how on earth he came by a quotation from Macaulay's *Lays of Ancient Rome*. I cannot believe that a well-bred woman such as the

Brushwood Boy's mother is supposed to be would speak to him of his father as 'the pater.' Sometimes the language used by the officers and officials in India is unconvincingly hearty. To my mind Kipling's dialogue is only beyond reproach when he is translating into measured, dignified English the speech of Indians. The reader will remember that as a child talking with his parents he had to translate what he had to say from Hindustani into English: it may be that that was the form of speech that came most naturally to him.

In 1887 Kipling, after five years as sub-editor of *The Civil and Military Gazette,* was sent to Allahabad, several hundred miles to the south, to work on the much more important sister-paper, *The Pioneer.* The proprietors were starting a weekly edition for home, and he was given the editorship. An entire page was devoted to fiction. The *Plain Tales from the Hills* had been restricted to twelve hundred words, but now he was allotted sufficient space to write stories up to five thousand. He wrote 'soldier tales, Indian tales, and tales of the opposite sex.' Among them were such powerful but gruesome stories as *The Mark of the Beast* and *The Return of Imray.*

The stories Kipling wrote during this period were published in six paper-covered volumes in Wheeler's Indian Railway Library, and with the money he thus earned and a commission to write travel sketches he left India for England 'by way of the Far East and the United States.' This was in 1889. He had spent seven years in India. His stories had become known in England and when he arrived in London, still a very young man, he found editors eager to accept whatever he wrote. He settled down in Villiers Street, Strand. The stories he produced there are of the highest quality, a quality which later he often achieved but never surpassed. Among them are *On Greenhow Hill, The Courting of Dinah Shadd, The Man Who Was, Without Benefit of Clergy* and *At the End of the Passage.* It looks as though the new surroundings in which he found himself brought into greater vividness his recollections of India. That is a likely enough thing to happen. When an author is living in the scene of his story, perhaps among the people who have suggested the characters of his invention, he may well find himself bewildered by the mass of his impressions. He cannot see the wood for the trees. But absence will erase from his memory redundant details and inessential facts. He will get then a bird's-eye view, as it were, of his subject and so, with less material to embarrass him, can get the form into his story which completes it.

It was then too that he wrote the tale which he called '*The Finest Story in the World.*' It is interesting because he dealt in it, for the first time, I think, with metempsychosis. It was natural that the theme should interest him, for the belief in it is ingrained in the Hindu sensibility. It is as little a matter of doubt to the people of India as were the Virgin Birth of Christ and the Resurrection to the Christians of the thirteenth century. No one can have travelled in India without discovering how deep-rooted the belief is not only among the uneducated, but among men of culture and of experience in world affairs. One hears in conversation, or reads in the papers, of men who claim to remember something of their past lives. In this story Kipling has dealt with it with great imaginative power. He returned to it in a story which is less well-known called *'Wireless.'* In this he made effective use of what was then a new toy for the scientifically minded amateur to persuade the reader of the possibility that the chemist's assistant of his tale, dying of tuberculosis, might under the effect of a drug recall that past life of his in which he was John Keats. To anyone who has stood in the little room in Rome overlooking the steps that lead down to the Piazza di Spagna and seen the drawing Joseph Severn made of the emaciated, beautiful head of the dead poet, Kipling's story is wonderfully pathetic. It is thrilling to watch the dying chemist's assistant, in love too, worrying out in a trance-like state, lines that Keats wrote in *The Eve of St. Agnes.* It is a lovely story admirably told.

Six years later Kipling, in the entrancing tale *The Tomb of his Ancestors,* to which I have already referred, took up once more the theme of metempsychosis and this time in such a way as not to outrage probability. It is the Bhils, the mountain tribes among whom the story is set, who believe that the young subaltern, its hero, is a reincarnation of his grandfather who spent many years in their midst and whose memory they still revere. It is here for the reader to read and enjoy so I need say no more about it. Kipling never succeeded better in creating that indefinable quality which for want of a better word we call atmosphere.

After spending two years in London, years of hard work, Kipling's health broke down, and he very sensibly decided to take the rest of a long journey. He returned to England to be married and with his bride started off on a tour of the world, but financial difficulties obliged him to cut it short, and he settled down in Vermont where his wife's family had long been established. This was in the summer of 1892. He stayed there off and on till 1896. During those four years he wrote a number of stories many of which were of a quality which only he could reach. It was then that he wrote *In the Rukh* in which Mowgli makes his first appearance. It was a propitious inspiration, for from it sprang the two *Jungle Books* in which, to my mind, his great and varied gifts found their most brilliant expression. They show his wonderful talent for telling a story, they have a delicate humour and they are romantic and plausible. The device of making animals talk is as old as Aesop's fables, and for all I know much older, and La Fontaine, as we know, employed it with charm and wit, but I think no one has performed the difficult feat of persuading the reader that it is as natural for animals to speak as for human beings more triumphantly than Kipling has done in *The Jungle Books.* He had used the same device in the story called *A Walking Delegate* in which horses indulge in political discussion, but there is in the story an obviously didactic element which prevents it from being successful.

It was during these fertile years that Kipling wrote *The Brushwood Boy,* a story which has deeply impressed so many people that, though it is not one of my favourites, I have thought it well to print it in this selection. He availed himself in this of a notion which has attracted writers of fiction both before and after him, the notion, namely, of two persons systematically dreaming the same dreams. The difficulty of it lies in making the dreams interesting. We listen restlessly when someone at the breakfast table insists on telling us of the dream he had during the night, and a dream described on paper is apt to arouse in us the same impatience. Kipling had before done the same sort of thing, though on a smaller scale, in *The Bridge-Builders.* There I think he made a mistake. He had a good story to tell. It is about a flood that suddenly rushes down on a bridge over the Ganges which, after three years of strenuous labour, is on the point of completion. There is doubt in the minds of the two white men in charge of the operations whether three of the spans, still unfinished, will stand the strain, and they fear that if the stone-boats go adrift the girders will be damaged. They have received by telegram warning that the flood is on the way, and with their army of workmen spend an agonized night doing what they can to strengthen the weak places. All this is described with force and the telling detail of which Kipling was a master. The bridge stands the strain and all is well. That is all. It may be that Kipling thought is wasn't enough. Findlayson, the chief engineer, has been too anxious and too fully occupied to bother about eating anything and by the second night is all in. His lascar aide persuades him to swallow some opium pills. Then news comes that a wire hawser has snapped and the stone-boats are loose. Findlayson and the lascar rush down to the bank and get into one of the stone-boats in the hope of preventing them from doing irreparable injury. The pair are swept down the river and landed half-drowned on an island. Exhausted and doped they fall asleep and dream the same dream in which they see the Hindu Gods in animal form, Ganesh the elephant, Hanuman the ape and finally Krishna himself, and hear them talk. When the two wake in the morning they are rescued. But the double dream is needless and because the conversation of the Gods is needless too it is tedious.

In *The Brushwood Boy* the identical dreams are an essential element in the story. It is here for the reader to read and I hope he will agree with me that Kipling has described these dreams with felicity. They are strange, romantic, frightening and mysterious. The long series of dreams which these two people have shared from their childhood seems, though you don't quite know why, so significant of something of high import that it is somewhat of a disappointment that such amazing occurrences should result in no more than 'boy meets girl.' It is of course the same difficulty that confronts the reader of the first part of Goethe's *Faust*. It seems hardly worth while for Faust to have bartered his soul to see Mephistopheles do conjuring tricks in a wine-cellar and to effect the seduction of a lowly maid. I find it difficult to look upon *The Brushwood Boy* as one of Kipling's best stories. The persons concerned in it are really too good to be true. The Brushwood Boy is heir to a fine estate. He is idolized by his parents, by the keeper who taught him to shoot, by the servants, by the tenants. He is a good shot, a good rider, a hard worker, a brave soldier adored by his men, and after a battle on the North-West Frontier is awarded a D.S.O. and becomes the youngest major in the British army. He is clever, sober and chaste. He is perfect and incredible. But though I carp I cannot deny that it remains a good and moving story admirably told. One must look upon it not as a tale that has any relation to real life, but as much of a fairy story as *The Sleeping Beauty* or *Cinderella*.

It was on his short periods of leave that Kipling came to know that Anglo-Indian society which he wrote about in *Plain Tales from the Hills,* but his experiences as a reporter, so well set forth in the passage I quoted earlier in this essay, surely made it plain to him that in those little stories he had described but one aspect of Anglo-Indian life. What he saw on his various assignments deeply impressed him. I have already spoken of *The Bridge-Builders* with its fine account of those men who on little pay, with small chance of recognition, gave their youth, their strength, their health to do to the best of their ability the job it was their business to do. In the unfortunately named *William the Conqueror* Kipling has written a tale in which he shows how two or three ordinary, rather commonplace men, and a woman, the William of the story, fought a disastrous famine all through the hot weather and saved a horde of children from dying of starvation. It is a tale of selfless, stubborn tenacity soberly narrated. In these two stories and in several more, Kipling has told of the obscure men and women who devoted their lives to the service of India. They made many mistakes, for they were but human. Many were stupid. Many were hidebound with prejudice. Many were unimaginative. They kept the peace. They administered justice. They built the roads, the bridges, the railways. They fought famine, flood and pestilence. They treated the sick. It remains to be seen whether those who have succeeded them, not in high place, but in those modest situations in the hands of whose occupants the lot of the common man depends will make as good a job of it as they did.

William the Conqueror is not only the story of a famine; it is a love story as well. I have mentioned the fact that Kipling seems to have shied away, like an unbroken colt, from any treatment of sex. In the Mulvaney stories he makes casual reference to the amours of the soldiery and in *Something of Myself* he has an indignant passage in which he remarks on the stupid and criminal folly of the authorities who counted it impious 'that bazaar prostitutes should be inspected; or that the men should be taught elementary precautions in their dealings with them. This official virtue cost our army in India nine thousand expensive white men a year always laid up from venereal disease.' But he is concerned then not with love, but with an instinct of normal man that demands its satisfaction. I can only remember two stories in which Kipling has attempted (successfully) to represent passion. One is *'Love-o'-Women,'* which for this reason I have inserted in this book. It is a terrible, perhaps brutal story, but it is finely and vigorously told, and the end, mysterious and left unexplained though it be, is powerful. Critics have found fault with this end. Matisse once showed a picture of his to a visitor who exclaimed: 'I've never seen a woman like that', to which he replied: 'It isn't a woman, madam, it's a picture.' If the painter is permitted certain distortions to achieve the effect he is aiming at, there can be no reason why the writer of fiction should not accord himself the same freedom. Probability is not something settled once for all; it is what you can get your readers to accept as such. Kipling was not writing an official report, he was writing a story. It was his right to make it dramatically effective, if that is what he wanted to do, and if the gentleman-ranker of the story might not have said in real life to the woman he had seduced and ruined the words Kipling has put into his mouth, that is no matter. It is plausible and the reader is moved as Kipling intended him to be.

The other story in which Kipling has depicted genuine passion is *Without Benefit of Clergy*. It is a beautiful and pathetic tale. If I had to choose for an anthology the best story Kipling ever wrote, this I believe is the one I would choose. Other stories are more characteristic, *The Head of the District*, for instance, but in this one he has come as near as the medium allows to what the story-teller aims at, but can hardly hope to achieve—perfection.

I have been led to write the above on account of the love scene which gives *William the Conqueror* its happy ending. It is strangely embarrassing. The two persons concerned are in love with one another; that is made clear; but there is nothing of ecstasy in their love, it is a rather humdrum affair, with already a kind of domestic quality about it. They are two very nice sensible people who will make a good job of married life. The love scene is adolescent. You would expect a schoolboy home for the holidays to talk like that with the local doctor's young daughter, not two grown, efficient persons who have just gone through a harrowing and dangerous experience.

As a rough generalization I would suggest that an author reaches the height of his powers when he is between thirty-five and forty. It takes him till then to learn what Kipling made a point of calling his trade. Till then his work is immature, tentative and experimental. By profiting by past mistakes, by the mere process of living, which brings him experience and a knowledge of human nature, by discovering his own limitations and learning what subjects he is competent to deal with and how best to deal with them, he acquires command over his medium. He is in possession of such talent as he has. He will produce the best work he is capable of for perhaps fifteen years, for twenty if he is lucky, and then his powers gradually dwindle. He loses the vigour of imagination which he had in his prime. He has given all he had to give. He will go on writing, for writing is a habit easy to contract, but hard to break, but what he writes will be only an increasingly pale reminder of what he wrote at his prime.

It was different with Kipling. He was immensely precocious. He was in full possession of his powers almost from the very beginning. Some of the stories in *Plain Tales from the Hills* are so trivial that later in life he would probably not have thought them worth writing, but they are told clearly, vividly and effectively. Technically there is no fault to find with them. Such faults as they have are owing to the callowness of his youth and not to his want of skill. And when, only just out of his teens, he was transferred to Allahabad and was able to express himself at greater length he wrote a series of tales which can justly be described as masterly. On his first arrival in London, the editor of *Macmillan's Magazine,* whom he had gone to see, asked him how old he was. It is no wonder that when Kipling told him that in a few months he would be twenty-four, he cried 'My God!' His accomplishment by then was truly amazing.

But all things have to be paid for in this world. By the end of the century, that is by the time Kipling was thirty-five, he had written his best stories. I do not mean that after that he wrote bad stories, he couldn't have done that if he'd tried, they were well enough in their way, but they lacked the magic with which the early Indian stories had been infused. It was only when, returning in fancy to the scene of his early life in India, he wrote *Kim,* that he regained it. *Kim* is his masterpiece. It must seem strange at first that Kipling after leaving Allahabad never went back to India except for a short visit to his parents at Lahore. After all it was his Indian stories that had brought him his immense fame. He himself called it notoriety, but it was fame. I can only suppose that he felt India had given him all the subjects he could deal with. Once, after he had spent a period in the West Indies he sent me a message to say that I should do well to go there, for there were plenty of stories to be written about the people of the islands, but they were not the sort of stories he could write. He must have felt that there were plenty of stories in India besides those he had written, but that they too were not the sort of stories he could write. For him the vein was worked out.

The Boer War came to pass and Kipling went to South Africa. In India he had conceived a boyish, touching if rather absurd admiration for the officers with whom he was brought in contact. But these gallant gentlemen who cut so fine a figure on the polo field, at gymkhanas, dances and picnics, showed a horrifying incapacity when it came to waging a war very different from the punitive expeditions they had conducted on the North-West Frontier. Officers and men were as brave as he had always thought them, but they were ill led. He surveyed the muddle of that unhappy war with consternation. Did he see that this was the first rent in that great fabric, the British Empire, which was his pride and to the awareness of which he had done so much, in verse and prose, to awaken his fellow-subjects? He wrote two stories, *The Captive* and *The Way that He Took,* in which he attacked the inefficiency of the authorities at home and the incompetence of the officers in command. They are good stories, and if I have not given them a place in this volume it is because of the strong element of propaganda in them and because like all stories that have a topical interest the passage of time has deprived them of significance.

I should warn the reader that my opinion that Kipling's best stories are those of which the scene is laid in India is by no means shared by eminent critics. They think those Kipling wrote in what they call his third period show a depth, an insight and a compassion of which they deplore the lack in his Indian tales. For them the height of his achievement is to be found in such stories as *An Habitation Enforced, A Madonna of the Trenches, The Wish House* and *Friendly Brook. An Habitation Enforced* is a charming story, but surely rather obvious; and though the other three are good enough they do not seem to me remarkable. It did not need an author of Kipling's great gifts to write them. *Just So Stories, Puck of Pook's Hill* and *Rewards and Fairies* are children's books and their worth must be judged by the pleasure they afforded children. This *Just So Stories* must have done. One can almost hear the squeals of laughter with which they listened to the story of how the elephant got his trunk. In the two other books Puck appears to a little boy and a little girl and produces for their instruction various characters by means of whom they may gain an elementary and romantic acquaintance with English history. I don't think this was a happy device. The stories are of course well contrived; I like best *On the Great Wall,* in which Parnesius, the Roman legionary, appears, but I should have liked it better if it had been a straightforward reconstruction of an episode in the Roman occupation of Britain.

The only story Kipling wrote after he settled down in England that I would on no account leave out of this selection is *'They.'* (In reading it you must keep in mind that his use of the House Beautiful for the country house in which the events he relates take place, reminding one of Ye Olde Tea-Shoppe and horrors of the same sort, had not been made obnoxious by the vulgar purveyors of whimsy and the pretty-pretty.) *'They'* is a fine and deeply moving effort of the imagination. In 1899 Kipling went with his wife and children to New York, and he and his elder daughter caught colds which turned into pneumonia. Those of us who are old enough can remember the world-wide concern when the cables told us that Kipling lay at death's door. He recovered, but his daughter died. It cannot be doubted that *'They'* was inspired by his enduring grief at her loss. Heine said: 'Out of my great griefs I make these little songs.' Kipling wrote an exquisite story. Some people have found it obscure and others sentimental. One of the hazards that confront the writer of fiction is the danger of slipping from sentiment into sentimentality. The distinction between the two is fine. It may be that sentimentality is merely sentiment that you don't happen to like. Kipling had the gift of drawing tears, but sometimes, in his stories not for children, but about children, they are tears you resent, for the emotion that draws them is mawkish. There is nothing obscure in *'They'* and to my mind nothing sentimental.

Kipling was deeply interested in the inventions and discoveries which were then transforming our civilization. The reader will remember what effective use he made of wireless in the story of that name. He was fascinated by machines and when he was fascinated by a subject he wrote stories about it. He took a great deal of trouble to get his facts right, and if sometimes he made mistakes, as all authors do, the facts were so unfamiliar to most readers that they did not know. He indulged in technical details for their own sake, not to show off, since though argumentative and self-opinionated as a man, he was modest and unassuming as an author, but for the fun of it. He was like a concert pianist rejoicing in the brilliant ease of his execution who chooses a piece not because of its musical value, but because it gives him an opportunity to exercise his special gift. In one of his stories Kipling says that he had to interrupt the narrator over and over again to ask him to explain his technical terms. The reader of these stories, and he wrote a number of them, unable to do this, remains perplexed. They would be more readable if their author had been less meticulous. In *'Their Lawful Occasions,'* for instance, I surmise that only a naval officer could fully understand what goes on, and I am quite prepared to believe that *he* would find it a jolly good yarn. .007 is a story about a locomotive, *The Ship that Found Herself,* a story about an ocean tramp; I think you would have to be respectively an engine-driver and a ship-builder to read them with comprehension. In *The Jungle Books,* and indeed in *The Maltese Cat,* Kipling made the various animals concerned talk in a highly convincing manner; he used the same device in the locomotive numbered .007 and in the ship named *Dimbula.* I do not think with advantage. I cannot believe that the ordinary reader knows (or cares) what a garboard strake is, or a bilge-stringer, a high-pressure cylinder or a web-frame.

These stories show another side of Kipling's varied talent, but I have not thought it necessary to include any of them in this selection. The object of fiction (from the reader's standpoint from which the author's may often be very different) is entertainment; and as such to my mind their value is small.

I have been more doubtful about those stories concerned with practical joking, ragging, and drunkenness which he wrote from time to time. There was a Rabelaisian streak in him which the hypocrisy of the times, with its deliberate turning away from what are known as the facts of life, constrained him to express in the description of horse-play and inebriation. In *Something of Myself* he tells how he showed a story about the 'opposite sex' to his mother, who 'abolished it' and wrote to him: 'Never you do that again.' From the context one may conclude that it dealt with adultery. Whether you find drunkenness amusing depends, I suppose, on your personal idiosyncrasies. It has been my ill-fortune to live much among drunkards, and for my part I have found them boring at their best and disgusting at their worst. But it is evident that this feeling of mine is rare. That stories dealing with drunkards have a strong allure is shown by the popularity of Brugglesmith, a crapulous ruffian, and of Pyecroft, a sottish petty officer, who amused Kipling so much that he wrote several tales about him. Practical joking, till the very recent past, seems to have had an appeal that was universal. Spanish literature of the Golden Age is full of it and everyone remembers the cruel practical jokes that were played on Don Quixote. In the Victorian Age it was still thought funny and from a recently published book we may learn that it was practised with delight in the highest circles. Here again it depends on your temperament whether it amuses you or whether it doesn't. I must confess that I read Kipling's stories which deal with this subject with discomfort. And the hilarity which overcomes the perpetrators of the exploit grates upon me; they are not content with laughing at the humiliation of their victim; they lean against one another helpless with laughter, they roll off their chairs, they collapse shrieking, they claw the carpet; and in one story the narrator takes a room at an inn so that he may have his laugh out. There is only one of these tales that I have found frankly amusing and since I thought it only right to give the reader at least one example of this kind of story I have printed it in this volume. It is called *The Village that Voted the Earth Was Flat*. Here the comedy is rich, the victim deserves his punishment, and his punishment is severe without being brutal.

I have in this essay only referred casually to Kipling's success. It was enormous. Nothing like it had been seen since Dickens took the reading world by storm with *The Pickwick Papers*. Nor did he have to wait for it. Already in 1890 Henry James was writing to Stevenson that Kipling, 'the star of the hour,' was Stevenson's nearest rival and Stevenson was writing to Henry James that Kipling was 'too clever to live.' It looks as though they were both a trifle taken aback by the appearance of this 'infant monster' as James called him. They acknowledged his brilliant parts, but with reservations. 'He amazes me by his precocity and various endowment,' wrote Stevenson. 'But he alarms me by his copiousness and haste. . . . I was never capable of—and surely never guilty of—such a debauch of production . . . I look on, I admire, I rejoice for myself; but in a kind of ambition we all have for our tongue and literature I am wounded. . . . Certainly Kipling has gifts; the fairy godmothers were all tipsy at his christening: what will he do with them?'

But copiousness is not a defect in a writer; it is a merit. All the greatest authors have had it. Of course all their production is not of value; only the mediocre can sustain a constant level. It is because the great authors wrote a great deal that now and then they produced great works. Kipling was no exception. I don't believe any writer is a good judge of the writing of his contemporaries, for he naturally likes best the sort of thing he does himself. It is difficult for him to appreciate merits that he does not possess. Stevenson and James were not ungenerous men and they recognized Kipling's great abilities, but from what we know of them we can guess how disconcerted they were by the boisterous exuberance and the sentimentality of some of his tales and the brutality and grimness of others.

Of course Kipling had his detractors. The plodding writers who after years of labour had achieved but a modest place in the literary world found it hard to bear that this young man, coming from nowhere, without any of the social graces, should win, apparently with little effort, so spectacular a success; and as we know, they consoled themselves by prophesying (as once before they had of Dickens) that as he had come up like a rocket he would go down like the stick. It was objected to Kipling that he put too much of himself into his stories. But when you come down to brass tacks what else has an author to give you but himself? Sometimes, like Sterne for instance, or Charles Lamb, he gives you himself with a beguiling frankness, it is both the inspiration and the mainstay of his creativity; but even though he tries his best to be objective what he writes is inevitably infused with his ego. You cannot read a dozen pages of *Madame Bovary* without receiving a strong impression of Flaubert's irascible, pessimistic, morbid and self-centred personality. Kipling's critics were wrong to blame him for introducing his personality into his stories. What they meant of course was that they did not like the personality he presented to them; and that is understandable. In his early work he exhibited characteristics which were offensive. You received the impression of a bumptious, arrogant young man, extravagantly cock-sure and knowing; and this necessarily excited the antagonism of his critics. For such an assumption of superiority as these rather unamiable traits indicate affronts one's self-esteem.

Kipling was widely accused of vulgarity: so were Balzac and Dickens; I think only because they dealt with aspects of life that offended persons of refinement. We are tougher now: when we call someone refined we do not think we are paying him a compliment. But one of the most absurd charges brought against him was that his stories were anecdotes, which the critics who made it thought was to condemn him (as they sometimes still do); but if they had troubled to consult the Oxford Dictionary they would have seen that a meaning it gives to the word is: 'The narration of a detached incident, or of a single event, told as being in itself interesting or striking.' That is a perfect definition of a short story. The story of Ruth, the story of the Matron of Ephesus, Boccaccio's story of Federigo degli Alberighi and his falcon are all anecdotes. So are *Boule de Suif, La Parure* and *L'Héritage.* An anecdote is the bony structure of a story which gives it form and coherence and which the author clothes with flesh, blood and nerves. No one is obliged to read stories, and if you don't like them unless there is something in them more than a story, there is nothing to do about it. You may not like oysters, no one can blame you for that, but it is unreasonable to condemn them because they don't possess the emotional quality of a beefsteak and kidney pudding. It is equally unreasonable to find fault with a story because it is only a story. That is just what some of Kipling's detractors have done. He was a very talented man, but not a profound thinker—indeed I cannot think of any great novelist who was; he had a consummate gift for telling a certain kind of story and he enjoyed telling it. He was wise enough for the most part to do what he could do best. As he was a sensible man, he was no doubt pleased when people liked his stories and took it with a shrug of the shoulders when they didn't.

Another fault found with him was that he had little power of characterization. I don't think the critics who did this quite understood the place of characterization in a short story. Of course you can write a story with the intention of displaying a character. Flaubert did it in *Un Coeur Simple* and Chekhov in *The Darling,* which Tolstoi thought so well of; though a purist might object that they are not short stories, but potted novels. Kipling was concerned with incident. In a tale so concerned you need only tell enough about the persons who take part in it to bring them to life; you show them at the moment you are occupied with; they are inevitably static. To show the development of character an author needs the passage of time and the elbow-room of a novel. Perhaps the most remarkable character in fiction is Julien Sorel, but how could Stendhal have shown the development of his complicated character in a short story? Now, I suggest that Kipling drew his characters quite firmly enough for his purpose. There is a distinction to be made between 'characters' and character. Mulvaney, Ortheris and Learoyd are 'characters.' It is easy enough to create them. Findlavson in *The Bridge-Builders,* and Scott and William in *William the Conquerer* have character; and to delineate that is much more difficult. It is true that they are very ordinary, commonplace people, but that gives point to the narrative, and surely Kipling was well aware of it. The father and mother of the Brushwood Boy are not, as Kipling thought, 'County,' landed gentry living on an ancestral estate, but a nice, worthy couple from Arnold Bennett's Five Towns who, after amassing a competence, had settled down in the country. Though lightly sketched, they are alive, recognizable human beings. Mrs. Hauksbee was not the fashionable and distinguished creature he thought her, she was a rather second-rate little woman with a very good opinion of herself, but she is far from a lay-figure. We have all met her. Yardley-Orde in *The Head of the District* dies four pages after the story opens, but so sufficiently has Kipling characterized him that anyone could write his life-history, after the pattern of one of Aubrey's *Lives,* with a very fair chance that it would be accurate. I hurry on so that I may not yield to the temptation of writing it here and now to show how easily it could be done.

A distinguished author not long ago told me that he disliked Kipling's style so much that he could not read him. The critics of his own day seem to have found it abrupt, jerky and mannered. One of them said that 'it must be insisted that slang is not strength, nor does the abuse of the full stop ensure crispness.' True. An author uses slang to reproduce conversation accurately and in the course of his narrative to give his prose a conversational air. The chief objection to it is that its vogue is transitory and in a few years it is dated and may even be incomprehensible. Sometimes of course it passes into the language and then gains a literary validity so that not even a purist can object to its use. Kipling wrote in shorter sentences than were at that time usual. That can no longer surprise us, and since the lexicographers tell us that a sentence is a series of words, forming the grammatically complete expression of a single thought, there seems no reason why, when an author has done just this, he should not point the fact with a full stop. He is indeed right to do so. George Moore, no lenient critic of his contemporaries, admired Kipling's style for its sonority and its rhythm. 'Others have written more beautifully, but no one that I can call to mind has written so copiously. . . . He writes with the whole language, with the language of the Bible, and with the language of the streets.' Kipling's vocabulary was rich. He chose his words, often very unexpected words, for their colour, their precision, their cadence. He knew what he wanted to say and said it incisively. His prose, with which alone I am concerned, had pace and vigour. Like every other author he had his mannerisms. Some, like his unseemly addiction to biblical phrases, he quickly discarded; others he retained. He continued throughout his life to begin a sentence with a relative. Which was a pity. He continued to make deplorable use of the poetic *ere* when it would have been more natural to say *before*. Once at least he wrote *e'en* for *even*. These are minor points. Kipling has so made his style his own that I don't suppose anyone to-day would care to write like him, even if he could, but I don't see how one can deny that the instrument he constructed was admirably suited to the purpose to which he put it. He seldom indulged in long descriptions, but with his seeing eye and quick perception he was able by means of this instrument to put before the reader with extreme vividness the crowded Indian scene in all its fantastic variety.

If in this essay I have not hesitated to point out what seemed to me Kipling's defects, I hope I have made it plain how great I think were his merits. The short story is not a form of fiction in which the English have on the whole excelled. The English, as their novels show, are inclined to diffuseness. They have never been much interested in form. Succinctness goes against their grain. But the short story demands form. It demands succinctness. Diffuseness kills it. It depends on construction. It does not admit of loose ends. It must be complete in itself. All these qualities you will find in Kipling's stories when he was at his magnificent best, and this, happily for us, he was in story after story. Rudyard Kipling is the only writer of short stories our country has produced who can stand comparison with Guy de Maupassant and Chekhov. He is our greatest story writer. I can't believe he will ever be equalled. I am sure he can never be excelled.

W. S. M.

'THE FINEST STORY IN THE WORLD'

'Or ever the knightly years were gone
  With the old world to the grave,
I was a king in Babylon
  And you were a Christian slave.'
W. E. Henley.

His name was Charlie Mears; he was the only son of his mother, who was a widow, and he lived in the north of London, coming into the City every day to work in a bank. He was twenty years old and was full of aspirations. I met him in a public billiard-saloon where the marker called him by his first name, and he called the marker 'Bullseye.' Charlie explained, a little nervously, that he had only come to the place to look on, and since looking on at games of skill is not a cheap amusement for the young, I suggested that Charlie should go back to his mother.

That was our first step towards better acquaintance. He would call on me sometimes in the evenings instead of running about London with his fellow-clerks; and before long, speaking of himself as a young man must, he told me of his aspirations, which were all literary. He desired to make himself an undying name chiefly through verse, though he was not above sending stories of love and death to the penny-in-the-slot journals. It was my fate to sit still while Charlie read me poems of many hundred lines, and bulky fragments of plays that would surely shake the world. My reward was his unreserved confidence, and the self-revelations and troubles of a young man are almost as holy as those of a maiden. Charlie had never fallen in love, but was anxious to do so on the first opportunity; he believed in all things good and all things honourable, but at the same time, was curiously careful to let me see that he knew his way about the world as befitted a bank-clerk on twenty-five shillings a week. He rhymed 'dove' with 'love' and 'moon' with 'June,' and devoutly believed that they had never so been rhymed before. The long lame gaps in his plays he filled up with hasty words of apology and description, and swept on, seeing all that he intended to do so clearly that he esteemed it already done, and turned to me for applause.

I fancy that his mother did not encourage his aspirations; and I know that his writing-table at home was the edge of his washstand. This he told me almost at the outset of our acquaintance—when he was ravaging my bookshelves, and a little before I was implored to speak the truth as to his chances of writing 'something really great, you know.' Maybe I encouraged him too much, for, one night, he called on me, his eyes flaming with excitement, and said, breathlessly:

'Do you mind—can you let me stay here and write all this evening? I won't interrupt you, I won't really. There's no place for me to write in at my mother's.'

'What's the trouble?' I said, knowing well what that trouble was.

'I've a notion in my head that would make the most splendid story that was ever written. Do let me write it out here. It's *such* a notion!'

There was no resisting the appeal. I set him a table; he hardly thanked me, but plunged into his work at once. For half an hour the pen scratched without stopping. Then Charlie sighed and tugged his hair. The scratching grew slower, there were more erasures, and at last ceased. The finest story in the world would not come forth.

'It looks such awful rot now,' he said mournfully. 'And yet it seemed so good when I was thinking about it. What's wrong?'

I could not dishearten him by saying the truth. So I answered: 'Perhaps you don't feel in the mood for writing.'

'Yes, I do—except when I look at this stuff. Ugh!'

'Read me what you've done,' I said.

He read, and it was wondrous bad, and he paused at all the specially turgid sentences, expecting a little approval; for he was proud of those sentences, as I knew he would be.

'It needs compression,' I suggested cautiously.

'I hate cutting my things down. I don't think you could alter a word here without spoiling the sense. It reads better aloud than when I was writing it.'

'Charlie, you're suffering from an alarming disease afflicting a numerous class. Put the thing by, and tackle it again in a week.'

'I want to do it at once. What do you think of it?'

'How can I judge from a half-written tale? Tell me the story as it lies in your head.'

Charlie told, and in the telling there was everything that his ignorance had so carefully prevented from escaping into the written word. I looked at him, wondering whether it were possible that he did not know the originality, the power of the notion that had come his way? It was distinctly a Notion among notions. Men had been puffed up with pride by ideas not a tithe as excellent and practicable. But Charlie babbled on serenely, interrupting the current of pure fancy with samples of horrible sentences that he purposed to use. I heard him out to the end. It would be folly to allow his thought to remain in his own inept hands, when I could do so much with it. Not all that could be done indeed; but oh, so much!

'What do you think?' he said at last. 'I fancy I shall call it "The Story of a Ship."'

'I think the idea's pretty good; but you won't be able to handle it for ever so long. Now I——'

'Would it be of any use to you? Would you care to take it? I should be proud,' said Charlie promptly.

There are few things sweeter in this world than the guileless, hotheaded, intemperate, open admiration of a junior. Even a woman in her blindest devotion does not fall into the gait of the man she adores, tilt her bonnet to the angle at which he wears his hat, or interlard her speech with his pet oaths. And Charlie did all these things. Still it was necessary to salve my conscience before I possessed myself of Charlie's thoughts.

'Let's make a bargain. I'll give you a fiver for the notion,' I said.

Charlie became a bank-clerk at once.

'Oh, that's impossible. Between two pals, you know, if I may call you so, and speaking as a man of the world, I couldn't. Take the notion if it's any use to you. I've heaps more.'

He had—none knew this better than I—but they were the notions of other men.

'Look at it as a matter of business—between men of the world,' I returned. 'Five pounds will buy you any number of poetry-books. Business is business, and you may be sure I shouldn't give that price unless——'

'Oh, if you put it *that* way,' said Charlie, visibly moved by the thought of the books. The bargain was clinched with an agreement that he should at unstated intervals come to me with all the notions that he possessed, should have a table of his own to write at, and unquestioned right to inflict upon me all his poems and fragments of poems. Then I said, 'Now tell me how you came by this idea.'

'It came by itself.' Charlie's eyes opened a little.

'Yes, but you told me a great deal about the hero that you must have read before somewhere.'

'I haven't any time for reading, except when you let me sit here, and on Sundays I'm on my bicycle or down the river all day. There's nothing wrong about the hero, is there?'

'Tell me again and I shall understand clearly. You say that your hero went pirating. How did he live?'

'He was on the lower deck of this ship-thing that I was telling you about.'

'What sort of ship?'

'It was the kind rowed with oars, and the sea spurts through the oar-holes, and the men row sitting up to their knees in water. Then there's a bench running down between the two lines of oars, and an overseer with a whip walks up and down the bench to make the men work.'

'How do you know that?'

'It's in the tale. There's a rope running overhead, looped to the upper deck, for the overseer to catch hold of when the ship rolls. When the overseer misses the rope once and falls among the rowers, remember the hero laughs at him and gets licked for it. He's chained to his oar, of course—the hero.'

'How is he chained?'

'With an iron band round his waist fixed to the bench he sits on, and a sort of handcuff on his left wrist chaining him to the oar. He's on the lower deck where the worst men are sent, and the only light comes from the hatchways and through the oar-holes. Can't you imagine the sunlight just squeezing through between the handle and the hole and wobbling about as the ship moves?'

'I can, but I can't imagine your imagining it.'

'How could it be any other way? Now you listen to me. The long oars on the upper deck are managed by four men to each bench, the lower ones by three, and the lowest of all by two. Remember it's quite dark on the lowest deck and all the men there go mad. When a man dies at his oar on that deck he isn't thrown overboard, but cut up in his chains and stuffed through the oar-hole in little pieces.'

'Why?' I demanded amazed, not so much at the information as the tone of command in which it was flung out.

'To save trouble and to frighten the others. It needs two overseers to drag a man's body up to the top deck; and if the men at the lower-deck oars were left alone, of course they'd stop rowing and try to pull up the benches by all standing up together in their chains.'

'You've a most provident imagination. Where have you been reading about galleys and galley-slaves?'

'Nowhere that I remember. I row a little when I get the chance. But, perhaps, if you say so, I may have read something.'

He went away shortly afterwards to deal with booksellers, and I wondered how a bank-clerk aged twenty could put into my hands with a profligate abundance of detail, all given with absolute assurance, the story of extravagant and bloodthirsty adventure, riot, piracy, and death in unnamed seas. He had led his hero a desperate dance through revolt against the overseers, to command of a ship of his own, and at last to the establishment of a kingdom on an island 'somewhere in the sea, you know'; and, delighted with my paltry five pounds, had gone out to buy the notions of other men, that these might teach him how to write. I had the consolation of knowing that this notion was mine by right of purchase, and I thought that I could make something of it.

When next he came to me he was drunk—royally drunk on many poets for the first time revealed to him. His pupils were dilated, his words tumbled over each other, and he wrapped himself in quotations—as a beggar would enfold himself in the purple of emperors. Most of all was he drunk with Longfellow.

'Isn't it splendid? Isn't it superb?' he cried, after hasty greetings. 'Listen to this—

' "Wouldst thou,"—so the helmsman answered,
"Learn the secret of the sea?
Only those who brave its dangers
Comprehend its mystery."

By gum!

' "Only those who brave its dangers
Comprehend its mystery," '

he repeated twenty times, walking up and down the room and forgetting me. 'But *I* can understand it too,' he said to himself. 'I don't know how to thank you for that fiver. And this; listen—

' "I remember the black wharves and the slips
And the sea-tides tossing free;
And Spanish sailors with bearded lips,
And the beauty and mystery of the ships,
And the magic of the sea."

I haven't braved any dangers, but I feel as if I knew all about it.'

'You certainly seem to have a grip of the sea. Have you ever seen it?'

'When I was a little chap I went to Brighton once; we used to live in Coventry, though, before we came to London. I never saw it,

' "When descends on the Atlantic
The gigantic
Storm-wind of the Equinox." '

He shook me by the shoulder to make me understand the passion that was shaking himself.

'When that storm comes,' he continued, 'I think that all the oars in the ship that I was talking about get broken, and the rowers have their chests smashed in by the oar-heads bucking. By the way, have you done anything with that notion of mine yet?'

'No. I was waiting to hear more of it from you. Tell me how in the world you're so certain about the fittings of the ship. You know nothing of ships.'

'I don't know. It's as real as anything to me until I try to write it down. I was thinking about it only last night in bed, after you had lent me *Treasure Island;* and I made up a whole lot of new things to go into the story.'

'What sort of things?'

'About the food the men ate; rotten figs and black beans and wine in a skin bag, passed from bench to bench.'

'Was the ship built so long ago as *that?*'

'As what? I don't know whether it was long ago or not. It's only a notion, but sometimes it seems just as real as if it was true. Do I bother you with talking about it?'

'Not in the least. Did you make up anything else?'

'Yes, but it's nonsense.' Charlie flushed a little.

'Never mind; let's hear about it.'

'Well, I was thinking over the story, and after a while I got out of bed and wrote down on a piece of paper the sort of stuff the men might be supposed to scratch on the oars with the edges of their handcuffs. It seemed to make the thing more life-like. It *is* so real to me, y'know.'

'Have you the paper on you?'

'Ye—es, but what's the use of showing it? It's only a lot of scratches. All the same, we might have 'em reproduced in the book on the front page.'

'I'll attend to those details. Show me what your men wrote.'

He pulled out of his pocket a sheet of notepaper, with a single line of scratches upon it, and I put this carefully away.

'What is it supposed to mean in English?' I said.

'Oh, I don't know. I mean it to mean "I'm beastly tired." It's great nonsense,' he repeated, 'but all those men in the ship seem as real as real people to me. Do do something to the notion soon; I should like to see it written and printed.'

'But all you've told me would make a long book.'

'Make it then. You've only to sit down and write it out.'

'Give me a little time. Have you any more notions?'

'Not just now. I'm reading all the books I've bought. They're splendid.'

When he had left I looked at the sheet of notepaper with the inscription upon it. Then I took my head tenderly between both hands, to make certain that it was not coming off or turning round. Then . . . but there seemed to be no interval between quitting my rooms and finding myself arguing with a policeman outside a door marked *Private* in a corner of the British Museum. All I demanded, as politely as possible, was 'the Greek antiquities man.' The policeman knew nothing except the rules of the Museum, and it became necessary to forage through all the houses and offices inside the gates. An elderly gentleman called away from his lunch put an end to my search by holding the notepaper between finger and thumb and sniffing at it scornfully.

'What does this mean? H'mm,' said he. 'So far as I can ascertain it is an attempt to write extremely corrupt Greek on the part'—here he glared at me with intention—'of an extremely illiterate—ah—person.' He read slowly from the paper, '*Pollick, Erckmann, Tauchnitz, Henniker*'—four names familiar to me.

'Can you tell me what the corruption is supposed to mean—the gist of the thing?' I asked.

' "I have been—many times—overcome with weariness in this particular employment." That is the meaning.' He returned me the paper, and I fled without a word of thanks, explanation, or apology.

I might have been excused for forgetting much. To me of all men had been given the chance to write the most marvellous tale in the world, nothing less than the story of a Greek galley-slave, as told by himself. Small wonder that his dreaming had seemed real to Charlie. The Fates that are so careful to shut the doors of each successive life behind us had, in this case, been neglectful, and Charlie was looking, though that he did not know, where never man had been permitted to look with full knowledge since Time began. Above all, he was absolutely ignorant of the knowledge sold to me for five pounds; and he would retain that ignorance, for bank-clerks do not understand metempsychosis, and a sound commercial education does not include Greek. He would supply me—here I capered among the dumb gods of Egypt and laughed in their battered faces—with material to make my tale sure—so sure that the world would hail it as an impudent and vamped fiction. And I—I alone would know that it was absolutely and literally true. I—I alone held this jewel to my hand for the cutting and polishing! Therefore I danced again among the gods of the Egyptian Court till a policeman saw me and took steps in my direction.

It remained now only to encourage Charlie to talk, and here there was no difficulty. But I had forgotten those accursed books of poetry. He came to me time after time, as useless as a surcharged phonograph—drunk on Byron, Shelley, or Keats. Knowing now what the boy had been in his past lives, and desperately anxious not to lose one word of his babble, I could not hide from him my respect and interest. He misconstrued both into respect for the present soul of Charlie Mears, to whom life was as new as it was to Adam, and interest in his readings; and stretched my patience to breaking-point by reciting poetry—not his own now, but that of others. I wished every English poet blotted out of the memory of mankind. I blasphemed the mightiest names of song because they had drawn Charlie from the path of direct narrative, and would, later, spur him to imitate them; but I choked down my impatience until the first flood of enthusiasm should have spent itself and the boy returned to his dreams.

'What's the use of my telling you what *I* think, when these chaps wrote things for the angels to read?' he growled, one evening. 'Why don't you write something like theirs?'

'I don't think you're treating me quite fairly,' I said, speaking under strong restraint.

'I've given you the story,' he said shortly, replunging into 'Lara.'

'But I want the details.'

'The things I make up about that damned ship you call a galley? They're quite easy. You can just make 'em up for yourself. Turn up the gas a little, I want to go on reading.'

I could have broken the gas-globe over his head for his amazing stupidity. I could indeed make up things for myself did I only know what Charlie did not know that he knew. But since the doors were shut behind me I could only wait his youthful pleasure and strive to keep him in good temper. One minute's want of guard might spoil a priceless revelation: now and again he would toss his books aside—he kept them in my rooms, for his mother would have been shocked at the waste of good money had she seen them—and launch into his sea-dreams. Again I cursed all the poets of England. The plastic mind of the bank-clerk had been overlaid, coloured, and distorted by that which he had read, and the result as delivered was a confused tangle of other voices most like the mutter and hum through a City telephone in the busiest part of the day.

He talked of the galley—his own galley had he but known it—with illustrations borrowed from 'The Bride of Abydos.' He pointed the experiences of his hero with quotations from 'The Corsair,' and threw in deep and desperate moral reflections from 'Cain' and 'Manfred,' expecting me to use them all. Only when the talk turned to on Longfellow were the jarring cross-currents dumb, and I knew that Charlie was speaking the truth as he remembered it.

'What do you think of this?' I said one evening, as soon as I understood the medium in which his memory worked best, and, before he could expostulate, read him nearly the whole of 'The Saga of King Olaf'!

He listened open-mouthed, flushed, his hands drumming on the back of the sofa where he lay, till I came to the Song of Einar Tamberskelver and the verse:—

> 'Einar then, the arrow taking
>   From the loosened string,
> Answered, "That was Norway breaking
>   From thy hand, O King!" '

He gasped with pure delight of sound.

'That's better than Byron, a little?' I ventured.

'Better! Why, it's *true!* How could he have known?'

I went back and repeated:—

> ' "What was that?" said Olaf, standing
>   On the quarter-deck.
> "Something heard I like the stranding
>   Of a shattered wreck." '

'How could he have know how the ships crash and the oars rip out and go *z-zzp* all along the line? Why, only the other night . . . But go back, please, and read "The Skerry of Shrieks" again.'

'No, I'm tired. Let's talk. What happened the other night?'

'I had an awful dream about that galley of ours. I dreamed I was drowned in a fight. You see, we ran alongside another ship in harbour. The water was dead still except where our oars whipped it up. You know where I always sit in the galley?' He spoke haltingly at first, under a fine English fear of being laughed at.

'No. That's news to me,' I answered meekly, my heart beginning to beat.

'On the fourth oar from the bow on the right side on the upper deck. There were four of us at that oar, all chained. I remember watching the water and trying to get my handcuffs off before the row began. Then we closed up on the other ship, and all their fighting men jumped over our bulwarks, and my bench broke and I was pinned down with the three other fellows on top of me, and the big oar jammed across our backs.'

'Well?' Charlie's eyes were alive and alight. He was looking at the wall behind my chair.

'I don't know how we fought. The men were trampling all over my back, and I lay low. Then our rowers on the left side–tied to their oars, you know–began to yell and back water. I could hear the watter sizzle, and we spun round like a cockchafer, and I knew, lying where I was, that there was a galley coming up bow-on to ram us on the left side. I could just lift up my head and see her sail over the bulwarks. We wanted to meet her bow to bow, but it was too late. We could only turn a little bit because the galley on our right had hooked herself on to us and stopped our moving. Then, by gum! there was a crash! Our left oars began to break as the other galley, the moving one y'know, stuck her nose into them. Then the lower-deck oars shot up through the deck planking, butt first, and one of them jumped clear up into the air and came down again close at my head.'

'How was that managed?'

'The moving galley's bow was plunking them back through their own oar-holes, and I could hear no end of a shindy on the decks below. Then her nose caught us nearly in the middle and we tilted sideways, and the fellows in the right-hand galley unhitched their hooks and ropes, and threw things on to our upper deck–arrows, and hot pitch or something that stung, and we went up and up on the left side, and the right side dipped, and I twisted my head round and saw the water stand still as it topped the right bulwarks, and then it curled over and crashed down on the whole lot of us on the right side, and I felt it hit my back, and I woke.'

'One minute, Charlie. When the sea topped the bulwarks, what did it look like?' I had my reasons for asking. A man of my acquaintance had once gone down with a leaking ship in a still sea, and had seen the water-level pause for an instant ere it fell on the deck.

'It looked just like a banjo-string drawn tight, and it seemed to stay there for years,' said Charlie.

Exactly! The other man had said: 'It looked like a silver wire laid down along the bulwarks, and I thought it was never going to break.' He had paid everything except the bare life for this little valueless piece of knowledge, and I had travelled ten thousand weary miles to meet him and take his knowledge at second hand. But Charlie, the bank-clerk on twenty-five shillings a week, who had never been out of sight of a made road, knew it all. It was no consolation to me that once in his lives he had been forced to die for his gains. I also must have died scores of times, but behind me, because I could have used my knowledge, the doors were shut.

'And then?' I said, trying to put away the devil of envy.

'The funny thing was, though, in all the row I didn't feel a bit astonished or frightened. It seemed as if I'd been in a good many fights, because I told my next man so when the row began. But that cad of an overseer on my deck wouldn't unloose our chains and give us a chance. He always said that we'd all be set free after a battle, but we never were; we never were.' Charlie shook his head mournfully.

'What a scoundrel!'

'I should say he was. He never gave us enough to eat, and sometimes we were so thirsty that we used to drink salt-water. I can taste that salt-water still.'

'Now tell me something about the harbour where the fight was fought.'

'I didn't dream about that. I know it was a harbour, though; because we were tied up to a ring on a white wall and all the face of the stone under water was covered with wood to prevent our ram getting chipped when the tide made us rock.'

'That's curious. Our hero commanded the galley, didn't he?'

'Didn't he just! He stood by the bows and shouted like a good 'un. He was the man who killed the overseer.'

'But you were all drowned together, Charlie, weren't you?'

'I can't make that fit quite,' he said, with a puzzled look. 'The galley must have gone down with all hands, and yet I fancy that the hero went on living afterwards. Perhaps he climbed into the attacking ship. I wouldn't see that, of course. I was dead, you know.'

He shivered slightly and protested that he could remember no more.

I did not press him further, but to satisfy myself that he lay in ignorance of the workings of his own mind, deliberately introduced him to Mortimer Collins's *Transmigration,* and gave him a sketch of the plot before he opened the pages.

'What rot it all is!' he said frankly, at the end of an hour. 'I don't understand his nonsense about the Red Planet Mars and the King, and the rest of it. Chuck me the Longfellow again.'

I handed him the book and wrote out as much as I could remember of his description of the sea-fight, appealing to him from time to time for confirmation of fact or detail. He would answer without raising his eyes from the book, as assuredly as though all his knowledge lay before him on the printed page. I spoke under the normal key of my voice that the current might not be broken, and I knew that he was not aware of what he was saying, for his thoughts were out on the sea with Longfellow.

'Charlie,' I asked, 'when the rowers on the galleys mutinied how did they kill their overseers?'

'Tore up the benches and brained 'em. That happened when a heavy sea was running. An overseer on the lower deck slipped from the centre plank and fell among the rowers. They choked him to death against the side of the ship with their chained hands quite quietly, and it was too dark for the other overseer to see what had happened. When he asked, he was pulled down too and choked, and the lower deck fought their way up deck by deck, with the pieces of the broken benches banging behind 'em. How they howled!'

'And what happened after that?'

'I don't know. The hero went away–red hair and red beard and all. That was after he had captured our galley, I think.'

The sound of my voice irritated him, and he motioned slightly with his left hand as a man does when interruption jars.

'You never told me he was red-headed before, or that he captured your galley,' I said, after a discreet interval.

Charlie did not raise his eyes.

'He was as red as a red bear,' said he abstractedly. 'He came from the north; they said so in the galley when he looked for rowers–not slaves, but free men. Afterwards–years and years afterwards–news came from another ship, or else he came back——'

His lips moved in silence. He was rapturously retasting some poem before him.

'Where had he been, then?' I was almost whispering that the sentence might come gently to whichever section of Charlie's brain was working on my behalf.

'To the Beaches–the Long and Wonderful Beaches!' was the reply after a minute of silence.

'To Furdurstrandi?' I asked, tingling from head to foot.

'Yes, to Furdurstrandi.' He pronounced the word in a new fashion. 'And I too saw——' The voice failed.

'Do you know what you have said?' I shouted incautiously.

He lifted his eyes, fully roused now. 'No!' he snapped. 'I wish you'd let a chap go on reading. Hark to this:—

' "But Othere, the old sea-captain,
He neither paused nor stirred
Till the King listened, and then
Once more took up his pen
And wrote down every word.

' "And to the King of the Saxons,
In witness of the truth,
Raising his noble head,
He stretched his brown hand and said,
'Behold this walrus-tooth!' "

By Jove, what chaps those must have been, to go sailing all over the shop never knowing where they'd fetch the land! Hah!'

'Charlie,' I pleaded, 'if you'll only be sensible for a minute or two I'll make our hero in our tale every inch as good as Othere.'

'Umph! Longfellow wrote that poem. I don't care about writing things any more. I want to read.' He was thoroughly out of tune now, and raging over my own ill-luck, I left him.

Conceive yourself at the door of the world's treasure-house guarded by a child—an idle, irresponsible child playing knuckle-bones—on whose favour depends the gift of the key, and you will imagine one-half my torment. Till that evening Charlie had spoken nothing that might not lie within the experiences of a Greek galley-slave. But now, or there was no virtue in books, he had talked of some desperate adventure of the Vikings, of Thorfin Karlsefne's sailing to Wineland, which is America, in the ninth or tenth century. The battle in the harbour he had seen; and his own death he had described. But this was a much more startling plunge into the past. Was it possible that he had skipped half a dozen lives, and was then dimly remembering some episode of a thousand years later? It was a maddening jumble, and the worst of it was that Charlie Mears in his normal condition was the last person in the world to clear it up. I could only wait and watch, but I went to bed that night full of the wildest imaginings. There was nothing that was not possible if Charlie's detestable memory only held good.

I might rewrite the Saga of Thorfin Karlsefne as it had never been written before, might tell the story of the first discovery of America, myself the discoverer. But I was entirely at Charlie's mercy, and so long as there was a three-and-sixpenny Bohn volume within his reach Charlie would not tell. I dared not curse him openly; I hardly dared jog his memory, for I was dealing with the experiences of a thousand years ago, told through the mouth of a boy of to-day; and a boy of to-day is affected by every change of tone and gust of opinion, so that he must lie even when he most desires to speak the truth.

I saw no more of Charlie for nearly a week. When next I met him it was in Gracechurch Street with a bill-book chained to his waist. Business took him over London Bridge, and I accompanied him. He was very full of the importance of that book and magnified it. As we passed over the Thames we paused to look at a steamer unloading great slabs of white and brown marble. A barge drifted under the steamer's stern and a lonely ship's cow in that barge bellowed. Charlie's face changed from the face of a bank-clerk to that of an unknown and—though he would not have believed this—a much shrewder man. He flung out his arm across the parapet of the bridge and, laughing very loudly, said:—

'When they heard *our* bulls bellow the Skrœlings ran away!'

I waited only for an instant, but the barge and the cow had disappeared under the bows of the steamer before I answered.

'Charlie, what do you suppose are Skrœlings?'

'Never heard of 'em before. They sound like a new kind of seagull. What a chap you are for asking questions!' he replied. 'I have to go to the cashier of the Omnibus Company yonder. Will you wait for me and we can lunch somewhere together? I've a notion for a poem.'

'No, thanks. I'm off. You're sure you know nothing about Skrœlings?'

'Not unless he's been entered for the Liverpool Handicap.' He nodded and disappeared in the crowd.

Now it is written in the Saga of Eric the Red or that of Thorfin Karlsefne, that nine hundred years ago, when Karlsefne's galleys came to Leif's booths, which Leif had erected in the unknown land called Markland, which may or may not have been Rhode Island, the Skrœlings—and the Lord He knows who these may or may not have been—came to trade with the Vikings, and ran away because they were frightened at the bellowing of the cattle which Thorfin had brought with him in the ships. But what in the world could a Greek slave know of that affair? I wandered up and down among the streets trying to unravel the mystery, and the more I considered it the more baffling it grew. One thing only seemed certain, and that certainty took away my breath for the moment. If I came to full knowledge of anything at all, it would not be one life of the soul in Charlie Mears's body, but half a dozen—half a dozen several and separate existences spent on blue water in the morning of the world!

Then I reviewed the situation.

Obviously if I used my knowledge I should stand alone and unapproachable until all men were as wise as myself. That would be something, but, manlike, I was ungrateful. It seemed bitterly unfair that Charlie's memory should fail me when I needed it most. Great Powers Above—I looked up at them through the fog-smoke—did the Lords of Life and Death know what this meant to me? Nothing less than eternal fame of the best kind, that comes from One, and shared by one alone. I would be content—remembering Clive, I stood astounded at my own moderation—with the mere right to tell one story, to work out one little contribution to the light literature of the day. If Charlie were permitted full recollection for one hour—for sixty short minutes—of existences that had extended over a thousand years—I would forgo all profit and honour from all that I should make of his speech. I would take no share in the commotion that would follow throughout the particular corner of the earth that calls itself 'the world.' The thing should be put forth anonymously. Nay, I would make other men believe that they had written it. They would hire bull-hided, self-advertising Englishmen to bellow it abroad. Preachers would found a fresh conduct of life upon it, swearing that it was new and that they had lifted the fear of death from all mankind. Every Orientalist in Europe would patronise it discursively with Sanskrit and Pali texts. Terrible women would invent unclean variants of the men's belief for the elevation of their sisters. Churches and religions would war over it. Between the hailing and restarting of an omnibus I foresaw the scuffles that would arise among half a dozen denominations all professing 'the doctrine of the True Metempsychosis as applied to the world and the New Era'; and saw, too, the respectable English newspapers shying, like frightened kine, over the beautiful simplicity of the tale. The mind leaped forward a hundred—two hundred—a thousand years. I saw with sorrow that men would mutilate and garble the story; that rival creeds would turn it upside down till, at last, the western world which clings to the dread of death more closely than the hope of life, would set it aside as an interesting superstition and stampede after some faith so long forgotten that it seemed altogether new. Upon this I changed the terms of the bargain that I would make with the Lords of Life and Death. Only let me know, let me write, the story with sure knowledge that I wrote the truth, and I would burn the manuscript as a solemn sacrifice. Five minutes after the last line was written I would destroy it all. But I must be allowed to write it with absolute certainty.

There was no answer. The flaming colours of an Aquarium poster caught my eye, and I wondered whether it would be wise or prudent to lure Charlie into the hands of the professional mesmerist there, and whether, if he were under his power, he would speak of his past lives. If he did, and if people believed him . . . but Charlie would be frightened and flustered, or made conceited by the interviews. In either case he would begin to lie through fear or vanity. He was safest in my own hands.

'They are very funny fools, your English,' said a voice at my elbow, and turning round I recognised a casual acquaintance, a young Bengali law student, called Grish Chunder, whose father had sent him to England to become civilised. The old man was a retired native official, and on an income of five pounds a month contrived to allow his son two hundred pounds a year, and the run of his teeth in a city where he could pretend to be the cadet of a royal house, and tell stories of the brutal Indian bureaucrats who ground the faces of the poor.

Grish Chunder was a young, fat, full-bodied Bengali, dressed with scrupulous care in frock coat, tall hat, light trousers, and tan gloves. But I had known him in the days when the brutal Indian Government paid for his university education, and he contributed cheap sedition to the *Sachi Durpan,* and intrigued with the wives of his fourteen-year-old schoolmates.

'That is very funny and very foolish,' he said nodding at the poster. 'I am going down to the Northbrook Club. Will you come too?'

I walked with him for some time. 'You are not well,' he said. 'What is there on your mind? You do not talk.'

'Grish Chunder, you've been too well educated to believe in a God, haven't you?'

'Oah, yes, *here!* But when I go home I must conciliate popular superstition, and make ceremonies of purification, and my women will anoint idols.'

'And hang up *tulsi* and feast the *purohit,* and take you back into caste again, and make a good *khuttri* of you again, you advanced Freethinker. And you'll eat *desi* food, and like it all, from the smell in the courtyard to the mustard oil over you.'

'I shall very much like it,' said Grish Chunder unguardedly. 'Once a

Hindu–always a Hindu. But I like to know what the English think they know.'

'I'll tell you something that one Englishman knows. It's an old tale to you.'

I began to tell the story of Charlie in English, but Grish Chunder put a question in the vernacular, and the history went forward naturally in the tongue best suited for its telling. After all, it could never have been told in English. Grish Chunder heard me, nodding from time to time, and then came up to my rooms, where I finished the tale.

'Beshak,' he said philosophically. *'Lekin darwaza band hai.* [Without doubt; but the door is shut.] I have heard of this remembering of previous existences among my people. It is of course an old tale with us, but to happen to an Englishman–a cow-fed *Mlechh*–an outcaste. By Jove, that is *most* peculiar!'

'Outcaste yourself, Grish Chunder! You eat cow-beef every day. Let's think the thing over. The boy remembers his incarnations.'

'Does he know that?' said Grish Chunder quietly, swinging his legs as he sat on my table. He was speaking in his English now.

'He does not know anything. Would I speak to you if he did? Go on!'

'There is no going on at all. If you tell that to your friends they will say you are mad and put it in the papers. Suppose, now, you prosecute for libel.'

'Let's leave that out of the question entirely. Is there any chance of his being made to speak?'

'There is a chance. Oah, yess! But *if* he spoke it would mean that all this world would end now–*instanto*–fall down on your head. These things are not allowed, you know. As I said, the door is shut.'

'Not a ghost of a chance?'

'How can there be? You are a Christi-án, and it is forbidden to eat, in your books, of the Tree of Life, or else you would never die. How shall you all fear death if you all know what your friend does not know that he knows? I am afraid to be kicked, but I am not afraid to die, because I know what I know. You are not afraid to be kicked, but you are afraid to die. If you were not, by God! you English would be all over the shop in an hour, upsetting the balances of power, and making commotions. It would not be good. But no fear. He will remember a little and a little less, and he will call it dreams. Then he will forget altogether. When I passed my First Arts Examination in Calcutta that was all in the cram-book on Wordsworth. "Trailing clouds of glory," you know.'

'This seems to be an exception to the rule.'

'There are no exceptions to rules. Some are not so hard-looking as others, but they are all the same when you touch. If this friend of yours said so-and-so and so-and-so, indicating that he remembered all his lost lives, or one piece of a lost life, he would not be in the bank another hour. He would be what you call sacked because he was mad, and they would send him to an asylum for lunatics. You can see that, my friend.'

'Of course I can, but I wasn't thinking of him. His name need never appear in the story.'

'Ah! I see. That story will never be written. You can try.'

'I am going to.'

'For your own credit and for the sake of money, *of* course?'

'No. For the sake of writing the story. On my honour that will be all.'

'Even then there is no chance. You cannot play with the gods. It is a very pretty story now. As they say, Let it go on that–I mean at that. Be quick; he will not last long.'

'How do you mean?'

'What I say. He has never, so far, thought about a woman.'

'Hasn't he, though!' I remembered some of Charlie's confidences.

'I mean no woman has thought about him. When that comes; *bus–hogya*–all up! I know. There are millions of women here. Housemaids, for instance. They kiss you behind doors.'

I winced at the thought of my story being ruined by a housemaid. And yet nothing was more probable.

Grish Chunder grinned.

'Yes–also pretty girls–cousins of his house, and perhaps *not* of his house. One kiss that he gives back again and remembers will cure all this nonsense, or else——'

'Or else what? Remember he does not know that he knows.'

'I know that. Or else, if nothing happens he will become immersed in the trade and the financial speculation like the rest. It must be so. You can see that it must be so. But the woman will come first, *I* think.'

There was a rap at the door, and Charlie charged in impetuously. He had been released from the office, and by the look in his eyes I could see that he had come over for a long talk; most probably with poems in his pockets. Charlie's poems were very wearying, but sometimes they led him to speak about the galley.

Grish Chunder looked at him keenly for a minute.

'I beg your pardon,' Charlie said uneasily; 'I didn't know you had any one with you.'

'I am going,' said Grish Chunder.

He drew me into the lobby as he departed.

'That is your man,' he said quickly. 'I tell you he will never speak all you wish. That is rot–bosh. But he would be most good to make to see things. Suppose now we pretend that it was only play'–I had never seen Grish Chunder so excited–'and pour the ink-pool into his hand. Eh, what do you think? I tell you that he could see *anything* that a man could see. Let me get the ink and the camphor. He is a seer and he will tell us very many things.'

'He may be all you say, but I'm not going to trust him to your gods and devils.'

'It will not hurt him. He will only feel a little stupid and dull when he wakes up. You have seen boys look into the ink-pool before.'

'That is the reason why I am not going to see it any more. You'd better go, Grish Chunder.'

He went, insisting far down the staircase that it was throwing away my only chance of looking into the future.

This left me unmoved, for I was concerned for the past, and no peering of hypnotised boys into mirrors and ink-pools would help me to that. But I recognised Grish Chunder's point of view and sympathised with it.

'What a big black brute that was!' said Charlie, when I returned to him. 'Well, look here, I've just done a poem; did it instead of playing dominoes after lunch. May I read it?'

'Let me read it to myself.'

'Then you miss the proper expression. Besides, you always make my things sound as if the rhymes were all wrong.'

'Read it aloud, then. You're like the rest of 'em.'

Charlie mouthed me his poem, and it was not much worse than the average of his verses. He had been reading his books faithfully, but he was not pleased when I told him that I preferred my Longfellow undiluted with Charlie.

Then we began to go through the MS. line by line, Charlie parrying every objection and correction with:

'Yes, that may be better, but you don't catch what I'm driving at.'

Charlie was, in one way at least, very like one kind of poet.

There was a pencil scrawl at the back of the paper, and 'What's that?' I said.

'Oh, that's not poetry at all. It's some rot I wrote last night before I went to bed, and it was too much bother to hunt for rhymes; so I made it a sort of blank verse instead.'

Here is Charlie's 'blank verse':—

'We pulled for you when the wind was against us and the sails were low.
Will you never let us go?
We ate bread and onions when you took towns, or ran aboard quickly when you were beaten back by the foe,
The captains walked up and down the deck in fair weather singing songs, but we were below.
We fainted with our chins on the oars and you did not see that we were idle, for we still swung to and fro.
Will you never let us go?
The salt made the oar-handles like shark-skin; our knees were cut to the bone with salt-cracks; our hair was stuck to our foreheads; and our lips were cut to our gums, and you whipped us because we could not row.
Will you never let us go?
But in a little time we shall run out of the portholes as the water runs along the oar-blade, and though you tell the others to row after us you will never catch us till you catch the oar-thresh and tie up the winds in the belly of the sail. Aho!
Will you never let us go?

'H'm. What's oar-thresh, Charlie?'

'The water washed up by the oars. That's the sort of song they might sing in the galley y' know. Aren't you ever going to finish that story and give me some of the profits?'

'It depends on yourself. If you had only told me more about your hero in the first instance it might have been finished by now. You're so hazy in your notions.'

'I only want to give you the general notion of it—the knocking about from place to place and the fighting and all that. Can't you fill in the rest yourself? Make the hero save a girl on a pirate-galley and marry her or do something.'

'You're a really helpful collaborator. I suppose the hero went through some few adventures before he married.'

'Well, then, make him a very artful card—a low sort of man—a sort of political man who went about making treaties and breaking them—a black-haired chap who hid behind the mast when the fighting began.'

'But you said the other day that he was red-haired.'

'I couldn't have. Make him black-haired of course. You've no imagination.'

Seeing that I had just discovered the entire principles upon which the half-memory falsely called imagination is based, I felt entitled to laugh, but forbore for the sake of the tale.

'You're right. *You're* the man with imagination. A black-haired chap in a decked ship,' I said.

'No, an open ship—like a big boat.'

This was maddening.

'Your ship has been built and designed, closed and decked in; you said so yourself,' I protested.

'No, no, not that ship. That was open or half-decked because—— By Jove, you're right. You made me think of the hero as a red-haired chap. Of course if he were red, the ship would be an open one with painted sails.'

Surely, I thought, he would remember now that he had served in two galleys at least—in a three-decked Greek one under the black-haired 'political man,' and again in a Viking's open sea-serpent under the man 'red as a red bear' who went to Markland. The Devil prompted me to speak.

'Why "of course," Charlie?' said I.

'I don't know. Are you making fun of me?'

The current was broken for the time being. I took up a notebook and pretended to make many entries in it.

'It's a pleasure to work with an imaginative chap like yourself,' I said, after a pause. 'The way that you've brought out the character of the hero is simply wonderful.'

'Do you think so?' he answered, with a pleased flush. 'I often tell myself that there's more in me than my mo—— than people think.'

'There's an enormous amount in you.'

'Then, won't you let me send an essay on The Ways of Bank-Clerks to *Tit-Bits,* and get the guinea prize?'

'That wasn't exactly what I meant, old fellow: perhaps it would be better to wait a little and go ahead with the galley-story.'

'Ah, but I shan't get the credit of that. *Tit-Bits* would publish my name and address if I win. What are you grinning at? They *would.*'

'I know it. Suppose you go for a walk. I want to look through my notes about our story.'

Now this reprehensible youth who left me, a little hurt and put aback, might for aught he or I knew have been one of the crew of the Argo—had been certainly slave or comrade to Thorfin Karlsefne. Therefore he was deeply interested in guinea competitions. Remembering what Grish Chunder had said I laughed aloud. The Lords of Life and Death would never allow Charlie Mears to speak with full knowledge of his pasts, and

I must even piece out what he had told me with my own poor inventions while Charlie wrote of the ways of bank-clerks.

I got together and placed on one file all my notes; and the net result was not cheering. I read them a second time. There was nothing that might not have been compiled at second hand from other people's books—except, perhaps, the story of the fight in the harbour. The adventures of a Viking had been written many times before; the history of a Greek galley-slave was no new thing, and though I wrote both, who could challenge or confirm the accuracy of my details? I might as well tell a tale of two thousand years hence. The Lords of Life and Death were as cunning as Grish Chunder had hinted. They would allow nothing to escape that might trouble or make easy the minds of men. Though I was convinced of this, yet I could not leave the tale alone. Exaltation followed reaction, not once, but twenty times in the next few weeks. My moods varied with the March sunlight and flying clouds. By night or in the beauty of a spring morning I perceived that I could write that tale and shift continents thereby. In the wet windy afternoons, I saw that the tale might indeed be written, but would be nothing more than a faked, false-varnished, sham-rusted piece of Wardour Street work in the end. Then I blessed Charlie in many ways—though it was no fault of his. He seemed to be busy with prize competitions, and I saw less and less of him as the weeks went by and the earth cracked and grew ripe to spring, and the buds swelled in their sheaths. He did not care to read or talk of what he had read, and there was a new ring of self-assertion in his voice. I hardly cared to remind him of the galley when we met; but Charlie alluded to it on every occasion, always as a story from which money was to be made.

'I think I deserve twenty-five per cent, don't I, at least?' he said, with beautiful frankness. 'I supplied all the ideas, didn't I?'

This greediness for silver was a new side in his nature. I assumed that it had been developed in the City, where Charlie was picking up the curious nasal drawl of the underbred City man.

'When the thing's done we'll talk about it. I can't make anything of it at present. Red-haired or black-haired heroes are equally difficult.'

He was sitting by the fire staring at the red coals. '*I* can't understand what you find so difficult. It's all as clear as mud to me,' he replied. A jet of gas puffed out between the bars, took light, and whistled softly. 'Suppose we take the red-haired hero's adventures first, from the time that he came south to my galley and captured it and sailed to the Beaches.'

I knew better now than to interrupt Charlie. I was out of reach of pen and paper, and dared not move to get them lest I should break the current. The gas-jet puffed and whinnied, Charlie's voice dropped almost to a whisper, and he told a tale of the sailing of an open galley to Furdurstrandi, of sunsets on the open sea, seen under the curve of the one sail evening after evening when the galley's beak was notched into the centre of the sinking disc, and 'we sailed by that, for we had no other guide,' quoth Charlie. He spoke of a landing on an island and explorations in its woods, where the crew killed three men whom they found asleep under the pines. Their ghosts, Charlie said, followed the galley, swimming and choking in the water, and the crew cast lots and threw one of their number overboard as a sacrifice to the strange gods whom they had offended. Then they ate sea-weed when their provisions failed, and their legs swelled, and their leader, the red-haired man, killed two rowers who mutinied, and after a year spent among the woods they set sail for their own country, and a wind that never failed carried them back so safely that they all slept at night. This and much more Charlie told. Sometimes the voice fell so low that I could not catch the words, though every nerve was on the strain. He spoke of their leader, the red-haired man, as a pagan speaks of his God; for it was he who cheered them and slew them impartially as he thought best for their needs; and it was he who steered them for three days among floating ice, each floe crowded with strange beasts that tried 'to sail with us,' said Charlie, 'and we beat them back with the handles of the oars.'

The gas-jet went out, a burnt coal gave way, and the fire settled with a tiny crash to the bottom of the grate. Charlie ceased speaking, and I said no word.

'By Jove!' he said at last, shaking his head. 'I've been staring at the fire till I'm dizzy. What was I going to say?'

'Something about the galley book.'

'I remember now. It's twenty-five per cent of the profits, isn't it?'

'It's anything you like when I've done the tale.'

'I wanted to be sure of that. I must go now. I've—I've an appointment.' And he left me.

Had not my eyes been held I might have known that that broken muttering over the fire was the swan-song of Charlie Mears. But I thought it the prelude to fuller revelation. At last and at last I should cheat the Lords of Life and Death!

When next Charlie came to me I received him with rapture. He was nervous and embarrassed, but his eyes were very full of light, and his lips a little parted.

'I've done a poem,' he said; and then, quickly: 'It's the best I've ever done. Read it.' He thrust it into my hand and retreated to the window.

I groaned inwardly. It would be the work of half an hour to criticise—that is to say, praise—the poem sufficiently to please Charlie. Then I had good reason to groan, for Charlie, discarding his favourite centipede metres, had launched into shorter and choppier verse, and verse with a motive at the back of it. This is what I read:—

'The day is most fair, the cheery wind
Halloos behind the hill,
Where he bends the wood as seemeth good,
And the sapling to his will!
Riot, O wind; there is that in my blood
That would not have thee still!

'She gave me herself, O Earth, O Sky;
Gray sea, she is mine alone!
Let the sullen boulders hear my cry,
And rejoice tho' they be but stone!

'Mine! I have won her, O good brown earth,
Make merry! 'Tis hard on Spring;
Make merry; my love is doubly worth
All worship your fields can bring!
Let the hind that tills you feel my mirth
At the early harrowing!'

'Yes, it's the early harrowing, past a doubt,' I said, with a dread at my heart. Charlie smiled, but did not answer.

'Red cloud of the sunset, tell it abroad;
I am victor. Greet me, O Sun,
Dominant master and absolute lord
Over the soul of one!'

'Well?' said Charlie, looking over my shoulder.

I thought it far from well, and very evil indeed, when he silently laid a photograph on the paper—the photograph of a girl with a curly head and a foolish slack mouth.

'Isn't it—isn't it wonderful?' he whispered, pink to the tips of his ears, wrapped in the rosy mystery of first love. 'I didn't know; I didn't think—it came like a thunderclap.'

'Yes. It comes like a thunderclap. Are you very happy, Charlie?'

'My God—she—she loves me!' He sat down repeating the last words to himself. I looked at the hairless face, the narrow shoulders already bowed by desk-work, and wondered when, where, and how he had loved in his past lives.

'What will your mother say?' I asked cheerfully.

'I don't care a damn what she says!'

At twenty the things for which one does not care a damn should, properly, be many, but one must not include mothers in the list. I told him this gently; and he described Her, even as Adam must have described to the newly-named beasts the glory and tenderness and beauty of Eve. Incidentally I learned that She was a tobacconist's assistant with a weakness for pretty dress, and had told him four or five times already that She had never been kissed by a man before.

Charlie spoke on and on, and on; while I, separated from him by thousands of years, was considering the beginnings of things. Now I understood why the Lords of Life and Death shut the doors so carefully behind us. It is that we may not remember our first and most beautiful wooings. Were this not so, our world would be without inhabitants in a hundred years.

'Now, about that galley-story,' I said still more cheerfully, in a pause in the rush of the speech.

Charlie looked up as though he had been hit. 'The galley—what galley? Good heavens, don't joke, man! This is serious! You don't know how serious it is!'

Grish Chunder was right. Charlie had tasted the love of woman that kills remembrance, and the finest story in the world would never be written.

THE MAN WHO WAS

The Earth gave up her dead that tide,
  Into our camp he came,
And said his say, and went his way,
  And left our hearts aflame.

Keep tally—on the gun-butt score
  The vengeance we must take,
When God shall bring full reckoning,
  For our dead comrade's sake.

Ballad.

LET IT be clearly understood that the Russian is a delightful person till he tucks in his shirt. As an Oriental he is charming. It is only when he insists upon being treated as the most easterly of western peoples instead of the most westerly of easterns that he becomes a racial anomaly extremely difficult to handle. The host never knows which side of his nature is going to turn up next.

Dirkovitch was a Russian—a Russian of the Russians—who appeared to get his bread by serving the Czar as an officer in a Cossack regiment, and corresponding for a Russian newspaper with a name that was never twice alike. He was a handsome young Oriental, fond of wandering through unexplored portions of the earth, and he arrived in India from nowhere in particular. At least no living man could ascertain whether it was by way of Balkh, Badakshan, Chitral, Baluchistan, or Nepal, or anywhere else. The Indian Government, being in an unusually affable mood, gave orders that he was to be civilly treated and shown everything that was to be seen. So he drifted, talking bad English and worse French, from one city to another, till he forgathered with Her Majesty's White Hussars in the city of Peshawur, which stands at the mouth of that narrow swordcut in the hills that men call the Khyber Pass. He was undoubtedly an officer, and he was decorated after the manner of the Russians with little enamelled crosses, and he could talk, and (though this has nothing to do with his merits) he had been given up as a hopeless task, or cask, by the Black Tyrone, who individually and collectively, with hot whisky and honey, mulled brandy, and mixed spirits of every kind, had striven in all hospitality to make him drunk. And when the Black Tyrone, who are exclusively Irish, fail to disturb the peace of head of a foreigner—that foreigner is certain to be a superior man.

The White Hussars were as conscientious in choosing their wine as in charging the enemy. All that they possessed, including some wondrous brandy, was placed at the absolute disposition of Dirkovitch, and he enjoyed himself hugely—even more than among the Black Tyrone.

But he remained distressingly European through it all. The White Hussars were 'My dear true friends,' 'Fellow-soldiers glorious,' and 'Brothers inseparable. He would unburden himself by the hour on the glorious future that awaited the combined arms of England and Russia when their hearts and their territories should run side by side, and the great mission of civilising Asia should begin. That was unsatisfactory, because Asia is not going to be civilised after the methods of the West. There is too much Asia and she is too old. You cannot reform a lady of many lovers, and Asia has been insatiable in her flirtations aforetime. She will never attend Sunday school or learn to vote save with swords for tickets.

Dirkovitch knew this as well as any one else, but it suited him to talk special-correspondently and to make himself as genial as he could. Now and then he volunteered a little, a very little information about his own sotnia of Cossacks, left apparently to look after themselves somewhere at the back of beyond. He had done rough work in Central Asia, and had seen rather more help-yourself fighting than most men of his years. But he was careful never to betray his superiority, and more than careful to praise on all occasions the appearance, drill, uniform, and organisation of Her Majesty's White Hussars. And indeed they were a regiment to be admired. When Lady Durgan, widow of the late Sir John Durgan, arrived in their station, and after a short time had been proposed to by every single man at mess, she put the public sentiment very neatly when she explained that they were all so nice that unless she could marry them all, including the Colonel and some Majors already married, she was not going to content herself with one hussar. Wherefore she wedded a little man in a rifle regiment, being by nature contradictious; and the White Hussars were going to wear crape on their arms, but compromised by attending the wedding in full force, and lining the aisle with unutterable reproach. She had jilted them all—from Basset-Holmer the senior Captain to little Mildred the junior subaltern, who could have given her four thousand a year and a title.

The only persons who did not share the general regard for the White Hussars were a few thousand gentlemen of Jewish extraction who lived across the border, and answered to the name of Pathan. They had once met the regiment officially and for something less than twenty minutes, but the interview, which was complicated with many casualties, had filled them with prejudice. They even called the White Hussars children of the devil and sons of persons whom it would be perfectly impossible to meet in decent society. Yet they were not above making their aversion fill their money-belts. The regiment possessed carbines—beautiful Martini-Henry carbines that would lob a bullet into an enemy's camp at one thousand yards, and were even handier than the long rifle. Therefore they were coveted all along the border, and since demand inevitably breeds supply, they were supplied at the risk of life and limb for exactly their weight in coined silver—seven and one half pounds weight of rupees, or sixteen pounds sterling reckoning the rupee at par. They were stolen at night by snaky-haired thieves who crawled on their stomachs under the nose of the sentries; they disappeared mysteriously from locked arm-racks, and in the hot weather, when all the barrack doors and windows were open, they vanished like puffs of their own smoke. The border people desired them for family vendettas and contingencies. But in the long cold nights of the northern Indian winter they were stolen most extensively. The traffic of murder was liveliest among the hills at that season and prices ruled high. The regimental guards were first doubled and then trebled. A trooper does not much care if he loses a weapon—Government must make it good—but he deeply resents the loss of his sleep. The regiment grew very angry, and one rifle-thief bears the visible marks of their anger upon him to this hour. That incident stopped the burglaries for a time and the guards were reduced accordingly, and the regiment devoted itself to polo with unexpected results; for it beat by two goals to one that very terrible polo corps the Lushkar Light Horse, though the latter had four ponies apiece for a short hour's fight, as well as a native officer who played like a lambent flame across the ground.

They gave a dinner to celebrate the event. The Lushkar team came, and Dirkovitch came, in the fullest full uniform of a Cossack officer, which is as full as a dressing-gown, and was introduced to the Lushkars, and opened his eyes as he regarded. They were lighter men than the Hussars, and they carried themselves with the swing that is the peculiar right of the Punjab Frontier Force and all Irregular Horse. Like everything else in the Service it has to be learnt, but, unlike many things, it is never forgotten, and remains on the body till death.

The great beam-roofed mess-room of the White Hussars was a sight to be remembered. All the mess plate was out on the long table—the same table that had served up the bodies of five officers after a forgotten fight long and long ago—the dingy, battered standards faced the door of entrance, clumps of winter-roses lay between the silver candlesticks, and the portraits of eminent officers deceased looked down on their successors from between the heads of sambhur, nilghai, markhor, and, pride of all the mess, two grinning snow-leopards that had cost Basset-Holmer four months' leave that he might have spent in England, instead of on the road to Thibet and the daily risk of his life by ledge, snow-slide, and grassy slope.

The servants in spotless white muslin with the crest of their regiments on the brow of their turbans waited behind their masters, who were clad in the scarlet and gold of the White Hussars, and the cream and silver of the Lushkar Light Horse. Dirkovitch's dull green uniform was the only dark spot at the board, but his big onyx eyes made up for it. He was fraternising effusively with the captain of the Lushkar team, who was wondering how many of Dirkovitch's Cossacks his own dark wiry downcountrymen could account for in a fair charge. But one does not speak of these things openly.

The talk rose higher and higher, and the regimental band played between the courses, as is the immemorial custom, till all tongues ceased for a moment with the removal of the dinner-slips and the first toast of obligation when an officer rising said, 'Mr. Vice, the Queen,' and little Mildred from the bottom of the table answered, 'The Queen, God bless her,' and the big spurs clanked as the big men heaved themselves up and drank the Queen upon whose pay they were falsely supposed to settle their mess-bills. That Sacrament of the Mess never grows old, and never ceases to bring a lump into the throat of the listener wherever he be by sea or by land. Dirkovitch rose with his 'brothers glorious,' but he could not understand. No one but an officer can tell what the toast means; and the bulk have more sentiment than comprehension. Immediately after the little silence that follows on the ceremony there entered the native officer who had played for the Lushkar team. He could not, of course, eat with the mess, but he came in at dessert, all six feet of him, with the blue and silver turban atop, and the big black boots below. The mess rose joyously as he thrust forward the hilt of his sabre in token of fealty for the Colonel of the White Hussars to touch, and dropped into a vacant chair amid shouts of: '*Rung ho,* Hira Singh!' (which being translated means 'Go in and win'). 'Did I whack you over the knee, old man?'

'Rissaldar Sahib, what the devil made you play that kicking pig of a pony in the last ten minutes?' '*Shabash*, Rissaldar Sahib!' Then the voice of the Colonel, 'The health of Rissaldar Hira Singh!'

After the shouting had died away Hira Singh rose to reply, for he was the cadet of a royal house, the son of a king's son, and knew what was due on these occasions. Thus he spoke in the vernacular:—'Colonel Sahib and officers of this regiment. Much honour have you done me. This will I remember. We came down from afar to play you. But we were beaten' ('No fault of yours, Rissaldar Sahib. Played on our own ground y' know. Your ponies were cramped from the railway. Don't apologise!') 'Therefore perhaps we will come again if it be so ordained.' ('Hear! Hear! Hear, indeed! Bravo! Hsh!') 'Then we will play you afresh' ('Happy to meet you') 'till there are left no feet upon our ponies. Thus far for sport.' He dropped one hand on his sword-hilt and his eye wandered to Dirkovitch lolling back in his chair. 'But if by the will of God there arises any other game which is not the polo game, then be assured, Colonel Sahib and officers, that we will play it out side by side, though *they*,' again his eye sought Dirkovitch, 'though *they*, I say, have fifty ponies to our one horse.' And with a deep-mouthed *Rung ho!* that sounded like a musket-butt on flagstones, he sat down amid leaping glasses.

Dirkovitch, who had devoted himself steadily to the brandy—the terrible brandy aforementioned—did not understand, nor did the expurgated translations offered to him at all convey the point. Decidedly Hira Singh's was the speech of the evening, and the clamour might have continued to the dawn had it not been broken by the noise of a shot without that sent every man feeling at his defenceless left side. Then there was a scuffle and a yell of pain.

'Carbine-stealing again!' said the Adjutant, calmly sinking back in his chair. 'This comes of reducing the guards. I hope the sentries have killed him.'

The feet of armed men pounded on the verandah flags, and it was as though something was being dragged.

'Why don't they put him in the cells till the morning?' said the Colonel testily. 'See if they've damaged him, sergeant.'

The mess sergeant fled out into the darkness and returned with two troopers and a corporal, all very much perplexed.

'Caught a man stealin' carbines, sir,' said the corporal. 'Leastways 'e was crawlin' towards the barricks, sir, past the main road sentries, an' the sentry 'e sez, sir——'

The limp heap of rags upheld by the three men groaned. Never was seen so destitute and demoralised an Afghan. He was turbanless, shoeless, caked with dirt, and all but dead with rough handling. Hira Singh started slightly at the sound of the man's pain. Dirkovitch took another glass of brandy.

'*What* does the sentry say?' said the Colonel.

'Sez 'e speaks English, sir,' said the corporal.

'So you brought him into mess instead of handing him over to the sergeant! If he spoke all the Tongues of the Pentecost you've no business——'

Again the bundle groaned and muttered. Little Mildred had risen from his place to inspect. He jumped back as though he had been shot.

'Perhaps it would be better, sir, to send the men away,' said he to the Colonel, for he was a much privileged subaltern. He put his arms round the rag-bound horror as he spoke, and dropped him into a chair. It may not have been explained that the littleness of Mildred lay in his being six feet four and big in proportion. The corporal seeing that an officer was disposed to look after the capture, and that the Colonel's eye was beginning to blaze, promptly removed himself and his men. The mess was left alone with the carbine-thief, who laid his head on the table and wept bitterly, hopelessly, and inconsolably, as little children wept.

Hira Singh leapt to his feet. 'Colonel Sahib,' said he, 'that man is no Afghan, for they weep *Ai! Ai!* Nor is he of Hindustan, for they weep *Oh! Ho!* He weeps after the fashion of the white men, who say *Ow! Ow!*'

'Now where the dickens did you get that knowledge, Hira Singh?' said the captain of the Lushkar team.

'Hear him!' said Hira Singh simply, pointing at the crumpled figure that wept as though it would never cease.

'He said, "My God!" said little Mildred. 'I heard him say it.'

The Colonel and the mess-room looked at the man in silence. It is a horrible thing to hear a man cry. A woman can sob from the top of her palate, or her lips, or anywhere else, but a man must cry from his diaphragm, and it rends him to pieces.

'Poor devil!' said the Colonel, coughing tremendously. 'We ought to send him to hospital. He's been man-handled.'

Now the Adjutant loved his carbines. They were to him as his grandchildren, the men standing in the first place. He grunted rebelliously: 'I can understand an Afghan stealing, because he's built that way. But I can't understand his crying. That makes it worse.'

The brandy must have affected Dirkovitch, for he lay back in his chair and stared at the ceiling. There was nothing special in the ceiling beyond a shadow as of a huge black coffin. Owing to some peculiarity in the construction of the mess-room this shadow was always thrown when the candles were lighted. It never disturbed the digestion of the White Hussars. They were in fact rather proud of it.

'Is he going to cry all night?' said the Colonel, 'or are we supposed to sit up with little Mildred's guest until he feels better?'

The man in the chair threw up his head and stared at the mess. 'Oh, my God!' he said, and every soul in the mess rose to his feet. Then the Lushkar captain did a deed for which he ought to have been given the Victoria Cross—distinguished gallantry in a fight against overwhelming curiosity. He picked up his team with his eyes as the hostess picks up the ladies at the opportune moment, and pausing only by the Colonel's chair to say, 'This isn't *our* affair, you know, sir,' led them into the verandah and the gardens. Hira Singh was the last to go and he looked at Dirkovitch. But Dirkovitch had departed into a brandy-paradise of his own. His lips moved without sound, and he was studying the coffin on the ceiling.

'White—white all over,' said Basset-Holmer, the Adjutant. 'What a pernicious renegade he must be! I wonder where he came from?'

The Colonel shook the man gently by the arm, and 'Who are you?' said he.

There was no answer. The man stared round the mess-room and smiled in the Colonel's face. Little Mildred, who was always more of a woman than a man till 'Boot and saddle' was sounded, repeated the question in a voice that would have drawn confidences from a geyser. The man only smiled. Dirkovitch at the far end of the table slid gently from his chair to the floor. No son of Adam in this present imperfect world can mix the Hussars' champagne with the Hussars' brandy by five and eight glasses of each without remembering the pit whence he was digged and descending thither. The band began to play the tune with which the White Hussars from the date of their formation have concluded all their functions. They would sooner be disbanded than abandon that tune; it is a part of their system. The man straightened himself in his chair and drummed on the table with his fingers.

'I don't see why we should entertain lunatics,' said the Colonel. 'Call a guard and send him off to the cells. We'll look into the business in the morning. Give him a glass of wine first though.'

Little Mildred filled a sherry-glass with the brandy and thrust it over to the man. He drank, and the tune rose louder, and he straightened himself yet more. Then he put out his long-taloned hands to a piece of plate opposite and fingered it lovingly. There was a mystery connected with that piece of plate, in the shape of a spring which converted what was a seven-branched candlestick, three springs on each side and one in the middle, into a sort of wheel-spoke candelabrum. He found the spring, pressed it, and laughed weakly. He rose from his chair and inspected a picture on the wall, then moved on to another picture, the mess watching him without a word. When he came to the mantelpiece he shook his head and seemed distressed. A piece of plate representing a mounted hussar in full uniform caught his eye. He pointed to it, and then to the mantelpiece with inquiry in his eyes.

'What is it–oh, what is it?' said little Mildred. Then as a mother might speak to a child, 'That is a horse. Yes, a horse.'

Very slowly came the answer in a thick, passionless guttural–'Yes, I –have seen. But–where is *the* horse?'

You could have heard the hearts of the mess beating as the men drew back to give the stranger full room in his wanderings. There was no question of calling the guard.

Again he spoke–very slowly, 'Where is *our* horse?'

There is but one horse in the White Hussars, and his portrait hangs outside the door of the mess-room. He is the piebald drum-horse, the king of the regimental band, that served the regiment for seven-and-thirty years, and in the end was shot for old age. Half the mess tore the thing down from its place and thrust it into the man's hands. He placed it above the mantelpiece, it clattered on the ledge as his poor hands dropped it, and he staggered towards the bottom of the table, falling into Mildred's chair. Then all the men spoke to one another something after this fashion, 'The drum-horse hasn't hung over the mantelpiece since '67.' 'How does he know?' 'Mildred, go and speak to him again.' 'Colonel, what are you going to do?' 'Oh, dry up, and give the poor devil a chance to pull himself together.' 'It isn't possible anyhow. The man's a lunatic.'

Little Mildred stood at the Colonel's side talking in his ear. 'Will you be good enough to take your seats, please, gentlemen!' he said, and the mess dropped into the chairs. Only Dirkovitch's seat, next to little Mildred's, was blank, and little Mildred himself had found Hira Singh's place. The wide-eyed mess-sergeant filled the glasses in dead silence. Once more the Colonel rose, but his hand shook, and the port spilled on the table as he looked straight at the man in little Mildred's chair and said hoarsely, 'Mr. Vice, the Queen.' There was a little pause, but the man sprang to his feet and answered without hesitation, 'The

Queen, God bless her!' and as he emptied the thin glass he snapped the shank between his fingers.

Long and long ago, when the Empress of India was a young woman and there were no unclean ideals in the land, it was the custom of a few messes to drink the Queen's toast in broken glass, to the vast delight of the mess-contractors. The custom is now dead, because there is nothing to break anything for, except now and again the word of a Government, and that has been broken already.

'That settles it,' said the Colonel, with a gasp. 'He's not a sergeant. What in the world is he?'

The entire mess echoed the word, and the volley of questions would have scared any man. It was no wonder that the ragged, filthy invader could only smile and shake his head.

From under the table, calm and smiling, rose Dirkovitch, who had been roused from healthful slumber by feet upon his body. By the side of the man he rose, and the man shrieked and grovelled. It was a horrible sight coming so swiftly upon the pride and glory of the toast that had brought the strayed wits together.

Dirkovitch made no offer to raise him, but little Mildred heaved him up in an instant. It is not good that a gentleman who can answer to the Queen's toast should lie at the feet of a subaltern of Cossacks.

The hasty action tore the wretch's upper clothing nearly to the waist, and his body was seamed with dry black scars. There is only one weapon in the world that cuts in parallel lines, and it is neither the cane nor the cat. Dirkovitch saw the marks, and the pupils of his eyes dilated. Also his face changed. He said something that sounded like *Shto ve takete,* and the man fawning answered, *Chetyre.*

'What's that?' said everybody together.

'His number. That is number four, you know.' Dirkovitch spoke very thickly.

'What has a Queen's officer to do with a qualified number?' said the Colonel, and an unpleasant growl ran round the table.

'How can I tell?' said the affable Oriental with a sweet smile. 'He is a –how you have it?–escape–run-a-way, from over there.' He nodded towards the darkness of the night.

'Speak to him if he'll answer you, and speak to him gently,' said little Mildred, settling the man in a chair. It seemed most improper to all present that Dirkovitch should sip brandy as he talked in purring, spitting Russian to the creature who answered so feebly and with such evident dread. But since Dirkovitch appeared to understand no one said a word. All breathed heavily, leaning forward, in the long gaps of the conversation. The next time that they have no engagements on hand the White Hussars intend to go to St. Petersburg in a body to learn Russian.

'He does not know how many years ago,' said Dirkovitch facing the mess, 'but he says it was very long ago in a war. I think that there was an accident. He says he was of this glorious and distinguished regiment in the war.'

'The rolls! The rolls! Holmer, get the rolls!' said little Mildred, and the Adjutant dashed off bare-headed to the orderly-room, where the muster-rolls of the regiment were kept. He returned just in time to hear Dirkovitch conclude, 'Therefore, my dear friends, I am most sorry to say there was an accident which would have been reparable if he had apologised to that our Colonel, which he had insulted.'

Then followed another growl which the Colonel tried to beat down. The mess was in no mood just then to weigh insults to Russian Colonels.

'He does not remember, but I think that there was an accident, and so he was not exchanged among the prisoners, but he was sent to another place—how do you say?—the country. *So,* he says, he came here. He does not know how he came. Eh? He was at Chepany'—the man caught the word, nodded, and shivered—'at Zhigansk and Irkutsk. I cannot understand how he escaped. He says, too, that he was in the forests for many years, but how many years he has forgotten—that with many things. It was an accident; done because he did not apologise to that our Colonel. Ah!'

Instead of echoing Dirkovitch's sigh of regret, it is sad to record that the White Hassars livelily exhibited un-Christian delight and other emotions, hardly restrained by their sense of hospitality. Holmer flung the frayed and yellow regimental rolls on the table, and the men flung themselves at these.

'Steady! Fifty-six—fifty-five—fifty-four,' said Holmer. 'Here we are. "Lieutenant Austin Limmason. *Missing.*" That was before Sebastopol. What an infernal shame! Insulted one of their Colonels, and was quietly shipped off. Thirty years of his life wiped out.'

'But he never apologised. Said he'd see him damned first,' chorused the mess.

'Poor chap! I suppose he never had the chance afterwards. How did he come here?' said the Colonel.

The dingy heap in the chair could give no answer.

'Do you know who you are?'

It laughed weakly.

'Do you know that you are Limmason—Lieutenant Limmason of the White Hussars?'

Swiftly as a shot came the answer, in a slightly surprised tone, 'Yes, I'm Limmason, of course.' The light died out in his eyes, and the man collapsed, watching every motion of Dirkovitch with terror. A flight from Siberia may fix a few elementary facts in the mind, but it does not seem to lead to continuity of thought. The man could not explain how, like a homing pigeon, he had found his way to his own old mess again. Of what he had suffered or seen he knew nothing. He cringed before Dirkovitch as instinctively as he had pressed the spring of the candlestick, sought the picture of the drum-horse, and answered to the toast of the Queen. The rest was a blank that the dreaded Russian tongue could only in part remove. His head bowed on his breast, and he giggled and cowered alternately.

The devil that lived in the brandy prompted Dirkovitch at this extremely inopportune moment to make a speech. He rose, swaying slightly, gripped the table-edge, while his eyes glowed like opals, and began:

'Fellow-soldiers glorious—true friends and hospitables. It was an accident, and deplorable—most deplorable.' Here he smiled sweetly all round the mess. 'But you will think of this little, little thing. So little, is it not? The Czar! Posh! I slap my fingers—I snap my fingers at him. Do I believe in him? No! But in us Slav who has done nothing, *him* I believe. Seventy—how much—millions peoples that have done nothing—not one thing. Posh! Napoleon was an episode.' He banged a hand on the table. 'Hear you, old peoples, we have done nothing in the world—out here. All our work is to do; and it shall be done, old peoples. Get a-way!' He waved his hand imperiously, and pointed to the man. 'You see him. He is not good to see. He was just one little—oh, so little—accident, that no one remembered. Now he is *That!* So will you be, brother soldiers so brave—so will you be. But you will never come back. You will all go where he is gone, or'—he pointed to the great coffin-shadow on the ceiling, and muttering, 'Seventy millions—get a-way, you old peoples,' fell asleep.

'Sweet, and to the point,' said little Mildred. 'What's the use of getting wroth? Let's make this poor devil comfortable.'

But that was a matter suddenly and swiftly taken from the loving hands of the White Hussars. The Lieutenant had returned only to go away again three days later, when the wail of the Dead March, and the tramp of the squadrons, told the wondering Station, who saw no gap in the mess-table, that an officer of the regiment had resigned his new-found commission.

And Dirkovitch, bland, supple, and always genial, went away too by a night train. Little Mildred and another man saw him off, for he was the guest of the mess, and even had he smitten the Colonel with the open hand, the law of that mess allowed no relaxation of hospitality.

'Good-bye, Dirkovitch, and a pleasant journey,' said little Mildred.

'*Au revoir,*' said the Russian.

'Indeed! But we thought you were going home?'

'Yes, but I will come again. My dear friends, is that road shut?' He pointed to where the North Star burned over the Khyber Pass.

'By Jove! I forgot. Of course. Happy to meet you, old man, any time you like. Got everything you want? Cheroots, ice, bedding? That's all right. Well, *au revoir,* Dirkovitch.'

'Um,' said the other man, as the tail-lights of the train grew small. 'Of—all—the—unmitigated——!'

Little Mildred answered nothing, but watched the North Star and hummed a selection from a recent Simla burlesque that had much delighted the White Hussars. It ran—

I'm sorry for Mister Bluebeard,
I'm sorry to cause him pain;
But a terrible spree there's sure to be
When he comes back again.

THE TOMB OF HIS ANCESTORS

SOME PEOPLE will tell you that if there were but a single loaf of bread in all India it would be divided equally between the Plowdens, the Trevors, the Beadons, and the Rivett-Carnacs. That is only one way of saying that certain families serve India generation after generation as dolphins follow in line across the open sea.

Let us take a small and obscure case. There has been at least one representative of the Devonshire Chinns in or near Central India since the days of Lieutenant-Fireworker Humphrey Chinn, of the Bombay European Regiment, who assisted at the capture of Seringapatam in 1799. Alfred Ellis Chinn, Humphrey's younger brother, commanded a regiment of Bombay Grenadiers from 1804 to 1813, when he saw some mixed fighting; and in 1834 John Chinn of the same family—we will call him John Chinn the First—came to light as a level-headed administrator in time of trouble at a place called Mundesur. He died young, but left his mark on the new country, and the Honourable the Board of Directors of the Honourable the East India Company embodied his virtues in a stately resolution, and paid for the expenses of his tomb among the Satpura hills.

He was succeeded by his son, Lionel Chinn, who left the little old Devonshire home just in time to be severely wounded in the Mutiny. He spent his working life within a hundred and fifty miles of John Chinn's grave, and rose to the command of a regiment of small, wild hill-men, most of whom had known his father. His son John was born in the small thatched-roofed, mud-walled cantonment, which is even to-day eighty miles from the nearest railway, in the heart of a scrubby, tigerish country. Colonel Lionel Chinn served thirty years and retired. In the Canal his steamer passed the outward-bound troopship, carrying his son eastward to the family duties.

The Chinns are luckier than most folk, because they know exactly what they must do. A clever Chinn passes for the Bombay Civil Service, and gets away to Central India, where everybody is glad to see him. A dull Chinn enters the Police Department or the Woods and Forests, and sooner or later, he, too, appears in Central India, and that is what gave rise to the saying 'Central India is inhabited by Bhils, Mairs, and Chinns, all very much alike.' The breed is small-boned, dark, and silent, and the stupidest of them are good shots. John Chinn the Second was rather clever, but as the eldest son he entered the army, according to Chinn tradition. His duty was to abide in his father's regiment, for the term of his natural life, though the corps was one which most men would have paid heavily to avoid. They were irregulars, small, dark, and blackish, clothed in rifle-green with black-leather trimmings; and friends called them the 'Wuddars,' which means a race of low-caste people who dug up rats to eat. But the Wuddars did not resent it. They were the only Wuddars, and their points of pride were these:

Firstly, they had fewer English officers than any native regiment. Secondly, their subalterns were not mounted on parade, as is the general rule, but walked at the head of their men. A man who can hold his own with the Wuddars at their quickstep must be sound in wind and limb. Thirdly, they were the most *pukka shikarries* (out-and-out hunters) in all India. Fourthly—up to one hundredthly—they were the Wuddars—Chinn's Irregular Bhil Levies of the old days, but now, henceforward and for ever, the Wuddars.

No Englishman entered their mess except for love or through family usage. The officers talked to their soldiers in a tongue not two hundred white folk in India understood; and the men were their children, all drawn from the Bhils, who are, perhaps, the strangest of the many strange races in India. They were, and at heart are, wild men, furtive, shy, full of untold superstitions. The races whom we call natives of the country found the Bhil in possession of the land when they first broke into that part of the world thousands of years ago. The books call them Pre-Aryan, Aboriginal, Dravidian, and so forth; and, in other words, that is what the Bhils call themselves. When a Rajput chief, whose bards can sing his pedigree backwards for twelve hundred years, is set on the throne, his investiture is not complete till he has been marked on the forehead with blood from the veins of a Bhil. The Rajputs say the ceremony has no meaning, but the Bhil knows that it is the last, last shadow of his old rights as the long-ago owner of the soil.

Centuries of oppression and massacre made the Bhil a cruel and half-crazy thief and cattle-stealer, and when the English came he seemed to be almost as open to civilisation as the tigers of his own jungles. But

John Chinn the First, father of Lionel, grandfather of our John, went into his country, lived with him, learned his language, shot the deer that stole his poor crops, and won his confidence, so that some Bhils learned to plough and sow, while others were coaxed into the Company's service to police their friends.

When they understood that standing in line did not mean instant execution, they accepted soldiering as a cumbrous but amusing kind of sport, and were zealous to keep the wild Bhils under control. That was the thin edge of the wedge. John Chinn the First gave them written promises that, if they were good from a certain date, the Government would overlook previous offences: and since John Chinn was never known to break his word—he promised once to hang a Bhil locally esteemed invulnerable, and hanged him in front of his tribe for seven proved murders—the Bhils settled down as steadily as they knew how. It was slow, unseen work, of the sort that is being done all over India to-day; and though John Chinn's only reward came, as I have said, in the shape of a grave at Government expense, the little people of the hills never forgot him.

Colonel Lionel Chinn knew and loved them too, and they were very fairly civilised, for Bhils, before his service ended. Many of them could hardly be distinguished from low-caste Hindu farmers; but in the south, where John Chinn the First was buried, the wildest still clung to the Satpura ranges, cherishing a legend that some day Jan Chinn, as they called him, would return to his own. In the meantime they mistrusted the white man and his ways. The least excitement would stampede them plundering at random, and now and then killing; but if they were handled discreetly they grieved like children, and promised never to do it again.

The Bhils of the regiment—the uniformed men—were virtuous in many ways, but they needed humouring. They felt bored and homesick unless taken after tigers as beaters; and their cold-blooded daring—all Wuddars shoot tigers on foot: it is their caste-mark—made even the officers wonder. They would follow up a wounded tiger as unconcernedly as though it were a sparrow with a broken wing; and this through a country full of caves and rifts and pits, where a wild beast could hold a dozen men at his mercy. Now and then some little man was brought to barracks with his head smashed in or his ribs torn away; but his companions never learned caution; they contented themselves with settling the tiger.

Young John Chinn was decanted at the verandah of the Wuddars' lonely mess-house from the back seat of a two-wheeled cart, his gun-cases cascading all round him. The slender, little, hooky-nosed boy looked forlorn as a strayed goat when he slapped the white dust off his knees, and the cart jolted down the glaring road. But in his heart he was contented. After all, this was the place where he had been born, and things were not much changed since he had been sent to England, a child, fifteen years ago.

There were a few new buildings, but the air and the smell and the sunshine were the same, and the little green men who crossed the parade-ground looked very familiar. Three weeks ago John Chinn would have said he did not remember a word of the Bhil tongue, but at the mess-door he found his lips moving in sentences that he did not understand —bits of old nursery rhymes, and tail-ends of such orders as his father used to give the men.

The Colonel watched him come up the steps, and laughed.

'Look!' he said to the Major. 'No need to ask the young un's breed. He's a *pukka* Chinn. Might be his father in the Fifties over again.'

'Hope he'll shoot as straight,' said the Major. 'He's brought enough ironmongery with him.'

'Wouldn't be a Chinn if he didn't. Watch him blowin' his nose. Regular Chinn beak. Flourishes his handkerchief like his father. It's the second edition—line for line.'

'Fairy tale, by Jove!' said the Major, peering through the slats of the jalousies. 'If he's the lawful heir, he'll . . . Now old Chinn could no more pass that chick without fiddling with it than . . .'

'His son!' said the Colonel, jumping up.

'Well, I be blowed!' said the Major. The boy's eye had been caught by a split reed screen that hung on a slew between the verandah pillars, and mechanically he had tweaked the edge to set it level. Old Chinn had sworn three times a day at that screen for many years; he could never get it to his satisfaction. His son entered the anteroom in the middle of a five-fold silence. They made him welcome for his father's sake and, as they took stock of him, for his own. He was ridiculously like the portrait of the Colonel on the wall, and when he had washed a little of the dust from his throat he went to his quarters with the old man's short, noiseless jungle-step.

'So much for heredity,' said the Major. 'That comes of three generations among the Bhils.'

'And the men know it,' said a Wing-officer. 'They've been waiting for this youth with their tongues hanging out. I am persuaded that, unless he absolutely beats 'em over the head, they'll lie down by companies and worship him.'

'Nothin' like havin' a father before you,' said the Major. 'I'm a parvenu with my chaps. I've only been twenty years in the regiment, and my revered parent he was a simple squire. There's no getting at the bottom of a Bhil's mind. Now, *why* is the superior bearer that young Chinn brought with him fleeing across country with his bundle?' He stepped into the verandah, and shouted after the man—a typical new-joined subaltern's servant who speaks English and cheats his master.

'What is it?' he called.

'Plenty bad men here. I going, sar,' was the reply. 'Have taken Sahib's keys, and say will shoot.'

'Doocid lucid—doocid convincin'. How those up-country thieves can leg it! He has been badly frightened by some one.' The Major strolled to his quarters to dress for mess.

Young Chinn, walking like a man in a dream, had fetched a compass round the entire cantonment before going to his own tiny cottage. The captains' quarters, in which he had been born, delayed him for a little; then he looked at the well on the parade-ground, where he had sat of evenings with his nurse, and at the ten-by-fourteen church, where the officers went to service if a chaplain of any official creed happened to come along. It seemed very small as compared with the gigantic building he used to stare up at, but it was the same place.

From time to time he passed a knot of silent soldiers, who saluted. They might have been the very men who had carried him on their backs when he was in his first knickerbockers. A faint light burned in his room, and, as he entered, hands clasped his feet, and a voice murmured from the floor.

'Who is it?' said young Chinn, not knowing he spoke in the Bhil tongue.

'I bore you in my arms, Sahib, when I was a strong man and you were a small one—crying, crying, crying! I am your servant, as I was your father's before you. We are all your servants.'

Young Chinn could not trust himself to reply, and the voice went on:

'I have taken your keys from that fat foreigner, and sent him away; and the studs are in the shirt for mess. Who should know, if I do not know? And so the baby has become a man, and forgets his nurse; but my nephew shall make a good servant, or I will beat him twice a day.'

Then there rose up, with a rattle, as straight as a Bhil arrow, a little white-haired wizened ape of a man, with medals and orders on his tunic, stammering, saluting, and trembling. Behind him a young and wiry Bhil, in uniform, was taking the trees out of Chinn's mess-boots.

Chinn's eyes were full of tears. The old man held out his keys.

'Foreigners are bad people. He will never come back again. We are all servants of your father's son. Has the Sahib forgotten who took him to see the trapped tiger in the village across the river when his mother was so frightened and he was so brave?'

The scene came back to Chinn in great magic-lantern flashes. 'Bukta!' he cried; and all in a breath: 'You promised nothing should hurt me. *Is* it Bukta?'

The man was at his feet a second time. 'He has not forgotten. He remembers his own people as his father remembered. Now can I die. But first I will live and show the Sahib how to kill tigers. That *that* yonder is my nephew. If he is not a good servant, beat him and send him to me, and I will surely kill him, for now the Sahib is with his own people. Ai, Jan *baba*–Jan *baba!* My Jan *baba!* I will stay here and see that this does his work well. Take off his boots, fool. Sit down upon the bed, Sahib, and let me look. It *is* Jan *baba!*'

He pushed forward the hilt of his sword as a sign of service, which is an honour paid only to viceroys, governors, generals, or to little children whom one loves dearly. Chinn touched the hilt mechanically with three fingers, muttering he knew not what. It happened to be the old answer of his childhood, when Bukta in jest called him the little General Sahib.

The Major's quarters were opposite Chinn's, and when he heard his servant gasp with surprise he looked across the room. Then the Major sat on the bed and whistled; for the spectacle of the senior native commissioned officer of the regiment, an 'unmixed' Bhil, a Companion of the Order of British India, with thirty-five years' spotless service in the army, and a rank among his own people superior to that of many Bengal princelings, valeting the last-joined subaltern, was a little too much for his nerves.

The throaty bugles blew the Mess-call that has a long legend behind it. First a few piercing notes like the shrieks of beaters in a far-away cover, and next, large, full, and smooth, the refrain of the wild song: 'And oh, and oh, the green pulse of Mundore–Mundore!'

'All little children were in bed when the Sahib heard the call last,' said Bukta, passing Chinn a clean handkerchief. The call brought back memories of his cot under the mosquito-netting, his mother's kiss, and the sound of footsteps growing fainter as he dropped asleep among his men. So he hooked the dark collar of his new mess-jacket, and went to dinner like a prince who has newly inherited his father's crown.

Old Bukta swaggered forth curling his whiskers. He knew his own value, and no money and no rank within the gift of the Government would have induced him to put studs in young officers' shirts, or to hand them clean ties. Yet, when he took off his uniform that night, and squatted among his fellows for a quiet smoke, he told them what he had done, and they said that he was entirely right. Thereat Bukta propounded a theory which to a white mind would have seemed raving insanity; but the whispering, level-headed little men of war considered it from every point of view, and thought that there might be a great deal in it.

At mess under the oil-lamps the talk turned as usual to the unfailing subject of *shikar*—big game shooting of every kind and under all sorts of conditions. Young Chinn opened his eyes when he understood that each one of his companions had shot several tigers in the Wuddar style—on foot, that is—making no more of the business than if the brute had been a dog.

'In nine cases out of ten,' said the Major, 'a tiger is almost as dangerous as a porcupine. But the tenth time you come home feet first.'

That set all talking, and long before midnight Chinn's brain was in a whirl with stories of tigers—man-eaters and cattle-killers each pursuing his own business as methodically as clerks in an office; new tigers that had lately come into such-and-such a district; and old, friendly beasts of great cunning, known by nicknames in the mess—such as 'Puggy,' who was lazy, with huge paws, and 'Mrs. Malaprop,' who turned up when you never expected her, and made female noises. Then they spoke of Bhil superstitions, a wide and picturesque field, till young Chinn hinted that they must be pulling his leg.

''Deed we aren't,' said a man on his left. 'We know all about you. You're a Chinn and all that, and you've a sort of vested right here; but if you don't believe what we're telling you, what will you do when old Bukta begins his stories? He knows about ghost-tigers, and tigers that go to a hell of their own; and tigers that walk on their hind feet; and your grandpapa's riding-tiger, as well. Odd he hasn't spoken of that yet.'

'You know you've an ancestor buried down Satpura way, don't you?' said the Major, as Chinn smiled irresolutely.

'Of course I do,' said Chinn, who had the chronicle of the Book of Chinn by heart. It lies in a worn old ledger on the Chinese lacquer table behind the piano in the Devonshire home, and the children are allowed to look at it on Sundays.

'Well, I wasn't sure. Your revered ancestor, my boy, according to the Bhils, has a tiger of his own—a saddle-tiger that he rides round the country whenever he feels inclined. *I* don't call it decent in an ex-collector's ghost; but that is what the Southern Bhils believe. Even our men, who might be called moderately cool, don't care to beat that country if they hear that Jan Chinn is running about on his tiger. It is supposed to be a clouded animal—not stripy, but blotchy, like a tortoise-shell tom-cat. No end of a brute, it is, and a sure sign of war or pestilence or—or something. There's a nice family legend for you.'

'What's the origin of it, d'you suppose?' said Chinn.

'Ask the Satpura Bhils. Old Jan Chinn was a mighty hunter before the Lord. Perhaps it was the tiger's revenge, or perhaps he's huntin' 'em still. You must go to his tomb one of these days and inquire. Bukta will probably attend to that. He was asking me before you came whether by any ill-luck you had already bagged your tiger. If not, he is going to enter you under his own wing. Of course, for you of all men it's imperative. You'll have a first-class time with Bukta.'

The Major was not wrong. Bukta kept an anxious eye on young Chinn at drill, and it was noticeable that the first time the new officer lifted up his voice in an order the whole line quivered. Even the Colonel was taken aback, for it might have been Lionel Chinn returned from Devonshire with a new lease of life. Bukta had continued to develop his peculiar theory among his intimates, and it was accepted as a matter of faith in the lines, since every word and gesture on young Chinn's part so confirmed it.

The old man arranged early that his darling should wipe out the reproach of not having shot a tiger; but he was not content to take the first or any beast that happened to arrive. In his own villages he dispensed the high, low, and middle justice, and when his people—naked and fluttered—came to him with word of a beast marked down, he bade them send spies to the kills and the watering-places, that he might be sure the quarry was such an one as suited the dignity of such a man.

Three or four times the reckless trackers returned most truthfully saying that the beast was mangy, undersized—a tigress worn with nursing, or a broken-toothed old male—and Bukta would curb young Chinn's impatience.

At last, a noble animal was marked down—a ten-foot cattle-killer with a huge roll of loose skin along the belly, glossy-hided, full-frilled about the neck, whiskered, frisky, and young. He had slain a man in pure sport, they said.

'Let him be fed,' quoth Bukta, and the villagers dutifully drove out cows to amuse him, that he might lie up near by.

Princes and potentates have taken ship to India and spent great moneys for the mere glimpse of beasts one-half as fine as this of Bukta's.

'It is not good,' said he to the Colonel, when he asked for shooting leave, 'that my Colonel's son who may be–that my Colonel's son should lose his maidenhead on any small jungle beast. That may come after. I have waited long for this which is a tiger. He has come in from the Mair country. In seven days we will return with the skin.'

The mess gnashed their teeth enviously. Bukta, had he chosen, might have invited them all. But he went out alone with Chinn, two days in a shooting-cart and a day on foot, till they came to a rocky, glary valley with a pool of good water in it. It was a parching day, and the boy very naturally stripped and went in for a bathe, leaving Bukta by the clothes. A white skin shows far against brown jungle, and what Bukta beheld on Chinn's back and right shoulder dragged him forward step by step with staring eyeballs.

'I'd forgotten it isn't decent to strip before a man of his position,' thought Chinn, flouncing in the water. 'How the little devil stares! What is it, Bukta?'

'The Mark!' was the whispered answer.

'It is nothing. You know how it is with my people!' Chinn was annoyed. The dull-red birth-mark on his shoulder, something like a conventionalised Tartar cloud, had slipped his memory, or he would not have bathed. It occurred, so they said at home, in alternate generations, appearing, curiously enough, eight or nine years after birth, and, save that it was part of the Chinn inheritance, would not be considered pretty. He hurried ashore, dressed again and went on till they met two or three Bhils, who promptly fell on their faces. 'My people,' grunted Bukta, not condescending to notice them. 'And so your people, Sahib. When I was a young man we were fewer, but not so weak. Now we are many, but poor stock. As may be remembered. How will you shoot him, Sahib? From a tree; from a shelter which my people shall build; by day or by night?'

'On foot and in the daytime,' said young Chinn.

'That was your custom, as I have heard,' said Bukta to himself. 'I will get news of him. Then you and I will go to him. I will carry one gun. You have yours. There is no need of more. What tiger shall stand against *thee*?'

He was marked down by a little water-hole at the head of a ravine, full-gorged and half asleep in the May sunlight. He was walked up like a partridge, and he turned to do battle for his life. Bukta made no motion to raise his rifle, but kept his eyes on Chinn, who met the shattering roar of the charge with a single shot—it seemed to him hours as he sighted—which tore through the throat, smashing the backbone below the neck and between the shoulders. The brute crouched, choked, and fell, and before Chinn knew well what had happened Bukta bade him stay still while he paced the distance between his feet and the ringing jaws.

'Fifteen,' said Bukta. 'Short paces. No need for a second shot, Sahib. He bleeds cleanly where he lies, and we need not spoil the skin. I said there would be no need of these, but they came—in case.'

Suddenly the sides of the ravine were crowned with the heads of Bukta's people—a force that could have blown the ribs out of the beast had Chinn's shot failed; but their guns were hidden, and they appeared as interested beaters, some five or six, waiting the word to skin. Bukta watched the life fade from the wild eyes, lifted one hand, and turned on his heel.

'No need to show that *we* care,' said he. 'Now, after this, we can kill what we choose. Put out your hand, Sahib.'

Chinn obeyed. It was entirely steady, and Bukta nodded. 'That also was your custom. My men skin quickly. They will carry the skin to cantonments. Will the Sahib come to my poor village for the night and, perhaps, forget that I am his officer?'

'But those men—the beaters. They have worked hard, and perhaps——'

'Oh, if they skin clumsily, we will skin them. They are my people. In the Lines I am one thing. Here I am another.'

This was very true. When Bukta doffed uniform and reverted to the fragmentary dress of his own people, he left his civilisation of drill in the next world. That night, after a little talk with his subjects, he devoted to an orgy; and a Bhil orgy is a thing not to be safely written about. Chinn, flushed with triumph, was in the thick of it, but the meaning of the mysteries was hidden. Wild folk came and pressed about his knees with offerings. He gave his flask to the elders of the village. They grew eloquent, and wreathed him about with flowers. Gifts and loans, not all seemly, were thrust upon him, and infernal music rolled and maddened round red fires, while singers sang songs of the ancient times, and danced peculiar dances. The aboriginal liquors are very potent, and Chinn was compelled to taste them often, but, unless the stuff had been drugged, how came he to fall asleep suddenly, and to waken late the next day—half a march from the village?

'The Sahib was very tired. A little before dawn he went to sleep,' Bukta explained. 'My people carried him here, and now it is time we should go back to cantonments.'

The voice, smooth and deferential, the step, steady and silent, made it hard to believe that only a few hours before Bukta was yelling and capering with naked fellow-devils of the scrub.

'My people were very pleased to see the Sahib. They will never forget. When next the Sahib goes out recruiting, he will go to my people, and they will give him as many men as we need.'

Chinn kept his own counsel, except as to the shooting of the tiger, and Bukta embroidered that tale with a shameless tongue. The skin was certainly one of the finest ever hung up in the mess, and the first of many. When Bukta could not accompany his boy on shooting-trips, he took care to put him in good hands, and Chinn learned more of the mind and desire of the wild Bhil in his marches and campings, by talks at twilight or at wayside pools, than an uninstructed man could have come at in a lifetime.

Presently his men in the regiment grew bold to speak of their relatives—mostly in trouble—and to lay cases of tribal custom before him. They would say, squatting in his verandah at twilight, after the easy, confidential style of the Wuddars, that such-and-such a bachelor had run away with such-and-such a wife at a far-off village. Now, how many cows would Chinn Sahib consider a just fine? Or, again, if written order came from the Government that a Bhil was to repair to a walled city of the plains to give evidence in a law-court, would it be wise to disregard that order? On the other hand, if it were obeyed, would the rash voyager return alive?

'But what have I to do with these things?' Chinn demanded of Bukta, impatiently. 'I am a soldier. I do not know the Law.'

'Hoo! Law is for fools and white men. Give them a large and loud order and they will abide by it. Thou art their Law.'

'But wherefore?'

Every trace of expression left Bukta's countenance. The idea might have smitten him for the first time. 'How can I say?' he replied. 'Perhaps it is on account of the name. A Bhil does not love strange things. Give them orders, Sahib—two, three, four words at a time such as they can carry away in their heads. That is enough.'

Chinn gave orders then, valiantly, not realising that a word spoken in haste before mess became the dread unappealable law of villages beyond the smoky hills—was, in truth, no less than the law of Jan Chinn the First, who, so the whispered legend ran, had come back to earth to oversee the third generation in the body and bones of his grandson.

There could be no sort of doubt in this matter. All the Bhils knew that Jan Chinn reincarnated had honoured Bukta's village with his presence after slaying his first—in this life—tiger; that he had eaten and drunk with the people, as he was used; and—Bukta must have drugged Chinn's liquor very deeply—upon his back and right shoulder all men had seen the same angry red Flying Cloud that the high Gods had set on the flesh of Jan Chinn the First when first he came to the Bhil. As concerned the foolish white world which has no eyes, he was a slim and young officer in the Wuddars; but his own people knew he was Jan Chinn, who had made the Bhil a man; and, believing, they hastened to carry his words, careful never to alter them on the way.

Because the savage and the child who plays lonely games have one horror of being laughed at or questioned, the little folk kept their convictions to themselves; and the Colonel, who thought he knew his regiment, never guessed that each one of the six hundred quick-footed, beady-eyed rank-and-file, at attention beside their rifles, believed serenely and unshakenly that the subaltern on the left flank of the line was a demigod twice born—tutelary deity of their land and people. The Earth-gods themselves had stamped the incarnation, and who would dare to doubt the handiwork of the Earth-gods?

Chinn, being practical above all things, saw that his family name served him well in the lines and in camp. His men gave no trouble—one does not commit regimental offences with a god in the chair of justice—and he was sure of the best beaters in the district when he needed them. They believed that the protection of Jan Chinn the First cloaked them, and were bold in that belief beyond the utmost daring of excited Bhils.

His quarters began to look like an amateur natural-history museum, in spite of duplicate heads and horns and skulls that he sent home to Devonshire. The people, very humanly, learned the weak side of their god. It is true he was unbribable, but bird-skins, flies, beetles, and, above all, news of big game pleased him. In other respects, too, he lived up to the Chinn tradition. He was feverproof. A night's sitting out over a tethered goat in a damp valley, that would have filled the Major with a month's malaria, had no effect on him. He was, as they said, 'salted before he was born.'

Now in the autumn of his second year's service an uneasy rumour crept out of the earth and ran about among the Bhils. Chinn heard nothing of it till a brother-officer said across the mess-table: 'Your revered ancestor's on the rampage in the Satpura country. You'd better look him up.'

'I don't want to be disrespectful, but I'm a little sick of my revered ancestor. Bukta talks of nothing else. What's the old boy supposed to be doing now?'

'Riding cross-country by moonlight on his processional tiger. That's the story. He's been seen by about two thousand Bhils, skipping along the tops of the Satpuras, and scaring people to death. They believe it devoutly, and all the Satpura chaps are worshipping away at his shrine—tomb, I mean—like good 'uns. You really ought to go down there. Must be a queer thing to see your grandfather treated as a god.'

'What makes you think there's any truth in the tale?' said Chinn.

'Because all our men deny it. They say they've never heard of Chinn's tiger. Now that's a manifest lie, because every Bhil *has*.'

'There's only one thing you've overlooked,' said the Colonel, thoughtfully. 'When a local god reappears on earth it's always an excuse for trouble of some kind; and those Satpura Bhils are about as wild as your grandfather left them, young 'un. It means something.'

'Meanin' they may go on the war-path?' said Chinn.

'Can't say—as yet. Shouldn't be surprised a little bit.'

'I haven't been told a syllable.'

'Proves it all the more. They are keeping something back.'

'Bukta tells me everything, too, as a rule. Now, why didn't he tell me that?'

Chinn put the question directly to the old man that night, and the answer surprised him.

'Why should I tell what is well known? Yes, the Clouded Tiger is out in the Satpura country.'

'What do the wild Bhils think that it means?'

'They do not know. They wait. Sahib, what *is* coming? Say only one little word, and we will be content.'

'We? What have tales from the south, where the jungly Bhils live, to do with drilled men?'

'When Jan Chinn wakes is no time for any Bhil to be quiet.'

'But he has not waked, Bukta.'

'Sahib'—the old man's eyes were full of tender reproof—'if he does not wish to be seen, why does he go abroad in the moonlight? We know he is awake, but we do not know what he desires. Is it a sign for all the Bhils, or one that concerns the Satpura folk alone? Say one little word, Sahib, that I may carry it to the lines, and send on to our villages. Why does Jan Chinn ride out? Who has done wrong? Is it pestilence? Is it murrain? Will our children die? Is it a sword? Remember, Sahib, we are thy people, and thy servants, and in this life I bore thee in my arms—not knowing.'

'Bukta has evidently looked on the cup this evening,' Chinn thought; 'but if I can do anything to soothe the old chap I must. It's like the Mutiny rumours on a small scale.'

He dropped into a deep wicker chair, over which was thrown his first tiger-skin, and his weight on the cushion flapped the clawed paws over his shoulders. He laid hold of them mechanically as he spoke, drawing the painted hide, cloak-fashion, about him.

'Now will I tell the truth, Bukta,' he said, leaning forward, the dried muzzle on his shoulder, to invent a specious lie.

'I see that it is the truth,' was the answer, in a shaking voice.

'Jan Chinn goes abroad among the Satpuras, riding on the Clouded Tiger, ye say? Be it so. Therefore the sign of the wonder is for the Satpura Bhils only, and does not touch the Bhils who plough in the north and east, the Bhils of the Khandesh, or any others, except the Satpura Bhils, who, as we know, are wild and foolish.'

'It is, then, a sign for *them*. Good or bad?'

'Beyond doubt, good. For why should Jan Chinn make evil to those whom he has made men? The nights over yonder are hot; it is ill to lie in one bed over long without turning, and Jan Chinn would look again upon his people. So he rises, whistles his Clouded Tiger, and goes abroad a little to breathe the cool air. If the Satpura Bhils kept to their villages, and did not wander after dark, they would not see him. Indeed, Bukta, it is no more than that he would see the light again in his own country. Send this news south, and say that it is my word.'

Bukta bowed to the floor. 'Good Heavens!' thought Chinn, 'and this blinking pagan is a first-class officer, and as straight as a die! I may as well round it off neatly.' He went on:

'If the Satpura Bhils ask the meaning of the sign, tell them that Jan Chinn would see how they kept their old promises of good living. Perhaps they have plundered; perhaps they mean to disobey the orders of the Government; perhaps there is a dead man in the jungle; and so Jan Chinn has come to see.'

'Is he, then, angry?'

'Bah! Am *I* ever angry with my Bhils? I say angry words, and threaten many things. *Thou* knowest, Bukta. I have seen thee smile behind the hand. I know, and thou knowest. The Bhils are my children. I have said it many times.'

'Ay. We be thy children,' said Bukta.

'And no otherwise is it with Jan Chinn, my father's father. He would see the land he loved and the people once again. It is a good ghost, Bukta. I say it. Go and tell them. And I do hope devoutly,' he added, 'that it will calm 'em down.' Flinging back the tiger-skin, he rose with a long, unguarded yawn that showed his well-kept teeth.

Bukta fled, to be received in the lines by a knot of panting inquirers.

'It is true,' said Bukta. 'He wrapped himself in the skin and spoke from it. He would see his own country again. The sign is not for us; and, indeed, he is a young man. How should he lie idle of nights? He says his bed is too hot and the air is bad. He goes to and fro for the love of night-running. He has said it.'

The grey-whiskered assembly shuddered.

'He says the Bhils are his children. Ye know he does not lie. He has said it to me.'

'But what of the Satpura Bhils? What means the sign for them?'

'Nothing. It is only night-running, as I have said. He rides to see if they obey the Government, as he taught them to do in his first life.'

'And what if they do not?'

'He did not say.'

The light went out in Chinn's quarters.

'Look,' said Bukta. 'Now he goes away. None the less it is a good ghost, as he has said. How shall we fear Jan Chinn, who made the Bhil a man? His protection is on us; and ye know Jan Chinn never broke a protection spoken or written on paper. When he is older and has found him a wife he will lie in his bed till morning.'

A commanding officer is generally aware of the regimental state of mind a little before the men; and this is why the Colonel said a few days later that some one had been putting the fear of God into the Wuddars. As he was the only person officially entitled to do this, it distressed him to see such unanimous virtue. 'It's too good to last,' he said. 'I only wish I could find out what the little chaps mean.'

The explanation, as it seemed to him, came at the change of the moon, when he received orders to hold himself in readiness to 'allay any possible excitement' among the Satpura Bhils, who were, to put it mildly, uneasy because a paternal Government had sent up against them a

Mahratta State-educated vaccinator, with lancets, lymph, and an officially registered calf. In the language of State, they had 'manifested a strong objection to all prophylactic measures,' had 'forcibly detained the vaccinator,' and 'were on the point of neglecting or evading their tribal obligations.'

'That means they are in a blue funk—same as they were at census-time,' said the Colonel; 'and if we stampede them into the hills we'll never catch 'em, in the first place, and, in the second, they'll whoop off plundering till further orders. Wonder who the God-forsaken idiot is who is trying to vaccinate a Bhil. I knew trouble was coming. One good thing is that they'll only use local corps, and we can knock up something we'll call a campaign, and let them down easy. Fancy us potting our best beaters because they don't want to be vaccinated! They're only crazy with fear.'

'Don't you think, sir,' said Chinn the next day, 'that perhaps you could give me a fortnight's shooting-leave?'

'Desertion in the face of the enemy, by Jove!' The Colonel laughed. 'I might, but I'd have to antedate it a little, because we're warned for service, as you might say. However, we'll assume that you applied for leave three days ago, and are now well on your way south.'

'I'd like to take Bukta with me.'

'Of course, yes. I think that will be the best plan. You've some kind of hereditary influence with the little chaps, and they may listen to you when a glimpse of our uniforms would drive them wild. You've never been in that part of the world before, have you? Take care they don't send you to your family vault in your youth and innocence. I believe you'll be all right if you can get 'em to listen to you.'

'I think so, sir; but if—if they should accidentally put an—make asses of 'emselves—they might, you know—I hope you'll represent that they were only frightened. There isn't an ounce of real vice in 'em, and I should never forgive myself if any one of—of my name got them into trouble.'

The Colonel nodded, but said nothing.

Chinn and Bukta departed at once. Bukta did not say that, ever since the official vaccinator had been dragged into the hills by indignant Bhils, runner after runner had skulked up to the lines, entreating, with forehead in the dust, that Jan Chinn should come and explain this unknown horror that hung over his people.

The portent of the Clouded Tiger was now too clear. Let Jan Chinn comfort his own, for vain was the help of mortal man. Bukta toned down these beseechings to a simple request for Chinn's presence. Nothing would have pleased the old man better than a rough-and-tumble campaign against the Satpuras, whom he, as an 'unmixed' Bhil, despised; but he had a duty to all his nation as Jan Chinn's interpreter, and he devoutly believed that forty plagues would fall on his village if he tampered with that obligation. Besides Jan Chinn knew all things, and he rode the Clouded Tiger.

They covered thirty miles a day on foot and pony, raising the blue wall-like line of the Satpuras as swiftly as might be. Bukta was very silent.

They began the steep climb a little after noon, but it was near sunset ere they reached the stone platform clinging to the side of a rifted, jungle-covered hill, where Jan Chinn the First was laid, as he had desired, that he might overlook his people. All India is full of neglected graves that date from the beginning of the eighteenth century–tombs of forgotten colonels of corps long since disbanded; mates of East Indiamen who went on shooting expeditions and never came back; factors, agents, writers, and ensigns of the Honourable the East India Company by hundreds and thousands and tens of thousands. English folk forget quickly, but natives have long memories, and if a man has done good in his life it is remembered after his death. The weathered marble four-square tomb of Jan Chinn was hung about with wild flowers and nuts, packets of wax and honey, bottles of native spirits, and infamous cigars, with buffalo horns and plumes of dried grass. At one end was a rude clay image of a white man, in the old-fashioned top-hat, riding on a bloated tiger.

Bukta salaamed reverently as they approached. Chinn bared his head and began to pick out the blurred inscription. So far as he could read it ran thus–word for word, and letter for letter:–

To the Memory of JOHN CHINN, ESQ.
Late Collector of . . . .
. . . . ithout Bloodshed or . . . error of Authority
Employ . only . . eans of Conciliat . . . and Confiden .
accomplished the . . . tire Subjection . . .
a Lawless and Predatory Peop . . .
. . . . taching them to . . . . ish Government
by a Conque . . over . . . . Minds
The most perma . . . and rational Mode of Domini . .
. . . Governor-General and Counc . . . engal
have ordered thi . . . . erected
. . . . arted this Life Aug. 19, 184 . Ag . . .

On the other side of the grave were ancient verses, also very worn. As much as Chinn could decipher said:

. . . . the savage band
Forsook their Haunts and b . . . . is Command
. . . . mended . . rals check a . . . . st for spoil
And . s . ing Hamlets prove his gene . . . . . toil
Humanit . . . survey . . . . . . ights restore . . .
A nation . . . ield . . subdued without a Sword.

For some little time he leaned on the tomb thinking of this dead man of his own blood, and of the house in Devonshire; then, nodding to the plains; 'Yes; it's a big work—all of it—even my little share. He must have been worth knowing. . . . Bukta, where are my people?'

'Not here, Sahib. No man comes here except in full sun. They wait above. Let us climb and see.'

But Chinn, remembering the first law of Oriental diplomacy, in an even voice answered: 'I have come this far only because the Satpura folk are foolish, and dared not visit our lines. Now bid them wait on me *here*. I am not a servant, but the master of Bhils.'

'I go—I go,' clucked the old man. Night was falling, and at any moment Jan Chinn might whistle up his dreaded steed from the darkening scrub.

Now for the first time in a long life Bukta disobeyed a lawful command and deserted his leader; for he did not come back but pressed to the flat table-top of the hill, and called softly. Men stirred all about him—little trembling men with bows and arrows who had watched the two since noon.

'Where is he?' whispered one.

'At his own place. He bids you come,' said Bukta.

'Now?'

'Now.'

'Rather let him loose the Clouded Tiger upon us. We do not go.'

'Nor I, though I bore him in my arms when he was a child in this his life. Wait here till the day.'

'But surely he will be angry.'

'He will be very angry, for he has nothing to eat. But he has said to me many times that the Bhils are his children. By sunlight I believe this, but—by moonlight I am not so sure. What folly have ye Satpura pigs compassed that ye should need him at all?'

'One came to us in the name of the Government with little ghost-knives and a magic calf, meaning to turn us into cattle by the cutting off of our arms. We were greatly afraid, but we did not kill the man. He is here, bound—a black man; and we think he comes from the West. He said it was an order to cut us all with knives—especially the women and the children. We did not hear that it was an order, so we were afraid, and kept to our hills. Some of our men have taken ponies and bullocks from the plains, and others pots and cloths and ear-rings.'

'Are any slain?'

'By our men? Not yet. But the young men are blown to and fro by many rumours like flames upon a hill. I sent runners asking for Jan Chinn lest worse should come to us. It was this fear that he foretold by the sign of the Clouded Tiger.'

'He says it is otherwise,' said Bukta; and he repeated, with amplifications, all that young Chinn had told him at the conference of the wicker chair.

'Think you,' said the questioner, at last, 'that the Government will lay hands on us?'

'Not I,' Bukta rejoined. 'Jan Chinn will give an order, and ye will obey. The rest is between the Government and Jan Chinn. I myself know something of the ghost-knives and the scratching. It is a charm against the Smallpox. But how it is done I cannot tell. Nor need that concern you.'

'If he stand by us and before the anger of the Government we will most strictly obey Jan Chinn, except—except we do not go down to that place to-night.'

They could hear young Chinn below them shouting for Bukta; but they cowered and sat still, expecting the Clouded Tiger. The tomb had been holy ground for nearly half a century. If Jan Chinn chose to sleep there, who had better right? But they would not come within eyeshot of the place till broad day.

At first Chinn was exceedingly angry, till it occurred to him that Bukta most probably had a reason (which, indeed, he had), and his own dignity might suffer if he yelled without answer. He propped himself against the foot of the grave, and, alternately dozing and smoking, came through the warm night proud that he was a lawful, legitimate, fever-proof Chinn.

He prepared his plan of action much as his grandfather would have done; and when Bukta appeared in the morning with a most liberal supply of food, said nothing of the overnight desertion. Bukta would have been relieved by an outburst of human anger; but Chinn finished his victual leisurely, and a cheroot, ere he made any sign.

'They are very much afraid,' said Bukta, who was not too bold himself. 'It remains only to give orders. They say they will obey if thou wilt only stand between them and the Government.'

'That I know,' said Chinn, strolling slowly to the table-land. A few of the elder men stood in an irregular semicircle in an open glade; but the ruck of people—women and children—were hidden in the thicket. They had no desire to face the first anger of Jan Chinn the First.

Seating himself on a fragment of split rock, he smoked his cheroot to the butt, hearing men breathe hard all about him. Then he cried so suddenly that they jumped:

'Bring the man that was bound!'

A scuffle and a cry were followed by the appearance of a Hindu vaccinator, quaking with fear, bound hand and foot, as the Bhils of old were accustomed to bind their human sacrifices. He was pushed cautiously before the presence; but young Chinn did not look at him.

'I said—the man that *was* bound. Is it a jest to bring me one tied like a buffalo? Since when could the Bhil bind folk at his pleasure? Cut!'

Half a dozen hasty knives cut away the thongs, and the man crawled to Chinn, who pocketed his case of lancets and tubes of lymph. Then, sweeping the semicircle with one comprehensive forefinger, and in the voice of compliment, he said, clearly and distinctly: 'Pigs!'

'Ai!' whispered Bukta. 'Now he speaks. Woe to foolish people!'

'I have come on foot from my house' (the assembly shuddered) 'to make clear a matter which any other than a Satpura Bhil would have seen with both eyes from a distance. Ye know the Smallpox, who pits and scars your children so that they look like wasp-combs. It is an order of the Government that whoso is scratched on the arm with these little knives which I hold up is charmed against Her. All Sahibs are thus charmed, and very many Hindus. This is the mark of the charm. Look!'

He rolled back his sleeve to the armpit and showed the white scars of the vaccination-mark on the white skin. 'Come, all, and look.'

A few daring spirits came up, and nodded their heads wisely. There was certainly a mark, and they knew well what other dread marks were hidden by the shirt. Merciful was Jan Chinn, that he had not then and there proclaimed his godhead.

'Now all these things the man whom ye bound told you.'

'I did—a hundred times; but they answered with blows,' groaned the operator, chafing his wrists and ankles.

'But, being pigs, ye did not believe; and so came I here to save you, first from Smallpox, next from a great folly of fear, and lastly, it may be, from the rope and the jail. It is no gain to me; but for the sake of that one who is yonder, who made the Bhil a man'—he pointed down the hill—'I, who am of his blood, the son of his son, come to turn your people. And I speak the truth, as did Jan Chinn.'

The crowd murmured reverently, and men stole out of the thicket by twos and threes to join it. There was no anger in their god's face.

'These are my orders. (Heaven send they'll take 'em, but I seem to have impressed them so far!) I myself will stay among you while this man scratches your arms with knives, after the order of the Government. In three, or it may be five or seven days, your arms will swell and itch and burn. That is the power of Smallpox fighting in your base blood against the orders of the Government. I will therefore stay among you till I see that Smallpox is conquered, and I will not go away till the men and the women and the little children show me upon their arms such marks as I have even now showed you. I bring with me two very good guns, and a man whose name is known among beasts and men. We will hunt together, I and he, and your young men and the others shall eat and lie still. This is my order.'

There was a long pause while victory hung in the balance. A white-haired old sinner, standing on one uneasy leg, piped up:

'There are ponies and some few bullocks and other things for which we need a *kowl* [protection]. They were *not* taken in the way of trade.'

The battle was won, and John Chinn drew a breath of relief. The young Bhils had been raiding, but if taken swiftly all could be put straight.

'I will write a *kowl* as soon as the ponies, the bullocks, and the other things are counted before me and sent back whence they came. But first we will put the Government mark on such as have not been visited by Smallpox.' In an undertone, to the vaccinator: 'If you show you are afraid you'll never see Poona again, my friend.'

'There is not sufficient ample supply of vaccine for all this population,' said the man. 'They have destroyed the offeecial calf.'

'They won't know the difference. Scrape 'em all round, and give me a couple of lancets; I'll attend to the elders.'

The aged diplomat who had demanded protection was the first victim. He fell to Chinn's hand, and dared not cry out. As soon as he was freed he dragged up a companion, and held him fast, and the crisis became, as it were, a child's sport; for the vaccinated chased the unvaccinated to treatment, vowing that all the tribe must suffer equally. The women shrieked, and the children ran howling; but Chinn laughed, and waved the pink-tipped lancet.

'It is an honour,' he cried. 'Tell them, Bukta, how great an honour it is that I myself should mark them. Nay, I cannot mark every one—the Hindu must also do his work—but I will touch all marks that he makes, so there will be an equal virtue in them. Thus do the Rajputs stick pigs. Ho, brother with one eye! Catch that girl and bring her to me. She need not run away yet, for she is not married, and I do not seek her in marriage. She will not come? Then she shall be shamed by her little brother, a fat boy, a bold boy. He puts out his arm like a soldier. Look! *He* does not flinch at the blood. Some day he shall be in my regiment. And now, mother of many, we will lightly touch thee, for Smallpox has been before us here. It is a true thing, indeed, that this charm breaks the power of Mata. There will be no more pitted faces among the Satpuras, and so ye can ask many cows for each maid to be wed.'

And so on and so on—quick-poured showman's patter, sauced in the Bhil hunting proverbs and tales of their own brand of coarse humour—till the lancets were blunted and both operators worn out.

But, nature being the same the world over, the unvaccinated grew jealous of their marked comrades, and came near to blows about it. Then Chinn declared himself a court of justice, no longer a medical board, and made formal inquiry into the late robberies.

'We are the thieves of Mahadeo,' said the Bhils, simply. 'It is our fate, and we were frightened. When we are frightened we always steal.'

Simply and directly as children, they gave in the tale of the plunder, all but two bullocks and some spirits that had gone a-missing (these Chinn promised to make good out of his own pocket), and ten ringleaders were despatched to the lowlands with a wonderful document, written on the leaf of a note-book, and addressed to an assistant district superintendent of police. There was warm calamity in that note, as Jan Chinn warned them, but anything was better than loss of liberty.

Armed with this protection, the repentant raiders went downhill.

They had no desire whatever to meet Mr. Dundas Fawne of the Police, aged twenty-two, and of a cheerful countenance, nor did they wish to revisit the scene of their robberies. Steering a middle course, they ran into the camp of the one Government chaplain allowed to the various irregular corps through a district of some fifteen thousand square miles, and stood before him in a cloud of dust. He was by way of being a priest they knew, and what was more to the point, a good sportsman who paid his beaters generously.

When he read Chinn's note he laughed, which they deemed a lucky omen, till he called up policemen, who tethered the ponies and the bullocks by the piled housegear, and laid stern hands upon three of that smiling band of the thieves of Mahadeo. The chaplain himself addressed them magisterially with a riding-whip. That was painful, but Jan Chinn had prophesied it. They submitted, but would not give up the written protection, fearing the jail. On their way back they met Mr. D. Fawne, who had heard about the robberies, and was not pleased.

'Certainly,' said the eldest of the gang, when the second interview was at an end, 'certainly Jan Chinn's protection has saved us our liberty, but it is as though there were many beatings in one small piece of paper. Put it away.'

One climbed into a tree, and stuck the letter into a cleft forty feet from the ground, where it could do no harm. Warmed, sore, but happy, the ten returned to Jan Chinn next day, where he sat among uneasy Bhils, all looking at their right arms, and all bound under terror of their god's disfavour not to scratch.

'It was a good *kowl,*' said the leader. 'First the chaplain, who laughed, took away our plunder, and beat three of us, as was promised. Next we met Fawne Sahib, who frowned, and asked for the plunder. We spoke the truth, and so he beat us all, one after another, and called us chosen names. He then gave us these two bundles'—they set down a bottle of whisky and a box of cheroots—'and we came away. The *kowl* is left in a tree, because its virtue is that so soon as we show it to a Sahib we are beaten.'

'But for that *kowl,*' said Jan Chinn, sternly, 'ye would all have been marching to jail with a policeman on either side. Ye come now to serve as beaters for me. These people are unhappy, and we will go hunting till they are well. To-night we will make a feast.'

It is written in the chronicles of the Satpura Bhils, together with many other matters not fit for print, that through five days, after the day that he had put his mark upon them, Jan Chinn the First hunted for his people; and on the five nights of those days the tribe was gloriously and entirely drunk. Jan Chinn bought country spirits of an awful strength, and slew wild pig and deer beyond counting, so that if any fell sick they might have two good reasons.

Between head- and stomach-aches they found no time to think of their arms, but followed Jan Chinn obediently through the jungles, and with each day's returning confidence men, women, and children stole away to their villages as the little army passed by. They carried news that it was good and right to be scratched with ghost-knives; that Jan Chinn was indeed reincarnated as a god of free food and drink, and that of all nations the Satpura Bhils stood first in his favour, if they would only refrain from scratching. Henceforward that kindly demi-god would be connected in their minds with great gorgings and the vaccine and lancets of a paternal Government.

'And to-morrow I go back to my home,' said Jan Chinn to his faithful few, whom neither spirits, over-eating, nor swollen glands could conquer. It is hard for children and savages to behave reverently at all times to the idols of their make-belief, and they had frolicked excessively with Jan Chinn. But the reference to his home cast a gloom on the people.

'And the Sahib will not come again?' said he who had been vaccinated first.

'That is to be seen,' answered Chinn, warily.

'Nay, but come as a white man—come as a young man whom we know and love; for, as thou alone knowest, we are a weak people. If we again saw thy—thy horse——' They were picking up their courage.

'I have no horse. I came on foot—with Bukta, yonder. What is this?'

'Thou knowest—the Thing that thou hast chosen for a night-horse.' The little men squirmed in fear and awe.

'Night-horse? Bukta, what is this last tale of children?'

Bukta had been a silent leader in Chinn's presence since the night of his desertion, and was grateful for a chance-flung question.

'They know, Sahib,' he whispered. 'It is the Clouded Tiger. That that comes from the place where thou didst once sleep. It is thy horse—as it has been these three generations.'

'My horse! That was a dream of the Bhils!'

'It is no dream. Do dreams leave the tracks of broad pugs on earth? Why make two faces before thy people? They know of the night ridings, and they—and they——'

'Are afraid, and would have them cease.'

Bukta nodded. 'If thou hast no further need of him. He is thy horse.'

'The thing leaves a trail, then?' said Chinn.

'We have seen it. It is like a village road under the tomb.'

'Can ye find and follow it for me?'

'By daylight—if one comes with us, and, above all, stands near by.'

'I will stand close, and we will see to it that Jan Chinn does not ride any more.'

The Bhils shouted the last words again and again.

From Chinn's point of view the stalk was nothing more than an ordinary one—down hill, through split and crannied rocks, unsafe, perhaps, if a man did not keep his wits by him, but no worse than twenty others he had undertaken. Yet his men—they refused absolutely to beat, and would only trail—dripped sweat at every move. They showed the marks of enormous pugs that ran, always down hill, to a few hundred feet below Jan Chinn's tomb, and disappeared in a narrow-mouthed cave. It was an insolently open road, a domestic highway, beaten without thought of concealment.

'The beggar might be paying rent and taxes,' Chinn muttered ere he asked whether his friend's taste ran to cattle or man.

'Cattle,' was the answer. 'Two heifers a week. We drive them for him at the foot of the hill. It is his custom. If we did not, he might seek us.'

'Blackmail and piracy,' said Chinn. 'I can't say I fancy going into the cave after him. What's to be done?'

The Bhils fell back as Chinn lodged himself behind a rock with his rifle ready. Tigers, he knew, were shy beasts, but one who had been long cattle-fed in this sumptuous style might prove overbold.

'He speaks!' some one whispered from the rear. 'He knows, too.'

'Well, of *all* the infernal cheek!' said Chinn. There was an angry growl from the cave—a direct challenge.

'Come out, then,' Chinn shouted. 'Come out of that! Let's have a look at you.'

The brute knew well enough that there was some connection between brown nude Bhils and his weekly allowance; but the white helmet in the sunlight annoyed him, and he did not approve of the voice that broke his rest. Lazily as a gorged snake he dragged himself out of the cave, and stood yawning and blinking at the entrance. The sunlight fell upon his flat right side, and Chinn wondered. Never had he seen a tiger marked after this fashion. Except for his head, which was staringly barred, he was dappled—not striped, but dappled like a child's rocking-horse in rich shades of smoky black on red gold. That portion of his belly and throat which should have been white was orange, and his tail and paws were black.

He looked leisurely for some ten seconds, and then deliberately lowered his head, his chin dropped and drawn in, staring intently at the man. The effect of this was to throw forward the round arch of his skull, with two broad bands across it, while below the bands glared the unwinking eyes; so that, head on, as he stood, he showed something like a diabolically scowling pantomime-mask. It was a piece of natural mesmerism that he had practised many times on his quarry, and though Chinn was by no means a terrified heifer, he stood for a while, held by the extraordinary oddity of the attack. The head—the body seemed to have been packed away behind it—the ferocious, skull-like head, crept nearer, to the switching of an angry tail-tip in the grass. Left and right the Bhils had scattered to let Jan Chinn subdue his own horse.

'My word!' he thought. 'He's trying to frighten me!' and fired between the saucer-like eyes, leaping aside upon the shot.

A big coughing mass, reeking of carrion, bounded past him up the hill, and he followed discreetly. The tiger made no attempt to turn into the jungle; he was hunting for sight and breath—nose up, mouth open, the tremendous fore-legs scattering the gravel in spurts.

'Scuppered!' said John Chinn, watching the flight. 'Now if he was a partridge he'd tower. Lungs must be full of blood.'

The brute had jerked himself over a boulder and fallen out of sight the other side. John Chinn looked over with a ready barrel. But the red trail led straight as an arrow even to his grandfather's tomb, and there, among the smashed spirit bottles and the fragments of the mud image, the life left with a flurry and a grunt.

'If my worthy ancestor could see that,' said John Chinn, 'he'd have been proud of me. Eyes, lower jaw, and lungs. A very nice shot.' He whistled for Bukta as he drew the tape over the stiffening bulk.

'Ten—six—eight—by Jove! It's nearly eleven—call it eleven. Fore-arm, twenty-four—five—seven and a half. A short tail, too; three feet one. But *what* a skin! Oh, Bukta! Bukta! The men with the knives swiftly.'

'Is he beyond question dead?' said an awestricken voice behind a rock.

'That was not the way I killed my first tiger,' said Chinn. 'I did not think that Bukta would run. I had no second gun.'

'It—it is the Clouded Tiger,' said Bukta, unheeding the taunt. 'He is dead.'

Whether all the Bhils, vaccinated and unvaccinated, of the Satpuras has lain by to see the kill, Chinn could not say; but the whole hill's flank rustled with little men, shouting, singing, and stamping. And yet, till he had made the first cut in the splendid skin, not a man would take a knife; and, when the shadows fell, they ran from the red-stained tomb, and no persuasion would bring them back till dawn. So Chinn spent a second night in the open, guarding the carcass from jackals, and thinking about his ancestor.

He returned to the lowlands to the triumphal chant of an escorting army three hundred strong, the Mahratta vaccinator close at his elbow, and the rudely dried skin a trophy before him. When that army suddenly and noiselessly disappeared, as quail in high corn, he argued he was near civilisation, and a turn in the road brought him upon the camp of a wing of his own corps. He left the skin on a cart-tail for the world to see, and sought the Colonel.

'They're perfectly right,' he explained earnestly. 'There isn't an ounce of vice in 'em. They were only frightened. I've vaccinated the whole boiling, and they like it awfully. What are–what are we doing here, sir?'

'That's what I'm trying to find out,' said the Colonel. 'I don't know yet whether we're a piece of a brigade or a police force. However, I think we'll call ourselves a police force. How did you manage to get a Bhil vaccinated?'

'Well, sir,' said Chinn, 'I've been thinking it over, and, as far as I can make out, I've got a sort of hereditary influence over 'em.'

'So I know, or I wouldn't have sent you; but *what,* exactly?'

'It's rather rummy. It seems, from what I can make out, that I'm my own grandfather reincarnated, and I've been disturbing the peace of the country by riding a pad-tiger of nights. If I hadn't done that, I don't think they'd have objected to the vaccination; but the two together were more than they could stand. And so, sir, I've vaccinated 'em, and shot my tiger-horse as a sort o' proof of good faith. You never saw such a skin in your life.'

The Colonel tugged his moustache thoughtfully. 'Now, how the deuce,' said he, 'am I to include that in my report?'

Indeed, the official version of the Bhils' anti-vaccination stampede said nothing about Lieutenant John Chinn, his godship. But Bukta knew, and the corps knew, and every Bhil in the Satpura hills knew.

And now Bukta is zealous that John Chinn shall swiftly be wedded and impart his powers to a son; for if the Chinn succession fails, and the little Bhils are left to their own imaginings, there will be fresh trouble in the Satpuras.

AT THE END OF THE PASSAGE

The sky is lead and our faces are red,
  And the gates of Hell are opened and riven,
  And the winds of Hell are loosened and driven,
And the dust flies up in the face of Heaven,
  And the clouds come down in a fiery sheet,
Heavy to raise and hard to be borne,
  And the soul of man is turned from his meat,
Turned from the trifles for which he has striven
  Sick in his body, and heavy-hearted,
  And his soul flies up like the dust in the street,
  Breaks from his flesh and is gone and departed,
As the blasts they blow on the cholera-horn.

Himalayan.

FOUR MEN, each entitled to 'life, liberty, and the pursuit of happiness,' sat at a table playing whist. The thermometer marked—for them—one hundred and one degrees of heat. The room was darkened till it was only just possible to distinguish the pips of the cards and the very white faces of the players. A tattered, rotten punkah of whitewashed calico was puddling the hot air and whining dolefully at each stroke. Outside lay gloom of a November day in London. There was neither sky, sun, nor horizon,—nothing but a brown purple haze of heat. It was as though the earth were dying of apoplexy.

From time to time clouds of tawny dust rose from the ground without wind or warning, flung themselves tablecloth-wise among the tops of the parched trees, and came down again. Then a whirling dust-devil would scutter across the plain for a couple of miles, break, and fall outward, though there was nothing to check its flight save a long low line of piled railway-sleepers white with the dust, a cluster of huts made of mud, condemned rails, and canvas, and the one squat four-roomed bungalow that belonged to the assistant engineer in charge of the section of a Gaudhari State line then under construction.

The four, stripped to the thinnest of sleeping-suits, played whist crossly, with wranglings as to leads and returns. It was not the best kind of whist, but they had taken some trouble to arrive at it. Mottram of the Indian Survey had ridden thirty and railed one hundred miles from his lonely post in the desert since the night before; Lowndes of the Civil Service, on special duty in the political department, had come as far to escape for an instant the miserable intrigues of an impoverished native State whose king alternately fawned and blustered for more money from the pitiful revenues contributed by hard-wrung peasants and despairing camel-breeders; Spurstow, the doctor of the line, had left a cholera-stricken camp of coolies to look after itself for forty-eight hours while he associated with white men once more. Hummil, the assistant engineer, was the host. He stood fast and received his friends thus every Sunday if they could come in. When one of them failed to appear, he would send a telegram to his last address, in order that he might know whether the defaulter were dead or alive. There are very many places in the East where it is not good or kind to let your acquaintances drop out of sight even for one short week.

The players were not conscious of any special regard for each other. They squabbled whenever they met; but they ardently desired to meet, as men without water desire to drink. They were lonely folk who understood the dread meaning of loneliness. They were all under thirty years of age,—which is too soon for any man to possess that knowledge.

'Pilsener?' said Spurstow, after the second rubber, mopping his forehead.

'Beer's out, I'm sorry to say, and there's hardly enough soda-water for to-night,' said Hummil.

'What filthy bad management!' Spurstow snarled.

'Can't help it. I've written and wired; but the trains don't come through regularly yet. Last week the ice ran out,—as Lowndes knows.'

'Glad I didn't come. I could ha' sent you some if I had known, though. Phew! it's too hot to go on playing bumblepuppy.' This with a savage scowl at Lowndes, who only laughed. He was a hardened offender.

Mottram rose from the table and looked out of a chink in the shutters.

'What a sweet day!' said he.

The company yawned all together and betook themselves to an aimless investigation of all Hummil's possessions,—guns, tattered novels, saddlery, spurs, and the like. They had fingered them a score of times before, but there was really nothing else to do.

'Got anything fresh?' said Lowndes.

'Last week's *Gazette of India,* and a cutting from a Home paper. My father sent it out. It's rather amusing.'

'One of those vestrymen that call 'emselves M.P.'s again, is it?' said Spurstow, who read his newspapers when he could get them.

'Yes. Listen to this. It's to your address, Lowndes. The man was making a speech to his constituents, and he piled it on. Here's a sample, "And I assert unhesitatingly that the Civil Service in India is the preserve—the pet preserve—of the aristocracy of England. What does the democracy—what do the masses—get from that country, which we have step by step fraudulently annexed? I answer, nothing whatever. It is farmed with a single eye to their own interests by the scions of the aristocracy. They take good care to maintain their lavish scale of incomes, to avoid or stifle any inquiries into the nature and conduct of their administration, while they themselves force the unhappy peasant to pay with the sweat of his brow for all the luxuries in which they are lapped." ' Hummil waved the cutting above his head. ' 'Ear! 'ear!' said his audience.

Then Lowndes, meditatively, 'I'd give—I'd give three months' pay to have that gentleman spend one month with me and see how the free and independent native prince works things. Old Timbersides'—this was his flippant title for an honoured and decorated feudatory prince—'has been wearing my life out this week past for money. By Jove, his latest performance was to send me one of his women as a bribe!'

'Good for you! Did you accept it?' said Mottram.

'No. I rather wish I had, now. She was a pretty little person, and she yarned away to me about the horrible destitution among the king's women-folk. The darlings haven't had any new clothes for nearly a month, and the old man wants to buy a new drag from Calcutta—solid silver railings and silver lamps, and trifles of that kind. I've tried to make him understand that he has played the deuce with the revenues for the last twenty years and must go slow. He can't see it.'

'But he has the ancestral treasure-vaults to draw on. There must be three millions at least in jewels and coin under his palace,' said Hummil.

'Catch a native king disturbing the family treasure! The priests forbid it except as the last resort. Old Timbersides has added something like a quarter of a million to the deposit in his reign.'

'Where the mischief does it all come from?' said Mottram.

'The country. The state of the people is enough to make you sick. I've known the taxmen wait by a milch-camel till the foal was born and then hurry off the mother for arrears. And what can I do? I can't get the court clerks to give me any accounts; I can't raise anything more than a fat smile from the commander-in-chief when I find out the troops are three months in arrears; and old Timbersides begins to weep when I speak to him. He has taken to the King's Peg heavily,—liqueur brandy for whisky, and Heidsieck for soda-water.'

'That's what the Rao of Jubela took to. Even a native can't last long at that,' said Spurstow. 'He'll go out.'

'And a good thing, too. Then I suppose we'll have a council of regency, and a tutor for the young prince, and hand him back his kingdom with ten years' accumulations.'

'Whereupon that young prince, having been taught all the vices of the English, will play ducks and drakes with the money and undo ten years' work in eighteen months. I've seen that business before,' said Spurstow. 'I should tackle the king with a light hand if I were you, Lowndes. They'll hate you quite enough under any circumstances.'

'That's all very well. The man who looks on can talk about the light hand; but you can't clean a pig-sty with a pen dipped in rose-water. I know my risks; but nothing has happened yet. My servant's an old Pathan, and he cooks for me. They are hardly likely to bribe him, and I don't accept food from my true friends, as they call themselves. Oh, but it's weary work! I'd sooner be with you, Spurstow. There's shooting near your camp.'

'Would you? I don't think it. About fifteen deaths a day don't incite a man to shoot anything but himself. And the worst of it is that the poor devils look at you as though you ought to save them. Lord knows, I've tried everything. My last attempt was empirical, but it pulled an old man through. He was brought to me apparently past hope, and I gave him gin and Worcester sauce with cayenne. It cured him; but I don't recommend it.'

'How do the cases run generally?' said Hummil.

'Very simply indeed. Chlorodyne, opium pill, chlorodyne, collapse, nitre, bricks to the feet, and then—the burning ghaut. The last seems to be the only thing that stops the trouble. It's black cholera, you know. Poor devils! But, I will say, little Bunsee Lal, my apothecary, works like a demon. I've recommended him for promotion if he comes through it all alive.'

'And what are your chances, old man?' said Mottram.

'Don't know; don't care much; but I've sent the letter in. What are you doing with yourself generally?'

'Sitting under a table in the tent and spitting on the sextant to keep it cool,' said the man of the Survey. 'Washing my eyes to avoid ophthalmia, which I shall certainly get, and trying to make a sub-surveyor understand that an error of five degrees in an angle isn't quite so small as it looks. I'm altogether alone, y' know, and shall be till the end of the hot weather.'

'Hummil's the lucky man,' said Lowndes, flinging himself into a long chair. 'He has an actual roof—torn as to the ceiling-cloth, but still a roof—over his head. He seen one train daily. He can get beer and soda-water and ice 'em when God is good. He has books, pictures,'—they were torn from the *Graphic*,—'and the society of the excellent sub-contractor Jevins, besides the pleasure of receiving us weekly.'

Hummil smiled grimly. 'Yes, I'm the lucky man, I suppose. Jevins is luckier.'

'How? Not——'

'Yes. Went out. Last Monday.'

'By his own hand?' said Spurstow quickly, hinting the suspicion that was in everybody's mind. There was no cholera near Hummil's section. Even fever gives a man at least a week's grace, and sudden death generally implied self-slaughter.

'I judge no man this weather,' said Hummil. 'He had a touch of the sun, I fancy; for last week, after you fellows had left, he came into the verandah and told me that he was going home to see his wife, in Market Street, Liverpool, that evening.

'I got the apothecary in to look at him, and we tried to make him lie down. After an hour or two he rubbed his eyes and said he believed he had had a fit,—hoped he hadn't said anything rude. Jevins had a great idea of bettering himself socially. He was very like Chucks in his language.'

'Well?'

'Then he went to his own bungalow and began cleaning a rifle. He told the servant that he was going to shoot buck in the morning. Naturally he fumbled with the trigger, and shot himself through the head—accidentally. The apothecary sent in a report to my chief, and Jevins is buried somewhere out there. I'd have wired to you, Spurstow, if you could have done anything.'

'You're a queer chap,' said Mottram. 'If you'd killed the man yourself you couldn't have been more quiet about the business.'

'Good Lord! what does it matter?' said Hummil calmly. 'I've got to do a lot of his overseeing work in addition to my own. I'm the only person that suffers. Jevins is out of it,—by pure accident, of course, but out of it.

The apothecary was going to write a long screed on suicide. Trust a babu to drivel when he gets the chance.'

'Why didn't you let it go in as suicide?' said Lowndes.

'No direct proof. A man hasn't many privileges in this country, but he might at least be allowed to mishandle his own rifle. Besides, some day I may need a man to smother up an accident to myself. Live and let live. Die and let die.'

'You take a pill,' said Spurstow, who had been watching Hummil's white face narrowly. 'Take a pill, and don't be an ass. That sort of talk is skittles. Anyhow, suicide is shirking your work. If I were Job ten times over, I should be so interested in what was going to happen next that I'd stay on and watch.'

'Ah! I've lost that curiosity,' said Hummil.

'Liver out of order?' said Lowndes feelingly.

'No. Can't sleep. That's worse.'

'By Jove, it is!' said Mottram. 'I'm that way every now and then, and the fit has to wear itself out. What do you take for it?'

'Nothing. What's the use? I haven't had ten minutes' sleep since Friday morning.'

'Poor chap! Spurstow, you ought to attend to this,' said Mottram. 'Now you mention it, your eyes are rather gummy and swollen.'

Spurstow, still watching Hummil, laughed lightly. 'I'll patch him up, later on. Is it too hot, do you think, to go for a ride?'

'Where to?' said Lowndes wearily. 'We shall have to go away at eight, and there'll be riding enough for us then. I hate a horse when I have to use him as a necessity. Oh, heavens! what is there to do?'

'Begin whist again, at chick points ['a chick' is supposed to be eight shillings] and a gold mohur on the rub,' said Spurstow promptly.

'Poker. A month's pay all round for the pool,—no limit,—and fifty-rupee raises. Somebody would be broken before we got up,' said Lowndes.

'Can't say that it would give me any pleasure to break any man in this company,' said Mottram. 'There isn't enough excitement in it, and it's foolish.' He crossed over to the worn and battered little camp-piano, —wreckage of a married household that had once held the bungalow,— and opened the case.

'It's used up long ago,' said Hummil. 'The servants have picked it to pieces.'

The piano was indeed hopelessly out of order, but Mottram managed to bring the rebellious notes into a sort of agreement, and there rose from the ragged keyboard something that might once have been the ghost of a popular music-hall song. The men in the long chairs turned with evident interest as Mottram banged the more lustily.

'That's good!' said Lowndes. 'By Jove! the last time I heard that song was in '79, or thereabouts, just before I came out.'

'Ah!' said Spurstow with pride, 'I was home in '80.' And he mentioned a song of the streets popular at that date.

Mottram executed it roughly. Lowndes criticised and volunteered emendations. Mottram dashed into another ditty, not of the music-hall character, and made as if to rise.

'Sit down,' said Hummil. 'I didn't know that you had any music in your composition. Go on playing until you can't think of anything more. I'll have that piano tuned up before you come again. Play something festive.'

Very simple indeed were the tunes to which Mottram's art and the limitations of the piano could give effect, but the men listened with pleasure, and in the pauses talked all together of what they had seen or heard when they were last at home. A dense dust-storm sprang up outside, and swept roaring over the house, enveloping it in the choking darkness of midnight, but Mottram continued unheeding, and the crazy tinkle reached the ears of the listeners above the flapping of the tattered ceiling-cloth.

In the silence after the storm he glided from the more directly personal songs of Scotland, half humming them as he played, into the Evening Hymn.

'Sunday,' said he, nodding his head.

'Go on. Don't apologise for it,' said Spurstow.

Hummil laughed long and riotously. 'Play it, by all means. You're full of surprises to-day. I didn't know you had such a gift of finished sarcasm. How does that thing go?'

Mottram took up the tune.

'Too slow by half. You miss the note of gratitude,' said Hummil. 'It ought to go to the "Grasshopper's Polka,"—this way.' And he chanted, *prestissimo*,—

> ' "Glory to thee, my God, this night,
> For all the blessings of the light."

That shows we really feel our blessings. How does it go on?—

> "If in the night I sleepless lie,
> My soul with sacred thoughts supply;
> May no ill dreams disturb my rest,"—

Quicker, Mottram!—

"Or powers of darkness me molest!"'

'Bah! what an old hypocrite you are!'

'Don't be an ass,' said Lowndes. 'You are at full liberty to make fun of anything else you like, but leave that hymn alone. It's associated in my mind with the most sacred recollections——'

'Summer evenings in the country,—stained-glass window,—light going out, and you and she jamming your heads together over one hymnbook,' said Mottram.

'Yes, and a fat old cockchafer hitting you in the eye when you walked home. Smell of hay, and a moon as big as a bandbox sitting on the top of a haycock; bats,—roses,—milk and midges,' said Lowndes.

'Also mothers. I can just recollect my mother singing me to sleep with that when I was a little chap,' said Spurstow.

The darkness had fallen on the room. They could hear Hummil squirming in his chair.

'Consequently,' said he testily, 'you sing it when you are seven fathom deep in Hell! It's an insult to the intelligence of the Deity to pretend we're anything but tortured rebels.'

'Take *two* pills,' said Spurstow; 'that's tortured liver.'

'The usually placid Hummil is in a vile bad temper. I'm sorry for his coolies to-morrow,' said Lowndes, as the servants brought in the lights and prepared the table for dinner.

As they were settling into their places about the miserable goat-chops, and the smoked tapioca pudding, Spurstow took occasion to whisper to Mottram, 'Well done, David!'

'Look after Saul, then,' was the reply.

'What are you two whispering about?' said Hummil suspiciously.

'Only saying that you are a damned poor host. This fowl can't be cut,' returned Spurstow with a sweet smile. 'Call this a dinner?'

'I can't help it. You don't expect a banquet, do you?'

Throughout the meal Hummil contrived laboriously to insult directly and pointedly all his guests in succession, and at each insult Spurstow kicked the aggrieved persons under the table; but he dared not exchange a glance of intelligence with either of them. Hummil's face was white and pinched, while his eyes were unnaturally large. No man dreamed for a moment of resenting his savage personalities, but as soon as the meal was over they made haste to get away.

'Don't go. You're just getting amusing, you fellows. I hope I haven't said anything that annoyed you. You're such touchy devils.' Then changing the note into one of almost abject entreaty, Hummil added, 'I say, you surely aren't going?'

'In the language of the blessed Jorrocks, where I dines I sleeps,' said Spurstow. 'I want to have a look at your coolies to-morrow, if you don't mind. You can give me a place to lie down in, I suppose?'

The others pleaded the urgency of their several duties next day, and, saddling up, departed together, Hummil begging them to come next Sunday. As they jogged off, Lowndes unbosomed himself to Mottram—

'. . . And I never felt so like kicking a man at his own table in my life. He said I cheated at whist, and reminded me I was in debt! 'Told you you were as good as a liar to your face! You aren't half indignant enough over it.'

'Not I,' said Mottram. 'Poor devil! Did you ever know old Hummy behave like that before or within a hundred miles of it?'

'That's no excuse. Spurstow was hacking my shin all the time, so I kept a hand on myself. Else I should have——'

'No, you wouldn't. You'd have done as Hummy did about Jevins; judge no man this weather. By Jove! the buckle of my bridle is hot in my hand! Trot out a bit, and 'ware rat-holes.'

Ten minutes' trotting jerked out of Lowndes one very sage remark when he pulled up, sweating from every pore—

' 'Good thing Spurstow's with him to-night.'

'Ye-es. Good man, Spurstow. Our roads turn here. See you again next Sunday, if the sun doesn't bowl me over.'

'S'pose so, unless old Timbersides' finance minister manages to dress some of my food. Good-night, and—God bless you!'

'What's wrong now?'

'Oh, nothing.' Lowndes gathered up his whip, and, as he flicked Mottram's mare on the flank, added, 'You're not a bad little chap,—that's all.' And the mare bolted half a mile across the sand, on the word.

In the assistant engineer's bungalow Spurstow and Hummil smoked the pipe of silence together, each narrowly watching the other. The capacity of a bachelor's establishment is as elastic as its arrangements are simple. A servant cleared away the dining-room table, brought in a couple of rude native bedsteads made of tape strung on a light wood frame, flung a square of cool Calcutta matting over each, set them side by side, pinned two towels to the punkah so that their fringes should just sweep clear of the sleeper's nose and mouth, and announced that the couches were ready.

The men flung themselves down, ordering the punkah-coolies by all the powers of Hell to pull. Every door and window was shut, for the outside air was that of an oven. The atmosphere within was only 104°, as the thermometer bore witness, and heavy with the foul smell of badly-trimmed kerosene lamps; and this stench, combined with that of native tobacco, baked brick, and dried earth, sends the heart of many a strong man down to his boots, for it is the smell of the Great Indian Empire when she turns herself for six months into a house of torment. Spurstow packed his pillows craftily so that he reclined rather than lay, his head at a safe elevation above his feet. It is not good to sleep on a low pillow in the hot weather if you happen to be of thick-necked build, for you may pass with lively snores and gugglings from natural sleep into the deep slumber of heat-apoplexy.

'Pack your pillows,' said the doctor sharply, as he saw Hummil preparing to lie down at full length.

The night-light was trimmed, the shadow of the punkah wavered across the room, and the '*flick*' of the punkah-towel and the soft whine of the rope through the wall-hole followed it. Then the punkah flagged, almost ceased. The sweat poured from Spurstow's brow. Should he go out and harangue the coolie? It started forward again with a savage jerk, and a pin came out of the towels. When this was replaced, a tom-tom in the coolie-lines began to beat with the steady throb of a swollen artery inside some brain-fevered skull. Spurstow turned on his side and swore gently. There was no movement on Hummil's part. The man had composed himself as rigidly as a corpse, his hands clinched at his sides. The respiration was too hurried for any suspicion of sleep. Spurstow looked at the set face. The jaws were clinched, and there was a pucker round the quivering eyelids.

'He's holding himself as tightly as ever he can,' thought Spurstow. 'What in the world is the matter with him?—Hummil!'

'Yes,' in a thick constrained voice.

'Can't you get to sleep?'

'No.'

'Head hot? 'Throat feeling bulgy? or how?'

'Neither, thanks. I don't sleep much, you know.'

''Feel pretty bad?'

'Pretty bad, thanks. There is a tomtom outside, isn't there? I thought it was my head at first. . . . Oh, Spurstow, for pity's sake give me something that will put me asleep,—sound asleep,—if it's only for six hours!'

He sprang up, trembling from head to foot. 'I haven't been able to sleep naturally for days, and I can't stand it!–I can't stand it!'

'Poor old chap!'

'That's no use. Give me something to make me sleep. I tell you I'm nearly mad. I don't know what I say half my time. For three weeks I've had to think and spell out every word that has come through my lips before I dared say it. Isn't that enough to drive a man mad? I can't see things correctly now, and I've lost my sense of touch. My skin aches–my skin aches! Make me sleep. Oh, Spurstow, for the love of God make me sleep sound. It isn't enough to merely let me dream. Let me sleep!'

'All right, old man, all right. Go slow; you aren't half as bad as you think.'

The flood-gates of reserve once broken, Hummil was clinging to him like a frightened child. 'You're pinching my arm to pieces.'

'I'll break your neck if you don't do something for me. No, I didn't mean that. Don't be angry, old fellow.' He wiped the sweat off himself as he fought to regain composure. 'I'm a bit restless and off my oats, and perhaps you could recommend some sort of sleeping mixture,–bromide of potassium.'

'Bromide of skittles! Why didn't you tell me this before? Let go of my arm, and I'll see if there's anything in my cigarette-case to suit your complaint.' Spurstow hunted among his day-clothes, turned up the lamp, opened a little silver cigarette-case, and advanced on the expectant Hummil with the daintiest of fairy squirts.

'The last appeal of civilisation,' said he, 'and a thing I hate to use. Hold out your arm. Well, your sleeplessness hasn't ruined your muscle; and what a thick hide it is! Might as well inject a buffalo subcutaneously. Now in a few minutes the morphia will begin working. Lie down and wait.'

A smile of unalloyed and idiotic delight began to creep over Hummil's face. 'I think,' he whispered,–'I think I'm going off now. Gad! it's positively heavenly! Spurstow, you must give me that case to keep; you——' The voice ceased as the head fell back.

'Not for a good deal,' said Spurstow to the unconscious form. 'And now, my friend, sleeplessness of your kind being very apt to relax the moral fibre in little matters of life and death, I'll just take the liberty of spiking your guns.'

He paddled into Hummil's saddle-room in his bare feet and uncased a twelve-bore rifle, an express, and a revolver. Of the first he unscrewed the nipples and hid them in the bottom of a saddlery-case; of the second he abstracted the lever, kicking it behind a big wardrobe. The third he merely opened, and knocked the doll-head bolt of the grip up with the heel of a riding-boot.

'That's settled,' he said, as he shook the sweat off his hands. 'These little precautions will at least give you time to turn. You have too much sympathy with gun-room accidents.'

And as he rose from his knees, the thick muffled voice of Hummil cried in the doorway, 'You fool!'

Such tones they use who speak in the lucid intervals of delirium to their friends a little before they die.

Spurstow started, dropping the pistol. Hummil stood in the doorway, rocking with helpless laughter.

'That was awf'ly good of you, I'm sure,' he said, very slowly, feeling for his words. 'I don't intend to go out by my own hand at present. I say, Spurstow, that stuff won't work. What shall I do? What shall I do?' And panic terror stood in his eyes.

'Lie down and give it a chance. Lie down at once.'

'I daren't. It will only take me half-way again, and I shan't be able to get away this time. Do you know it was all I could do to come out just now? Generally I am as quick as lightning; but you had clogged my feet. I was nearly caught.'

'Oh, yes, I understand. Go and lie down.'

'No, it isn't delirium; but it was an awfully mean trick to play on me. Do you know I might have died?'

As a sponge rubs a slate clean, so some power unknown to Spurstow had wiped out of Hummil's face all that stamped it for the face of a man, and he stood at the doorway in the expression of his lost innocence. He had slept back into terrified childhood.

'Is he going to die on the spot?' thought Spurstow. Then, aloud, 'All right, my son. Come back to bed, and tell me all about it. You couldn't sleep; but what was all the rest of the nonsense?'

'A place,—a place down there,' said Hummil, with simple sincerity. The drug was acting on him by waves, and he was flung from the fear of a strong man to the fright of a child as his nerves gathered sense or were dulled.

'Good God! I've been afraid of it for months past, Spurstow. It has made every night hell to me; and yet I'm not conscious of having done anything wrong.'

'Be still, and I'll give you another dose. We'll stop your nightmares, you unutterable idiot!'

'Yes, but you must give me so much that I can't get away. You must make me quite sleepy,—not just a little sleepy. It's so hard to run then.'

'I know it; I know it. I've felt it myself. The symptoms are exactly as you describe.'

'Oh, don't laugh at me, confound you! Before this awful sleeplessness came to me I've tried to rest on my elbow and put a spur in the bed to sting me when I fell back. Look!'

'By Jove! the man has been rowelled like a horse! Ridden by the night-mare with a vengeance! And we all thought him sensible enough. Heaven send us understanding! You like to talk, don't you?'

'Yes, sometimes. Not when I'm frightened. *Then* I want to run. Don't you?'

'Always. Before I give you your second dose try to tell me exactly what your trouble is.'

Hummil spoke in broken whispers for nearly ten minutes, whilst Spurstow looked into the pupils of his eyes and passed his hand before them once or twice.

At the end of the narrative the silver cigarette-case was produced, and the last words that Hummil said as he fell back for the second time were, 'Put me quite to sleep; for if I'm caught I die,—I die!'

'Yes, yes; we all do that sooner or later,—thank Heaven who has set a term to our miseries,' said Spurstow, settling the cushions under the head. 'It occurs to me that unless I drink something I shall go out before my time. I've stopped sweating, and—I wear a seventeen-inch collar.' He brewed himself scalding hot tea, which is an excellent remedy against heat-apoplexy if you take three or four cups of it in time. Then he watched the sleeper.

'A blind face that cries and can't wipe its eyes, a blind face that chases him down corridors! H'm! Decidedly, Hummil ought to go on leave as soon as possible; and, sane or otherwise, he undoubtedly did rowel himself most cruelly. Well, Heaven send us understanding!'

At mid-day Hummil rose, with an evil taste in his mouth, but an unclouded eye and a joyful heart.

'I was pretty bad last night, wasn't I?' said he.

'I have seen healthier men. You must have had a touch of the sun. Look here: if I write you a swingeing medical certificate will you apply for leave on the spot?'

'No.'

'Why not? You want it.'

'Yes, but I can hold on till the weather's a little cooler.'

'Why should you, if you can get relieved on the spot?'

'Burkett is the only man who could be sent; and he's a born fool.'

'Oh, never mind about the line. You aren't so important as all that. Wire for leave, if necessary.'

Hummil looked very uncomfortable.

'I can hold on till the Rains,' he said evasively.

'You can't. Wire to headquarters for Burkett.'

'I won't. If you want to know why, particularly, Burkett is married, and his wife's just had a kid, and she's up at Simla, in the cool, and Burkett has a very nice billet that takes him into Simla from Saturday to Monday. That little woman isn't at all well. If Burkett was transferred she'd try to follow him. If she left the baby behind she'd fret herself to death. If she came,—and Burkett's one of those selfish little beasts who are always talking about a wife's place being with her husband,—she'd die. It's murder to bring a woman here just now. Burkett hasn't the physique of a rat. If he came here he'd go out; and I know she hasn't any money, and I'm pretty sure she'd go out too. I'm salted in a sort of way, and I'm not married. Wait till the Rains, and then Burkett can get thin down here. It'll do him heaps of good.'

'Do you mean to say that you intend to face—what you have faced, till the Rains break?'

'Oh, it won't be so bad, now you've shown me a way out of it. I can always wire to you. Besides, now I've once got into the way of sleeping, it'll be all right. Anyhow, I shan't put in for leave. That's the long and the short of it.'

'My great Scott! I thought all that sort of thing was dead and done with.'

'Bosh! You'd do the same yourself. I feel a new man, thanks to that cigarette-case. You're going over to camp now, aren't you?'

'Yes; but I'll try to look you up every other day, if I can.'

'I'm not bad enough for that. I don't want you to bother. Give the coolies gin and ketchup.'

'Then you feel all right?'

'Fit to fight for my life, but not to stand out in the sun talking to you. Go along, old man, and bless you!'

Hummil turned on his heel to face the echoing desolation of his bungalow, and the first thing he saw standing in the verandah was the figure of himself. He had met a similar apparition once before, when he was suffering from overwork and the strain of the hot weather.

'This is bad,—already,' he said, rubbing his eyes. 'If the thing slides away from me all in one piece, like a ghost, I shall know it is only my eyes and stomach that are out of order. If it walks—my head is going.

He approached the figure, which naturally kept at an unvarying distance from him, as is the use of all spectres that are born of overwork. It slid through the house and dissolved into swimming specks within the eyeball as soon as it reached the burning light of the garden. Hummil went about his business till even. When he came in to dinner he found himself sitting at the table. The vision rose and walked out hastily. Except that it cast no shadow it was in all respects real.

No living man knows what that week held for Hummil. An increase of the epidemic kept Spurstow in camp among the coolies, and all he could do was to telegraph to Mottram, bidding him go to the bungalow and sleep there. But Mottram was forty miles away from the nearest telegraph, and knew nothing of anything save the needs of the Survey till he met, early on Sunday morning, Lowndes and Spurstow heading towards Hummil's for the weekly gathering.

'Hope the poor chap's in a better temper,' said the former, swinging himself off his horse at the door. 'I suppose he isn't up yet.'

'I'll just have a look at him,' said the doctor. 'If he's asleep there's no need to wake him.'

And an instant later, by the tone of Spurstow's voice calling upon them to enter, the men knew what had happened. There was no need to wake him.

The punkah was still being pulled over the bed, but Hummil had departed this life at least three hours.

The body lay on its back, hands clinched by the side, as Spurstow had seen it lying seven nights previously. In the staring eyes was written terror beyond the expression of any pen.

Mottram, who had entered behind Lowndes, bent over the dead and touched the forehead lightly with his lips. 'Oh, you lucky, lucky devil!' he whispered.

But Lowndes had seen the eyes, and withdrew shuddering to the other side of the room.

'Poor chap! poor old chap! And the last time I met him I was angry. Spurstow, we should have watched him. Has he——?'

Deftly Spurstow continued his investigations, ending by a search round the room.

'No, he hasn't,' he snapped. 'There's no trace of anything. Call the servants.'

They came, eight or ten of them, whispering and peering over each other's shoulders.

'When did your Sahib go to bed?' said Spurstow.

'At eleven or ten, we think,' said Hummil's personal servant.

'He was well then? But how should you know?'

'He was not ill, as far as our comprehension extended. But he had slept very little for three nights. This I know, because I saw him walking much, and specially in the heart of the night.'

As Spurstow was arranging the sheet, a big straight-necked hunting-spur tumbled on the ground. The doctor groaned. The personal servant peeped at the body.

'What do you think, Chuma?' said Spurstow, catching the look on the dark face.

'Heaven-born, in my poor opinion, this that was my master has descended into the Dark Places, and there has been caught because he was not able to escape with sufficient speed. We have the spur for evidence that he fought with Fear. Thus have I seen men of my race do with thorns when a spell was laid upon them to overtake them in their sleeping hours and they dared not sleep.'

'Chuma, you're a mud-head. Go out and prepare seals to be set on the Sahib's property.'

'God has made the Heaven-born. God has made me. Who are we, to inquire into the dispensations of God? I will bid the other servants hold aloof while you are reckoning the tale of the Sahib's property. They are all thieves, and would steal.'

'As far as I can make out, he died from—oh, anything; stoppage of the heart's action, heat-apoplexy, or some other visitation,' said Spurstow to his companions. 'We must make an inventory of his effects, and so on.'

'He was scared to death,' insisted Lowndes. 'Look at those eyes! For pity's sake don't let him be buried with them open!'

'Whatever it was, he's clear of all the trouble now,' said Mottram softly.

Spurstow was peering into the open eyes.

'Come here,' said he. 'Can you see anything there?'

'I can't face it!' whimpered Lowndes. 'Cover up the face! Is there any fear on earth that can turn a man into that likeness? It's ghastly. Oh, Spurstow, cover it up!'

'No fear—on earth,' said Spurstow. Mottram leaned over his shoulder and looked intently.

'I see nothing except some grey blurs in the pupil. There can be nothing there, you know.'

'Even so. Well, let's think. It'll take half a day to knock up any sort of coffin; and he must have died at midnight. Lowndes, old man, go out and tell the coolies to break ground next to Jevins's grave. Mottram, go round the house with Chuma and see that the seals are put on things. Send a couple of men to me here, and I'll arrange.'

The strong-armed servants when they returned to their own kind told a strange story of the doctor Sahib vainly trying to call their master back to life by magic arts,—to wit, the holding of a little green box that clicked to each of the dead man's eyes, and of a bewildered muttering on the part of the doctor Sahib, who took the little green box away with him.

The resonant hammering of a coffin-lid is no pleasant thing to hear, but those who have experience maintain that much more terrible is the soft swish of the bed-linen, the reeving and unreeving of the bed-tapes, when he who has fallen by the roadside is apparelled for burial, sinking gradually as the tapes are tied over, till the swaddled shape touches the floor and there is no protest against the indignity of hasty disposal.

At the last moment Lowndes was seized with scruples of conscience. 'Ought you to read the service,—from beginning to end?' said he to Spurstow.

'I intend to. You're my senior as a civilian. You can take it if you like.'

'I didn't mean that for a moment. I only thought if we could get a chaplain from somewhere,—I'm willing to ride anywhere,—and give poor Hummil a better chance. That's all.'

'Bosh!' said Spurstow, as he framed his lips to the tremendous words that stand at the head of the burial service.

After breakfast they smoked a pipe in silence to the memory of the dead. Then Spurstow said absently—

''Tisn't in medical science.'

'What?'

'Things in a dead man's eye.'

'For goodness' sake leave that horror alone!' said Lowndes. 'I've seen a native die of pure fright when a tiger chivvied him. I know what killed Hummil.'

'The deuce you do! I'm going to try to see.' And the doctor retreated into the bathroom with a Kodak camera. After a few minutes there was the sound of something being hammered to pieces, and he emerged, very white indeed.

'Have you got a picture?' said Mottram. 'What does the thing look like?'

'It was impossible, of course. You needn't look, Mottram. I've torn up the films. There was nothing there. It was impossible.'

'That,' said Lowndes, very distinctly, watching the shaking hand striving to relight the pipe, 'is a damned lie.'

Mottram laughed uneasily. 'Spurstow's right,' he said. 'We're all in such a state now that we'd believe anything. For pity's sake let's try to be rational.'

There was no further speech for a long time. The hot wind whistled without, and the dry trees sobbed. Presently the daily train, winking brass, burnished steel, and spouting steam, pulled up panting in the intense glare. 'We'd better go on on that,' said Spurstow. 'Go back to work. I've written my certificate. We can't do any more good here, and work'll keep our wits together. Come on.'

No one moved. It is not pleasant to face railway journeys at mid-day in June. Spurstow gathered up his hat and whip, and, turning in the doorway, said—

'There may be Heaven,—there must be Hell.
Meantime, there is our life here. We-ell?'

Neither Mottram nor Lowndes had any answer to the question.

'WIRELESS'

IT'S A funny thing, this Marconi business, isn't it?' said Mr. Shaynor, coughing heavily. 'Nothing seems to make any difference, by what they tell me—storms, hills, or anything; but if that's true we shall know before morning.'

'Of course it's true,' I answered, stepping behind the counter. 'Where's old Mr. Cashell?'

'He's had to go to bed on account of his influenza. He said you'd very likely drop in.'

'Where's his nephew?'

'Inside, getting the things ready. He told me that the last time they experimented they put the pole on the roof of one of the big hotels here, and the batteries electrified all the water-supply, and'—he giggled—'the ladies got shocks when they took their baths.'

'I never heard of that.'

'The hotel wouldn't exactly advertise it, would it? Just now, by what Mr. Cashell tells me, they're trying to signal from here to Poole, and they're using stronger batteries than ever. But, you see, he being the guvnor's nephew and all that (and it will be in the papers too), it doesn't matter how they electrify things in this house. Are you going to watch?'

'Very much. I've never seen this game. Aren't you going to bed?'

'We don't close till ten on Saturdays. There's a good deal of influenza in town, too, and there'll be a dozen prescriptions coming in before morning. I generally sleep in the chair here. It's warmer than jumping out of bed every time. Bitter cold, isn't it?'

'Freezing hard. I'm sorry your cough's worse.'

'Thank you. I don't mind cold so much. It's this wind that fair cuts me to pieces.' He coughed again hard and hackingly, as an old lady came in for ammoniated quinine. 'We've just run out of it in bottles, madam,' said Mr. Shaynor, returning to the professional tone, 'but if you will wait two minutes, I'll make it up for you, madam.'

I had used the shop for some time, and my acquaintance with the proprietor had ripened into friendship. It was Mr. Cashell who revealed to me the purpose and power of Apothecaries' Hall what time a fellow-chemist had made an error in a prescription of mine, had lied to cover his sloth, and when error and lie were brought home to him had written vain letters.

'A disgrace to our profession,' said the thin, mild-eyed man, hotly, after studying the evidence. 'You couldn't do a better service to the profession than report him to Apothecaries' Hall.'

I did so, not knowing what djinns I should evoke; and the result was such an apology as one might make who had spent a night on the rack. I conceived great respect for Apothecaries' Hall, and esteem for Mr. Cashell, a zealous craftsman who magnified his calling. Until Mr. Shaynor came down from the North his assistants had by no means agreed with Mr. Cashell. 'They forget,' said he, 'that, first and foremost, the compounder is a medicine-man. On him depends the physician's reputation. He holds it literally in the hollow of his hand, sir.'

Mr. Shaynor's manners had not, perhaps, the polish of the grocery and Italian warehouse next door, but he knew and loved his dispensary work in every detail. For relaxation he seemed to go no farther afield than the romance of drugs—their discovery, preparation, packing, and export—but it led him to the ends of the earth, and on this subject, and the Pharmaceutical Formulary, and Nicholas Culpepper, most confident of physicians, we met.

Little by little I grew to know something of his beginnings and his hopes—of his mother, who had been a school-teacher in one of the northern counties, and of his red-headed father, a small job-master at Kirby Moors, who died when he was a child; of the examinations he had passed and of their exceeding and increasing difficulty; of his dreams of a shop in London; of his hate for the price-cutting Co-operative stores; and, most interesting, of his mental attitude towards customers.

'There's a way you get into,' he told me, 'of serving them carefully, and I hope, politely, without stopping your own thinking. I've been reading Christy's *New Commercial Plants* all this autumn, and that needs keeping your mind on it, I can tell you. So long as it isn't a prescription, of course, I can carry as much as half a page of Christy in my head, and at the same time I could sell out all that window twice over, and not a penny wrong at the end. As to prescriptions, I think I could make up the general run of 'em in my sleep, almost.'

For reasons of my own, I was deeply interested in Marconi experiments at their outset in England; and it was of a piece with Mr. Cashell's unvarying thoughtfulness that, when his nephew the electrician appropriated the house for a long-range installation, he should, as I have said, invite me to see the result.

The old lady went away with her medicine, and Mr. Shaynor and I stamped on the tiled floor behind the counter to keep ourselves warm. The shop, by the light of the many electrics, looked like a Paris-diamond mine, for Mr. Cashell believed in all the ritual of his craft. Three superb glass jars—red, green, and blue—of the sort that led Rosamond to parting with her shoes—blazed in the broad plate-glass windows, and there was a confused smell of orris, Kodak films, vulcanite, tooth-powder, sachets, and almond-cream in the air. Mr. Shaynor fed the dispensary stove, and we sucked cayenne-pepper jujubes and menthol lozenges. The brutal east wind had cleared the streets, and the few passers-by were muffled to their puckered eyes. In the Italian warehouse next door some gay feathered birds and game, hung upon hooks, sagged to the wind across the left edge of our window-frame.

'They ought to take these poultry in—all knocked about like that,' said Mr. Shaynor. 'Doesn't it make you feel fair perishing? See that old hare! The wind's nearly blowing the fur off him.'

I saw the belly-fur of the dead beast blown apart in ridges and streaks as the wind caught it, showing bluish skin underneath. 'Bitter cold,' said Mr. Shaynor, shuddering. 'Fancy going out on a night like this! Oh, here's young Mr. Cashell.'

The door of the inner office behind the dispensary opened, and an energetic, spade-bearded man stepped forth, rubbing his hands.

'I want a bit of tin-foil, Shaynor,' he said. 'Good-evening. My uncle told me you might be coming.' This to me, as I began the first of a hundred questions.

'I've everything in order,' he replied. 'We're only waiting until Poole calls us up. Excuse me a minute. You can come in whenever you like—but I'd better be with the instruments. Give me that tin-foil. Thanks.'

While we were talking, a girl—evidently no customer—had come into the shop, and the face and bearing of Mr. Shaynor changed. She leaned confidently across the counter.

'But I can't,' I heard him whisper uneasily—the flush on his cheek was dull red, and his eyes shone like a drugged moth's. 'I can't. I tell you I'm alone in the place.'

'No, you aren't. Who's *that?* Let him look after it for half an hour. A brisk walk will do you good. Ah, come now, John.'

'But he isn't——'

'I don't care. I want you to; we'll only go round by St. Agnes'. If you don't——'

He crossed to where I stood in the shadow of the dispensary counter, and began some sort of broken apology about a lady-friend.

'Yes,' she interrupted. 'You take the shop for half an hour—to oblige *me,* won't you?'

She had a singularly rich and promising voice that well matched her outline.

'All right,' I said. 'I'll do it—but you'd better wrap yourself up, Mr. Shaynor.'

'Oh, a brisk walk ought to help me. We're only going round by the church.' I heard him cough grievously as they went out together.

I refilled the stove, and, after reckless expenditure of Mr. Cashell's coal, drove some warmth into the shop. I explored many of the glass-knobbed drawers that lined the walls, tasted some disconcerting drugs, and, by the aid of a few cardamoms, ground ginger, chloric-ether, and dilute alcohol, manufactured a new and wildish drink, of which I bore a glassful to young Mr. Cashell, busy in the back office. He laughed shortly when I told him that Mr. Shaynor had stepped out—but a frail coil of wire held all his attention, and he had no word for me bewildered among the batteries and rods. The noise of the sea on the beach began to make itself heard as the traffic in the street ceased. Then briefly, but very lucidly, he gave me the names and uses of the mechanism that crowded the tables and the floor.

'When do you expect to get the message from Poole?' I demanded, sipping my liquor out of a graduated glass.

'About midnight, if everything is in order. We've got our installation-pole fixed to the roof of the house. I shouldn't advise you to turn on a tap or anything to-night. We've connected up with the plumbing, and all the water will be electrified.' He repeated to me the history of the agitated ladies at the hotel at the time of the first installation.

'But what *is* it?' I asked. 'Electricity is out of my beat altogether.'

'Ah, if you knew *that* you'd know something nobody knows. It's just It—what we call Electricity, but the magic—the manifestations—the Hertzian waves—are all revealed by *this.* The coherer, we call it.'

He picked up a glass tube not much thicker than a thermometer, in which, almost touching, were two tiny silver plugs, and between them an infinitesimal pinch of metallic dust. 'That's all,' he said, proudly, as though himself responsible for the wonder. 'That is the thing that will reveal to us the Powers—whatever the Powers may be—at work—through space—a long distance away.'

Just then Mr. Shaynor returned alone and stood coughing his heart out on the mat.

'Serves you right for being such a fool,' said young Mr. Cashell, as annoyed as myself at the interruption. 'Never mind—we've all the night before us to see wonders.'

Shaynor clutched the counter, his handkerchief to his lips. When he brought it away I saw two bright red stains.

'I—I've got a bit of a rasped throat from smoking cigarettes,' he panted. 'I think I'll try a cubeb.'

'Better take some of this. I've been compounding while you've been away.' I handed him the brew.

''Twon't make me drunk, will it? I'm almost a teetotaller. My word! That's grateful and comforting.'

He set down the empty glass to cough afresh.

'Brr! But it was cold out there! I shouldn't care to be lying in my grave a night like this. Don't *you* ever have a sore throat from smoking?' He pocketed the handkerchief after a furtive peep.

'Oh, yes, sometimes,' I replied, wondering, while I spoke, into what agonies of terror I should fall if ever I saw those bright-red danger-signals under my nose. Young Mr. Cashell among the batteries coughed slightly to show that he was quite ready to continue his scientific explanations, but I was thinking still of the girl with the rich voice and the significantly cut mouth, at whose command I had taken charge of the shop. It flashed across me that she distantly resembled the seductive shape on a gold-framed toilet-water advertisement whose charms were unholily heightened by the glare from the red bottle in the window. Turning to make sure, I saw Mr. Shaynor's eyes bent in the same direction, and by instinct recognised that the flamboyant thing was to him a shrine. 'What do you take for your—cough?' I asked.

'Well, I'm the wrong side of the counter to believe much in patent medicines. But there are asthma cigarettes and there are pastilles. To tell you the truth, if you don't object to the smell, which is very like incense, I believe, though I'm not a Roman Catholic, Blaudett's Cathedral Pastilles relieve me as much as anything.'

'Let's try.' I had never raided a chemist's shop before, so I was thorough. We unearthed the pastilles—brown, gummy cones of benzoin—and set them alight under the toilet-water advertisement, where they fumed in thin blue spirals.

'Of course,' said Mr. Shaynor, to my question, 'what one uses in the shop for one's self comes out of one's pocket. Why, stocktaking in our business is nearly the same as with jewellers—and I can't say more than that. But one gets them'—he pointed to the pastille-box—'at trade prices.' Evidently the censing of the gay, seven-tinted wench with the teeth was an established ritual which cost something.

'And when do we shut up shop?'

'We stay like this all night. The guv—old Mr. Cashell—doesn't believe in locks and shutters as compared with electric light. Besides, it brings trade. I'll just sit here in the chair by the stove and write a letter, if you don't mind. Electricity isn't my prescription.'

The energetic young Mr. Cashell snorted within, and Shaynor settled himself up in his chair over which he had thrown a staring red, black, and yellow Austrian jute blanket, rather like a table-cover. I cast about, amid patent-medicine pamphlets, for something to read, but finding little, returned to the manufacture of the new drink. The Italian warehouse took down its game and went to bed. Across the street blank shutters flung back the gaslight in cold smears; the dried pavement seemed to rough up in goose-flesh under the scouring of the savage wind, and we could hear, long ere he passed, the policeman flapping his arms to keep himself warm. Within, the flavours of cardamoms and chloric-ether disputed those of the pastilles and a score of drugs and perfume and soap scents. Our electric lights, set low down in the windows before the tun-bellied Rosamond jars, flung inward three monstrous daubs of red, blue, and green, that broke into kaleidoscopic lights on the faceted knobs of the drug-drawers, the cut-glass scent flagons, and the bulbs of the sparklet bottles. They flushed the white-tiled floor in gorgeous patches; splashed along the nickel-silver counter-rails, and turned the polished mahogany counter-panels to the likeness of intricate grained marbles—slabs of porphyry and malachite. Mr. Shaynor unlocked a drawer, and ere he began to write, took out a meagre bundle of letters. From my place by the stove, I could see the scalloped edges of the paper with a flaring monogram in the corner and could even smell the reek of chypre. At each page he turned toward the toilet-water lady of the advertisement and devoured her with over-luminous eyes. He had drawn the Austrian blanket over his shoulders, and among those warring lights he looked more than ever the incarnation of a drugged moth—a tiger-moth as I thought.

He put his letter into an envelope, stamped it with stiff mechanical movements, and dropped it in the drawer. Then I became aware of the silence of a great city asleep—the silence that underlay the even voice of the breakers along the sea-front—a thick, tingling quiet of warm life stilled down for its appointed time, and unconsciously I moved about the glittering shop as one moves in a sick-room. Young Mr. Cashell was adjusting some wire that crackled from time to time with the tense, knuckle-stretching sound of the electric spark. Upstairs, where a door shut and opened swiftly, I could hear his uncle coughing abed.

'Here,' I said, when the drink was properly warmed, 'take some of this, Mr. Shaynor.'

He jerked in his chair with a start and a wrench, and held out his hand for the glass. The mixture, of a rich port-wine colour, frothed at the top.

'It looks,' he said, suddenly, 'it looks—those bubbles—like a string of pearls winking at you—rather like the pearls round that young lady's neck.' He turned again to the advertisement where the female in the dove-coloured corset had seen fit to put on all her pearls before she cleaned her teeth.

'Not bad, is it?' I said.

'Eh?'

He rolled his eyes heavily full on me, and, as I stared, I beheld all meaning and consciousness die out of the swiftly dilating pupils. His figure lost its stark rigidity, softened into the chair, and, chin on chest, hands dropped before him, he rested open-eyed, absolutely still.

'I'm afraid I've rather cooked Shaynor's goose,' I said, bearing the fresh drink to young Mr. Cashell. 'Perhaps it was the chloric-ether.'

'Oh, he's all right.' The spade-bearded man glanced at him pityingly. 'Consumptives go off in those sort of dozes very often. It's exhaustion . . . I don't wonder. I daresay the liquor will do him good. It's grand stuff.' He finished his share appreciatively. 'Well, as I was saying—before he interrupted—about this little coherer. The pinch of dust, you see, is nickel-filings. The Hertzian waves, you see, come out of space from the station that despatches 'em, and all these little particles are attracted together—cohere, we call it—for just so long as the current passes through them. Now, it's important to remember that the current is an induced current. There are a good many kinds of induction——'

'Yes, but what *is* induction?'

'That's rather hard to explain untechnically. But the long and the short of it is that when a current of electricity passes through a wire there's a lot of magnetism present round that wire; and if you put another wire parallel to, and within what we call its magnetic field—why, then the second wire will also become charged with electricity.'

'On its own account?'

'On its own account.'

'Then let's see if I've got it correctly. Miles off, at Poole, or wherever it is——'

'It will be anywhere in ten years.'

'You've got a charged wire——'

'Charged with Hertzian waves which vibrate, say, two hundred and thirty million times a second.' Mr. Cashell snaked his forefinger rapidly through the air.

'All right—a charged wire at Poole, giving out these waves into space. Then this wire of yours sticking out into space—on the roof of the house—in some mysterious way gets charged with those waves from Poole——'

'Or anywhere—it only happens to be Poole tonight.'

'And those waves set the coherer at work, just like an ordinary telegraph-office ticker?'

'No! That's where so many people make the mistake. The Hertzian waves wouldn't be strong enough to work a great heavy Morse instrument like ours. They can only just make that dust cohere, and while it coheres (a little while for a dot and a longer while for a dash) the current from this battery—the home battery'—he laid his hand on the thing—'can get through to the Morse printing-machine to record the dot or dash. Let me make it clearer. Do you know anything about steam?'

'Very little. But go on.'

'Well, the coherer is like a steam-valve. Any child can open a valve and start a steamer's engines, because a turn of the hand lets in the main steam, doesn't it? Now, this home battery here ready to print is the main steam. The coherer is the valve, always ready to be turned on. The Hertzian wave is the child's hand that turns it.'

'I see. That's marvellous.'

'Marvellous, isn't it? And, remember, we're only at the beginning. There's nothing we shan't be able to do in ten years. I want to live—my God, how I want to live, and see it develop!' He looked through the door at Shaynor breathing lightly in his chair. 'Poor beast! And he wants to keep company with Fanny Brand.'

'Fanny *who?*' I said, for the name struck an obscurely familiar chord in my brain—something connected with a stained handkerchief, and the word 'arterial.'

'Fanny Brand—the girl you kept shop for.' He laughed. 'That's all I know about her, and for the life of me I can't see what Shaynor sees in her, or she in him.'

'*Can't* you see what he sees in her?' I insisted.

'Oh, yes, if *that's* what you mean. She's a great, big, fat lump of a girl, and so on. I suppose that's why he's so crazy after her. She isn't his sort. Well, it doesn't matter. My uncle says he's bound to die before the year's out. Your drink's given him a good sleep, at any rate.' Young Mr. Cashell could not catch Mr. Shaynor's face, which was half turned to the advertisement.

I stoked the stove anew, for the room was growing cold, and lighted another pastille. Mr. Shaynor in his chair, never moving, looked through and over me with eyes as wide and lustreless as those of a dead hare.

'Poole's late,' said young Mr. Cashell, when I stepped back. 'I'll just send them a call.'

He pressed a key in the semi-darkness, and with a rending crackle there leaped between two brass knobs a spark, streams of sparks, and sparks again.

'Grand, isn't it? *That's* the Power—our unknown Power—kicking and fighting to be let loose,' said young Mr. Cashell. 'There she goes—kick—kick—kick into space. I never get over the strangeness of it when I work a sending-machine—waves going into space, you know. T. R. is our call. Poole ought to answer with L. L. L.'

We waited two, three, five minutes. In that silence, of which the boom of the tide was an orderly part, I caught the clear *'kiss—kiss—kiss'* of the halliards on the roof, as they were blown against the installation-pole.

'Poole is not ready. I'll stay here and call you when he is.'

I returned to the shop, and set down my glass on a marble slab with a careless clink. As I did so, Shaynor rose to his feet, his eyes fixed once more on the advertisement, where the young woman bathed in the light from the red jar simpered pinkly over her pearls. His lips moved without cessation. I stepped nearer to listen. 'And threw—and threw—and threw,' he repeated, his face all sharp with some inexplicable agony.

I moved forward astonished. But it was then he found words—delivered roundly and clearly. These:—

> 'And threw warm gules on Madeleine's young breast.'

The trouble passed off his countenance, and he returned lightly to his place, rubbing his hands.

It had never occurred to me, though we had many times discussed reading and prize-competitions as a diversion, that Mr. Shaynor ever read Keats, or could quote him at all appositely. There was, after all, a certain stained-glass effect of light on the high bosom of the highly-polished picture which might, by stretch of fancy, suggest, as a vile chromo recalls some incomparable canvas, the line he had spoken. Night, my drink, and solitude were evidently turning Mr. Shaynor into a poet. He sat down again and wrote swiftly on his villainous notepaper, his lips quivering.

I shut the door into the inner office and moved up behind him. He made no sign that he saw or heard. I looked over his shoulder, and read, amid half-formed words, sentences, and wild scratches:—

—— Very cold it was. Very cold
The hare—the hare—the hare—
The birds——

He raised his head sharply, and frowned toward the blank shutters of the poulterer's shop where they jutted out against our window. Then one clear line came:—

The hare, in spite of fur, was very cold.

The head, moving machine-like, turned right to the advertisement where the Blaudett's Cathedral pastille reeked abominably. He grunted, and went on:—

Incense in a censer—
Before her darling picture framed in gold—
Maiden's picture—angel's portrait—

'Hsh!' said Mr. Cashell guardedly from the inner office, as though in the presence of spirits. 'There's something coming through from somewhere; but it isn't Poole.' I heard the crackle of sparks as he depressed the keys of the transmitter. In my own brain, too, something crackled, or it might have been the hair on my head. Then I heard my own voice, in a harsh whisper: 'Mr. Cashell, there is something coming through here, too. Leave me alone till I tell you.'

'But I thought you'd come to see this wonderful thing—sir,' indignantly at the end.

'Leave me alone till I tell you. Be quiet.'

I watched—I waited. Under the blue-veined hand—the dry hand of the consumptive—came away clear, without erasure:—

And my weak spirit fails
To think how the dead must freeze—

he shivered as he wrote—

Beneath the churchyard mould.

Then he stopped, laid the pen down, and leaned back.

For an instant, that was half an eternity, the shop spun before me in a rainbow-tinted whirl, in and through which my own soul most dispassionately considered my own soul as that fought with an over-mastering fear. Then I smelt the strong smell of cigarettes from Mr. Shaynor's clothing, and heard, as though it had been the rending of trumpets, the rattle of his breathing. I was still in my place of observation, much as one would watch a rifle-shot at the butts, half-bent, hands on my knees, and head within a few inches of the black, red, and yellow blanket of his shoulder. I was whispering encouragement, evidently to my other self, sounding sentences, such as men pronounce in dreams.

'If he has read Keats, it proves nothing. If he hasn't—like causes *must* beget like effects. There is no escape from this law. *You* ought to be grateful that you know "St. Agnes' Eve" without the book; because, given the circumstances, such as Fanny Brand, who is the key of the enigma, and approximately represents the latitude and longitude of Fanny Brawne; allowing also for the bright red colour of the arterial blood upon the handkerchief, which was just what you were puzzling over in the shop just now; and counting the effect of the professional environment, here almost perfectly duplicated—the result is logical and inevitable. As inevitable as induction.'

Still, the other half of my soul refused to be comforted. It was cowering in some minute and inadequate corner—at an immense distance.

Hereafter, I found myself one person again, my hands still gripping my knees, and my eyes glued on the page before Mr. Shaynor. As dreamers accept and explain the upheaval of landscapes and the resurrection of the dead, with excerpts from the evening hymn or the multiplication-table, so I had accepted the facts, whatever they might be, that I should witness, and had devised a theory, sane and plausible to my mind, that explained them all. Nay, I was even in advance of my facts, walking hurriedly before them, assured that they would fit my theory. And all that I now recall of that epoch-making theory are the lofty words: 'If he has read Keats it's the chloric-ether. If he hasn't, it's the identical bacillus, or Hertzian wave of tuberculosis, *plus* Fanny Brand and the professional status which, in conjunction with the main-stream of subconscious thought common to all mankind, has thrown up temporarily an induced Keats.'

Mr. Shaynor returned to his work, erasing and rewriting as before with swiftness. Two or three blank pages he tossed aside. Then he wrote, muttering:—

The little smoke of a candle that goes out.

'No,' he muttered. 'Little smoke–little smoke–little smoke. What else?' He thrust his chin forward toward the advertisement, whereunder the last of the Blaudett's Cathedral pastilles fumed in its holder. 'Ah!' Then with relief:–

The little smoke that dies in moonlight cold.

Evidently he was snared by the rhymes of his first verse, for he wrote and rewrote 'gold–cold–mould' many times. Again he sought inspiration from the advertisement, and set down, without erasure, the line I had overheard:–

And threw warm gules on Madeleine's young breast.

As I remembered the original it is 'fair'–a trite word–instead of 'young,' and I found myself nodding approval, though I admitted that the attempt to reproduce 'Its little smoke in pallid moonlight died' was a failure.

Followed without a break ten or fifteen lines of bald prose–the naked soul's confession of its physical yearning for its beloved–unclean as we count uncleanliness; unwholesome, but human exceedingly; the raw material, so it seemed to me in that hour and in that place, whence Keats wove the twenty-sixth, seventh, and eighth stanzas of his poem. Shame I had none in overseeing this revelation; and my fear had gone with the smoke of the pastille.

'That's it,' I murmured. 'That's how it's blocked out. Go on! Ink it in, man. Ink it in!'

Mr. Shaynor returned to broken verse wherein 'loveliness' was made to rhyme with a desire to look upon 'her empty dress.' He picked up a fold of the gay, soft blanket, spread it over one hand, caressed it with infinite tenderness, thought, muttered, traced some snatches which I could not decipher, shut his eyes drowsily, shook his head, and dropped the stuff. Here I found myself at fault, for I could not then see (as I do now) in what manner a red, black, and yellow Austrian blanket coloured his dreams.

In a few minutes he laid aside his pen, and, chin on hand, considered the shop with thoughtful and intelligent eyes. He threw down the blanket, rose, passed along a line of drug-drawers, and read the names on the labels aloud. Returning, he took from his desk Christy's *New Commercial Plants* and the old Culpepper that I had given him, opened and laid them side by side with a clerky air, all trace of passion gone from his face, read first in one and then in the other, and paused with pen behind his ear.

'What wonder of Heaven's coming now?' I thought.

'Manna—manna—manna,' he said at last, under wrinkled brows. 'That's what I wanted. Good! Now then! Now then! Good! Good! Oh, by God, that's good!' His voice rose and he spoke rightly and fully without a falter:—

'Candied apple, quince and plum and gourd,
With jellies smoother than the creamy curd,
And lucent syrops tinct with cinnamon;
Manna and dates in argosy transferred
From Fez; and spicèd dainties, every one
From silken Samarcand to cedared Lebanon.'

He repeated it once more, using 'blander' for 'smoother' in the second line; then wrote it down without erasure, but this time (my set eyes missed no stroke of any word) he substituted 'soother' for his atrocious second thought, so that it came away under his hand as it is written in the book—as it is written in the book.

A wind went shouting down the street, and on the heels of the wind followed a spurt and rattle of rain.

After a smiling pause—and good right had he to smile—he began anew, always tossing the last sheet over his shoulder:—

The sharp rain falling on the window-pane,
Rattling sleet—the wind-blown sleet.

Then prose: 'It is very cold of mornings when the wind brings rain and sleet with it. I heard the sleet on the window-pane outside, and thought of you, my darling. I am always thinking of you. I wish we could both run away like two lovers into the storm and get that little cottage by the sea which we are always thinking about, my own dear darling. We could sit and watch the sea beneath our windows. It would be a fairyland all of our own—a fairy sea—a fairy sea. . . .'

He stopped, raised his head, and listened. The steady drone of the Channel along the sea-front that had borne us company so long leaped up a note to the sudden fuller surge that signals the change from ebb to flood. It beat in like the change of step throughout an army—this renewed pulse of the sea—and filled our ears till they, accepting it, marked it no longer.

A fairyland for you and me
Across the foam—beyond . . .
A magic foam, a perilous sea.

He grunted again with effort and bit his underlip. My throat dried, but I dared not gulp to moisten it lest I should break the spell that was drawing him nearer and nearer to the high-water mark but two of the sons of Adam have reached. Remember that in all the millions permitted there are no more than five—five little lines—of which one can say: 'These are the pure Magic. These are the clear Vision. The rest is only poetry.' And Mr. Shaynor was playing hot and cold with two of them!

I vowed no unconscious thought of mine should influence the blindfold soul, and pinned myself desperately to the other three, repeating and re-repeating:—

'A savage place! as holy and enchanted
As e'er beneath a waning moon was haunted
By woman wailing for her demon-lover.'

But though I believed my brain thus occupied, my every sense hung upon the writing under the dry, bony hand, all brown-fingered with chemicals and cigarette-smoke.

Our windows fronting on the dangerous foam,

(he wrote, after long, irresolute snatches), and then—

Our open casements facing desolate seas
Forlorn—forlorn—

Here again his face grew peaked and anxious with that sense of loss I had first seen when the Power snatched him. But this time the agony was tenfold keener. As I watched it mounted like mercury in the tube. It lighted his face from within till I thought the visibly scourged soul must leap forth naked between his jaws, unable to endure. A drop of sweat trickled from my forehead down my nose and splashed on the back of my hand.

Our windows facing on the desolate seas
And pearly foam of magic fairyland—

'Not yet—not yet,' he muttered, 'wait a minute. *Please* wait a minute. I shall get it then—

Our magic windows fronting on the sea,
The dangerous foam of desolate seas . . .
For aye.

Ouh, my God!'

From head to heel he shook—shook from the marrow of his bones outwards—then leaped to his feet with raised arms, and slid the chair screeching across the tiled floor where it struck the drawers behind and fell with a jar. Mechanically, I stooped to recover it.

As I rose, Mr. Shaynor was stretching and yawning at leisure.

'I've had a bit of a doze,' he said. 'How did I come to knock the chair over? You look rather——'

'The chair startled me,' I answered. 'It was so sudden in this quiet.'

Young Mr. Cashell behind his shut door was offendedly silent.

'I suppose I must have been dreaming,' said Mr. Shaynor.

'I suppose you must,' I said. 'Talking of dreams–I–I noticed you writing–before——'

He flushed consciously.

'I meant to ask you if you've ever read anything written by a man called Keats.'

'Oh! I haven't much time to read poetry, and I can't say that I remember the name exactly. Is he a popular writer?'

'Middling. I thought you might know him because he's the only poet who was ever a druggist. And he's rather what's called the lover's poet.'

'Indeed. I must dip into him. What did he write about?'

'A lot of things. Here's a sample that may interest you.'

Then and there, carefully, I repeated the verse he had twice spoken and once written not ten minutes ago.

'Ah! Anybody could see he was a druggist from that line about the tinctures and syrups. It's a fine tribute to our profession.'

'I don't know,' said young Mr. Cashell, with icy politeness, opening the door one half-inch, 'if you still happen to be interested in our trifling experiments. But, should such be the case——'

I drew him aside, whispering, 'Shaynor seemed going off into some sort of fit when I spoke to you just now. I thought, even at the risk of being rude, it wouldn't do to take you off your instruments just as the call was coming through. Don't you see?'

'Granted–granted as soon as asked,' he said, unbending. 'I *did* think it a shade odd at the time. So that was why he knocked the chair down?'

'I hope I haven't missed anything,' I said.

'I'm afraid I can't say that, but you're just in time for the end of a rather curious performance. You can come in too, Mr. Shaynor. Listen, while I read it off.'

The Morse instrument was ticking furiously. Mr. Cashell interpreted: '"*K.K.V. Can make nothing of your signals.*"' A pause. '"*M.M.V. M.M.V. Signals unintelligible. Purpose anchor Sandown Bay. Examine instruments to-morrow.*" Do you know what that means? It's a couple of men-o'-war working Marconi signals off the Isle of Wight. They are trying to talk to each other. Neither can read the other's messages, but all their messages are being taken in by our receiver here. They've been going on for ever so long. I wish you could have heard it.'

'How wonderful!' I said. 'Do you mean we're overhearing Portsmouth ships trying to talk to each other—that we're eavesdropping across half South England?'

'Just that. Their transmitters are all right, but their receivers are out of order, so they only get a dot here and a dash there. Nothing clear.'

'Why is that?'

'God knows—and Science will know tomorrow. Perhaps the induction is faulty; perhaps the receivers aren't tuned to receive just the number of vibrations per second that the transmitter sends. Only a word here and there. Just enough to tantalise.'

Again the Morse sprang to life.

'That's one of 'em complaining now. Listen: *"Disheartening—most disheartening."* It's quite pathetic. Have you ever seen a spiritualistic séance? It reminds me of that sometimes—odds and ends of messages coming out of nowhere—a word here and there—no good at all.'

'But mediums are all impostors,' said Mr. Shaynor, in the doorway, lighting an asthma-cigarette. 'They only do it for the money they can make. I've seen 'em.'

'Here's Poole, at last—clear as a bell. L.L.L. *Now* we shan't be long.' Mr. Cashell rattled the keys merrily. 'Anything you'd like to tell 'em?'

'No, I don't think so,' I said. 'I'll go home and get to bed. I'm feeling a little tired.'

ON GREENHOW HILL

To Love's low voice she lent a careless ear;
Her hand within his rosy fingers lay,
A chilling weight. She would not turn or hear;
But with averted face went on her way.
But when pale Death, all featureless and grim,
Lifted his bony hand, and beckoning
Held out his cypress-wreath, she followed him,
And Love was left forlorn and wondering,
That she who for his bidding would not stay,
At Death's first whisper rose and went away.

Rivals.

O*hé, Ahmed Din! Shafiz Ullah ahoo!* Bahadur Khan, where are you? Come out of the tents, as I have done, and fight against the English. Don't kill your own kin! Come out to me!'

The deserter from a native corps was crawling round the outskirts of the camp, firing at intervals, and shouting invitations to his old comrades. Misled by the rain and the darkness, he came to the English wing of the camp, and with his yelping and rifle-practice disturbed the men. They had been making roads all day, and were tired.

Ortheris was sleeping at Learoyd's feet. 'Wot's all that?' he said thickly. Learoyd snored, and a Snider bullet ripped its way through the tent wall. The men swore. 'It's that bloomin' deserter from the Aurangabadis,' said Ortheris. 'Git up, some one, an' tell 'im 'e's come to the wrong shop.'

'Go to sleep, little man,' said Mulvaney, who was steaming nearest the door. 'I can't arise an' expaytiate with him. 'Tis rainin' entrenchin' tools outside.'

' 'Tain't because you bloomin' can't. It's 'cause you bloomin' won't, ye long, limp, lousy, lazy beggar, you. 'Ark to 'im 'owlin'!'

'Wot's the good of argifying? Put a bullet into the swine! 'E's keepin' us awake!' said another voice.

A subaltern shouted angrily, and a dripping sentry whined from the darkness—

' 'Tain't no good, sir. I can't see 'im. 'E's 'idin' somewhere down 'ill.'

Ortheris tumbled out of his blanket. 'Shall I try to get 'im, sir?' said he.

'No,' was the answer. 'Lie down. I won't have the whole camp shooting all round the clock. Tell him to go and pot his friends.'

Ortheris considered for a moment. Then, putting his head under the tent wall, he called, as a 'bus conductor calls in a block, ' 'Igher up, there! 'Igher up!'

The men laughed, and the laughter was carried down wind to the deserter, who, hearing that he had made a mistake, went off to worry his own regiment half a mile away. He was received with shots; the Aurangabadis were very angry with him for disgracing their colours.

'An' that's all right,' said Ortheris, withdrawing his head as he heard the hiccough of the Sniders in the distance. 'S'elp me Gawd, tho', that man's not fit to live–messin' with my beauty-sleep this way.'

'Go out and shoot him in the morning, then,' said the subaltern incautiously. 'Silence in the tents now. Get your rest, men.'

Ortheris lay down with a happy little sigh, and in two minutes there was no sound except the rain on the canvas and the all-embracing and elemental snoring of Learoyd.

The camp lay on a bare ridge of the Himalayas, and for a week had been waiting for a flying column to make connection. The nightly rounds of the deserter and his friends had become a nuisance.

In the morning the men dried themselves in hot sunshine and cleaned their grimy accoutrements. The native regiment was to take its turn of road-making that day while the Old Regiment loafed.

'I'm goin' to lay for a shot at that man,' said Ortheris, when he had finished washing out his rifle. ' 'E comes up the watercourse every evenin' about five o'clock. If we go and lie out on the north 'ill a bit this afternoon we'll get 'im.'

'You're a bloodthirsty little mosquito,' said Mulvaney, blowing blue clouds into the air. 'But I suppose I will have to come wid you. Fwhere's Jock?'

'Gone out with the Mixed Pickles, 'cause 'e thinks 'isself a bloomin' marksman,' said Ortheris with scorn.

The 'Mixed Pickles' were a detachment of pickled shots, generally employed in clearing spurs of hills when the enemy were too impertinent. This taught the young officers how to handle men, and did not do the enemy much harm. Mulvaney and Ortheris strolled out of camp, and passed the Aurangabadis going to their road-making.

'You've got to sweat to-day,' said Ortheris genially. 'We're going to get your man. You didn't knock 'im out last night by any chance, any of you?'

'No. The pig went away mocking us. I had one shot at him,' said a private. 'He's my cousin, and *I* ought to have cleared our dishonour. But good luck to you.'

They went cautiously to the north hill, Ortheris leading, because, as he explained, 'this is a long-range show, an' I've got to do it.' His was an almost passionate devotion to his rifle, which, by barrack-room report, he was supposed to kiss every night before turning in. Charges and scuffles he held in contempt, and, when they were inevitable, slipped between Mulvaney and Learoyd, bidding them to fight for his skin as well as their own. They never failed him. He trotted along, questing like a hound on a broken trail, through the wood of the north hill. At last he was satisfied, and threw himself down on the soft pine-needled slope that commanded a clear view of the watercourse and a brown, bare hillside beyond it. The trees made a scented darkness in which an army corps could have hidden from the sun-glare without.

''Ere's the tail o' the wood, said Ortheris. ''E's got to come up the watercourse, 'cause it gives 'im cover. We'll lay 'ere. 'Tain't not arf so bloomin' dusty neither.'

He buried his nose in a clump of scentless white violets. No one had come to tell the flowers that the season of their strength was long past, and they had bloomed merrily in the twilight of the pines.

'This is something like,' he said luxuriously. 'Wot a 'evinly clear drop for a bullet acrost. How much d'you make it, Mulvaney?'

'Seven hunder. Maybe a trifle less, bekaze the air's so thin.'

Wop! wop! wop! went a volley of musketry in the rear face of the north hill.

'Curse them Mixed Pickles firin' at nothin'! They'll scare arf the country.'

'Thry a sightin' shot in the middle of the row,' said Mulvaney, the man of many wiles. 'There's a red rock yonder he'll be sure to pass. Quick!'

Ortheris ran his sight up to six hundred yards and fired. The bullet threw up a feather of dust by a clump of gentians at the base of the rock.

'Good enough!' said Ortheris, snapping the scale down. 'You snick your sights to mine or a little lower. You're always firin' high. But remember, first shot to me. O Lordy! but it's a lovely afternoon.'

The noise of the firing grew louder, and there was a tramping of men in the wood. The two lay very quiet, for they knew that the British soldier is desperately prone to fire at anything that moves or calls. Then Learoyd appeared, his tunic ripped across the breast by a bullet, looking ashamed of himself. He flung down on the pine-needles, breathing in snorts.

'One o' them damned gardeners o' th' Pickles,' said he, fingering the rent. 'Firin' to th' right flank, when he knowed I was there. If I knew who he was I'd 'a' rippen the hide offan him. Look at ma tunic!'

'That's the spishil trustability av a marksman. Train him to hit a fly wid a stiddy rest at seven hunder, an' he'll loose on anythin' he sees or hears up to th' mile. You're well out av that fancy-firin' gang, Jock. Stay here.'

'Bin firin' at the bloomin' wind in the bloomin' treetops,' said Ortheris with a chuckle. 'I'll show you some firin' later on.'

They wallowed in the pine-needles, and the sun warmed them where they lay. The Mixed Pickles ceased firing, and returned to camp, and left the wood to a few scared apes. The watercourse lifted up its voice in the silence, and talked foolishly to the rocks. Now and again the dull thump of a blasting charge three miles away told that the Aurangabadis were in difficulties with their road-making. The men smiled as they listened and lay still, soaking in the warm leisure. Presently Learoyd, between the whiffs of his pipe—

'Seems queer—about 'im yonder—desertin' at all.'

''E'll be a bloomin' side queerer when I've done with 'im,' said Ortheris. They were talking in whispers, for the stillness of the wood and the desire of slaughter lay heavy upon them.

'I make no doubt he had his reasons for desertin'; but, my faith! I make less doubt ivry man has good reason for killin' him,' said Mulvaney.

'Happen there was a lass tewed up wi' it. Men do more than more for th' sake of a lass.'

'They make most av us 'list. They've no manner av right to make us desert.'

'Ah; they make us 'list, or their fathers do,' said Learoyd softly, his helmet over his eyes.

Ortheris's brows contracted savagely. He was watching the valley. 'If it's a girl I'll shoot the beggar twice over, an' second time for bein' a fool. You're blasted sentimental all of a sudden. Thinkin' o' your last near shave?'

'Nay, lad; ah was but thinkin' o' what has happened.'

'An fwhat has happened, ye lumberin' child av calamity, that you're lowing like a cow-calf at the back av the pasture, an' suggestin' invidious excuses for the man Stanley's goin' to kill. Ye'll have to wait another hour yet, little man. Spit it out, Jock, an' bellow melojus to the moon. It takes an earthquake or a bullet graze to fetch aught out av you. Discourse, Don Juan! The a-moors av Lotharius Learoyd! Stanley, kape a rowlin' rig'mental eye on the valley.'

'It's along o' yon hill there,' said Learoyd, watching the bare sub-Himalayan spur that reminded him of his Yorkshire moors. He was speaking more to himself than his fellows. 'Ay,' said he, 'Rumbolds Moor stands up ower Skipton town, an' Greenhow Hill stands up ower Pately Brig. I reckon you've never heard tell o' Greenhow Hill, but yon bit o' bare stuff if there was nobbut a white road windin' is like ut; strangely like. Moors an' moors an' moors, wi' never a tree for shelter, an' grey houses wi' flagstone rooves, and peewits cryin', an' a windhover goin' to and fro just like these kites. And cold! A wind that cuts you like a knife. You could tell Greenhow Hill folk by the red-apple colour o' their cheeks an' nose tips, and their blue eyes, driven into pin-points by the wind. Miners mostly, burrowin' for lead i' th' hillsides, followin' the trail of th' ore vein same as a field-rat. It was the roughest minin' I ever seen. Yo'd come on a bit o' creakin' wood windlass like a well-head, an' you was let down i' th' bight of a rope, fendin' yoursen off the side wi' one hand, carryin' a candle stuck in a lump o' clay with t'other, an' clickin' hold of a rope with t'other hand.

'An' that's three of them,' said Mulvaney. 'Must be a good climate in those parts.'

Learoyd took no heed.

'An' then yo' came to a level, where you crept on your hands and knees through a mile o' windin' drift, an' you come out into a cave-place as big as Leeds Town Hall, with a engine pumpin' water from workin's 'at went deeper still. It's a queer country, let alone minin', for the hill is full of those natural caves, an' the rivers an' the becks drops into what they call pot-holes, an' come out again miles away.'

'Wot was you doin' there?' said Ortheris.

'I was a young chap then, an' mostly went wi' 'osses, leadin' coal and lead ore; but at th' time I'm tellin' on I was drivin' the waggon-team i' th' big sumph. I didn't belong to that country-side by rights. I went there because of a little difference at home, an' at fust I took up wi' a rough lot. One night we'd been drinkin', an' I must ha' hed more than I could stand, or happen th' ale was none so good. Though i' them days, By for God, I never seed bad ale. He flung his arms over his head, and gripped a vast handful of white violets. 'Nah,' said he, 'I never seed the ale I could not drink, the bacca I could not smoke, nor the lass I could not kiss. Well, we mun have a race home, the lot on us. I lost all th' others, an' when I was climbin' ower one of them walls built o' loose stones, I comes down into the ditch, stones and all, an' broke my arm. Not as I knawed much about it, for I fell on th' back of my head, an' was knocked stupid like. An' when I come to mysen it were mornin', an' I were lyin' on the settle i' Jesse Roantree's house-place, an' 'Liza Roantree was settin' sewin'. I ached all ovver, and my mouth were like a lime-kiln. She gave me a drink out of a china mug wi' gold letters—"A Present from Leeds" —as I looked at many and many a time at after. "Yo're to lie still while Dr. Warbottom comes, because your arm's broken, and father has sent a lad to fetch him. He found yo' when he was goin' to work, an' carried you here on his back," sez she. "Oa!" sez I; an' I shet my eyes, for I felt ashamed o' mysen. "Father's gone to his work these three hours, an' he said he'd tell 'em to get somebody to drive the tram." The clock ticked, an' a bee comed in the house, an' they rung i' my head like mill-wheels. An' she gave me another drink an' settled the pillow. "Eh, but yo're young to be getten drunk an' such like, but yo' won't do it again, will yo'?"—Noa, sez I, I wouldn't if she'd not but stop they mill-wheels clatterin'.'

'Faith, it's a good thing to be nursed by a woman when you're sick!' said Mulvaney. 'Dir' cheap at the price av twenty broken heads.'

Ortheris turned to frown across the valley. He had not been nursed by many women in his life.

'An' then Dr. Warbottom comes ridin' up, an' Jesse Roantree along with 'im. He was a high-larned doctor, but he talked wi' poor folk same as theirsens. "What's ta bin agaate on naa?" he sings out. "Brekkin' tha thick head?" An' he felt me all ovver. "That's none broken. Tha's nobbut knocked a bit sillier than ordinary, an' that's daaft eneaf." An' soa he went on, callin' me all the names he could think on, but settin' my arm, wi' Jesse's help, as careful as could be. "Yo' mun let the big oaf bide here a bit, Jesse," he says, when he hed strapped me up an' given me a dose o' physic; "an' you an' 'Liza will tend him, though he's scarcelins worth the trouble. An' tha'll lose tha work," sez he, "an' tha'll be upon th' Sick Club for a couple o' months an' more. Doesn't tha think tha's a fool?"'

'But whin was a young man, high or low, the other av a fool, I'd like to know?' said Mulvaney. 'Sure, folly's the only safe way to wisdom, for I've thried it.'

'Wisdom!' grinned Ortheris, scanning his comrades with uplifted chin. 'You're bloomin' Solomons, you two, ain't you?'

Learoyd went calmly on, with a steady eye like an ox chewing the cud. 'And that was how I comed to know 'Liza Roantree. There's some tunes as she used to sing—aw, she were always singin'—that fetches Greenhow Hill before my eyes as fair as yon brow across there. And she would learn me to sing bass, an' I was to go to th' chapel wi' 'em, where Jesse and she led the singin', th' old man playin' the fiddle. He was a strange chap, old Jesse, fair mad wi' music, an' he made me promise to learn the big fiddle when my arm was better. It belonged to him, and it stood up in a big case alongside o' th' eight-day clock, but Willie Satterthwaite, as played it in the chapel, had getten deaf as a door-post, and it vexed Jesse, as he had to rap him ower his head wi' th' fiddlestick to make him give ower sawin' at the' right time.

'But there was a black drop in it all, an' it was a man in a black coat that brought it. When th' Primitive Methodist preacher came to Greenhow, he would always stop wi' Jesse Roantree, an' he laid hold of me from th' beginning. It seemed I wor a soul to be saved, and he meaned to do it. At th' same time I jealoused 'at he were keen o' savin' 'Liza Roantree's soul as well, and I could ha' killed him many a time. An' this went on till one day I broke out, an' borrowed th' brass for a drink from 'Liza. After fower days I come back, wi' my tail between my legs, just to see 'Liza again. But Jesse were at home an' th' preacher—th' Reverend Amos Barraclough. 'Liza said naught, but a bit o' red come into her face as were white of a regular thing. Says Jesse, tryin' his best to be civil, "Nay, lad, it's like this. You've getten to choose which way it's goin' to be. I'll ha' nobody across ma doorstep as goes a-drinkin', an' borrows my lass's money to spend i' their drink. Ho'd tha tongue, 'Liza," sez he, when she wanted to put in a word 'at I were welcome to th' brass, and she were none afraid that I wouldn't pay it back. Then the Reverend cuts in, seein' as Jesse were losin' his temper, an' they fair beat me among them. But it were 'Liza, as looked an' said naught, as did more than either o' their tongues, an' soa I concluded to get converted.'

'Fwhat!' shouted Mulvaney. Then checking himself, he said softly, 'Let be! Let be! Sure the Blessed Virgin is the mother of all religion an' most women; an' there's a dale av piety in a girl if the men would only let ut stay there. I'd ha' been converted myself under the circumstances.'

'Nay, but,' pursued Learoyd with a blush, 'I meaned it.'

Ortheris laughed as loudly as he dared, having regard to his business at the time.

'Ay, Ortheris, you may laugh, but you didn't know yon preacher Barraclough—a little white-faced chap, wi' a voice as 'ud wile a bird offan a bush, and a way o' layin' hold of folks as made them think they'd never had a live man for a friend before. You never saw him, an'—an'—you never seed 'Liza Roantree—never seed 'Liza Roantree. . . . Happen it was as much 'Liza as th' preacher and her father, but anyways they all meaned it, an' I was fair shamed o' mysen, an' so I become what they called a changed character. And when I think on, it's hard to believe as yon chap going to prayer-meetin's, chapel, and class-meetin's were me. But I never had naught to say for mysen, though there was a deal o' shoutin', and old Sammy Strother, as were almost clemmed to death and doubled up with the rheumatics, would sing out "Joyful! Joyful!" and 'at it were better to go up to heaven in a coal-basket than down to hell i' a coach an' six. And he would put his poor old claw on my shoulder, sayin', "Doesn't tha feel it, tha great lump? Doesn't tha feel it?" An' sometimes I thought I did, and then again I thought I didn't, an' how was that?'

'The iverlastin' nature av mankind,' said Mulvaney. 'An', furthermore, I misdoubt you were built for the Primitive Methodians. They're a new corps anyways. I hold by the Ould Church, for she's the mother of them all—ay, an' the father, too. I like her bekaze she's most remarkable regimental in her fittings. I may die in Honolulu, Nova Zambra, or Cape Cayenne, but wherever I die, me bein' fwhat I am, an' a priest handy, I go under the same orders an' the same words an' the same unction as tho' the Pope himself come down from the roof av St. Peter's to see me off. There's neither high nor low, nor broad nor deep, nor betwixt nor between wid her, an' that's what I like. But mark you, she's no manner av Church for a wake man, bekaze she takes the body and the soul av him, onless he has his proper work to do. I remember when my father died that was three months comin' to his grave; begad he'd ha' sold the shebeen above our heads for ten minutes' quittance of purgathory. An' he did all he could. That's why I say ut takes a strong man to deal with the Ould Church, an' for that reason you'll find so many women go there. An' that same's a conundrum.'

'Wot's the use o' worrittin' 'bout these things?' said Ortheris. 'You're bound to find all out quicker nor you want to, any'ow.' He jerked the cartridge out of the breech-block into the palm of his hand. ''Ere's my chaplain,' he said, and made the venomous black-headed bullet bow like a marionette. ''E's goin' to teach a man all about which is which, an' wot's true, after all, before sundown. But wot 'appened after that, Jock?'

'There was one thing they boggled at, and almost shut th' gate i' my face for, and that were my dog Blast, th' only one saved out o' a litter o' pups as was blowed up when a keg o' minin' powder loosed off in th' store-keeper's hut. They liked his name no better than his business, which were fightin' every dog he comed across; a rare good dog, wi' spots o' black and pink on his face, one ear gone, and lame o' one side wi' being driven in a basket through an iron roof, a matter of half a mile.

'They said I mun give him up 'cause he were worldly and low; and would I let mysen be shut out of heaven for the sake on a dog? "Nay," says I, "if th' door isn't wide enough for th' pair on us, we'll stop outside, for we'll none be parted." And th' preacher spoke up for Blast, as had a likin' for him from th' first—I reckon that was why I come to like th' preacher—and wouldn't hear o' changin' his name to Bless, as some o' them wanted. So th' pair on us became reg'lar chapel-members. But it's hard for a young chap o' my build to cut traces from the world, th' flesh, an' the devil all uv a heap. Yet I stuck to it for a long time, while th' lads as used to stand about th' town-end an' lean ower th' bridge, spittin' into th' beck o' a Sunday, would call after me, "Sitha, Learoyd, when's ta bean to preach, 'cause we're comin' to hear tha?"—"Ho'd tha jaw. He hasn't getten th' white choaker on ta morn," another lad would say, and I had to double my fists hard i' th' bottom of my Sunday coat, and say to mysen, "If 'twere Monday and I warn't a member o' the Primitive Methodists, I'd leather all th' lot of yond'." That was th' hardest of all—to know that I could fight and I mustn't fight.'

Sympathetic grunts from Mulvaney.

'So what wi' singin', practisin', and class-meetin's, and th' big fiddle, as he made me take between my knees, I spent a deal o' time i' Jesse Roantree's house-place. But often as I was there, th' preacher fared to me to go oftener, and both th' old man an' th' young woman were pleased to have him. He lived i' Pately Brig, as were a goodish step off, but he come. He come all the same. I liked him as well or better as any man I'd ever seen i' one way, and yet I hated him wi' all my heart i' t'other, and we watched each other like cat and mouse, but civil as you please, for I was on my best behaviour, and he was that fair and open that I was bound to be fair with him. Rare good company he was, if I hadn't wanted to wring his clever little neck half of the time. Often and often when he was goin' from Jesse's I'd set him a bit on the road.'

'See 'im 'ome, you mean?' said Ortheris.

'Ay. It's a way we have i' Yorkshire o' seein' friends off. Yon was a friend as I didn't want to come back, and he didn't want me to come back neither, and so we'd walk together towards Pately, and then he'd set me back again, and there we'd be wal two o'clock i' the mornin' settin' each other to an' fro like a blasted pair o' pendulums twixt hill and valley, long after th' light had gone out i' 'Liza's window, as both on us had been looking at, pretending to watch the moon.'

'Ah!' broke in Mulvaney, 'ye'd no chanst against the maraudin' psalm-singer. They'll take the airs an' the graces instid av the man nine times out av ten, an' they only find the blunder later—the wimmen.'

'That's just where yo're wrong,' said Learoyd, reddening under the freckled tan of his cheeks. 'I was th' first wi' 'Liza, an' yo'd think that were enough. But th' parson were a steady-gaited sort o' chap, and Jesse were strong o' his side, and all th' women i' the congregation dinned it to 'Liza 'at she were fair fond to take up wi' a wastrel ne'er-do-weel like me, as was scarcelins respectable an' a fighting dog at his heels. It was all very well for her to be doing me good and saving my soul, but she must mind as she didn't do herself harm. They talk o' rich folk bein' stuck-up an' genteel, but for cast-iron pride o' respectability there's naught like poor chapel folk. It's as cold as th' wind o' Greenhow Hill—ay, and colder, for 'twill never change. And now I come to think on it, one o' t' strangest things I know is 'at they couldn't abide th' thought o' soldiering. There's a vast o' fightin' i' th' Bible, and there's a deal of Methodists i' th' army; but to hear chapel folk talk yo'd think that soldierin' were next door, an' t'other side, to hangin'. I' their meetin's all their talk is o' fightin'. When Sammy Strother were stuck for summat to say in his prayers, he'd sing out, "Th' sword o' th' Lord and o' Gideon." They were allus at it about puttin' on th' whole armour o' righteousness, an' fightin' the good fight o' faith. And then, atop o' 't all, they held a prayer-meetin' ower a young chap as wanted to 'list, and nearly deafened him, till he picked up his hat and fair ran away. And they'd tell tales in th' Sunday-school o' bad lads as had been thumped and brayed for bird-nesting o' Sundays and playin' truant o' week-days, and how they took to wrestlin', dog-fightin', rabbit-runnin', and drinkin', till at last, as if 'twere a hepitaph on a gravestone, they damned him across th' moors wi', "an' then he went and 'listed for a soldier," an' they'd all fetch a deep breath, and throw up their eyes like a hen drinkin'.'

'Fwhy is ut?' said Mulvaney, bringing down his hand on his thigh with a crack. 'In the name av God, fwhy is ut? I've seen ut, tu. They cheat an' they swindle an' they lie an' they slander, an' fifty things fifty times worse; but the last an' the worst by their reckonin' is to serve the Widdy honest. It's like the talk av childer—seein' things all round.'

'Plucky lot of fightin' good fights of whatsername they'd do if we didn't see they had a quiet place to fight in. And such fightin' as theirs is! Cats on the tiles. T'other callin' to which to come on. I'd give a month's pay to get some o' them broad-backed beggars in London sweatin' through a day's road-makin' an' a night's rain. They'd carry on a deal afterwards–same as we're supposed to carry on. I've bin turned out of a measly arf-licence pub down Lambeth way, full o' greasy keb-men, 'fore now,' said Ortheris with an oath.

'Maybe you were dhrunk,' said Mulvaney soothingly.

'Worse nor that. The Forders were drunk. *I* was wearin' the Queen's uniform.'

'I'd no particular thought to be a soldier i' them days,' said Learoyd, still keeping his eye on the bare hill opposite, 'but this sort o' talk put it i' my head. They was so good, th' chapel folk, that they tumbled ower t'other side. But I stuck to it for 'Liza's sake, specially as she was learning me to sing the bass part in a horotorio as Jesse were gettin' up. She sung like a throstle hersen, and we had practisin's night after night for a matter of three months.'

'I know what a horotorio is,' said Ortheris pertly. 'It's a sort of chap-lain's sing-song–words all out of the Bible, and hullabaloojah choruses.'

'Most Greenhow Hill folks played some instrument or t'other, an' they all sung so you might have heard them miles away, and they were so pleased wi' the noise they made they didn't fare to want anybody to listen. The preacher sung high seconds when he wasn't playin' the flute, an' they set me, as hadn't got far with big fiddle, again' Willie Satterth-waite, to jog his elbow when he had to get agate playin'. Old Jesse was happy if ever a man was, for he were th' conductor an' th' first fiddle an' th' leadin' singer, beatin' time wi' his fiddle-stick, till at times he'd rap with it on the table, and cry out, "Now, you mun all stop; it's my turn." And he'd face round to his front, fair sweating wi' pride, to sing th' tenor solos. But he were grandest i' th' choruses, waggin' his head, flinging his arms round like a windmill, and singin' hisself black in the face. A rare singer were Jesse.

'Yo' see, I was not o' much account wi' 'em all exceptin' to 'Liza Roan-tree, and I had a deal o' time settin' quiet at meetings and horotorio practices to harken their talk, and if it were strange to me at beginnin', it got stranger still at after, when I was shut on it, and could study what it meaned.

'Just after th' horotorios came off, 'Liza, as had allus been weakly like, was took very bad. I walked Dr. Warbottom's horse up and down a deal of times while he were inside, where they wouldn't let me go, though I fair ached to see her.

'"She'll be better i' noo, lad—better i' noo," he used to say. "Tha mun ha' patience." Then they said if I was quiet I might go in, and th' Reverend Amos Barraclough used to read to her lyin' propped up among th' pillows. Then she began to mend a bit, and they let me carry her on to th' settle, and when it got warm again she went about same as afore. Th' preacher and me and Blast was a deal together i' them days, and i' one way we was rare good comrades. But I could ha' stretched him time and again with a good will. I mind one day he said he would like to go down into th' bowels o' th' earth, and see how th' Lord had builded th' framework o' th' everlastin' hills. He were one of them chaps as had a gift o' sayin' things. They rolled off the tip of his clever tongue, same as Mulvaney here, as would ha' made a rare good preacher if he had nobbut given his mind to it. I lent him a suit o' miner's kit as almost buried th' little man, and his white face down i' th' coat-collar and hat-flap looked like the face of a boggart, and he cowered down i' th' bottom o' the waggon. I was drivin' a tram as led up a bit of an incline up to th' cave where the engine was pumpin', and where th' ore was brought up and put into th' waggons as went down o' themselves, me puttin' th' brake on and th' horses a-trottin' after. Long as it was daylight we were good friends, but when we got fair into th' dark, and could nobbut see th' day shinin' at the hole like a lamp at a street-end, I feeled downright wicked. Ma religion dropped all away from me when I looked back at him as were always comin' between me and 'Liza. The talk was 'at they were to be wed when she got better, an' I couldn't get her to say yes or nay to it. He began to sing a hymn in his thin voice, and I came out wi' a chorus that was all cussin' an' swearin' at my horses, an' I began to know how I hated him. He were such a little chap, too. I could drop him wi' one hand down Garstang's Copper-hole—a place where th' beck slithered ower th' edge on a rock, and fell wi' a bit of a whisper into a pit as no rope i' Greenhow could plumb.'

Again Learoyd rooted up the innocent violets. 'Ay, he should see th' bowels o' th' earth an' never naught else. I could take him a mile or two along th' drift, and leave him wi' his candle doused to cry hallelujah, wi' none to hear him and say amen. I was to lead him down th' ladder-way to th' drift where Jesse Roantree was workin', and why shouldn't he slip on th' ladder, wi' my feet on his fingers till they loosed grip, and I put him down wi' my heel? If I went fust down th' ladder I could click hold on him and chuck him over my head, so as he should go squushin' down the shaft, breakin' his bones at ev'ry timberin' as Bill Appleton did when he was fresh, and hadn't a bone left when he wrought to th' bottom.

Niver a blasted leg to walk from Pately. Niver an arm to put round 'Liza Roantree's waist. Niver no more—niver no more.'

The thick lips curled back over the yellow teeth, and that flushed face was not pretty to look upon. Mulvaney nodded sympathy, and Ortheris, moved by his comrade's passion, brought up the rifle to his shoulder, and searched the hillside for his quarry, muttering ribaldry about a sparrow, a spout, and a thunder-storm. The voice of the watercourse supplied the necessary small talk till Learoyd picked up his story.

'But it's none so easy to kill a man like yon. When I'd given up my horses to th' lad as took my place and I was showin' th' preacher th' workin's, shoutin' into his ear across th' clang o' th' pumpin' engines, I saw he were afraid o' naught; and when the lamplight showed his black eyes, I could feel as he was masterin' me again. I were no better nor Blast chained up short and growlin' i' the depths of him while a strange dog went safe past.

' "Th'art a coward and a fool," I said to mysen; an' I wrestled i' my mind again' him till, when we come to Garstang's Copper-hole, I laid hold o' the preacher and lifted him up over my head and held him into the darkest on it. "Now, lad," I says, "it's to be one or t'other on us—thee or me—for 'Liza Roantree. Why, isn't thee afraid for thysen?" I says, for he were still i' my arms as a sack. "Nay; I'm but afraid for thee, my poor lad, as knows naught," says he. I set him down on th' edge, an' th' beck run stiller, an' there was no more buzzin' in my head like when th' bee come through th' window o' Jesse's house. "What dost tha mean?" says I.

' "I've often thought as thou ought to know," says he, "but 'twas hard to tell thee. 'Liza Roantree's for neither on us, nor for nobody o' this earth. Dr. Warbottom says—and he knows her, and her mother before her—that she is in a decline, and she cannot live six months longer. He's known it for many a day. Steady, John! Steady!" says he. And that weak little man pulled me further back and set me again' him, and talked it all over quiet and still, me turnin' a bunch o' candles in my hand, and counting them ower and ower again as I listened. A deal on it were th' regular preachin' talk, but there were a vast lot as made me begin to think as he were more of a man than I'd ever given him credit for, till I were cut as deep for him as I were for mysen.

'Six candles we had, and we crawled and climbed all that day while they lasted, and I said to mysen, " 'Liza Roantree hasn't six months to live." And when we came into th' daylight again we were like dead men to look at, an' Blast come behind us without so much as waggin' his tail. When I saw 'Liza again she looked at me a minute and says, "Who's telled tha? For I see tha knows." And she tried to smile as she kissed me, and I fair broke down.

'Yo' see, I was a young chap i' them days, and had seen naught o' life, let alone death, as is allus a-waitin'. She telled me as Dr. Warbottom said as Greenhow air was too keen, and they were goin' to Bradford, to Jesse's brother David, as worked i' a mill, and I mun hold up like a man and a Christian, and she'd pray for me. Well, and they went away, and the preacher that same back end o' th' year were appointed to another circuit, as they call it, and I were left alone on Greenhow Hill.

'I tried, and I tried hard, to stick to th' chapel, but 'tweren't th' same thing at after. I hadn't 'Liza's voice to follow i' th' singin', nor her eyes a-shinin' acrost their heads. And i' th' class-meetings they said as I mun have some experiences to tell, and I hadn't a word to say for mysen.

'Blast and me moped a good deal, and happen we didn't behave ourselves over well, for they dropped us and wondered however they'd come to take us up. I can't tell how we got through th' time, while i' th' winter I gave up my job and went to Bradford. Old Jesse were at th' door o' th' house, in a long street o' little houses. He'd been sendin' th' children 'way as were clatterin' their clogs in th' causeway, for she were asleep.

' "Is it thee?" he says; "but you're not to see her. I'll none have her wakened for a nowt like thee. She's goin' fast, and she mun go in peace. Thou'lt never be good for naught i' th' world, and as long as thou lives thou'll never play the big fiddle. Get away, lad, get away!" So he shut the door softly i' my face.

'Nobody never made Jesse my master, but it seemed to me he was about right, and I went away into the town and knocked up against a recruiting sergeant. The old tales o' th' chapel folk came buzzin' into my head. I was to get away, and this were th' regular road for the likes o' me. I 'listed there and then, took th' Widow's shillin', and had a bunch o' ribbons pinned i' my hat.

'But next day I found my way to David Roantree's door, and Jesse came to open it. Says he, "Thou's come back again wi' th' devil's colours flyin'—thy true colours, as I always telled thee."

'But I begged and prayed of him to let me see her nobbut to say good-bye, till a woman calls down th' stairway, "She says John Learoyd's to come up." Th' old man shifts aside in a flash, and lays his hand on my arm, quite gentle like. "But thou'lt be quiet, John," says he, "for she's rare and weak. Thou was allus a good lad."

'Her eyes were all alive wi' light, and her hair was thick on the pillow round her, but her cheeks were thin—thin to frighten a man that's strong. "Nay, father, yo' mayn't say th' devil's colours. Them ribbons is pretty." An' she held out her hands for th' hat, an' she put all straight as a woman will wi' ribbons. "Nay, but what they're pretty," she says. "Eh, but I'd ha' liked to see thee i' thy red coat, John, for thou was allus my own lad—my very own lad, and none else."

'She lifted up her arms, and they come round my neck i' a gentle grip, and they slacked away, and she seemed fainting. "Now yo' mun get away, lad," says Jesse, and I picked up my hat and I came downstairs.

'Th' recruiting sergeant were waitin' for me at the corner public-house. "You've seen your sweetheart?" says he. "Yes, I've seen her," says I. "Well, we'll have a quart now, and you'll do your best to forget her," says he, bein' one o' them smart, bustlin' chaps. "Ay, sergeant," says I. "Forget her." And I've been forgettin' her ever since.'

He threw away the wilted clump of white violets as he spoke. Ortheris suddenly rose to his knees, his rifle at his shoulder, and peered across the valley in the clear afternoon light. His chin cuddled the stock, and there was a twitching of the muscles of the right cheek as he sighted; Private Stanley Ortheris was engaged on his business. A speck of white crawled up the watercourse.

'See that beggar? . . . Got 'im.'

Seven hundred yards away, and a full two hundred down the hillside, the deserter of the Aurangabadis pitched forward, rolled down a red rock, and lay very still, with his face in a clump of blue gentians, while a big raven flapped out of the pine wood to make investigation.

'That's a clean shot, little man,' said Mulvaney.

Learoyd thoughtfully watched the smoke clear away. 'Happen there was a lass tewed up wi' him, too,' said he.

Ortheris did not reply. He was staring across the valley, with the smile of the artist who looks on the completed work.

'LOVE-O'-WOMEN'

'A lamentable tale of things
Done long ago, and ill done.'

THE HORROR, the confusion, and the separation of the murderer from his comrades were all over before I came. There remained only on the barrack-square the blood of man calling from the ground. The hot sun had dried it to a dusky goldbeater's-skin film, cracked lozenge-wise by the heat; and as the wind rose, each lozenge, rising a little, curled up at the edges as if it were a dumb tongue. Then a heavier gust blew all away down wind in grains of dark-coloured dust. It was too hot to stand in the sunshine before breakfast. The men were in barracks talking the matter over. A knot of soldiers' wives stood by one of the entrances to the married quarters, while inside a woman shrieked and raved with wicked filthy words.

A quiet and well-conducted sergeant had shot down, in broad daylight just after early parade, one of his own corporals, had then returned to barracks and sat on a cot till the guard came for him He would, therefore, in due time be handed over to the High Court for trial. Further, but this he could hardly have considered in his scheme of revenge, he would horribly upset my work; for the reporting of that trial would fall on me without a relief. What that trial would be like I knew even to weariness. There would be the rifle carefully uncleaned, with the fouling-marks about breech and muzzle, to be sworn to by half a dozen superfluous privates; there would be heat, reeking heat, till the wet pencil slipped sideways between the fingers; and the punkah would swish and the pleaders would jabber in the verandahs and his Commanding Officer would put in certificates to the prisoner's moral character, while the jury would pant and the summer uniforms of the witnesses would smell of dye and soaps; and some abject barrack-sweeper would lose his head in cross-examination, and the young barrister who always defended soldiers' cases for the credit that they never brought him, would say and do wonderful things, and would then quarrel with me because I had not reported him correctly. At the last, for he surely would not be hanged, I might meet the prisoner again, ruling blank account-forms in the Central Jail, and cheer him with the hope of his being made a warder in the Andamans.

The Indian Penal Code and its interpreters do not treat murder, under any provocation whatever, in a spirit of jest. Sergeant Raines would be very lucky indeed if he got off with seven years, I thought. He had slept the night upon his wrongs, and killed his man at twenty yards before any talk was possible. That much I knew. Unless, therefore, the case was doctored a little, seven years would be his least; and I fancied it was exceedingly well for Sergeant Raines that he had been liked by his Company.

That same evening–no day is so long as the day of a murder–I met Ortheris with the dogs, and he plunged defiantly into the middle of the matter. 'I'll be one o' the witnesses,' said he. 'I was in the verandah when Mackie come along. 'E come from Mrs. Raines's quarters. Quigley, Parsons, an' Trot, they was in the inside verandah, so *they* couldn't ave 'eard nothing. Sergeant Raines was in the verandah talkin' to me, an' Mackie 'e come along acrost the square an' 'e sez, "Well," sez 'e, " 'ave they pushed your 'elmet off yet, Sergeant?" 'e sez. An' at that Raines 'e catches 'is breath an' 'e sez, "My Gawd, I can't stand this!" sez 'e, an' 'e picks up my rifle an' shoots Mackie. See?'

'But what were you doing with your rifle in the outer verandah an hour after parade?'

'Cleanin' 'er,' said Ortheris, with the sullen brassy stare that always went with his choicer lies.

He might as well have said that he was dancing naked, for at no time did his rifle need hand or rag on her twenty minutes after parade. Still, the High Court would not know his routine.

'Are you going to stick to that–on the Book?' I asked.

'Yes. Like a bloomin' leech.'

'All right, I don't want to know any more. Only remember that Quigley, Parsons, and Trot couldn't have been where you say without hearing something; and there's nearly certain to be a barrack-sweeper who was knocking about the square at the time. There always is.'

' 'Twasn't the sweeper. It was the beastie. 'E's all right.'

Then I knew that there was going to be some spirited doctoring, and I felt sorry for the Government Advocate who would conduct the prosecution.

When the trial came on I pitied him more, for he was always quick to lose his temper and made a personal matter of each lost cause. Raines's young barrister had for once put aside his unslaked and welling passion for alibis and insanity, had forsworn gymnastics and fireworks, and worked soberly for his client. Mercifully the hot weather was yet young, and there had been no flagrant cases of barrack-shootings up to the time; and the jury was a good one, even for an Indian jury, where nine men out of every twelve are accustomed to weighing evidence. Ortheris stood firm and was not shaken by any cross-examination. The one weak point in his tale—the presence of his rifle in the outer verandah—went unchallenged by civilian wisdom, though some of the witnesses could not help smiling. The Government Advocate called for the rope, contending throughout that the murder had been a deliberate one. Time had passed, he argued, for that reflection which comes so naturally to a man whose honour is lost. There was also the Law, ever ready and anxious to right the wrongs of the common soldier if, indeed, wrong had been done. But he doubted much whether there had been any sufficient wrong. Causeless suspicion over-long brooded upon had led, by his theory, to deliberate crime. But his attempts to minimise the motive failed. The most disconnected witness knew—had known for weeks—the causes of offence; and the prisoner, who naturally was the last of all to know, groaned in the dock while he listened. The one question that the trial circled round was whether Raines had fired under sudden and blinding provocation given that very morning; and in the summing-up it was clear that Ortheris's evidence told. He had contrived most artistically to suggest that he personally hated the Sergeant, who had come into the verandah to give him a talking-to for insubordination. In a weak moment the Government Advocate asked one question too many. 'Beggin' *your* pardon, sir,' Ortheris replied, ''e was callin' me a dam' impudent little lawyer.' The Court shook. The jury brought it in a killing, but with every provocation and extenuation known to God or man, and the Judge put his hand to his brow before giving sentence, and the Adam's apple in the prisoner's throat went up and down like mercury pumping before a cyclone.

In consideration of all considerations, from his Commanding Officer's certificate of good conduct to the sure loss of pension, service, and honour, the prisoner would get two years, to be served in India, and—there need be no demonstration in Court. The Government Advocate scowled and picked up his papers; the guard wheeled with a clash, and the prisoner was relaxed to the Secular Arm, and driven to the jail in a broken-down *ticca-gharri*.

His guard and some ten or twelve military witnesses, being less important, were ordered to wait till what was officially called the cool of the evening before marching back to cantonments. They gathered together in one of the deep red-brick verandahs of a disused lock-up and congratulated Ortheris, who bore his honours modestly. I sent my work in to the office and joined them. Ortheris watched the Government Advocate driving off to lunch.

'That's a nasty little bald-'eaded little butcher, that is,' he said. ''E don't please me. 'E's got a collie dog wot do, though. I'm goin' up to Murree in a week. That dawg'll bring fifteen rupees anywheres.'

'You had better spend ut in Masses,' said Terence, unbuckling his belt; for he had been on the prisoner's guard, standing helmeted and bolt upright for three long hours.

'Not me,' said Ortheris cheerfully. 'Gawd'll put it down to B Comp'ny's barrick-damages one o' these days. You look strapped, Terence.'

'Faith, I'm not so young as I was. That guard-mountin' wears on the sole av the fut, and this'—he sniffed contemptuously at the brick verandah—'is as hard setting as standin'!'

'Wait a minute. I'll get the cushions out of my cart,' I said.

''Strewth—sofies. We're going it gay, said Ortheris, as Terence dropped himself section by section on the leather cushions, saying prettily, 'May ye niver want a soft place wheriver you go, an' power to share ut wid a frind. Another for yourself? That's good. It lets me sit longways. Stanley, pass me a pipe. Augrrh! An' that's another man gone all to pieces bekaze av a woman. I must ha' been on forty or fifty prisoners' gyards, first an' last; an I hate ut new ivry time.'

'Let's see. You were on Losson's, Lancey's, Dugard's, and Stebbins's, that I can remember,' I said.

'Ay, an' before that an' before that—scores av thim,' he answered with a worn smile. ''Tis better to die than to live for them, though. Whin Raines comes out—he'll be changin' his kit at the jail now—he'll think that too. He shud ha' shot himself an' the woman by rights an' made a clean bill av all. Now he's left the woman—she tuk tay wid Dinah Sunday gone last—an' he's left himself. Mackie's the lucky man.'

'He's probably getting it hot where he is,' I ventured, for I knew something of the dead Corporal's record.

'Be sure av that,' said Terence, spitting over the edge of the verandah. 'But fwhat he'll get there is light marchin'-ordher to fwhat he'd ha' got here if he'd lived.'

'Surely not. He'd have gone on and forgotten—like the others.'

'Did ye know Mackie well, sorr?' said Terence.

'He was on the Patiala guard of honour last winter, and I went out shooting with him in an *ekka* for the day, and I found him rather an amusing man.'

'Well, he'll ha' got shut av amusemints, excipt turnin' from wan side to the other, these few years to come. I knew Mackie, an' I've seen too many to be mistuk in the muster av wan man. He might ha' gone on an' forgot as you say, sorr, but he was a man wid an educashin, an' he used ut for his schames; an' the same educashin, an' talkin', an' all that made him able to do fwhat he had a mind to wid a woman, that same wud turn back again in the long run an' tear him alive. I can't say fwhat that I mane to say bekaze I don't know how, but Mackie was the spit an' livin' image av a man that I saw march the same march *all but;* an' 'twas worse for him that he did not come by Mackie's ind. Wait while I remember now. 'Twas whin I was in the Black Tyrone, an' he was drafted us from Portsmouth; an' fwhat was his misbegotten name? Larry—Larry Tighe ut was; an' wan of the draft said he was a gentleman-ranker, an' Larry tuk an' three-parts killed him for saying so. An' he was a big man, an' a strong man, an' a handsome man, an' that tells heavy in practice wid some women, but, takin' them by an' large, not wid all. Yet 'twas wid all that Larry dealt—*all*—for he cud put the comether on any woman that trod the green earth av God, an' he knew ut. Like Mackie that's roastin' now, he knew ut, an' niver did he put the comether on any woman save an' excipt for the black shame. 'Tis not me that shud be talkin', dear knows, dear knows, but the most av my mis—misallinces was for pure devilry, an' mighty sorry I have been whin harm came; an' time an' again wid a girl, ay, an' a woman too, for the matter av that, whin I have seen by the eyes av her, that I was makin' more throuble than I talked, I have hild off an' let be for the sake av the mother that bore me. But Larry, I'm thinkin', he was suckled by a she-devil, for he never let wan go that came nigh to listen to him. 'Twas his business, as if it might ha' ben sinthry-go. He was a good soldier too. Now there was the Colonel's governess—an' he a privit too!—that was never known in barricks; an' wan av the Major's maids, and she was promised to a man; an' some more outside; an' fwhat ut was amongst *us* we'll never know till Judgment Day. 'Twas the nature av the baste to put the comether on the best av thim—not the prettiest by any manner av manes—but the like av such women as you cud lay your hand on the Book an' swear there was niver thought av foolishness in. An' for that very reason, mark you, he was niver caught. He came close to ut wanst or twice, but caught he niver was, an' that cost him more at the ind than the beginnin'. He talked to me more than most, bekaze he tould me, barrin' the accident av my educashin, I'd av been the same kind av divil he was. "An' is ut like," he wud say, houldin' his head high—"is ut like that I'd iver be thrapped? For fwhat am I when all's said an' done?" he sez. "A damned privit," sez he. "An' is ut like, think you, that thim I know wud be connect wid a privit like me? Number tin thousand four hundred an' sivin," he sez grinnin'. I knew by the turn av his spache when he was not takin' care to talk rough-shod that he was a gentleman-ranker.

' "I do not undherstan' ut at all," I sez; "but I know," sez I, "that the divil looks out av your eyes, an' I'll have no share wid you. A little fun by way av amusemint where 'twill do no harm, Larry, is right and fair, but I am mistook if 'tis any amusemint to you," I sez.

' "You are much mistook," he sez. "An' I counsel you not to judge your betters."

' "My betthers!" I sez. "God help you, Larry. There's no betther in this; 'tis all bad, as ye will find for yoursilf."

' "You're not like me," he says, tossin' his head.

' "Praise the Saints, I am not," I sez. "Fwhat I have done I have done an' been crool sorry for. Fwhin your time comes," sez I, "ye'll remimber fwhat I say."

' "An' whin that time comes," sez he, "I'll come to you for ghostly consolation, Father Terence," an' at that he went off afther some more divil's business—for to get expayrience, he tould me. He was wicked—rank wicked—wicked as all Hell! I'm not construct by nature to go in fear av any man, but, begad, I was afraid av Larry. He'd come into barricks wid his cap on three hairs, an' lie on his cot and stare at the ceilin', and now an' again he'd fetch a little laugh, the like av a splash in the bottom av a well, an' by that I knew he was schamin' new wickedness, an' I'd be afraid. All this was long an' long ago, but ut hild me straight—for a while.

'I tould you, did I not, sorr, that I was caressed an' pershuaded to lave the Tyrone on account av a throuble?'

'Something to do with a belt and a man's head, wasn't it?' Terence had never given me the tale in full.

'It was. Faith, ivry time I go on prisoner's gyard in coort I wondher fwhy I was not where the pris'ner is. But the man I struk tuk it in fair fight, an' he had the good sinse not to die. Considher now, fwhat wud ha' come to the Arrmy if he had! I was enthreated to exchange, an' my Commandin' Orf'cer pled wid me. I wint, not to be disobligin', an' Larry tould me he was powerful sorry to lose me, though fwhat I'd done to make him sorry I do not know. So to the Ould Rig'mint I came, lavin' Larry to go to the divil his own way, an' niver expectin' to see him again excipt as a shootin'-case in barracks. . . . Who's that quittin' the compound?' Terence's quick eye had caught sight of a white uniform skulking behind the hedge.

'The Sergeant's gone visiting,' said a voice.

'Thin I command here, an' I will have no sneakin' away to the bazar, an' huntin' for you wid a pathrol at midnight. Nalson, for I know ut's you, come back to the verandah.'

Nalson, detected, slunk back to his fellows. There was a grumble that died away in a minute or two, and Terence turning on the other side went on:—

'That was the last I saw av Larry for a while. Exchange is the same as death for not thinkin', an' by token I married Dinah, an' that kept me from remimberin' ould times. Thin we went up to the Front, an' ut tore my heart in tu to lave Dinah at the Depôt in Pindi. Consequint, whin I was at the Front I fought circumspectuous till I warrmed up, an' thin I fought double tides. You remember fwhat I tould you in the gyard-gate av the fight at Silver's Theatre?'

'Wot's that about Silver's Theayter?' said Ortheris quickly, over his shoulder.

'Nothin', little man. A tale that ye know. As I was sayin', afther that fight, us av the Ould Rig'mint an' the Tyrone was all mixed together takin' shtock av the dead, an' av coorse I wint about to find if there was any man that remimbered me. The second man I came acrost—an' how I'd missed him in the fight I do not know—was Larry, an' a fine man he looked, but oulder, by reason that he had fair call to be. "Larry," sez I, "how is ut wid you?"

' "Ye're callin' the wrong man," he sez, wid his gentleman's smile. "Larry has been dead these three years. They call him 'Love-o'-Women' now," he sez. By that I knew the ould divil was in him yet, but the ind av a fight is no time for the beginnin' av confession, so we sat down an' talked av times.

' "They tell me you're a married man," he sez, puffin' slow at his poipe. "Are ye happy?"

'"I will be whin I get back to Depôt," I sez. "'Tis a reconnaissance-honeymoon now."

'"I'm married too," he sez, puffin' slow an' more slow, an' stopperin' wid his forefinger.

'"Send you happiness," I sez. "That's the best hearin' for a long time."

'"Are ye av that opinion?" he sez; an' thin he began talkin' av the campaign. The sweat av Silver's Theatre was not dhry upon him an' he was prayin' for more work. I was well contint to lie and listen to the cook-pot lids.

'Whin he got up off the ground he shtaggered a little, an' laned over all twisted.

'"Ye've got more than ye bargained for," I sez. "Take an inventory, Larry. 'Tis like you're hurt."

'He turned round stiff as a ramrod an' damned the eyes av me up an' down for an impartinent Irish-faced ape. If that had been in barracks, I'd ha' stretched him an' no more said; but 'twas at the Front, an' afther such a fight as Silver's Theatre I knew there was no callin' a man to account for his tempers. He might as well ha' kissed me. Afterwards I was well pleased I kept my fists home. Thin our Captain Crook—Cruik-na-bulleen—came up. He'd been talkin' to the little orf'cer bhoy av the Tyrone. "We're all cut to windystraws," he sez, "but the Tyrone are damned short for non-coms. Go you over there, Mulvaney, an' be Deputy-Sergeant, Corp'ral, Lance, an' everything else ye can lay hands on till I bid you stop."

'I wint over an' tuk hould. There was wan sergeant left standin', an' they'd pay no heed to him. The remnint was me, an' 'twas full time I came. Some I talked to, an' some I did not, but before night the bhoys av the Tyrone stud to attention, begad, if I sucked on my poipe above a whisper. Betune you an' me an' Bobs I was commandin' the Company, an' that was what Crook had thransferred me for; an' the little orf'cer bhoy knew ut, and I knew ut, but the Comp'ny did not. And *there*, mark you, is the vartue that no money an' no dhrill can buy—the vartue av the ould soldier that knows his orf'cer's work an' does ut for him at the salute!

'Thin the Tyrone, wid the Ould Rig'mint in touch, was sint maraudin' an' prowlin' acrost the hills promishcuous an' onsatisfactory. 'Tis my privit opinion that a gin'ral does not know half his time fwhat to do wid three-quarthers his command. So he shquats on his hunkers an' bids them run round an' round forninst him while he considhers on it. Whin by the process av nature they get sejuced into a big fight that was none av their seekin', he sez: "Obsarve my shuperior janius. I meant ut to come so." We ran round an' about, an' all we got was shootin' into the camp at night, an' rushin' empty *sungars* wid the long bradawl, an' bein' hit from behind rocks till we was wore out—all excipt Love-o'-Women. That puppy-dog business was mate an' dhrink to him. Begad, he cud niver get enough av ut. Me well knowin' that it is just this desultorial campaignin' that kills the best men, an' suspicionin' that if I was cut, the little orf'cer bhoy wud expind all his men in thryin' to get me out, I wud lie most powerful doggo whin I heard a shot, an' curl my long legs behind a bowlder, an' run like blazes whin the ground was clear. Faith, if I led the Tyrone in rethreat wanst I led thim forty times! Love-o'-Women wud stay pottin' an' pottin' from behind a rock, and wait till the fire was heaviest, an' thin stand up an' fire man-height clear. He wud lie out in camp too at night, snipin' at the shadows, for he never tuk a mouthful av slape. My commandin' orf'cer—save his little soul!—cud not see the beauty av my strategims, an' whin the Ould Rig'ment crossed us, an' that was wanst a week, he'd throt off to Crook, wid his big blue eyes as round as saucers, an' lay an information against me. I heard thim wanst talkin' through the tent-wall, an' I nearly laughed.

'"He runs—runs like a hare," sez the little orf'cer bhoy. "'Tis demoralisin' my men."

'"Ye damned little fool," sez Crook, laughin', "he's larnin' you your business. Have ye been rushed at night yet?"

'"No," sez that child; wishful he had been.

'"Have you any wounded?" sez Crook.

'"No," he sez. "There was no chanst for that. They follow Mulvaney too quick," he sez.

'"Fwhat more do you want, thin?" sez Crook. "Terence is bloodin' you neat an' handy," he sez. "He knows fwhat you do not, an' that's that there's a time for ivrything. He'll not lead you wrong," he sez, "but I'd give a month's pay to larn fwhat he thinks av you."

'That kept the babe quiet, but Love-o'-Women was pokin' at me for ivrything I did, an' specially my manœuvres.

'"Mr. Mulvaney," he sez wan evenin', very contempshus, "you're growin' very *jeldy* on your feet. Among gentlemen," he sez, "among gentlemen that's called no pretty name."

'"Among privits 'tis different," I sez. "Get back to your tent. I'm sergeant here," I sez.

'There was just enough in the voice av me to tell him he was playin' wid his life betune his teeth. He wint off, an' I noticed that this man that was contempshus set off from the halt wid a shunt as tho' he was bein' kicked behind. That same night there was a Paythan picnic in the hills about, an' firin' into our tents fit to wake the livin' dead. "Lie down all," I sez. "Lie down an' kape still. They'll no more than waste ammunition."

'I heard a man's feet on the ground, an' thin a 'Tini joinin' in the chorus. I'd been lyin' warm, thinkin' av Dinah an' all, but I crup out wid the bugle for to look round in case there was a rush; an' the 'Tini was flashin' at the fore-ind av the camp, an' the hill near by was fair flickerin' wid long-range fire. Undher the starlight I behild Love-o'-Women settin' on a rock wid his belt and helmet off. He shouted wanst or twice, an' thin I heard him say: "They shud ha' got the range long ago. Maybe they'll fire at the flash." Thin he fired again, an' that dhrew a fresh volley, and the long slugs that they chew in their teeth came floppin' among the rocks like tree-toads av a hot night. "That's better," sez Love-o'-Women. "Oh Lord, how long, how long!" he sez, an' at that he lit a match an' held ut above his head.

' "Mad," thinks I, "mad as a coot," an' I tuk wan stip forward, an' the nixt I knew was the sole av my boot flappin' like a cavalry gydon an' the funny-bone av my toes tinglin'. 'Twas a clane-cut shot–a slug–that niver touched sock or hide, but set me barefut on the rocks. At that I tuk Love-o'-Women by the scruff and threw him under a bowlder, an' whin I sat down I heard the bullets patterin' on that same good stone.

' "Ye may dhraw your own wicked fire," I sez, shakin' him, "but 'Im not goin' to be kilt too."

' "Ye've come too soon," he sez. "Ye've come too soon. In another minute they cudn't ha' missed me. Mother av' God," he sez, "fwhy did ye not lave me be? Now 'tis all to do again," an' he hides his face in his hands.

' "So that's it," I sez, shakin' him again. "That's the manin' av your disobeyin' ordhers."

' "I dare not kill meself," he sez, rockin' to and fro. "My own hand wud not let me die, and there's not a bullet this month past wud touch me. I'm to die slow," he sez. "I'm to die slow. But I'm in hell now," he sez, shriekin' like a woman. "I'm in hell now!"

' "God be good to us all," I sez, for I saw his face. "Will ye tell a man the throuble? If 'tis not murder, maybe we'll mend it yet."

'At that he laughed. "D'you remember fwhat I said in the Tyrone barricks about comin' to you for ghostly consolation. I have not forgot," he sez. "That came back, and the rest av my time is on me now, Terence. I've fought ut off for months an' months, but the liquor will not bite any more. Terence," he sez, "I can't get dhrunk!"

'Thin I knew he spoke the truth about bein' in hell, for whin liquor does not take hould the sowl av a man is rotten in him. But me bein' such as I was, fwhat could I say to him?

' "Di'monds an' pearls," he begins again. "Di'monds an' pearls I have thrown away wid both hands—an' fwhat have I left? Oh, fwhat have I left?"

'He was shakin' an' tremblin' up against my shouldher, an' the slugs were singin' overhead, an' I was wonderin' whether my little bhoy wud have sinse enough to kape his men quiet through all this firin'.

' "So long as I did not think," sez Love-o'-Women, "so long I did not see—I wud not see, but I can now, what I've lost. The time an' the place," he sez, "an' the very words I said whin ut pleased me to go off alone to hell. But thin, even thin," he sez, wrigglin' tremenjous, "I wud not ha' been happy. There was too much behind av me. How cud I ha' believed her sworn oath—me that have bruk mine again an' again for the sport av seein' thim cry? An' there are the others," he sez. "Oh, what will I do—what will I do?" He rocked back an' forward again, an' I think he was cryin' like wan av the women he talked av.

'The full half of fwhat he said was Brigade Ordhers to me, but from the rest an' the remnint I suspicioned somethin' av his throuble. 'Twas the judgment av God had grup the heel av him, as I tould him 'twould in the Tyrone barricks. The slugs was singin' over our rock more an' more, an' I sez for to divart him: "Let bad alone," I sez. "They'll be tryin' to rush the camp in a minut'."

'I had no more than said that whin a Paythan man crep' up on his belly wid his knife betune his teeth, not twinty yards from us. Love-o'-Women jumped up an' fetched a yell, an' the man saw him an' ran at him (he'd left his rifle under the rock) wid the knife. Love-o'-Women niver turned a hair, but by the Living Power, for I saw ut, a stone twisted under the Paythan man's feet an' he came down full sprawl, an' his knife wint tinkling across the rocks! "I tould you I was Cain," sez Love-o'-Women. "Fwhat's the use av killin' him? He's an honust man—by compare."

'I was not dishputin' about the morils av Paythans that tide, so I dhropped Love-o'-Women's butt acrost the man's face, an' "Hurry into camp," I sez, "for this may be the first av a rush."

'There was no rush after all, though we waited undher arms to give them a chanst. The Paythan man must ha' come alone for the mischief, an' afther a while Love-o'-Women wint back to his tint wid that quare lurchin' sind-off in his walk that I cud niver understand. Begad, I pitied him, an' the more bekaze he made me think for the rest av the night av the day whin I was confirmed Corp'ril, not actin' Lef'tinant, an' my thoughts was not good to me.

'Ye can ondersthand that afther that night we came to talkin' a dale together, an' bit by bit ut came out fwhat I'd suspicioned. The whole av his carr'in's on an' divilments had come back on him hard, as liquor comes back whin you've been on the dhrink for a wake. All he'd said an' all he'd done, an' only he cud tell how much that was, come back, and there was niver a minut's peace in his sowl. 'Twas the Horrors widout any cause to see, an' yet, an' yet—fwhat am I talkin' av? He'd ha' taken the Horrors wid thankfulness. Beyon' the repentince av the man, an' that was beyon' the nature av man—awful, awful, to behould!—there was more that was worse than any repentince. Av the scores an' scores that he called over in his mind (an' they were drivin' him mad), there was, mark you, wan woman av all, an' she was not his wife, that cut him to the quick av his marrow. 'Twas there he said he'd thrown away di'monds an' pearls past count, an' thin he'd begin again like a blind *byle* in an oil-mill, walkin' round and round to considher (him that was beyond all touch av bein' happy this side hell!) how happy he wud ha' been wid *her*. The more he considhered the more he'd consate himself that he'd lost mighty happiness, an' thin he wud work ut all backwards, an' cry that he niver cud ha' been happy anyway.

'Time an' time an' again in camp, on p'rade, ay, an' in action, I've seen that man shut his eyes an' duck his head as ye wud duck to the flicker av a baynit. For 'twas thin, he tould me, that the thought av all he'd missed came an' stud forninst him like red-hot irons. For what he'd done wid the others he was sorry, but he did not care; but this wan woman that I've tould of, by the Hilts av God, she made him pay for all the others twice over! Niver did I know that a man cud enjure such tormint widout his heart crackin' in his ribs, an' I have been'—Terence turned the pipe-stem slowly between his teeth—'I have been in some black cells. All I iver suffered tho' was not to be talked of alongside av *him* . . . an' what could I do? Paternosters was no more than peas on plates for his sorrows.

'Evenshually we finished our prom'nade acrost the hills, and, thanks to me for the same, there was no casualties an' no glory. The campaign was comin' to an ind, an' all the rig'mints was being drawn together for to be sint back home. Love-o'-Women was mighty sorry bekaze he had no work to do, an' all his time to think in. I've heard that man talkin' to his belt-plate an' his side-arms while he was soldierin' thim, all to prevent himself from thinkin', an' ivry time he got up afther he had been settin' down or wint on from the halt, he'd start wid that kick an' traverse that I tould you av—his legs sprawlin' all ways to wanst. He wud niver go see the docthor, tho' I tould him to be wise. He'd curse me up an' down for my advice; but I knew he was no more a man to be reckoned wid than the little bhoy was a commandin' orf'cer, so I let his tongue run if it aised him.

'Wan day—'twas on the way back—I was walkin' round camp wid him an' he stopped an' struck ground wid his right fut three or four times doubtful. "Fwhat is ut?" I sez. "Is that ground?" sez he; an' while I was thinkin' his mind was goin', up comes the docthor, who'd been anatomisin' a dead bullock. Love-o'-Women starts to go on quick, an' lands me a kick on the knee while his legs were gettin' into marchin' ordher.

' "Hould on there," sez the docthor; an' Love-o'-Women's face, that was lined like a gridiron, turns red as brick.

' " 'Tention," says the docthor; an' Love-o'-Women stud so. "Now shut your eyes," sez the docthor. "No, ye must not hould by your comrade."

' " 'Tis all up," sez Love-o'-Women, thrying to smile. "I'd fall, docthor, an' you know ut."

' "Fall?" I sez. "Fall at attention wid your eyes shut! Fwhat do you mane?"

' "The docthor knows," he sez. "I've hild up as long as I can, but begad I'm glad 'tis all done. But I will die slow," he sez, "I will die very slow."

'I cud see by the docthor's face that he was mortial sorry for the man, an' he ordered him to hospital. We wint back together, an' I was dumbstruck. Love-o'-Women was cripplin' and crumblin' at ivry step. He walked wid a hand on my shoulder all slued sideways, an' his right leg swingin' like a lame camel. Me not knowin' more than the dead fwhat ailed him, 'twas just as though the docthor's word had done ut all—as if Love-o'-Women had but been waitin' for the word to let go.

'In hospital he sez somethin' to the docthor that I could not catch.

' "Holy Shmoke!" sez the docthor, "an' who are you to be givin' names to your diseases? 'Tis agin' all the reg'lations."

' "I'll nat be a privit much longer," sez Love-o'-Women in his gentleman's voice, an' the docthor jumped.

' "Thrate me as a study, Doctor Lowndes," he sez; an' that was the first time I'd iver heard a docthor called his name.

' "Good-bye, Terence," sez Love-o'-Women. " 'Tis a dead man I am widout the pleasure av dyin'. You'll come an' set wid me sometimes for the peace av my sowl."

'Now I had been minded for to ask Crook to take me back to the Ould Rig'mint; the fightin' was over, an' I was wore out wid the ways av the bhoys in the Tyrone; but I shifted my will, an' hild on, and wint to set wid Love-o'-Women in the hospital. As I have said, sorr, the man bruk all to little pieces under my hand. How long he had hild up an' forced himself fit to march I cannot tell, but in hospital but two days later he was such as I hardly knew. I shuk hands wid him, an' his grip was fair strong, but his hands wint all ways to wanst, an' he cud not button his tunic.

' "I'll take long an' long to die yet," he sez, "for the wages av sin they're like interest in the rig'mintal savin's-bank–sure, but a damned long time bein' paid."

'The docthor sez to me, quiet one day, "Has Tighe there anythin' on his mind?" he sez. "He's burnin' himself out."

' "How shud I know, sorr?" I sez, as innocint as putty.

' "They call him Love-o'-Women in the Tyrone, do they not?" he sez. "I was a fool to ask. Be wid him all you can. He's houldin' on to your strength."

' "But fwhat ails him, docthor?" I sez.

' "They call ut Locomotus attacks us," he sez, "bekaze," sez he, "ut attacks us like a locomotive, if ye know fwhat that manes. An' ut comes," sez he, lookin' at me, "ut comes from bein' called Love-o'-Women."

' "You're jokin', docthor," I sez.

' "Jokin'!" sez he. "If iver you feel that you've got a felt sole in your boot instid av a Government bull's-wool, come to me," he sez, "an' I'll show you whether 'tis a joke."

'You would not belave ut, sorr, but that, an' seein' Love-o'-Women overtuk widout warnin', put the cowld fear av Attacks-us on me so strong that for a week an' more I was kickin' my toes against stones an' stumps for the pleasure av feelin' thim hurt.

'An' Love-o'-Women lay in the cot (he might have gone down wid the wounded before an' before, but he asked to stay wid me), and fwhat there was in his mind had full swing at him night an' day an' ivry hour av the day an' the night, and he shrivelled like beef-rations in a hot sun, an' his eyes was like owls' eyes, an' his hands was mut'nous.

'They was getting the rig'mints away wan by wan, the campaign bein' inded, but as ushuil they was behavin' as if niver a rig'mint had been moved before in the mem'ry av man. Now, fwhy is that, sorr? There's fightin', in an' out, nine months av the twelve somewhere in the army. There has been—for years an' years an' years; an' I wud ha' thought they'd begin to get the hang av providin' for throops. But no! Ivry time 'tis like a girls' school meetin' a big red bull whin they're goin' to church; and, "Mother av God," sez the Commissariat an' the Railways an' the Barrick-masters, "fwhat will we do now?" The ordhers came to us av the Tyrone an' the Ould Rig'mint an' half a dozen more to go down, an' there the ordhers stopped dumb. We wint down, by the special grace av God—down the Khyber anyways. There was sick wid us, an' I'm thinkin' that some av thim was jolted to death in the doolies, but they was anxious to be kilt so if they cud get to Peshawur alive the sooner. I walked by Love-o'-Women—there was no marchin', an' Love-o'-Women was not in a stew to get on. "If I'd only ha' died up there," sez he through the dooli-curtains, an' thin he'd twist up his eyes an' duck his head for the thoughts that come an' raked him.

'Dinah was in Depôt at Pindi, but I wint circumspectuous, for well I knew 'tis just at the rump-ind av all things that his luck turns on a man. By token I had seen a dhriver of a batthery goin' by at a trot singin' "Home, swate home" at the top av his shout, and takin' no need to his bridle-hand—I had seen that man dhrop under the gun in the middle of a word, and come out by the limber like—like a frog on a pave-stone. No. I wud *not* hurry, though, God knows, my heart was all in Pindi. Love-o'-Women saw fwhat was in my mind, an' "Go on, Terence," he sez, "I know fwhat's waitin' for you." "I will not," I sez. " 'Twill kape a little yet."

'Ye know the turn of the pass forninst Jumrood and the nine-mile road on the flat to Peshawur? All Peshawur was along that road day and night waitin' for frinds—men, women, childer, and bands. Some av the throops was camped round Jumrood, an' some wint to Peshawur to get away down to their cantonmints. We came through in the early mornin', havin' been awake the night through, and we dhruv sheer into the middle av the mess. Mother av Glory, will I iver forget that comin' back? The light was not fair lifted, and the first we heard was "For 'tis my delight av a shiny night," frum a band that thought we was the second four comp'nies av the Lincolnshire. At that we was forced to sind them a yell to say who we was, an' thin up wint "The Wearin' av the Green." It made me crawl all up my backbone, not havin' taken my brequist. Then right smash into our rear came fwhat was left av the Jock Elliotts—wid four pipers an' not half a kilt among thim, playin' for the dear life, an' swingin' their rumps like buck-rabbits, an' a native rig'mint shriekin' blue murther. Ye niver heard the like! There was men cryin' like women that did—an' faith I do not blame them! Fwhat bruk me down was the Lancers' Band—shinin' an' spick like angils, wid the ould dhrum-horse at the head an' the silver kettle-dhrums an' all an' all, waitin' for their men that was behind us. They shtruck up the Cavalry Canter; an' begad those poor ghosts that had not a sound fut in a throop they answered to ut; the men rockin' in their saddles. We thried to cheer them as they wint by, but ut came out like a big gruntin' cough, so there must have been many that was feelin' like me. Oh, but I'm forgettin'! The Fly-by-Nights was waitin' for their second battalion, an' whin ut came out, there was the Colonel's horse led at the head—saddle-empty. The men fair worshipped him, an' he'd died at Ali Musjid on the road down. They waited till the remnint av the battalion was up, and thin—clane against ordhers, for who wanted *that* chune that day?—they wint back to Peshawur slow-time an' tearin' the bowils out av ivry man that heard, wid "The Dead March." Right acrost our line they wint, an' ye know their uniforms are as black as the Sweeps, crawlin' past like the dead, an' the other bands damnin' them to let be.

'Little they cared. The carpse was wid them, an' they'd ha' taken ut so through a Coronation. Our ordhers was to go into Peshawur, an' we wint hot-fut past the Fly-by-Nights, not singin', to lave that chune behind us. That was how we tuk the road of the other corps.

' 'Twas ringin' in my ears still whin I felt in the bones av me that Dinah was comin', an' I heard a shout, an' thin I saw a horse an' a tattoo latherin' down the road, hell-to-shplit, under women. I knew—I knew! Wan was the Tyrone Colonel's wife—ould Beeker's lady—her gray hair flyin' an' her fat round carkiss rowlin' in the saddle, an' the other was Dinah, that shud ha' been at Pindi. The Colonel's lady she charged the head av our column like a stone wall, an' she all but knocked Beeker off his horse, throwin' her arms round his neck an' blubberin', "Me bhoy! me bhoy!" an' Dinah wheeled left an' came down our flank, an' I let a yell that had suffered inside av me for months and—Dinah came! Will I iver forget that while I live! She'd come on pass from Pindi, an' the Colonel's lady had lint her the tattoo. They'd been huggin' an' cryin' in each other's arms all the long night.

'So she walked along wid her hand in mine, asking forty questions to wanst, an' beggin' me on the Virgin to make oath that there was not a bullet consaled in me, unbeknownst somewhere, an' thin I remembered Love-o'-Women. He was watchin' us, an' his face was like the face av a divil that has been cooked too long. I did not wish Dinah to see ut, for whin a woman's runnin' over with happiness she's like to be touched, for harm afterwards, by the laste little thing in life. So I dhrew the curtain, an' Love-o'-Women lay back and groaned.

'Whin we marched into Peshawur Dinah wint to barracks to wait for me, an', me feelin' so rich that tide, I wint on to take Love-o'-Women to hospital. It was the last I cud do, an' to save him the dust an' the smother I turned the dooli-men down a road well clear av the rest av the throops, an' we wint along, me talkin' through the curtains. Av a sudden I heard him say:

' "Let me look. For the mercy av Hiven, let me look." I had been so tuk up wid gettin' him out av the dust an' thinkin' av Dinah that I had not kept my eyes about me. There was a woman ridin' a little behind av us; an' talkin' ut over wid Dinah afterwards, that same woman must ha' rid out far on the Jumrood road. Dinah said that she had been hoverin' like a kite on the left flank av the columns.

'I halted the dooli to set the curtains, an' she rode by, walkin' pace, an' Love-o'-Women's eyes wint afther her as if he wud fair haul her down from the saddle.

' "Follow there," was all he sez, but I niver heard a man speak in that voice before or since; an' I knew by those two wan words an' the look in his face that she was Di'monds-an'-Pearls that he'd talked av in his disthresses.

'We followed till she turned into the gate av a little house that stud near the Edwardes Gate. There was two girls in the verandah, an' they ran in whin they saw us. Faith, at long eye-range it did not take me a wink to see fwhat kind av house ut was. The throops bein' there an' all, there was three or four such; but aftherwards the polis bade thim go. At the verandah Love-o'-Women sez, catchin' his breath, "Stop here," an' thin, an' thin, wid a grunt that must ha' tore the heart up from his stomick, he swung himself out av the dooli, an' my troth he stud up on his feet wid the sweat pourin' down his face! If Mackie was to walk in here now I'd be less tuk back than I was thin. Where he'd dhrawn his power from, God knows—or the Divil—but 'twas a dead man walkin' in the sun, wid the face av a dead man and the breath av a dead man, hild up by the Power, an' the legs an' the arms av the carpse obeyin' ordhers.

'The woman stud in the verandah. She'd been a beauty too, though her eyes was sunk in her head, an' she looked Love-o'-Women up an' down terrible. "An'," she sez, kicking back the tail av her habit,—"An'," she sez, "fwhat are you doin' *here,* married man?"

'Love-o'-Women said nothin', but a little froth came to his lips, an' he wiped ut off wid his hand an' looked at her an' the paint on her, an' looked, an' looked, an' looked.

' "An' yet," she sez, wid a laugh—(Did you hear Raines's wife laugh whin Mackie died? Ye did not? Well for you.) "An' yet," she sez, "who but you have betther right?" sez she. "You taught me the road. You showed me the way," she sez. "Ay, look," she sez, "for 'tis your work; you that tould me—d'you remimber it?—that a woman who was false to wan man cud be false to two. I have been that," she sez, "that an' more, for you always said I was a quick learner, Ellis. Look well," she sez, "for it is me that you called your wife in the sight av God long since." An' she laughed.

'Love-o'-Women stud still in the sun widout answerin'. Thin he groaned an' coughed to wanst, an' I thought 'twas the death-rattle, but he niver tuk his eyes off her face, not for a blink. Ye cud ha' put her eyelashes through the flies av an E.P. tent, they were so long.

' "Fwhat do you do here?" she sez, word by word, "that have taken away my joy in my man this five years gone—that have broken my rest an' killed my body an' damned my soul for the sake av seein' how 'twas done. Did your expayrience aftherwards bring you acrost any woman that give you more than I did? Wud I not ha' died for you, an' wid you, Ellis? Ye know that, man! If iver your lyin' sowl saw truth in uts life ye know that."

'An' Love-o'-Women lifted up his head and said, "I knew," an' that was all. While she was spakin' the Power hild him up parade-set in the sun, an' the sweat dhripped undher his helmet. 'Twas more an' more throuble for him to talk, an' his mouth was running twistways.

' "Fwhat do you do *here?"* she sez, an' her voice wint up. 'Twas like bells tollin' before. "Time was whin you were quick enough wid your words,—you that talked me down to hell. Are ye dumb now?" An' Love-o'-Women got his tongue, an' sez simple, like a child, "May I come in?" he sez.

' "The house is open day an' night," she sez, wid a laugh; an' Love-o'-Women ducked his head an' hild up his hand as tho' he was gyardin'. The Power was on him still—it hild him up still, for, by my sowl, as I'll never save ut, he walked up the verandah steps that had been a livin' carpse in hospital for a month!

'"An' now?" she sez, lookin' at him; an' the red paint stud lone on the white av her face like a bull's-eye on a target.

'He lifted up his eyes, slow an' very slow, an' he looked at her long an' very long, an' he tuk his spache betune his teeth wid a wrench that shuk him.

'"I'm dyin', Aigypt—dyin'," he sez. Ay, those were his words, for I remimber the name he called her. He was turnin' the death-colour, but his eyes niver rowled. They were set—set on her. Widout word or warnin' she opened her arms full stretch, an' "Here!" she sez. (Oh, fwhat a golden mericle av a voice ut was!) "Die here!" she sez; an' Love-o'-Women dhropped forward, an' she hild him up, for she was a fine big woman.

'I had no time to turn, bekaze that minut' I heard the sowl quit him —tore out in the death-rattle—an' she laid him back in a long chair, an' she sez to me, "Misther soldier," she sez, "will ye not wait an' talk to wan av the girls? This sun's too much for him."

'Well I knew there was no sun he'd iver see, but I cud not spake, so I wint away wid the empty dooli to find the docthor. He'd been breakfastin' an' lunchin' iver since we'd come in, an' he was full as a tick.

'"Faith, ye've got dhrunk mighty soon," he sez, whin I'd tould him, "to see that man walk. Barrin' a puff or two av life, he was a carpse before we left Jumrood. I've a great mind," he sez, "to confine you."

'"There's a dale av liquor runnin' about, docthor," I sez, solemn as a hard-boiled egg. "Maybe tis so; but will ye not come an' see the carpse at the house?"

'"'Tis dishgraceful," he sez, "that I would be expected to go to a place like that. Was she a pretty woman?" he sez, an' at that he set off double-quick.

'I cud see that the two was in the verandah where I'd left them, an' I knew by the hang av her head an' the noise av the crows fwhat had happened. 'Twas the first and the last time that I'd iver known woman to use the pistol. They fear the shot as a rule, but Di'monds-an'-Pearls she did not—she did not.

'The docthor touched the long black hair av her head ('twas all loose upon Love-o'-Women's tunic), an' that cleared the liquor out av him. He stud considherin' a long time, his hands in his pockets, an' at last he sez to me, "Here's a double death from naturil causes, most naturil causes; an' in the present state av affairs the rig'mint will be thankful for wan grave the less to dig. *Issiwasti,*" he sez. "*Issiwasti,* Privit Mulvaney, these two will be buried together in the Civil Cemet'ry at my expinse; an' may the good God," he sez, "make it so much for me whin my time comes. Go you to your wife," he sez. "Go an' be happy. I'll see to this all."

'I left him still considherin'. They was buried in the Civil Cemet'ry together, wid a Church av England service. There was too many buryin's thin to ask questions, an' the docthor—he ran away wid Major—Major Van Dyce's lady that year—he saw to ut all. Fwhat the right an' the wrong av Love-o'-Women an' Di'monds-an'-Pearls was I niver knew, an' I will niver know; but I've tould ut as I came acrost ut—here an' there in little pieces. *So,* being fwhat I am, an' knowin' fwhat I knew, that's fwhy I say in this shootin'-case here, Mackie that's dead an' in hell is the lucky man. There are times, sorr, whin 'tis betther for the man to die than to live, an' by consequince forty million times betther for the woman.'

'H'up there!' said Ortheris. 'It's time to go.'

The witnesses and guard formed up in the thick white dust of the parched twilight and swung off, marching easy and whistling. Down the road to the green by the church I could hear Ortheris, the black Book-lie still uncleansed on his lips, setting, with a fine sense of the fitness of things, the shrill quickstep that runs—

'Oh, do not despise the advice of the wise,
Learn wisdom from those that are older,
And don't try for things that are out of your reach—
An' that's what the Girl told the Soldier!
Soldier! Soldier!
Oh, that's what the Girl told the Soldier!'

THE BRUSHWOOD BOY

Girls and boys, come out to play:
The moon is shining as bright as day!
Leave your supper and leave your sleep,
And come with your playfellows out in the street!
Up the ladder and down the wall—

A CHILD of three sat up in his crib and screamed at the top of his voice, his fists clinched and his eyes full of terror. At first no one heard, for his nursery lay in the west wing, and the nurse was talking to a gardener among the laurels. Then the housekeeper passed that way, and hurried to soothe him. He was her special pet, and she disapproved of the nurse.

'What was it, then? What was it, then? There's nothing to frighten him, Georgie dear.'

'It was—it was a policeman! He was on the Down—I saw him! He came in. Jane *said* he would.'

'Policemen don't come into houses, dearie. Turn over, and take my hand.'

'I saw him—on the Down. He came here. Where is your hand, Harper?'

The housekeeper waited till the sobs changed to the regular breathing of sleep before she stole out.

'Jane, what nonsense have you been telling Master Georgie about policemen?'

'I haven't told him anything.'

'You have. He's been dreaming about them.'

'We met Tisdall on Dowhead when we were in the donkey-cart this morning. P'raps that's what put it into his head.'

'Oh! Now you aren't going to frighten the child into fits with your silly tales, and the master know nothing about it. If ever I catch you again,' etc.

A child of six was telling himself stories as he lay in bed. It was a new power, and he kept it a secret. A month before it had occurred to him to carry on a nursery tale left unfinished by his mother, and he was delighted to find the tale as it came out of his own head just as surprising as though he were listening to it 'all new from the beginning.' There was a prince in that tale, and he killed dragons, but only for one night. Ever afterwards Georgie dubbed himself prince, pasha, giant-killer, and all the rest (you see, he could not tell any one, for fear of being laughed at), and his tales faded gradually into dreamland, where adventures were so many that he could not recall the half of them. They all began in the same way, or, as Georgie explained to the shadows of the night-light, there was 'the same starting-off place'—a pile of brushwood stacked somewhere near a beach; and round this pile Georgie found himself running races with little boys and girls. These ended, ships ran high up the dry land and opened into cardboard boxes; or gilt-and-green iron railings that surrounded beautiful gardens turned all soft, and could be walked through and overthrown so long as he remembered it was only a dream. He could never hold that knowledge more than a few seconds ere things became real, and instead of pushing down houses full of grown-up people (a just revenge), he sat miserably upon gigantic door-steps trying to sing the multiplication-table up to four times six.

The princess of his tales was a person of wonderful beauty (she came from the old illustrated edition of Grimm, now out of print), and as she always applauded Georgie's valour among the dragons and buffaloes, he gave her the two finest names he had ever heard in his life—Annie and Louise, pronounced 'Annie*an*louise.' When the dreams swamped the stories, she would change into one of the little girls round the brushwood-pile, still keeping her title and crown. She saw Georgie drown once in a dream-sea by the beach (it was the day after he had been taken to bathe in a real sea by his nurse); and he said as he sank: 'Poor Annie*an*louise! She'll be sorry for me now!' But 'Annie*an*louise,' walking slowly on the beach, called, ' "Ha! ha!" said the duck, laughing,' which to a waking mind might not seem to bear on the situation. It consoled Georgie at once, and must have been some kind of spell, for it raised the bottom of the deep, and he waded out with a twelve-inch flower-pot on each foot. As he was strictly forbidden to meddle with flower-pots in real life, he felt triumphantly wicked.

The movement of the grown-ups, whom Georgie tolerated, but did not pretend to understand, removed his world, when he was seven years old, to a place called 'Oxford-on-a-visit.' Here were huge buildings surrounded by vast prairies, with streets of infinite length, and, above all, something called the 'buttery,' which Georgie was dying to see, because he knew it must be greasy, and therefore delightful. He perceived how correct were his judgments when his nurse led him through a stone arch into the presence of an enormously fat man, who asked him if he would like some bread and cheese. Georgie was used to eating all round the clock, so he took what 'buttery' gave him, and would have taken some brown liquid called 'auditale,' but that his nurse led him away to an afternoon performance of a thing called 'Pepper's Ghost.' This was intensely thrilling. People's heads came off and flew all over the stage, and skeletons danced bone by bone, while Mr. Pepper himself, beyond question a man of the worst, waved his arms and flapped a long gown, and in a deep bass voice (Georgie had never heard a man sing before) told of his sorrows unspeakable. Some grown-up or other tried to explain that the illusion was made with mirrors, and that there was no need to be frightened. Georgie did not know what illusions were, but he did know that a mirror was the looking-glass with the ivory handle on his mother's dressing-table. Therefore the 'grown-up' was 'just saying things' after the distressing custom of 'grown-ups,' and Georgie cast about for amusement between scenes. Next to him sat a little girl dressed all in black, her hair combed off her forehead exactly like the girl in the book called 'Alice in Wonderland,' which had been given him on his last birthday. The little girl looked at Georgie and Georgie looked at her. There seemed to be no need of any further introduction.

'I've got a cut on my thumb,' said he. It was the first work of his first real knife, a savage triangular hack, and he esteemed it a most valuable possession.

'I'm tho thorry!' she lisped. 'Let me look—pleathe.'

'There's a di-ack-lum plaster on, but it's all raw under,' Georgie answered, complying.

'Dothent it hurt?'—her grey eyes were full of pity and interest.

'Awf'ly. Perhaps it will give me lockjaw.'

'It lookth very horrid. I'm *tho* thorry!' She put a forefinger to his hand, and held her head sidewise for a better view.

Here the nurse turned and shook him severely. 'You mustn't talk to strange little girls, Master Georgie.'

'She isn't strange. She's very nice. I like her, an' I've showed her my new cut.'

'The idea! You change places with me.'

She moved him over, and shut out the little girl from his view, while the grown-up behind renewed the futile explanations.

'I am *not* afraid, truly,' said the boy, wriggling in despair; 'but why don't you go to sleep in the afternoons, same as Provostoforiel?'

'Georgie had been introduced to a grown-up of that name, who slept in his presence without apology. Georgie understood that he was the most important grown-up in Oxford; hence he strove to gild his rebuke with flatteries. This grown-up did not seem to like it, but he collapsed, and Georgie lay back in his seat, silent and enraptured. Mr. Pepper was singing again, and the deep, ringing voice, the red fire, and the misty, waving gown all seemed to be mixed up with the little girl who had been so kind about his cut. When the performance was ended she nodded to Georgie and Georgie nodded in return. He spoke no more than was necessary till bedtime, but meditated on new colours, and sounds, and lights, and music, and things as far as he understood them; the deep-mouthed agony of Mr. Pepper mingling with the little girl's lisp. That night he made a new tale, from which he shamelessly removed the Rapunzel-Rapunzel-let-down-your-hair princess, gold crown, Grimm edition, and all, and put a new Annie*an*louise in her place. So it was perfectly right and natural that when he came to the brushwood-pile he should find her waiting for him, her hair combed off her forehead, more like Alice in Wonderland than ever, and the races and adventures began.

Ten years at an English public school do not encourage dreaming. Georgie won his growth and chest measurement, and a few other things which did not appear in the bills, under a system of cricket, football, and paper-chases, from four to five days a week, which provided for three lawful cuts of a ground-ash if any boy absented himself from these entertainments. He became a rumple-collared, dusty-hatted fag of the Lower Third, and a light half-back at Little Side football; was pushed and prodded through the slack backwaters of the Lower Fourth, where the raffle of a school generally accumulates; won his Second Fifteen cap at football, enjoyed the dignity of a study with two companions in it, and began to look forward to office as a sub-prefect. At last he blossomed into full glory as head of the school, ex-officio captain of the games; head of his house, where he and his lieutenants preserved discipline and decency among seventy boys from twelve to seventeen; general arbiter in the quarrels that spring up among the touchy Sixth—and intimate friend and ally of the Head himself. When he stepped forth in the black jersey, white knickers, and black stockings of the First Fifteen, the new match-ball under his arm, and his old and frayed cap at the back of his head, the small fry of the lower forms stood apart and worshipped, and the 'new caps' of the team talked to him ostentatiously, that the world might see. And so, in summer, when he came back to the pavilion after a slow but eminently safe game, it mattered not whether he had made nothing, or, as once happened, a hundred and three, the school shouted just the same, and womenfolk who had come to look at the match looked at Cottar—Cottar *major;* 'that's Cottar!' Above all, he was responsible for that thing called the tone of the school, and few realise with what passionate devotion a certain type of boy throws himself into this work. Home was a far-away country, full of ponies and fishing, and shooting, and men-visitors who interfered with one's plans; but school was his real world, where things of vital importance happened and crises arose that must be dealt with promptly and quietly. Not for nothing was it written, 'Let the Consuls look to it that the Republic takes no harm,' and Georgie was glad to be back in authority when the holidays ended. Behind him, but not too near, was the wise and temperate Head, now suggesting the wisdom of the serpent, now counselling the mildness of the dove; leading him on to see, more by half-hints than by any direct word, how boys and men are all of a piece, and how he who can handle the one will assuredly in time control the other.

For the rest, the school was not encouraged to dwell on its emotions, but rather to keep in hard condition, to avoid false quantities, and to enter the army direct, without the help of the expensive London crammer, under whose roof young blood learns too much. Cottar *major* went the way of hundreds before him. The Head gave him six months' final polish, taught him what kind of answers best please a certain kind of examiners, and handed him over to the properly constituted authorities, who passed him into Sandhurst. Here he had sense enough to see that he was in the Lower Third once more, and behaved with respect towards his seniors, till they in turn respected him, and he was promoted to the rank of corporal, and sat in authority over mixed people with all the vices of men and boys combined. His reward was another string of athletic cups, a good-conduct sword, and, at last, Her Majesty's Commission as a subaltern in a first-class line regiment. He did not know that he bore with him from school and college a character worth much fine gold, but was pleased to find his mess so kindly. He had plenty of money of his own; his training had set the public-school mask upon his face, and had taught him how many were the 'things no fellow can do.' By virtue of the same training he kept his pores open and his mouth shut.

The regular working of the Empire shifted his world to India, where he tasted utter loneliness in subaltern's quarters—one room and one bullock-trunk—and, with his mess, learned the new life from the beginning. But there were horses in the land—ponies at reasonable price; there was polo for such as could afford it; there were the disreputable remnants of a pack of hounds, and Cottar worried his way along without too much despair. It dawned on him that a regiment in India was nearer the chance of active service than he had conceived, and that a man might as well study his profession. A Major of the new school backed this idea with enthusiasm, and he and Cottar accumulated a library of military works, and read and argued and disputed far into the nights. But the Adjutant said the old thing: 'Get to know your men, young 'un, and they'll follow you anywhere. That's all you want—know your men.' Cottar thought he knew them fairly well at cricket and the regimental sports, but he never realised the true inwardness of them till he was sent off with a detachment of twenty to sit down in a mud fort near a rushing river which was spanned by a bridge of boats. When the floods came they went forth and hunted strayed pontoons along the banks. Otherwise there was nothing to do, and the men got drunk, gambled and quarrelled. They were a sickly crew, for a junior subaltern is by custom saddled with the worst men. Cottar endured their rioting as long as he could, and then sent down-country for a dozen pairs of boxing-gloves.

'I wouldn't blame you for fightin',' said he, 'if you only knew how to use your hands; but you don't. Take these things and I'll show you.' The men appreciated his efforts. Now, instead of blaspheming and swearing at a comrade, and threatening to shoot him, they could take him apart and soothe themselves to exhaustion. As one explained whom Cottar found with a shut eye and a diamond-shaped mouth spitting blood through an embrasure: 'We tried it with the gloves, sir, for twenty minutes, and *that* done us no good, sir. Then we took off the gloves and tried it that way for another twenty minutes, same as you showed us, sir, an' that done us a world o' good. 'Twasn't fightin', sir; there was a bet on.'

Cottar dared not laugh, but he invited his men to other sports, such as racing across country in shirt and trousers after a trail of torn paper, and to single-stick in the evenings, till the native population, who had a lust for sport in every form, wished to know whether the white men understood wrestling. They sent in an ambassador, who took the soldiers by the neck and threw them about the dust; and the entire command were all for this new game. They spent money on learning new falls and holds, which was better than buying other doubtful commodities; and the peasantry grinned five deep round the tournaments.

That detachment, who had gone up in bullock-carts, returned to headquarters at an average rate of thirty miles a day, fair heel-and-toe; no sick, no prisoners, and no court-martials pending. They scattered themselves among their friends, singing the praises of their Lieutenant and looking for causes of offence.

'How did you do it, young 'un?' the Adjutant asked.

'Oh, I sweated the beef off 'em, and then I sweated some muscle on to 'em. It was rather a lark.'

'If that's your way of lookin' at it, we can give you all the larks you want. Young Davies isn't feelin' quite fit, and he's next for detachment duty. Care to go for him?'

'Sure he wouldn't mind? I don't want to shove myself forward, you know.'

'You needn't bother on Davies's account. We'll give you the sweepin's of the corps, and you can see what you can make of 'em.'

'All right,' said Cottar. 'It's better fun than loafin' about cantonments.'

'Rummy thing,' said the Adjutant, after Cottar had returned to his wilderness with twenty other devils worse than the first. 'If Cottar only knew it, half the women in the station would give their eyes—confound 'em!—to have the young 'un in tow.'

'That accounts for Mrs. Elery sayin' I was workin' my nice new boy too hard,' said a Wing-Commander.

'Oh yes; and "Why doesn't he come to the band-stand in the evenings?" and "Can't I get him to make up a four at tennis with the Hammon girls?" ' the Adjutant snorted. 'Look at young Davies makin' an ass of himself over mutton-dressed-as-lamb old enough to be his mother!'

'No one can accuse young Cottar of runnin' after women, white *or* black,' the Major replied thoughtfully. 'But, then, that's the kind that generally goes the worst mucker in the end.'

'Not Cottar. I've only run across one of his muster before—a fellow called Ingles, in South Africa. He was just the same hard-trained, athletic-sports build of animal. Always kept himself in the pink of condition. Didn't do him much good, though. Shot at Wesselstroom the week before Majuba. Wonder how the young 'un will lick his detachment into shape.'

Cottar turned up six weeks later, on foot, with his pupils. He never told his experiences, but the men spoke enthusiastically, and fragments of it leaked back to the Colonel through sergeants, batmen, and the like.

There was great jealousy between the first and second detachments, but the men united in adoring Cottar, and their way of showing it was by sparing him all the trouble that men know how to make for an unloved officer. He sought popularity as little as he had sought it at school, and therefore it came to him. He favoured no one—not even when the company sloven pulled the company cricket-match out of the fire with an unexpected forty-three at the last moment. There was very little getting round him, for he seemed to know by instinct exactly when and where to head off a malingerer; but he did not forget that the difference between a dazed and sulky junior of the upper school and a bewildered, brow-beaten lump of a private fresh from the depôt was very small indeed. The sergeants, seeing these things, told him secrets generally hid from young officers. His words were quoted as barrack authority on bets in canteen and at tea; and the veriest shrew of the corps, bursting with charges against other women who had used the cooking-ranges out of turn, forbore to speak when Cottar, as the regulations ordained, asked of a morning if there were 'any complaints.'

'I'm full o' complaints,' said Mrs. Corporal Morrison, 'an' I'd kill O'Halloran's fat cow of a wife any day, but ye know how it is. 'E puts 'is head just inside the door, an' looks down 'is blessed nose so bashful, an' 'e whispers, "Any complaints?" Ye can't complain after that. *I* want to kiss him. Some day I think I will. Heigh-ho! She'll be a lucky woman that gets Young Innocence. See 'im now, girls. Do yer blame me?'

Cottar was cantering across to polo, and he looked a very satisfactory figure of a man as he gave easily to the first excited bucks of his pony, and slipped over a low mud wall to the practice-ground. There were more than Mrs. Corporal Morrison who felt as she did. But Cottar was busy for eleven hours of the day. He did not care to have his tennis spoiled by petticoats in the court; and after one long afternoon at a garden-party, he explained to his Major that this sort of thing was 'futile piffle,' and the Major laughed. Theirs was not a married mess, except for the Colonel's wife, and Cottar stood in awe of the good lady. She said 'my regiment,' and the world knows what that means. None the less, when they wanted her to give away the prizes after a shooting-match, and she refused because one of the prize-winners was married to a girl who had made a jest of her behind her broad back, the mess ordered Cottar to 'tackle her,' in his best calling-kit. This he did, simply and laboriously, and she gave way altogether.

'She only wanted to know the facts of the case,' he explained. 'I just told her, and she saw at once.'

'Ye-es,' said the Adjutant. 'I expect that's what she did. 'Comin' to the Fusiliers' dance to-night, Galahad?'

'No, thanks. I've got a fight on with the Major.' The virtuous apprentice sat up till midnight in the Major's quarters, with a stop-watch and a pair of compasses, shifting little painted lead blocks about a four-inch map.

Then he turned in and slept the sleep of innocence, which is full of healthy dreams. One peculiarity of his dreams he noticed at the beginning of his second hot weather. Two or three times a month they duplicated or ran in series. He would find himself sliding into dreamland by the same road—a road that ran along a beach near a pile of brushwood. To the right lay the sea, sometimes at full tide, sometimes withdrawn to the very horizon; but he knew it for the same sea. By that road he would travel over a swell of rising ground covered with short, withered grass, into valleys of wonder and unreason. Beyond the ridge, which was crowned with some sort of street-lamp, anything was possible; but up to the lamp it seemed to him that he knew the road as well as he knew the parade-ground. He learned to look forward to the place; for, once there, he was sure of a good night's rest, and Indian hot weather can be rather trying. First, shadowy under closing eyelids, would come the outline of the brushwood-pile; next the white sand of the beach road, almost overhanging the black, changeful sea; then the turn inland and uphill to the single light. When he was unrestful for any reason, he would tell himself how he was sure to get there—sure to get there—if he shut his eyes and surrendered to the drift of things. But one night after a foolishly hard hour's polo (the thermometer was 94° in his quarters at ten o'clock), sleep stood away from him altogether, though he did his best to find the well-known road, the point where true sleep began. At last he saw the brushwood-pile, and hurried along to the ridge, for behind him he felt was the wide-awake, sultry world. He reached the lamp in safety, tingling with drowsiness, when a policeman—a common country policeman—sprang up before him and touched him on the shoulder ere he could dive into the dim valley below. He was filled with terror,—the hopeless terror of dreams,—for the policeman said, in the awful, distinct voice of the dream-people, 'I am Policeman Day coming back from the City of Sleep. You come with me.' Georgie knew it was true—that just beyond him in the valley lay the lights of the City of Sleep, where he would have been sheltered, and that this Policeman Thing had full power and authority to head him back to miserable wakefulness. He found himself looking at the moonlight on the wall, dripping with fright; and he never overcame that horror, though he met the policeman several times that hot weather, and his coming was the forerunner of a bad night.

But other dreams—perfectly absurd ones—filled him with an incommunicable delight. All those that he remembered began by the brushwood-pile. For instance, he found a small clockwork steamer (he had noticed it many nights before) lying by the sea-road, and stepped into it, whereupon it moved with surpassing swiftness over an absolutely level sea. This was glorious, for he felt he was exploring great matters; and it stopped by a lily carved in stone, which, most naturally, floated on the water. Seeing the lily was labelled 'Hong-Kong,' Georgie said: 'Of course. This is precisely what I expected Hong-Kong would be like. How magnificent!' Thousands of miles farther on it halted at yet another stone lily, labelled 'Java'; and this again delighted him hugely, because he knew that now he was at the world's end. But the little boat ran on and on till it stopped in a deep fresh-water lock, the sides of which were carven marble, green with moss. Lily-pads lay on the water, and reeds arched above. Some one moved among the reeds—some one whom Georgie knew he had travelled to this world's end to reach. Therefore everything was entirely well with him. He was unspeakably happy, and vaulted over the ship's side to find this person. When his feet touched that still water, it changed, with the rustle of unrolling maps, to nothing less than a sixth quarter of the globe, beyond the most remote imaginings of man—a place where islands were coloured yellow and blue, their lettering strung across their faces. They gave on unknown seas, and Georgie's urgent desire was to return swiftly across this floating atlas to known bearings. He told himself repeatedly that it was no good to hurry; but still he hurried desperately, and the islands slipped and slid under his feet, the straits yawned and widened, till he found himself utterly lost in the world's fourth dimension, with no hope of return. Yet only a little distance away he could see the old world with the rivers and mountain-chains marked according to the Sandhurst rules of map-making. Then that person for whom he had come to the Lily Lock (that was its name) ran up across unexplored territories, and showed him a way. They fled hand in hand till they reached a road that spanned ravines, and ran along the edge of precipices, and was tunnelled through mountains. 'This goes to our brushwood-pile,' said his companion; and all his trouble was at an end. He took a pony, because he understood that this was the Thirty-Mile-Ride, and he must ride swiftly; and raced through the clattering tunnels and round the curves, always downhill, till he heard the sea to his left, and saw it raging under a full moon against sandy cliffs. It was heavy going, but he recognised the nature of the country, the dark purple downs inland, and the bents that whistled in the wind. The road was eaten away in places, and the sea lashed at him —black, foamless tongues of smooth and glossy rollers; but he was sure that there was less danger from the sea than from 'Them,' whoever 'They' were, inland to his right. He knew, too, that he would be safe if he could reach the down with the lamp on it. This came as he expected: he saw the one light a mile ahead along the beach, dismounted, turned to the right, walked quietly over to the brushwood-pile, found the little steamer had returned to the beach whence he had unmoored it, and— must have fallen asleep, for he could remember no more. 'I'm gettin' the hang of the geography of that place,' he said to himself, as he shaved next morning. 'I must have made some sort of circle. Let's see. The Thirty-Mile-Ride (now how the deuce did I know it was called the Thirty-Mile-Ride?) joins the sea-road beyond the first down where the lamp is. And that atlas-country lies at the back of the Thirty-Mile-Ride, somewhere out to the right beyond the hills and tunnels. Rummy thing, dreams. 'Wonder what makes mine fit into each other so?'

He continued on his solid way through the recurring duties of the seasons. The regiment was shifted to another station, and he enjoyed road-marching for two months, with a good deal of mixed shooting thrown in; and when they reached their new cantonments he became a member of the local Tent Club, and chased the mighty boar on horseback with a short stabbing-spear. There he met the *mahseer* of the Poonch, beside whom the tarpon is as a herring, and he who lands him can say that he is a fisherman. This was as new and as fascinating as the big game shooting that fell to his portion, when he had himself photographed for the mother's benefit, sitting on the flank of his first tiger.

Then the Adjutant was promoted, and Cottar rejoiced with him, for he admired the Adjutant greatly, and marvelled who might be big enough to fill his place; so that he nearly collapsed when the mantle fell on his own shoulders, and the Colonel said a few sweet things that made him blush. An Adjutant's position does not differ materially from that of head of the school, and Cottar stood in the same relation to the Colonel as he had to his old Head in England. Only, tempers wear out in hot weather, and things were said and done that tried him sorely, and he made glorious blunders, from which the regimental sergeant-major pulled him with a loyal soul and a shut mouth. Slovens and incompetents raged against him; the weak-minded strove to lure him from the ways of justice; the small-minded—yea, men who Cottar believed would never do 'things no fellow can do'—imputed motives mean and circuitous to actions that he had not spent a thought upon; and he tasted injustice, and it made him very sick. But his consolation came on parade, when he looked down the full companies, and reflected how few were in hospital or cells, and wondered when the time would come to try the machine of his love and labour. But they needed and expected the whole of a man's working day, and maybe three or four hours of the night. Curiously enough, he never dreamed about the regiment as he was popularly supposed to. The mind, set free from the day's doings, generally ceased working altogether, or, if it moved at all, carried him along the old beach road to the downs, the lamp-post, and, once in a while, to terrible Policeman Day. The second time that he returned to the world's lost continent (this was a dream that repeated itself again and again, with variations, on the same ground) he knew that if he only sat still the person from the Lily Lock would help him; and he was not disappointed. Sometimes he was trapped in mines of vast depth hollowed out of the heart of the world, where men in torment chanted echoing songs; and he heard this person coming along through the galleries, and everything was made safe and delightful. They met again in low-roofed Indian railway carriages that halted in a garden surrounded by gilt-and-green railings, where a mob of stony white people, all unfriendly, sat at breakfast-tables covered with roses, and separated Georgie from his companion, while underground voices sang deep-voiced songs. Georgie was filled with enormous despair till they two met again. They foregathered in the middle of an endless hot tropic night and crept into a huge house that stood, he knew, somewhere north of the railway station where the people ate among the roses. It was surrounded with gardens, all moist and dripping; and in one room, reached through leagues of whitewashed passages, a Sick Thing lay in bed. Now the least noise, Georgie knew, would unchain some waiting horror, and his companion knew it too; but when their eyes met across the bed, Georgie was disgusted to see that she was a child—a little girl in strapped shoes, with her black hair combed back from her forehead.

'What disgraceful folly!' he thought. 'Now she could do nothing whatever if Its head came off.'

Then the thing coughed, and the ceiling shattered down in plaster on the mosquito-netting, and 'They' rushed in from all quarters. He dragged the child through the stifling garden, voices chanting behind them, and they rode the Thirty-Mile-Ride under whip and spur along the sandy beach by the booming sea, till they came to the downs, the lamp-post, and the brushwood-pile, which was safety. Very often dreams would break up about them in this fashion, and they would be separated, to endure awful adventures alone. But the most amusing times were when he and she had a clear understanding that it was all make-believe, and walked through mile-wide roaring rivers without even taking off their shoes, or set light to populous cities to see how they would burn, and were rude as any children to the vague shadows met in their rambles. Later in the night they were sure to suffer for this, either at the hands of the Railway People eating among the roses, or in the tropic uplands at the far end of the Thirty-Mile-Ride. Together, this did not much affright them; but often Georgie would hear her shrill cry of 'Boy! Boy!' half a world away, and hurry to her rescue before 'They' maltreated her.

He and she explored the dark purple downs as far inland from the brushwood-pile as they dared, but that was always a dangerous matter. The interior was filled with 'Them,' and 'They' went about singing in the hollows, and Georgie and she felt safer on or near the seaboard. So thoroughly had he come to know the place of his dreams that even waking he accepted it as a real country, and made a rough sketch of it. He kept his own counsel, of course; but the permanence of the land puzzled him. His ordinary dreams were as formless and as fleeting as any healthy dreams could be, but once at the brushwood-pile he moved within known limits and could see where he was going. There were months at a time when nothing notable crossed his sleep. Then the dreams would come in a batch of five or six, and next morning the map that he kept in his writing-case would be written up to date, for Georgie was a most methodical person. There was, indeed, a danger—his seniors said so—of his developing into a regular 'Auntie Fuss' of an Adjutant, and when an officer once takes to old-maidism there is more hope for the virgin of seventy than for him.

But fate sent the change that was needed, in the shape of a little winter campaign on the border, which, after the manner of little campaigns, flashed out into a very ugly war; and Cottar's regiment was chosen among the first.

'Now,' said a Major, 'this'll shake the cobwebs out of us all—especially you, Galahad; and we can see what your hen-with-one-chick attitude has done for the regiment.'

Cottar nearly wept with joy as the campaign went forward. They were fit—physically fit beyond the other troops; they were good children in camp, wet or dry, fed or unfed; and they followed their officers with the quick suppleness and trained obedience of a first-class football fifteen. They were cut off from their apology for a base, and cheerfully cut their way back to it again; they crowned and cleaned out hills full of the enemy with the precision of well-broken dogs of chase; and in the hour of retreat, when, hampered with the sick and wounded of the column, they were persecuted down eleven miles of waterless valley, they, serving as rearguard, covered themselves with a great glory in the eyes of fellow-professionals. Any regiment can advance, but few know how to retreat with a sting in the tail. Then they turned to and made roads, most often under fire, and dismantled some inconvenient mud redoubts. They were the last corps to be withdrawn when the rubbish of the campaign was all swept up; and after a month in standing camp, which tries morals severely, they departed to their own place singing—

> 'E's goin' to do without 'em—
>   Don't want 'em any more;
> 'E's goin' to do without 'em,
>   As 'e's often done before,
> 'E's goin' to be a martyr
>   On a 'ighly novel plan,
> An' all the boys and girls will say,
>   'Ow! what a nice young man—man—man!
>   Ow! what a nice young man!'

There came out a *Gazette*, in which Cottar found that he had been behaving with 'courage and coolness and discretion' in all his capacities; that he had assisted the wounded under fire, and blown in a gate, also under fire. Net result, his captaincy and a brevet majority, coupled with the Distinguished Service Order.

As to his wounded, he explained that they were both heavy men, whom he could lift more easily than any one else. 'Otherwise, of course, I should have sent out one of my chaps; and, of course, about that gate business, we were safe the minute we were well under the walls.' But this did not prevent his men from cheering him furiously whenever they saw him, or the mess from giving him a dinner on the eve of his departure to England. (A year's leave was among the things he had 'snaffled out of the campaign,' to use his own words.) The doctor, who had taken quite as much as was good for him, quoted poetry about 'a good blade carving the casques of men,' and so on, and everybody told Cottar that he was an excellent person; but when he rose to make his maiden speech they shouted so that he was understood to say, 'It isn't any use tryin' to speak with you chaps rottin' me like this. Let's have some pool.'

It is not unpleasant to spend eight-and-twenty days in an easy-going steamer on warm waters, in the company of a woman who lets you see that you are head and shoulders superior to the rest of the world, even though that woman may be, and most often is, ten counted years your senior. P. & O. boats are not lighted with the disgustful particularity of Atlantic liners. There is more phosphorescence at the bows, and greater silence and darkness by the hand-steering gear aft.

Awful things might have happened to Georgie, but for the little fact that he had never studied the first principles of the game he was expected to play. So when Mrs. Zuleika, at Aden, told him how motherly an interest she felt in his welfare, medals, brevet, and all, Georgie took her at the foot of the letter, and promptly talked of his own mother, three hundred miles nearer each day, of his home, and so forth, all the way up the Red Sea. It was much easier than he had supposed to converse with a woman for an hour at a time. Then Mrs. Zuleika, turning from parental affection, spoke of love in the abstract as a thing not unworthy of study, and in discreet twilights after dinner demanded confidences. Georgie would have been delighted to supply them, but he had none, and did not know it was his duty to manufacture them. Mrs. Zuleika expressed surprise and unbelief, and asked those questions which deep asks of deep. She learned all that was necessary to conviction, and, being very much a woman, resumed (Georgie never knew that she had abandoned) the motherly attitude.

'Do you know,' she said, somewhere in the Mediterranean, 'I think you're the very dearest boy I have ever met in my life, and I'd like you to remember me a little. You will when you are older, but I want you to remember me now. You'll make some girl very happy.'

'Oh! 'Hope so,' said Georgie, gravely; 'but there's heaps of time for marryin', an' all that sort of thing, ain't there?'

'That depends. Here are your bean-bags for the Ladies' Competition. I think I'm growing too old to care for these *tamashas*.'

They were getting up sports, and Georgie was on the committee. He never noticed how perfectly the bags were sewn, but another woman did, and smiled—once. He liked Mrs. Zuleika greatly. She was a bit old, of course, but uncommonly nice. There was no nonsense about her.

A few nights after they passed Gibraltar his dream returned to him.

She who waited by the brushwood-pile was no longer a little girl, but a woman with black hair that grew into a 'widow's peak,' combed back from her forehead. He knew her for the child in black, the companion of the last six years, and, as it had been in the time of the meetings on the Lost Continent, he was filled with delight unspeakable. 'They,' for some dreamland reason, were friendly or had gone away that night, and the two flitted together over all their country, from the brushwood-pile up the Thirty-Mile-Ride, till they saw the House of the Sick Thing, a pin-point in the distance to the left; stamped through the Railway Waiting-room where the roses lay on the spread breakfast-tables; and returned, by the ford and the city they had once burned for sport, to the great swells of the downs under the lamp-post. Wherever they moved a strong singing followed them underground, but this night there was no panic. All the land was empty except for themselves, and at the last (they were sitting by the lamp-post hand in hand) she turned and kissed him. He woke with a start, staring at the waving curtain of the cabin door; he could almost have sworn that the kiss was real.

Next morning the ship was rolling in a Biscay sea, and people were not happy; but as Georgie came to breakfast, shaven, tubbed, and smelling of soap, several turned to look at him because of the light in his eyes and the splendour of his countenance.

'Well, you look beastly fit,' snapped a neighbour. 'Any one left you a legacy in the middle of the Bay?'

Georgie reached for the curry, with a seraphic grin. 'I suppose it's the gettin' so near home, and all that. I do feel rather festive this mornin'. 'Rolls a bit, doesn't she?'

Mrs. Zuleika stayed in her cabin till the end of the voyage, when she left without bidding him farewell, and wept passionately on the dock-head for pure joy of meeting her children, who, she had often said, were so like their father.

Georgie headed for his own county, wild with delight of first long furlough after the lean seasons. Nothing was changed in that orderly life, from the coachman who met him at the station to the white peacock that stormed at the carriage from the stone wall above the shaven lawns. The house took toll of him with due regard to precedence—first the mother; then the father; then the housekeeper, who wept and praised God; then the butler; and so on down to the under-keeper, who had been dog-boy in Georgie's youth, and called him 'Master Georgie,' and was reproved by the groom who had taught Georgie to ride.

'Not a thing changed,' he sighed contentedly, when the three of them sat down to dinner in the late sunlight, while the rabbits crept out upon the lawn below the cedars, and the big trout in the ponds by the home paddock rose for their evening meal.

'*Our* changes are all over, dear,' cooed the mother; 'and now I am getting used to your size and your tan (you're very brown, Georgie), I see you haven't changed in the least. You're exactly like the pater.'

The father beamed on this man after his own heart,—'Youngest Major in the army, and should have had the V.C., sir,'—and the butler listened with his professional mask off when Master Georgie spoke of war as it is waged to-day, and his father cross-questioned.

They went out on the terrace to smoke among the roses, and the shadow of the old house lay long across the wonderful English foliage, which is the only living green in the world.

'Perfect! By Jove, it's perfect!' Georgie was looking at the round-bosomed woods beyond the home paddock, where the white pheasant-boxes were ranged; and the golden air was full of a hundred sacred scents and sounds. Georgie felt his father's arm tighten in his.

'It's not half bad—but *hodie mihi, cras tibi,* isn't it? I suppose you'll be turning up some fine day with a girl under your arm, if you haven't one now, eh?'

'You can make your mind easy, sir. I haven't one.'

'Not in all these years?' said the mother.

'I hadn't time, mummy. They keep a man pretty busy, these days, in the service, and most of our mess are unmarried, too.'

'But you must have met hundreds in society—at balls, and so on?'

'I'm like the Tenth, mummy: I don't dance.'

'Don't dance! What have you been doing with yourself, then—backing other men's bills?' said the father.

'Oh yes; I've done a little of that too; but you see, as things are now, a man has all his work cut out for him to keep abreast of his profession, and my days were always too full to let me lark about half the night.'

'Hmm!'—suspiciously.

'It's never too late to learn. We ought to give some kind of house-warming for the people about, now you've come back. Unless you want to go straight up to town, dear?'

'No. I don't want anything better than this. Let's sit still and enjoy ourselves. I suppose there will be something for me to ride if I look for it?'

'Seeing I've been kept down to the old brown pair for the last six weeks because all the others were being got ready for Master Georgie,

I should say there might be,' the father chuckled. 'They're reminding me in a hundred ways that I must take the second place now.'

'Brutes!'

'The pater doesn't mean it, dear; but every one has been trying to make your home-coming a success; and you *do* like it, don't you?'

'Perfect! Perfect! There's no place like England—when you've done your work.'

'That's the proper way to look at it, my son.'

And so up and down the flagged walk till their shadows grew long in the moonlight, and the mother went indoors and played such songs as a small boy once clamoured for, and the squat silver candlesticks were brought in, and Georgie climbed to the two rooms in the west wing that had been his nursery and his play-room in the beginning. Then who should come to tuck him up for the night but the mother? And she sat down on the bed, and they talked for a long hour, as mother and son should, if there is to be any future for our empire. With a simple woman's deep guile she asked questions and suggested answers that should have waked some sign in the face on the pillow, but there was neither quiver of eyelid nor quickening of breath, neither evasion nor delay in reply. So she blessed him and kissed him on the mouth, which is not always a mother's property, and said something to her husband later, at which he laughed profane and incredulous laughs.

All the establishment waited on Georgie next morning, from the tallest six-year-old, 'with a mouth like a kid glove, Master Georgie,' to the under-keeper strolling carelessly along the horizon, Georgie's pet rod in his hand, and 'There's a four-pounder risin' below the lasher. You don't 'ave 'em in Injia, Mast—Major Georgie.' It was all beautiful beyond telling, even though the mother insisted on taking him out in the landau (the leather had the hot Sunday smell of his youth), and showing him off to her friends at all the houses for six miles round; and the pater bore him up to town and a lunch at the club, where he introduced him, quite carelessly, to not less than thirty ancient warriors whose sons were not the youngest Majors in the army, and had not the D.S.O. After that it was Georgie's turn; and remembering his friends, he filled up the house with that kind of officer who lived in cheap lodgings at Southsea or Montpelier Square, Brompton—good men all, but not well off. The mother perceived that they needed girls to play with; and as there was no scarcity of girls, the house hummed like a dovecote in spring. They tore up the place for amateur theatricals; they disappeared in the gardens when they ought to have been rehearsing; they swept off every available horse and vehicle, especially the governess-cart and the fat pony; they fell into the trout-pond; they picnicked and they tennised; and they sat on gates in the twilight, two by two, and Georgie found that he was not in the least necessary to their entertainment.

'My word!' said he, when he saw the last of their dear backs. 'They told me they'd enjoyed 'emselves, but they haven't done half the things they said they would.'

'I know they've enjoyed themselves—immensely,' said the mother. 'You're a public benefactor, dear.'

'Now we can be quiet again, can't we?'

'Oh, quite. I've a very dear friend of mine that I want you to know. She couldn't come with the house so full, because she's an invalid, and she was away when you first came. She's a Mrs. Lacy.'

'Lacy! I don't remember the name about here.'

'No; they came after you went to India—from Oxford. Her husband died there, and she lost some money, I believe. They bought The Firs on the Bassett Road. She's a very sweet woman, and we're very fond of them both.'

'She's a widow, didn't you say?'

'She has a daughter. Surely I said so, dear?'

'Does she fall into trout-ponds, and gas and giggle, and "Oh, Major Cottah!" and all that sort of thing?'

'No, indeed. She's a very quiet girl, and very musical. She always came over here with her music-books—composing, you know; and she generally works all day, so you won't——'

' 'Talking about Miriam?' said the pater, coming up. The mother edged toward him within elbow reach. There was no finesse about Georgie's father. 'Oh, Miriam's a dear girl. Plays beautifully. Rides beautifully, too. She's a regular pet of the household. 'Used to call me——' The elbow went home, and ignorant, but obedient always, the pater shut himself off.

'What used she to call you, sir?'

'All sorts of pet names. I'm very fond of Miriam.'

'Sounds Jewish—Miriam.'

'Jew! You'll be calling yourself a Jew next. She's one of the Herefordshire Lacys. When her aunt dies——' Again the elbow.

'Oh, you won't see anything of her, Georgie. She's busy with her music or her mother all day. Besides, you're going up to town to-morrow, aren't you? I thought you said something about an Institute meeting?' The mother spoke.

'Going up to town *now?* What nonsense!' Once more the pater was silenced.

'I had some idea of it, but I'm not quite sure,' said the son of the house. Why did the mother try to get him away because a musical girl and her invalid parent were expected? He did not approve of unknown females calling his father pet names. He would observe these pushing persons who had been only seven years in the county.

All of which the delighted mother read in his countenance, herself keeping an air of sweet disinterestedness.

'They'll be here this evening for dinner. I'm sending the carriage over for them, and they won't stay more than a week.'

'Perhaps I shall go up to town. I don't quite know yet.' Georgie moved away irresolutely. There was a lecture at the United Services Institute on the supply of ammunition in the field, and the one man whose theories most irritated Major Cottar would deliver it. A heated discussion was sure to follow, and perhaps he might find himself moved to speak. He took his rod that afternoon and went down to thrash it out among the trout.

'Good sport, dear!' said the mother, from the terrace.

''Fraid it won't be, mummy. All those men from town, and the girls particularly, have put every trout off his feed for weeks. There isn't one of 'em that cares for fishin'—really. Fancy stampin' and shoutin' on the bank, and tellin' every fish for half a mile exactly what you're goin' to do, and then chuckin' a brute of a fly at him! By Jove, it would scare *me* if I was a trout!'

But things were not as bad as he had expected. The black gnat was on the water, and the water was strictly preserved. A three-quarter-pounder at the second cast set him for the campaign, and he worked down-stream, crouching behind the reed and meadow-sweet; creeping between a hornbeam hedge and a foot-wide strip of bank, where he could see the trout, but where they could not distinguish him from the background; lying on his stomach to switch the blue-upright sidewise through the checkered shadows of a gravelly ripple under overarching trees. But he had known every inch of the water since he was four feet high. The aged and astute between sunk roots, with the large and fat that lay in the frothy scum below some strong rush of water, sucking lazily as carp, came to trouble in their turn, at the hand that imitated so delicately the flicker and wimple of an egg-dropping fly. Consequently, Georgie found himself five miles from home when he ought to have been dressing for dinner. The housekeeper had taken good care that her boy should not go empty; and before he changed to the white moth he sat down to excellent claret with sandwiches of potted egg and things that adoring women make and men never notice. Then back, to surprise the otter grubbing for fresh-water mussels, the rabbits on the edge of the beechwoods foraging in the clover, and the policeman-like white owl stooping to the little field-mice, till the moon was strong, and he took his rod apart, and went home through well-remembered gaps in the hedges. He fetched a compass round the house, for, though he might have broken every law of the establishment every hour, the law of his boyhood was unbreakable: after fishing you went in by the south garden back-door, cleaned up in the outer scullery, and did not present yourself to your elders and your betters till you had washed and changed.

'Half-past ten, by Jove! Well, we'll make the sport an excuse. They wouldn't want to see me the first evening, at any rate. Gone to bed, probably.' He skirted by the open French windows of the drawing-room. 'No, they haven't. They look very comfy in there.'

He could see his father in his own particular chair, the mother in hers, and the back of a girl at the piano by the big potpourri-jar. The garden showed half divine in the moonlight, and he turned down through the roses to finish his pipe.

A prelude ended, and there floated out a voice of the kind that in his childhood he used to call 'creamy'—a full, true contralto; and this is the song that he heard, every syllable of it:

Over the edge of the purple down,
  Where the single lamplight gleams,
Know ye the road to the Merciful Town
  That is hard by the Sea of Dreams—
Where the poor may lay their wrongs away,
  And the sick may forget to weep?
But we—pity us! Oh, pity us!—
  We wakeful; ah, pity us!—
We must go back with Policeman Day—
  Back from the City of Sleep!

Weary they turn from the scroll and crown,
  Fetter and prayer and plough—
They that go up to the Merciful Town,
  For her gates are closing now.
It is their right in the Baths of Night
  Body and soul to steep;
But we—pity us! ah, pity us!—
  We wakeful; oh, pity us!—
We must go back with Policeman Day—
  Back from the City of Sleep!

Over the edge of the purple down,
  Ere the tender dreams begin,
Look—we may look—at the Merciful Town,
  But we may not enter in!
Outcasts all, from her guarded wall
  Back to our watch we creep:
We—pity us! ah, pity us!—
  We wakeful; oh, pity us!—
We that go back with Policeman Day—
  Back from the City of Sleep!

At the last echo he was aware that his mouth was dry and unknown pulses were beating in the roof of it. The housekeeper, who would have it that he must have fallen in and caught a chill, was waiting to advise him on the stairs, and, since he neither saw nor answered her, carried a wild tale abroad that brought his mother knocking at the door.

'Anything happened, dear? Harper said she thought you weren't——'

'No; it's nothing. I'm all right, mummy. *Please* don't bother.'

He did not recognise his own voice, but that was a small matter beside what he was considering. Obviously, most obviously, the whole coincidence was crazy lunacy. He proved it to the satisfaction of Major George Cottar, who was going up to town to-morrow to hear a lecture on the supply of ammunition in the field; and having so proved it, the soul and brain and heart and body of Georgie cried joyously: 'That's the Lily Lock girl—the Lost Continent girl—the Thirty-Mile-Ride girl—the Brushwood girl! *I* know her!'

He waked, stiff and cramped in his chair, to reconsider the situation by sunlight, when it did not appear normal. But a man must eat, and he went to breakfast, his heart between his teeth, holding himself severely in hand.

'Late, as usual,' said the mother. 'My boy, Miriam.'

A tall girl in black raised her eyes to his, and Georgie's life training deserted him—just as soon as he realised that she did not know. He stared coolly and critically. There was the abundant black hair, growing in a widow's peak, turned back from the forehead, with that peculiar ripple over the right ear; there were the grey eyes set a little close together; the short upper lip, resolute chin, and the known poise of the head. There was also the small, well-cut mouth that had kissed him.

'Georgie—*dear!*' said the mother, amazedly, for Miriam was flushing under the stare.

'I—I beg your pardon!' he gulped. 'I don't know whether the mother has told you, but I'm rather an idiot at times, specially before I've had my breakfast. It's—it's a family failing.' He turned to explore among the hot-water dishes on the sideboard, rejoicing that she did not know—she did not know.

His conversation for the rest of the meal was mildly insane, though the mother thought she had never seen her boy look half so handsome. How could any girl, least of all one of Miriam's discernment, forbear to fall down and worship? But deeply Miriam was displeased. She had never been stared at in that fashion before, and promptly retired into her shell when Georgie announced that he had changed his mind about going to town, and would stay to play with Miss Lacy if she had nothing better to do.

'Oh, but don't let me throw you out. I'm at work. I've things to do all the morning.'

'What possessed Georgie to behave so oddly?' the mother sighed to herself. 'Miriam's a bundle of feelings—like her mother.'

'You compose, don't you? Must be a fine thing to be able to do that. ('Pig—oh, pig!' thought Miriam.) I think I heard you singin' when I came in last night after fishin'. All about a Sea of Dreams, wasn't it? (Miriam shuddered to the core of the soul that afflicted her.) Awfully pretty song. How d'you think of such things?'

'You only composed the music, dear, didn't you?'

'The words too, mummy. I'm sure of it,' said Georgie, with a sparkling eye. No; she did not know.

'Yeth; I wrote the words too.' Miriam spoke slowly, for she knew she lisped when she was nervous.

'Now how *could* you tell, Georgie?' said the mother, as delighted as though the youngest Major in the army were ten years old, showing off before company.

'I was sure of it, somehow. Oh, there are heaps of things about me, mummy, that you don't understand. Looks as if it were goin' to be a hot day—for England. Would you care for a ride this afternoon, Miss Lacy? We can start out after tea, if you'd like it.'

Miriam could not in decency refuse, but any woman might see she was not filled with delight.

'That will be very nice, if you take the Bassett Road. It will save me sending Martin down to the village,' said the mother, filling in gaps.

Like all good managers, the mother had her one weakness—a mania for little strategies that should economise horses and vehicles. Her men-folk complained that she turned them into common carriers, and there was a legend in the family that she had once said to the pater on the morning of a meet: 'If you *should* kill near Bassett, dear, and if it isn't too late, would you mind just popping over and matching me this?'

'I knew that was coming. You'd never miss a chance, mother. If it's fish or a trunk, I won't.' Georgie laughed.

'It's only a duck. They can do it up very neatly at Mallett's,' said the mother simply. 'You won't mind, will you? We'll have a scratch dinner at nine, because it's so hot.'

The long summer day dragged itself out for centuries; but at last there was tea on the lawn, and Miriam appeared.

She was in the saddle before he could offer to help, with the clean spring of the child who mounted the pony for the Thirty-Mile-Ride. The day held mercilessly, though Georgie got down thrice to look for imaginary stones in Rufus's foot. One cannot say even simple things in broad light, and this that Georgie meditated was not simple. So he spoke seldom, and Miriam was divided between relief and scorn. It annoyed her that the great hulking thing should know she had written the words of the over-night song; for though a maiden may sing her most secret fancies aloud, she does not care to have them trampled over by the male Philistine. They rode into the little red-brick street of Bassett, and Georgie made untold fuss over the disposition of that duck. It must go in just such a package, and be fastened to the saddle in just such a manner, though eight o'clock had passed and they were miles from dinner.

'We must be quick!' said Miriam, bored and angry.

'There's no great hurry; but we can cut over Dowhead Down, and let 'em out on the grass. That will save us half an hour.'

The horses capered on the short, sweet-smelling turf, and the delaying shadows gathered in the valley as they cantered over the great dun down that overhangs Bassett and the Western coaching-road. Insensibly the pace quickened without thought of molehills; Rufus, gentleman that he was, waiting on Miriam's Dandy till they should have cleared the rise. Then down the two-mile slope they raced together, the wind whistling in their ears, to the steady throb of eight hoofs and the light click-click of the shifting bits.

'Oh, that was glorious!' Miriam cried, reining in. 'Dandy and I are old friends, but I don't think we've ever gone better together.'

'No; but you've gone quicker, once or twice.'

'Really? When?'

Georgie moistened his lips. 'Don't you remember the Thirty-Mile-Ride—with me—when "They" were after us—on the beach road, with the sea to the left—going toward the Lamp-post on the Downs?'

The girl gasped. 'What—what do you mean?' she said hysterically.

'The Thirty-Mile-Ride, and—and all the rest of it.'

'You mean——? I didn't sing anything about the Thirty-Mile-Ride. I know I didn't. I have never told a living soul.'

'You told about Policeman Day, and the lamp at the top of the downs, and the City of Sleep. It all joins on, you know—it's the same country—and it was easy enough to see where you had been.'

'Good God!—It joins on—of course it does; but—I have been—you have been—— Oh, let's walk, please, or I shall fall off!'

Georgie ranged alongside, and laid a hand that shook below her bridle-hand, pulling Dandy into a walk. Miriam was sobbing as he had seen a man sob under the touch of the bullet.

'It's all right—it's all right,' he whispered feebly. 'Only—only it's true, you know.'

'True! Am I mad?'

'Not unless I'm mad as well. *Do* try to think a minute quietly. How could any one conceivably know anything about the Thirty-Mile-Ride having anything to do with you, unless he had been there?'

'But where? But *where?* Tell me!'

'There—wherever it may be—in our country, I suppose. Do you remember the first time you rode it—the Thirty-Mile-Ride, I mean? You must.'

'It was all dreams—all dreams!'

'Yes, but tell, please; because I know.'

'Let me think. I—we were on no account to make any noise—on no account to make any noise.' She was staring between Dandy's ears with eyes that did not see, and suffocating heart.

'Because "It" was dying in the big house?' Georgie went on, reining in again.

'There was a garden with green-and-gilt railings—all hot. Do *you* remember?'

'I ought to. I was sitting on the other side of the bed before "It" coughed and "They" came in.'

'You!'—the deep voice was unnaturally full and strong and the girl's wide-opened eyes burned in the dusk as she stared him through and through. 'Then you're the Boy—my Brushwood Boy, and I've known you all my life!'

She fell forward on Dandy's neck. Georgie forced himself out of the weakness that was overmastering his limbs, and slid an arm round her waist. The head dropped on his shoulder, and he found himself with parched lips saying things that up till then he believed existed only in printed works of fiction. Mercifully the horses were quiet. She made no attempt to draw herself away when she recovered, but lay still, whispering, 'Of course you're the Boy, and I didn't know—I didn't know.'

'I knew last night; and when I saw you at breakfast——'

'Oh, *that* was why! I wondered at the time. You would, of course.'

'I couldn't speak before this. Keep your head where it is, dear. It's all right now—all right now, isn't it?'

'But how was it *I* didn't know—after all these years and years? I remember—oh, what lots of things I remember!'

'Tell me some. I'll look after the horses.'

'I remember waiting for you when the steamer came in. Do you?'

'At the Lily Lock, beyond Hong-Kong and Java?'

'Do *you* call it that, too?'

'You told me it was when I was lost in the continent. That was you that showed me the way through the mountains?'

'When the islands slid? It must have been, because you're the only one I remember. All the others were "Them." '

'Awful brutes they were, too.'

'Yes, I remember showing you the Thirty-Mile-Ride the first time. You ride just as you used to—then. You *are* you!'

'That's odd. I thought that of you this afternoon. Isn't it wonderful?'

'What does it all mean? Why should you and I of the millions of people in the world have this—this thing between us? What does it mean? I'm frightened.'

'This!' said Georgie. The horses quickened their pace. They thought they had heard an order. 'Perhaps when we die we may find out more, but it means this now.'

There was no answer. What could she say? As the world went, they had known each other rather less than eight and a half hours, but the matter was one that did not concern the world. There was a very long silence, while the breath in their nostrils drew cold and sharp as it might have been fumes of ether.

'That's the second,' Georgie whispered. 'You remember, don't you?'

'It's not!'—furiously. 'It's not!'

'On the downs the other night—months ago. You were just as you are now, and we went over the country for miles and miles.'

'It was all empty, too. "They" had gone away. Nobody frightened us. I wonder why, Boy?'

'Oh, if you remember *that*, you must remember the rest. Confess!'

'I remember lots of things, but I *know* I didn't. I never have—till just now.'

'You *did,* dear.'

'I know I didn't, because—oh, it's no use keeping anything back!—because I truthfully meant to.'

'And truthfully did.'

'No; meant to; but some one else came by.'

'There wasn't any one else. There never has been.'

'There was—there always is. It was another woman—out there on the sea. I saw her. It was the 26th of May. I've got it written down somewhere.'

'Oh, *you've* kept a record of your dreams, too? That's odd about the other woman, because I happened to be on the sea just then.'

'I was right. How do I know what you've done—when you were awake? And I thought it was only *you!*'

'You never were more wrong in your life. What a little temper you've got! Listen to me a minute, dear.' And Georgie, though he knew it not, committed black perjury. 'It—it isn't the kind of thing one says to any one, because they'd laugh; but on my word and honour, darling, I've never been kissed by a living soul outside my own people in all my life. Don't laugh, dear. I wouldn't tell any one but you, but it's the solemn truth.'

'I knew! You are you. Oh, I *knew* you'd come some day; but I didn't know you were you in the least till you spoke.'

'Then give me another.'

'And you never cared or looked anywhere? Why, all the round world must have loved you from the very minute they saw you, Boy.'

'They kept it to themselves if they did. No; I never cared.'

'And we shall be late for dinner—horribly late. Oh, how can I look at you in the light before your mother—and mine!'

'We'll play you're Miss Lacy till the proper time comes. What's the shortest limit for people to get engaged? S'pose we have got to go through all the fuss of an engagement, haven't we?'

'Oh, I don't want to talk about that. It's so commonplace. I've thought of something that you don't know. I'm sure of it. What's my name?'

'Miri—no, it isn't, by Jove! Wait half a second, and it'll come back to me. You aren't—you can't? Why, *those* old tales—before I went to school! I've never thought of 'em from that day to this. Are you the original, only Annie*an*louise?'

'It was what you always called me ever since the beginning. Oh! We've turned into the avenue, and we must be an hour late.'

'What does it matter? The chain goes as far back as those days? It must, of course—of course it must. I've got to ride round with this pestilent old bird—confound him!'

' "Ha! ha!" said the duck, laughing. Do you remember *that?*'

'Yes, I do—flower-pots on my feet, and all. We've been together all this while; and I've got to say good-bye to you till dinner. *Sure* I'll see you at dinner-time? *Sure* you won't sneak up to your room, darling, and leave me all the evening? Good-bye, dear—good-bye.'

'Good-bye, Boy, good-bye. Mind the arch! Don't let Rufus bolt into his stable. Good-bye. Yes, I'll come down to dinner; but—what shall I do when I see you in the light!'

THE MAN WHO WOULD BE KING

Brother to a Prince and fellow to a beggar if he be found worthy.

The law, as quoted, lays down a fair conduct of life, and one not easy to follow. I have been fellow to a beggar again and again under circumstances which prevented either of us finding out whether the other was worthy. I have still to be brother to a Prince, though I once came near to kinship with what might have been a veritable King, and was promised the reversion of a Kingdom—army, law-courts, revenue, and policy all complete. But, to-day, I greatly fear that my King is dead, and if I want a crown I must go hunt it for myself.

The beginning of everything was in a railway train upon the road to Mhow from Ajmir. There had been a Deficit in the Budget, which necessitated travelling, not Second-class, which is only half as dear as First-class, but by Intermediate, which is very awful indeed. There are no cushions in the Intermediate class, and the population are either Intermediate, which is Eurasian, or Native, which for a long night journey is nasty, or Loafer, which is amusing though intoxicated. Intermediates do not buy from refreshment-rooms. They carry their food in bundles and pots, and buy sweets from the native sweetmeat-sellers, and drink the roadside water. That is why in the hot weather Intermediates are taken out of the carriages dead, and in all weathers are most properly looked down upon.

My particular Intermediate happened to be empty till I reached Nasirabad, when a big black-browed gentleman in shirt-sleeves entered, and, following the custom of Intermediates, passed the time of day. He was a wanderer and a vagabond like myself, but with an educated taste for whisky. He told tales of things he had seen and done, of out-of-the-way corners of the Empire into which he had penetrated, and of adventures in which he risked his life for a few days' food.

'If India was filled with men like you and me, not knowing more than the crows where they'd get their next day's rations, it isn't seventy millions of revenue the land would be paying—it's seven hundred millions,' said he; and as I looked at his mouth and chin I was disposed to agree with him.

We talked politics—the politics of Loaferdom, that sees things from the underside where the lath and plaster is not smoothed off—and we talked postal arrangements because my friend wanted to send a telegram back from the next station to Ajmir, the turning-off place from the Bombay to the Mhow line as you travel westward. My friend had no money beyond eight annas, which he wanted for dinner, and I had no money at all, owing to the hitch in the Budget before mentioned. Further, I was going into a wilderness where, though I should resume touch wth the Treasury, there were no telegraph offices. I was, therefore, unable to help him in any way.

'We might threaten a Station-master, and make him send a wire on tick,' said my friend, 'but that'd mean inquiries for you and for me, and *I*'ve got my hands full these days. Did you say you are travelling back along this line within any days?'

'Within ten,' I said.

'Can't you make it eight?' said he. 'Mine is rather urgent business.'

'I can send your telegram within ten days if that will serve you,' I said.

'I couldn't trust the wire to fetch him, now I think of it. It's this way. He leaves Delhi on the 23rd for Bombay. That means he'll be running through Ajmir about the night of the 23rd.'

'But I'm going into the Indian Desert,' I explained.

'Well *and* good,' said he. 'You'll be changing at Marwar Junction to get into Jodhpore territory—you must do that—and he'll be coming through Marwar Junction in the early morning of the 24th by the Bombay Mail. Can you be at Marwar Junction on that time? 'Twon't be inconveniencing you because I know that there's precious few pickings to be got out of these Central India States—even though you pretend to be correspondent of the *Backwoodsman*.'

'Have you ever tried that trick?' I asked.

'Again and again, but the Residents find you out, and then you get escorted to the border before you've time to get your knife into them.

But about my friend here. I *must* give him a word o' mouth to tell him what's come to me or else he won't know where to go. I would take it more than kind of you if you was to come out of Central India in time to catch him at Marwar Junction, and say to him: "He has gone South for the week." He'll know what that means. He's a big man with a red beard, and a great swell he is. You'll find him sleeping like a gentleman with all his luggage round him in a second-class compartment. But don't you be afraid. Slip down the window, and say: "He has gone South for the week," and he'll tumble. It's only cutting your time of stay in those parts by two days. I ask you as a stranger—going to the West,' he said with emphasis.

'Where have *you* come from?' said I.

'From the East,' said he, 'and I am hoping that you will give him the message on the Square—for the sake of my Mother as well as your own.'

Englishmen are not usually softened by appeals to the memory of their mothers, but for certain reasons, which will be fully apparent, I saw fit to agree.

'It's more than a little matter,' said he, 'and that's why I asked you to do it—and now I know that I can depend on you doing it. A second-class carriage at Marwar Junction, and a red-haired man asleep in it. You'll be sure to remember. I get out at the next station, and I must hold on there till he comes or sends me what I want.'

'I'll give the message if I catch him,' I said, 'and for the sake of your Mother as well as mine I'll give you a word of advice. Don't try to run the Central India States just now as the correspondent of the *Backwoodsman*. There's a real one knocking about there, and it might lead to trouble.'

'Thank you,' said he simply, 'and when will the swine be gone? I can't starve because he's ruining my work. I wanted to get hold of the Degumber Rajah down here about his father's widow, and give him a jump.'

'What did he do to his father's widow, then?'

'Filled her up with red pepper and slippered her to death as she hung from a beam. I found that out myself, and I'm the only man that would dare going into the State to get hush-money for it. They'll try to poison me, same as they did in Chortumna when I went on the loot there. But you'll give the man at Marwar Junction my message?'

He got out at a little roadside station, and I reflected. I had heard, more than once, of men personating correspondents of newspapers and bleeding small Native States with threats of exposure, but I had never met any of the caste before. They lead a hard life, and generally die with great suddenness. The Native States have a wholesome horror of English newspapers which may throw light on their peculiar methods of government, and do their best to choke correspondents with champagne, or drive them out of their mind with four-in-hand barouches. They do not understand that nobody cares a straw for the internal administration of Native States so long as oppression and crime are kept within decent limits, and the ruler is not drugged, drunk, or diseased from one end of the year to the other. They are the dark places of the earth, full of unimaginable cruelty, touching the Railway and the Telegraph on one side, and, on the other, the days of Harun-al-Raschid. When I left the train I did business with divers Kings, and in eight days passed through many changes of life. Sometimes I wore dress-clothes and consorted with Princes and Politicals, drinking from crystal and eating from silver. Sometimes I lay out upon the ground and devoured what I could get, from a plate made of leaves, and drank the running water, and slept under the same rug as my servant. It was all in the day's work.

Then I headed for the Great Indian Desert upon the proper date, as I had promised, and the night mail set me down at Marwar Junction, where a funny, little, happy-go-lucky, native-managed railway runs to Jodhpore. The Bombay Mail from Delhi makes a short halt at Marwar. She arrived as I got in, and I had just time to hurry to her platform and go down the carriages. There was only one second-class on the train. I slipped the window and looked down upon a flaming red beard, half covered by a railway rug. That was my man, fast asleep, and I dug him gently in the ribs. He woke with a grunt, and I saw his face in the light of the lamps. It was a great and shining face.

'Tickets again?' said he.

'No,' said I. 'I am to tell you that he has gone South for the week. He has gone South for the week!'

The train had begun to move out. The red man rubbed his eyes. 'He has gone South for the week,' he repeated. 'Now that's just like his impidence. Did he say that I was to give you anything? 'Cause I won't.'

'He didn't,' I said, and dropped away, and watched the red lights die out in the dark. It was horribly cold because the wind was blowing off the sands. I climbed into my own train—not an Intermediate carriage this time—and went to sleep.

If the man with the beard had given me a rupee I should have kept it as a memento of a rather curious affair. But the consciousness of having done my duty was my only reward.

Later on I reflected that two gentlemen like my friends could not do any good if they foregathered and personated correspondents of newspapers, and might, if they blackmailed one of the little rat-trap states of Central India or Southern Rajputana, get themselves into serious difficulties. I therefore took some trouble to describe them as accurately as I could remember to people who would be interested in deporting them; and succeeded, so I was later informed, in having them headed back from the Degumber borders.

Then I became respectable, and returned to an office where there were no Kings and no incidents outside the daily manufacture of a newspaper. A newspaper office seems to attract every conceivable sort of person, to the prejudice of discipline. Zenana-mission ladies arrive, and beg that the Editor will instantly abandon all his duties to describe a Christian prize-giving in a back-slum of a perfectly inaccessible village; Colonels who have been overpassed for command sit down and sketch the outline of a series of ten, twelve, or twenty-four leading articles on Seniority *versus* Selection; missionaries wish to know why they have not been permitted to escape from their regular vehicles of abuse and swear at a brother-missionary under special patronage of the editorial We; stranded theatrical companies troop up to explain that they cannot pay for their advertisements, but on their return from New Zealand or Tahiti will do so with interest; inventors of patent punkah-pulling machines, carriage couplings, and unbreakable swords and axle-trees, call with specifications in their pockets and hours at their disposal; tea-companies enter and elaborate their prospectuses with the office pens; secretaries of ball-committees clamour to have the glories of their last dance more fully described; strange ladies rustle and say, 'I want a hundred lady's cards printed *at once*, please,' which is manifestly part of an Editor's duty; and every dissolute ruffian that ever tramped the Grand Trunk Road makes it his business to ask for employment as a proof-reader. And, all the time, the telephone-bell is ringing madly, and Kings are being killed on the Continent, and Empires are saying, 'You're another,' and Mister Gladstone is calling down brimstone upon the British Dominions and the little black copy-boys are whining, *'kaa-pi chay-ha-yeh'* [copy wanted] like tired bees, and most of the paper is as blank as Modred's shield.

But that is the amusing part of the year. There are six other months when none ever comes to call, and the thermometer walks inch by inch up to the top of the glass, and the office is darkened to just above reading-light, and the press-machines are red-hot of touch, and nobody writes anything but accounts of amusements in the Hill-stations or obituary notices. Then the telephone becomes a tinkling terror, because it tells you of the sudden deaths of men and women that you knew intimately, and the prickly-heat covers you with a garment, and you sit down and write: 'A slight increase of sickness is reported from the Khuda Janta Khan District. The outbreak is purely sporadic in its nature, and, thanks to the energetic efforts of the District authorities, is now almost at an end. It is, however, with deep regret we record the death, etc.'

Then the sickness really breaks out, and the less recording and reporting the better for the peace of the subscribers. But the Empires and the Kings continue to divert themselves as selfishly as before, and the Foreman thinks that a daily paper really ought to come out once in twenty-four hours, and all the people at the Hill-stations in the middle of their amusements say: 'Good gracious! Why can't the paper be sparkling? I'm sure there's plenty going on up here.'

That is the dark half of the moon, and, as the advertisements say, 'must be experienced to be appreciated.'

It was in that season, and a remarkably evil season, that the paper began running the last issue of the week on Saturday night, which is to say Sunday morning, after the custom of a London paper. This was a great convenience, for immediately after the paper was put to bed, the dawn would lower the thermometer from 96° to almost 84° for half an hour, and in that chill—you have no idea how cold is 84° on the grass until you begin to pray for it—a very tired man could get off to sleep ere the heat roused hm.

One Saturday night it was my pleasant duty to put the paper to bed alone. A King or a courtier or courtesan of a Community was going to die or get a new Constitution, or do something that was important on the other side of the world, and the paper was to be held open till the latest possible minute in order to catch the telegram.

It was a pitchy black night, as stifling as a June night can be, and the *loo,* the red-hot wind from the westward, was booming among the tinder-dry trees and pretending that the rain was on its heels. Now and again a spot of almost boiling water would fall on the dust with the flop of a frog, but all our weary world knew that was only pretence. It was a shade cooler in the press-room than the office, so I sat there, while the type ticked and clicked, and the night-jars hooted at the windows, and the all but naked compositors wiped the sweat from their foreheads, and called for water. The thing that was keeping us back, whatever it was, would not come off, though the *loo* dropped and the last type was set, and the whole round earth stood still in the choking heat, with its finger on its lip, to wait the event. I drowsed, and wondered whether the telegraph was a blessing, and whether this dying man, or struggling people, might be aware of the inconvenience the delay was causing. There was no special reason beyond the heat and worry to make tension, but, as the clock-hands crept up to three o'clock, and the machines spun their fly-wheels two or three times to see that all was in order before I said the word that would set them off, I could have shrieked aloud.

Then the roar and rattle of the wheels shivered the quiet into little bits. I rose to go away, but two men in white clothes stood in front of me. The first one said: 'It's him!' The second said: 'So it is!' And they both laughed almost as loudly as the machinery roared, and mopped their foreheads. 'We seed there was a light burning across the road, and we were sleeping in that ditch there for coolness, and I said to my friend here, "The office is open. Let's come along and speak to him as turned us back from the Degumber State,"' said the smaller of the two. He was the man I had met in the Mhow train, and his fellow was the red-haired man of Marwar Junction. There was no mistaking the eyebrows of the one or the beard of the other.

I was not pleased, because I wished to go to sleep, not to squabble with loafers. 'What do you want?' I asked.

'Half an hour's talk with you, cool and comfortable, in the office,' said the red-bearded man. 'We'd *like* some drink—the Contrack doesn't begin yet, Peachey, so you needn't look—but what we really want is advice. We don't want money. We ask you as a favour, because we found out you did us a bad turn about Degumber State.'

I led from the press-room to the stifling office with the maps on the walls, and the red-haired man rubbed his hands. 'That's something like,' said he. 'This was the proper shop to come to. Now, sir, let me introduce to you Brother Peachey Carnehan, that's him, and Brother Daniel Dravot, that is *me*, and the less said about our professions the better, for we have been most things in our time. Soldier, sailor, compositor, photographer, proof-reader, street-preacher, *and* correspondent of the *Backwoodsman* when we thought the paper wanted one. Carnehan is sober, and so am I. Look at us first, and see that's sure. It will save you cutting into my talk. We'll take one of your cigars apiece, and you shall see us light up.'

I watched the test. The men were absolutely sober, so I gave them each a tepid whisky and soda.

'Well *and* good,' said Carnehan of the eyebrows, wiping the froth from his moustache. 'Let *me* talk now, Dan. We have been all over India, mostly on foot. We have been boiler-fitters, engine-drivers, petty contractors, and all that, and we have decided that India isn't big enough for such as us.'

They certainly were too big for the office. Dravot's beard seemed to fill half the room and Carnehan's shoulders the other half, as they sat on the big table. Carnehan continued: 'The country isn't half worked out because they that governs it won't let you touch it. They spend all their blessed time in governing it, and you can't lift a spade, nor chip a rock, nor look for oil, nor anything like that, without all the Government saying, "Leave it alone, and let us govern." Therefore, such *as* it is, we will let it alone, and go away to some other place where a man isn't crowded and can come to his own. We are not little men, and there is nothing that we are afraid of except Drink, and we have signed a Contrack on that. *Therefore,* we are going away to be Kings.'

'Kings in our own right,' muttered Dravot.

'Yes, of course,' I said. 'You've been tramping in the sun, and it's a very warm night, and hadn't you better sleep over the notion? Come to-morrow.'

'Neither drunk nor sunstruck,' said Dravot. 'We have slept over the notion half a year, and require to see Books and Atlases, and we have decided that there is only one place now in the world that two strong men can Sar-a-*whack*. They call it Kafiristan. By my reckoning it's the top right-hand corner of Afghanistan, not more than three hundred miles from Peshawur. They have two-and-thirty heathen idols there, and we'll be the thirty-third and fourth. It's a mountainous country, and the women of those parts are very beautiful.'

'But that is provided against in the Contrack,' said Carnehan. 'Neither Women nor Liqu-or, Daniel.'

'And that's all we know, except that no one has gone there, and they fight; and in any place where they fight, a man who knows how to drill men can always be a King. We shall go to those parts and say to any King we find—"D'you want to vanquish your foes?" and we will show him how to drill men; for that we know better than anything else. Then we will subvert that King and seize his Throne and establish a Dynasty.'

'You'll be cut to pieces before you're fifty miles across the Border,' I said. 'You have to travel through Afghanistan to get to that country. It's one mass of mountains and peaks and glaciers, and no Englishman has been through it. The people are utter brutes, and even if you reached them you couldn't do anything.'

'That's more like,' said Carnehan. 'If you could think us a little more mad we would be more pleased. We have come to you to know about this country, to read a book about it, and to be shown maps. We want you to tell us that we are fools and to show us your books.' He turned to the bookcases.

'Are you at all in earnest?' I said.

'A little,' said Dravot sweetly. 'As big a map as you have got, even if it's all blank where Kafiristan is, and any books you've got. We can read, though we aren't very educated.'

I uncased the big thirty-two-miles-to-the-inch map of India, and two smaller Frontier maps, hauled down volume INF-KAN of the *Encyclopædia Britannica,* and the men consulted them.

'See here!' said Dravot, his thumb on the map. 'Up to Jagdallak, Peachey and me know the road. We was there with Roberts' Army. We'll have to turn off to the right at Jagdallak through Laghman territory. Then we get among the hills—fourteen thousand feet—fifteen thousand—it will be cold work there, but it don't look very far on the map.'

I handed him Wood on the *Sources of the Oxus*. Carnehan was deep in the *Encyclopædia.*

'They're a mixed lot,' said Dravot reflectively; 'and it won't help us to know the names of their tribes. The more tribes the more they'll fight, and the better for us. From Jagdallak to Ashang—H'mm!'

'But all the information about the country is as sketchy and inaccurate as can be,' I protested. 'No one knows anything about it really. Here's the file of the *United Services' Institute*. Read what Bellew says.'

'Blow Bellew!' said Carnehan. 'Dan, they're a stinkin' lot of heathens, but this book here says they think they're related to us English.'

I smoked while the men pored over Raverty, Wood, the maps, and the *Encyclopædia.*

'There is no use your waiting,' said Dravot politely. 'It's about four o'clock now. We'll go before six o'clock if you want to sleep, and we won't steal any of the papers. Don't you sit up. We're two harmless lunatics, and if you come to-morrow evening down to the Serai we'll say good-bye to you.'

'You *are* two fools,' I answered. 'You'll be turned back at the Frontier or cut up the minute you set foot in Afghanistan. Do you want any money or a recommendation down-country? I can help you to the chance of work next week.'

'Next week we shall be hard at work ourselves, thank you,' said Dravot. 'It isn't so easy being a King as it looks. When we've got our Kingdom in going order we'll let you know, and you can come up and help us to govern it.'

'Would two lunatics make a Contrack like that?' said Carnehan, with subdued pride, showing me a greasy half-sheet of notepaper on which was written the following. I copied it, then and there, as a curiosity:—

This Contrack between me and you persuing witnesseth in the name of God—Amen and so forth.

(One) That me and you will settle this matter together; i.e. *to be Kings of Kafiristan.*

(Two) That you and me will not, while this matter is being settled, look at any Liquor, nor any Woman black, white, or brown, so as to get mixed up with one or the other harmful.

(Three) That we conduct ourselves with Dignity and Discretion, and if one of us gets into trouble the other will stay by him.

Signed by you and me this day.

Peachey Taliaferro Carnehan.
Daniel Dravot.
Both Gentlemen at Large.

'There was no need for the last article,' said Carnehan, blushing modestly; 'but it looks regular. Now you know the sort of men that loafers are—we *are* loafers, Dan, until we get out of India—and *do* you think that we would sign a Contrack like that unless we was in earnest? We have kept away from the two things that make life worth having.'

'You won't enjoy your lives much longer if you are going to try this idiotic adventure. Don't set the office on fire,' I said, 'and go away before nine o'clock.'

I left them still poring over the maps and making notes on the back of the 'Contrack.' 'Be sure to come down to the Serai to-morrow,' were their parting words.

The Kumharsen Serai is the great four-square sink of humanity where the strings of camels and horses from the North load and unload. All the nationalities of Central Asia may be found there, and most of the folk of India proper. Balkh and Bokhara there meet Bengal and Bombay, and try to draw eye-teeth. You can buy ponies, turquoises, Persian pussy-cats, saddle-bags, fat-tailed sheep and musk in the Kumharsen Serai, and get many strange things for nothing. In the afternoon I went down to see whether my friends intended to keep their word or were lying there drunk.

A priest attired in fragments of ribbons and rags stalked up to me, gravely twisting a child's paper whirligig. Behind him was his servant bending under the load of a crate of mud toys. The two were loading up two camels, and the inhabitants of the Serai watched them with shrieks of laughter.

'The priest is mad,' said a horse-dealer to me. 'He is going up to Kabul to sell toys to the Amir. He will either be raised to honour or have his head cut off. He came in here this morning and has been behaving madly ever since.'

'The witless are under the protection of God,' stammered a flat-cheeked Uzbeg in broken Hindi. 'They foretell future events.'

'Would they could have foretold that my caravan would have been cut up by the Shinwaris almost within shadow of the Pass!' grunted the Yusufzai agent of a Rajputana trading-house whose goods had been diverted into the hands of other robbers just across the Border, and whose misfortunes were the laughing-stock of the bazaar. 'Ohé, priest, whence come you and whither do you go?'

'From Roum have I come,' shouted the priest, waving his whirligig; 'from Roum, blown by the breath of a hundred devils across the sea! O thieves, robbers, liars, the blessing of Pir Khan on pigs, dogs, and perjurers! Who will take the Protected of God to the North to sell charms that are never still to the Amir? The camels shall not gall, the sons shall not fall sick, and the wives shall remain faithful while they are away, of the men who give me place in their caravan. Who will assist me to slipper the King of the Roos with a golden slipper with a silver heel? The protection of Pir Khan be upon his labours!' He spread out the skirts of his gaberdine and pirouetted between the lines of tethered horses.

'There starts a caravan from Peshawur to Kabul in twenty days, *Huzrut*,' said the Yusufzai trader. 'My camels go therewith. Do thou also go and bring us good luck.'

'I will go even now!' shouted the priest. 'I will depart upon my winged camels, and be at Peshawur in a day! Ho! Hazar Mir Khan,' he yelled to his servant, 'drive out the camels, but let me first mount my own.'

He leaped on the back of his beast as it knelt, and, turning round to me, cried: 'Come thou also, Sahib, a little along the road, and I will sell thee a charm—an amulet that shall make thee King of Kafiristan.'

Then the light broke upon me, and I followed the two camels out of the Serai till we reached open road and the priest halted.

'What'd you think o' that?' said he in English. 'Carnehan can't talk their patter, so I've made him my servant. He makes a handsome servant. 'Tisn't for nothing that I've been knocking about the country for fourteen years. Didn't I do that talk neat? We'll hitch on to a caravan at Peshawur till we get to Jagdallak, and then we'll see if we can get donkeys for our camels, and strike into Kafiristan. Whirligigs for the Amir, oh, Lor'! Put your hand under the camel-bags and tell me what you feel.'

I felt the butt of a Martini, and another and another.

'Twenty of 'em,' said Dravot placidly. 'Twenty of 'em and ammunition to correspond, under the whirligigs and the mud dolls.'

'Heaven help you if you are caught with those things!' I said. 'A Martini is worth her weight in silver among the Pathans.'

'Fifteen hundred rupees of capital—every rupee we could beg, borrow, or steal—are invested on these two camels,' said Dravot. 'We won't get caught. We're going through the Khyber with a regular caravan. Who'd touch a poor mad priest?'

'Have you got everything you want?' I asked, overcome with astonishment.

'Not yet, but we shall soon. Give us a memento of your kindness, *Brother*. You did me a service, yesterday, and that time in Marwar. Half my Kingdom shall you have, as the saying is.' I slipped a small charm compass from my watch-chain and handed it up to the priest.

'Good-bye,' said Dravot, giving me hand cautiously. 'It's the last time we'll shake hands with an Englishman these many days. Shake hands with him, Carnehan,' he cried, as the second camel passed me.

Carnehan leaned down and shook hands. Then the camels passed away along the dusty road, and I was left alone to wonder. My eye could detect no failure in the disguises. The scene in the Serai proved that they were complete to the native mind. There was just the chance, therefore, that Carnehan and Dravot would be able to wander through Afghanistan without detection. But, beyond, they would find death—certain and awful death.

Ten days later a native correspondent, giving me the news of the day from Peshawur, wound up his letter with: 'There has been much laughter here on account of a certain mad priest who is going in his estimation to sell petty gauds and insignificant trinkets which he ascribes as great charms to H.H. the Amir of Bokhara. He passed through Peshawur and associated himself to the Second Summer caravan that goes to Kabul. The merchants are pleased because through superstition they imagine that such mad fellows bring good fortune.'

The two, then, were beyond the Border. I would have prayed for them, but, that night, a real King died in Europe, and demanded an obituary notice.

The wheel of the world swings through the same phases again and again. Summer passed and winter thereafter, and came and passed again. The daily paper continued and I with it, and upon the third summer there fell a hot night, a night-issue, and a strained waiting for something to be telegraphed from the other side of the world, exactly as had happened before. A few great men had died in the past two years, the machines worked with more clatter, and some of the trees in the office garden were a few feet taller. But that was all the difference.

I passed over to the press-room, and went through just such a scene as I have already described. The nervous tension was stronger than it had been two years before, and I felt the heat more acutely. At three o'clock I cried, 'Print off,' and turned to go, when there crept to my chair what was left of a man. He was bent into a circle, his head was sunk between his shoulders, and he moved his feet one over the other like a bear. I could hardly see whether he walked or crawled—this rag-wrapped, whining cripple who addressed me by name, crying that he was come back. 'Can you give me a drink?' he whimpered. 'For the Lord's sake give me a drink!'

I went back to the office, the man following with groans of pain, and I turned up the lamp.

'Don't you know me?' he gasped, dropping into a chair, and he turned his drawn face, surmounted by a shock of grey hair, to the light.

I looked at him intently. Once before had I seen eyebrows that met over the nose in an inch-broad black band, but for the life of me I could not recall where.

'I don't know you,' I said, handing him the whisky. 'What can I do for you?'

He took a gulp of the spirit raw, and shivered in spite of the suffocating heat.

'I've come back,' he repeated; 'and I was the King of Kafiristan—me and Dravot—crowned Kings we was! In this office we settled it—you setting there and giving us the books. I am Peachey—Peachey Taliaferro Carnehan, and you've been setting here ever since—oh, Lord!'

I was more than a little astonished, and expressed my feelings accordingly.

'It's true,' said Carnehan, with a dry cackle, nursing his feet, which were wrapped in rags. 'True as gospel. Kings we were, with crowns upon our heads—me and Dravot—poor Dan—oh, poor, poor Dan, that would never take advice, not though I begged of him!'

'Take the whisky,' I said, 'and take your own time. Tell me all you can recollect of everything from beginning to end. You got across the Border on your camels, Dravot dressed as a mad priest and you his servant. Do you remember that?'

'I ain't mad—yet, but I shall be that way soon. Of course I remember. Keep looking at me, or maybe my words will go all to pieces. Keep looking at me in my eyes and don't say anything.'

I leaned forward and looked into his face as steadily as I could. He dropped one hand upon the table and I grasped it by the wrist. It was twisted like a bird's claw, and upon the back was a ragged red diamond-shaped scar.

'No, don't look there. Look at *me,*' said Carnehan. 'That comes afterwards, but for the Lord's sake don't distrack me. We left with that caravan, me and Dravot playing all sorts of antics to amuse the people we were with. Dravot used to make us laugh in the evenings when all the people was cooking their dinners—cooking their dinners, and . . . what did they do then? They lit little fires with sparks that went into Dravot's beard, and we all laughed—fit to die. Little red fires they was, going into Dravot's big red beard—so funny.' His eyes left mine and he smiled foolishly.

'You went as far as Jagdallak with that caravan,' I said at a venture, 'after you had lit those fires. To Jagdallak where you turned off to try to get into Kafiristan.'

'No, we didn't neither. What are you talking about? We turned off before Jagdallak, because we heard the roads was good. But they wasn't good enough for our two camels—mine and Dravot's. When we left the caravan, Dravot took off all his clothes and mine too, and said we would be heathen, because the Kafirs didn't allow Mohammedans to talk to them. So we dressed betwixt and between, and such a sight as Daniel Dravot I never saw yet nor expect to see again. He burned half his beard, and slung a sheep-skin over his shoulder, and shaved his head into patterns. He shaved mine, too, and made me wear outrageous things to look like a heathen. That was in a most mountainous country, and our camels couldn't go along any more because of the mountains. They were tall and black, and coming home I saw them fight like wild goats—there are lots of goats in Kafiristan. And these mountains, they never keep still, no more than the goats. Always fighting they are, and don't let you sleep at night.'

'Take some more whisky,' I said very slowly. 'What did you and Daniel Dravot do when the camels could go no farther because of the rough roads that led into Kafiristan?'

'What did which do? There was a party called Peachey Taliaferro Carnehan that was with Dravot. Shall I tell you about him? He died out there in the cold. Slap from the bridge fell old Peachey, turning and twisting in the air like a penny whirligig that you can sell to the Amir.—No; they was two for three-ha'pence, those whirligigs, or I am much mistaken and woeful sore. . . . And then these camels were no use, and Peachey said to Dravot—"For the Lord's sake let's get out of this before our heads are chopped off," and with that they killed the camels all among the mountains, not having anything in particular to eat, but first they took off the boxes with the guns and ammunition, till two men came along driving four mules. Dravot up and dances in front of them, singing: "Sell me four mules." Says the first man: "If you are rich enough to buy, you are rich enough to rob"; but before ever he could put his hand to his knife, Dravot breaks his neck over his knee, and the other party runs away. So Carnehan loaded the mules with the rifles that was taken off the camels, and together we starts forward into those bitter cold mountaineous parts, and never a road broader than the back of your hand.'

He paused for a moment, while I asked him if he could remember the nature of the country through which he had journeyed.

'I am telling you as straight as I can, but my head isn't as good as it might be. They drove nails through it to make me hear better how Dravot died. The country was mountaineous, and the mules were most contrary, and the inhabitants was dispersed and solitary. They went up and up, and down and down, and that other party, Carnehan, was imploring of Dravot not to sing and whistle so loud, for fear of bringing down the tremenjus avalanches. But Dravot says that if a King couldn't sing it wasn't worth being King, and whacked the mules over the rump, and never took no heed for ten cold days. We came to a big level valley all among the mountains, and the mules were near dead, so we killed them, not having anything special for them or us to eat. We sat upon the boxes, and played odd and even with the cartridges that was jolted out.

'Then ten men with bows and arrows ran down that valley, chasing twenty men with bows and arrows, and the row was tremenjus. They was fair men—fairer than you or me—with yellow hair and remarkable well built. Says Dravot, unpacking the guns: "This is the beginning of the business. We'll fight for the ten men," and with that he fires two rifles at the twenty men, and drops one of them at two hundred yards from the rock where he was sitting. The other men began to run, but Carnehan and Dravot sits on the boxes picking them off at all ranges, up and down the valley. Then we goes up to the ten men that had run across the snow too, and they fires a footy little arrow at us. Dravot he shoots above their heads and they all falls down flat. Then he walks over them and kicks them, and then he lifts them up and shakes hands all round to make them friendly like. He calls them and gives them the boxes to carry, and waves his hand for all the world as though he was King already. They takes the boxes and him across the valley and up the hill into a pine-wood on the top, where there was half-a-dozen big stone idols. Dravot he goes to the biggest—a fellow they call Imbra—and lays a rifle and a cartridge at his feet, rubbing his nose respectful with his own nose, patting him on the head, and saluting in front of it. He turns round to the men and nods his head and says: "That's all right. I'm in the know too, and all these old jim-jams are my friends." Then he opens his mouth and points down it, and when the first man brings him food, he says: "No"; and when the second man brings him food, he says: "No"; but when one of the old priests and the boss of the village brings him food, he says: "Yes," very haughty, and eats it slow. That was how we came to our first village, without any trouble, just as though we had tumbled from the skies. But we tumbled from one of those damned rope-bridges, you see, and—you couldn't expect a man to laugh much after that?'

'Take some more whisky and go on,' I said. 'That was the first village you came into. How did you get to be King?'

'I wasn't King,' said Carnehan. 'Dravot he was the King, and a handsome man he looked with the gold crown on his head and all. Him and the other party stayed in that village, and every morning Dravot sat by the side of old Imbra, and the people came and worshipped. That was Dravot's order. Then a lot of men came into the valley, and Carnehan and Dravot picks them off with the rifles before they knew where they was, and runs down into the valley and up again the other side and finds another village, same as the first one, and the people all falls down flat on their faces, and Dravot says: "Now what is the trouble between you two villages?" and the people points to a woman, as fair as you or me, that was carried off, and Dravot takes her back to the first village and counts up the dead—eight there was. For each dead man Dravot pours a little milk on the ground and waves his arms like a whirligig, and "That's all right," says he. Then he and Carnehan takes the big boss of each valley by the arm and walks them down into the valley, and shows them how to scratch a line with a spear right down the valley, and gives each a sod of turf from both sides of the line. Then all the people comes down and shouts like the devil and all, and Dravot says: "Go and dig the land, and be fruitful and multiply," which they did, though they didn't understand. Then we asks the names of things in their lingo—bread and water and fire and idols and such, and Dravot leads the priest of each village up to the idol, and says he must sit there and judge the people, and if anything goes wrong he is to be shot.

'Next week they was all turning up the land in the valley as quiet as bees and much prettier, and the priests heard all the complaints and told Dravot in dumb show what it was about. "That's just the beginning," says Dravot. "They think we're Gods." He and Carnehan picks out twenty good men and shows them how to click off a rifle, and form fours, and advance in line, and they was very pleased to do so, and clever to see the hang of it. Then he takes out his pipe and his baccy-pouch and leaves one at one village, and one at the other, and off we two goes to see what was to be done in the next valley. That was all rock, and there was a little village there, and Carnehan says: "Send 'em to the old valley to plant," and takes 'em there, and gives 'em some land that wasn't took before. They were a poor lot, and we blooded 'em with a kid before letting 'em into the new Kingdom. That was to impress the people, and then they settled down quiet, and Carnehan went back to Dravot, who had got into another valley, all snow and ice and most mountaineous. There was no people there and the Army got afraid, so Dravot shoots one of them, and goes on till he finds some people in a village, and the Army explains that unless the people wants to be killed they had better not shoot their little matchlocks; for they had matchlocks. We makes friends with the priest, and I stays there alone with two of the Army, teaching the men how to drill, and a thundering big Chief comes across the snow with kettle-drums and horns twanging, because he heard there was a new God kicking about. Carnehan sights for the brown of the men half a mile across the snow and wings one of them. Then he sends a message to the Chief that, unless he wished to be killed, he must come and shake hands with me and leave his arms behind. The Chief comes alone first, and Carnehan shakes hands with him and whirls his arms about, same as Dravot used, and very much surprised that Chief was, and strokes my eyebrows. Then Carnehan goes alone to the Chief, and asks him in dumb show if he had an enemy he hated. "I have," says the Chief. So Carnehan weeds out the pick of his men, and sets the two of the Army to show them drill, and at the end of two weeks the men can manœuvre about as well as Volunteers. So he marches with the Chief to a great big plain on the top of a mountain, and the Chief's men rushes into a village and takes it; we three Martinis firing into the brown of the enemy. So we took that village too, and I gives the Chief a rag from my coat and says, "Occupy till I come"; which was scriptural. By way of a reminder, when me and the Army was eighteen hundred yards away, I drops a bullet near him standing on the snow, and all the people falls flat on their faces. Then I sends a letter to Dravot wherever he be by land or by sea.'

At the risk of throwing the creature out of train I interrupted: 'How could you write a letter up yonder?'

'The letter?—Oh!—The letter! Keep looking at me between the eyes, please. It was a string-talk letter, that we'd learned the way of it from a blind beggar in the Punjab.'

I remembered that there had once come to the office a blind man with a knotted twig and a piece of string which he wound round the twig according to some cipher of his own. He could, after the lapse of days or weeks, repeat the sentence which he had reeled up. He had reduced the alphabet to eleven primitive sounds, and tried to teach me his method, but I could not understand.

'I sent that letter to Dravot,' said Carnehan; 'and told him to come back because this Kingdom was growing too big for me to handle, and then I struck for the first valley, to see how the priests were working. They called the village we took along with the Chief, Bashkai, and the first village we took, Er-Heb. The priests at Er-Heb was doing all right, but they had a lot of pending cases about land to show me, and some men from another village had been firing arrows at night. I went out and looked for that village, and fired four rounds at it from a thousand yards. That used all the cartridges I cared to spend, and I waited for Dravot, who had been away two or three months, and I kept my people quiet.

'One morning I heard the devil's own noise of drums and horns, and Dan Dravot marches down the hill with his Army and a tail of hundreds of men, and, which was the most amazing, a great gold crown on his head. "My Gord, Carnehan," says Daniel, "this is a tremenjus business, and we've got the whole country as far as it's worth having. I am the son of Alexander by Queen Semiramis, and you're my younger brother and a God too! It's the biggest thing we've ever seen. I've been marching and fighting for six weeks with the Army, and every footy little village for fifty miles has come in rejoiceful; and more than that, I've got the key of the whole show, as you'll see, and I've got a crown for you! I told 'em to make two of 'em at a place called Shu, where the gold lies in the rock like suet in mutton. Gold I've seen, and turquoise I've kicked out of the cliffs, and there's garnets in the sands of the river, and here's a chunk of amber that a man brought me. Call up all the priests and, here, take your crown."

'One of the men opens a black hair bag, and I slips the crown on. It was too small and too heavy, but I wore it for the glory. Hammered gold it was–five pound weight, like a hoop of a barrel.

' "Peachey," says Dravot, "we don't want to fight no more. The Craft's the trick, so help me!" and he brings forward that same Chief that I left at Bashkai–Billy Fish we called him afterwards, because he was so like Billy Fish that drove the big tank-engine at Mach on the Bolan in the old days. "Shake hands with him," says Dravot, and I shook hands and nearly dropped, for Billy Fish gave me the Grip. I said nothing, but tried him with the Fellow Craft Grip. He answers all right, and I tried the Master's Grip, but that was a slip. "A Fellow Craft he is!" I says to Dan. "Does he know the Word?"–"He does," says Dan, "and all the priests know. It's a miracle! The Chiefs and the priests can work a Fellow Craft Lodge in a way that's very like ours, and they've cut the marks on the rocks, but they don't know the Third Degree, and they've come to find out. It's Gord's Truth! I've known these long years that the Afghans knew up to the Fellow Craft Degree, but this is a miracle. A God and a Grand-Master of the Craft am I, and a Lodge in the Third Degree I will open, and we'll raise the head priests and the Chiefs of the villages."

' "It's against all the law," I says, "holding a Lodge without warrant from any one; and you know we never held office in any Lodge."

' "It's a master-stroke o' policy," says Dravot. "It means running the country as easy as a four-wheeled bogie on a down grade. We can't stop to inquire now, or they'll turn against us. I've forty Chiefs at my heel, and passed and raised according to their merit they shall be. Billet these men on the villages, and see that we run up a Lodge of some kind. The temple of Imbra will do for the Lodge-room. The women must make aprons as you show them. I'll hold a levee of Chiefs to-night and Lodge to-morrow."

'I was fair run off my legs, but I wasn't such a fool as not to see what a pull this Craft business gave us. I showed the priests' families how to make aprons of the degrees, but for Dravot's apron the blue border and marks was made of turquoise lumps on white hide, not cloth. We took a great square stone in the temple for the Master's chair, and little stones for the officers' chairs, and painted the black pavement with white squares, and did what we could to make things regular.

'At the levee which was held that night on the hillside with big bonfires, Dravot gives out that him and me were Gods and sons of Alexander, and Past Grand-Masters in the Craft, and was come to make Kafiristan a country where every man should eat in peace and drink in quiet, and 'specially obey us. Then the Chiefs come round to shake hands, and they were so hairy and white and fair it was just shaking hands with old friends. We gave them names according as they was like men we had known in India—Billy Fish, Holly Dilworth, Pikky Kergan, that was Bazaar-master when I was at Mhow, and so on, and so on.

'*The* most amazing miracles was at Lodge next night. One of the old priests was watching us continuous, and I felt uneasy, for I knew we'd have to fudge the Ritual, and I didn't know what the men knew. The old priest was a stranger come in from beyond the village of Bashkia. The minute Dravot puts on the Master's apron that the girls had made for him, the priest fetches a whoop and a howl, and tries to overturn the stone that Dravot was sitting on. "It's all up now," I says. "That comes of meddling with the Craft without warrant!' Dravot never winked an eye, not when ten priests took and tilted over the Grand-Master's chair—which was to say the stone of Imbra. The priest begins rubbing the bottom end of it to clear away the black dirt, and presently he shows all the other priests the Master's Mark, same as was on Dravot's apron, cut into the stone. Not even the priests of the temple of Imbra knew it was there. The old chap falls flat on his face at Dravot's feet and kisses 'em. "Luck again," says Dravot, across the Lodge to me. "They say it's the missing Mark that no one could understand the why of. We're more than safe now.' Then he bangs the butt of his gun for a gavel and says: "By virtue of the authority vested in me by my own right hand and the help of Peachey, I declare myself Grand-Master of all Free-masonry in Kafiristan in this the Mother Lodge o' the country, and King of Kafiristan equally with Peachey!" At that he puts on his crown and I puts on mine—I was doing Senior Warden—and we opens the Lodge in most ample form. It was an amazing miracle!

The priests moved in Lodge through the first two degrees almost without telling, as if the memory was coming back to them. After that, Peachey and Dravot raised such as was worthy—high priests and Chiefs of far-off villages. Billy Fish was the first, and I can tell you we scared the soul out of him. It was not in any way according to Ritual, but it served our turn. We didn't raise more than ten of the biggest men, because we didn't want to make the Degree common. And they was clamouring to be raised.

'"In another six months," says Dravot, "we'll hold another Communication, and see how you are working." Then he asks them about their villages, and learns that they was fighting one against the other, and was sick and tired of it. And when they wasn't doing that they was fighting with the Mohammedans. "You can fight those when they come into our country," says Dravot. "Tell off every tenth man of your tribes for a Frontier guard, and send two hundred at a time to this valley to be drilled. Nobody is going to be shot or speared any more so long as he does well, and I know that you won't cheat me, because you're white people—sons of Alexander—and not like common, black Mohammedans. You are *my* people, and by God," says he, running off into English at the end, "I'll make a damned fine Nation of you, or I'll die in the making!"

'I can't tell all we did for the next six months, because Dravot did a lot I couldn't see the hang of, and he learned their lingo in a way I never could. My work was to help the people plough, and now and again go out with some of the Army and see what the other villages were doing, and make 'em throw rope-bridges across the ravines which cut up the country horrid. Dravot was very kind to me, but when he walked up and down in the pine-wood pulling that bloody red beard of his with both fists I knew he was thinking plans I could not advise about, and I just waited for orders.

'But Dravot never showed me disrespect before the people. They were afraid of me and the Army, but they loved Dan. He was the best of friends with the priests and the Chiefs; but any one could come across the hills with a complaint, and Dravot would hear him out fair, and call four priests together and say what was to be done. He used to call in Billy Fish from Bashkai, and Pikky Kergan from Shu, and an old Chief we called Kafoozelum—it was like enough to his real name—and hold councils with 'em when there was any fighting to be done in small villages. That was his Council of War, and the four priests of Bashkai, Shu, Khawak, and Madora was his Privy Council.

Between the lot of 'em they sent me, with forty men and twenty rifles and sixty men carrying turquoises, into the Ghorband country to buy those hand-made Martini rifles, that come out of the Amir's workshops at Kabul, from one of the Amir's Herati regiments that would have sold the very teeth out of their mouths for turquoises.

'I stayed in Ghorband a month, and gave the Governor there the pick of my baskets for hush-money, and bribed the Colonel of the regiment some more, and, between the two and the tribes-people, we got more than a hundred hand-made Martinis, a hundred good Kohat *jezails* that'll throw to six hundred yards, and forty man-loads of very bad ammunition for the rifles. I came back with what I had, and distributed 'em among the men that the Chiefs sent in to me to drill. Dravot was too busy to attend to those things, but the old Army that we first made helped me, and we turned out five hundred men that could drill, and two hundred that knew how to hold arms pretty straight. Even those corkscrewed, hand-made guns was a miracle to them. Dravot talked big about power-shops and factories, walking up and down in the pine-wood when the winter was coming on.

' "I won't make a Nation," says he. "I'll make an Empire! These men aren't niggers; they're English! Look at their eyes—look at their mouths. Look at the way they stand up. They sit on chairs in their own houses. They're the Lost Tribes, or something like it, and they've grown to be English. I'll take a census in the spring if the priests don't get frightened. There must be a fair two million of 'em in these hills. The villages are full o' little children. Two million people—two hundred and fifty thousand fighting men—and all English! They only want the rifles and a little drilling. Two hundred and fifty thousand men, ready to cut in on Russia's right flank when she tries for India! Peachey, man," he says, chewing his beard in great hunks, "we shall be Emperors—Emperors of the Earth! Rajah Brooke will be a suckling to us. I'll treat with the Viceroy on equal terms. I'll ask him to send me twelve picked English—twelve that I know of—to help us govern a bit. There's Mackray, Sergeant-pensioner at Segowli—many's the good dinner he's given me, and his wife a pair of trousers. There's Donkin, the Warder of Tounghoo Jail. There's hundreds that I could lay my hand on if I was in India. The Viceroy shall do it for me. I'll send a man through in the spring for those men, and I'll write for a Dispensation from the Grand Lodge for what I've done as Grand-Master. That—and all the Sniders that'll be thrown out when the native troops in India take up the Martini. They'll be worn smooth, but they'll do for fighting in these hills. Twelve English, a hundred thousand Sniders run through the Amir's country in driblets—I'd be content with twenty thousand in one year—and we'd be an Empire. When everything was ship-shape, I'd hand over the crown—this crown I'm wearing now—to Queen Victoria on my knees, and she'd say: 'Rise up, Sir Daniel Dravot.' Oh, it's big! It's big, I tell you! But there's so much to be done in every place—Bashkai, Khawak, Shu, and everywhere else."

'"What is it?" I says. "There are no more men coming in to be drilled this autumn. Look at those fat, black clouds. They're bringing the snow."

'"It isn't that," says Daniel, putting his hand very hard on my shoulder; "and I don't wish to say anything that's against you, for no other living man would have followed me and made me what I am as you have done. You're a first-class Commander-in-Chief and the people know you; but—it's a big country, and somehow you can't help me, Peachey, in the way I want to be helped."

'"Go to your blasted priests, then!" I said, and I was sorry when I made that remark, but it did hurt me sore to find Daniel talking so superior, when I'd drilled all the men, and done all he told me.

'"Don't let's quarrel, Peachey," says Daniel without cursing. "You're a King too, and the half of this Kingdom is yours; but can't you see, Peachey, we want cleverer men than us now—three or four of 'em, that we can scatter about for our Deputies. It's a hugeous great State, and I can't always tell the right thing to do, and I haven't time for all I want to do, and here's winter coming on and all." He stuffed half his beard into his mouth, all red like the gold of his crown.

'"I'm sorry, Daniel," says I. "I've done all I could. I've drilled the men and shown the people how to stack their oats better; and I've brought in those tinware rifles from Ghorband—but I know what you're driving at. I take it Kings always feel oppressed that way."

'"There's another thing too," says Dravot, walking up and down. "The winter's coming and these people won't be giving much trouble, and if they do we can't move about. I want a wife."

'"For Gord's sake, leave the women alone!" I says. "We've both got all the work we can, though I *am* a fool. Remember the Contrack, and keep clear o' women."

'"The Contrack only lasted till such time as we was Kings; and Kings we have been these months past," says Dravot, weighing his crown in his hand. "You go get a wife, too, Peachey—a nice strappin', plump girl that'll keep you warm in the winter. They're prettier than English girls, and we can take the pick of 'em. Boil 'em once or twice in hot water and they'll come out like chicken and ham."

'"Don't tempt me!" I says. "I will not have any dealings with a woman not till we are a dam' sight more settled than we are now. I've been doing the work o' two men, and you've been doing the work o' three. Let's lie off a bit, and see if we can get some better tobacco from Afghan country and run in some good liquor; but no women."

'"Who's talking o' *women?*" says Dravot. "I said *wife*—a Queen to breed a King's son for the King. A Queen out of the strongest tribe, that'll make them your blood-brothers, and that'll lie by your side and tell you all the people thinks about you and their own affairs. That's what I want."

'"Do you remember that Bengali woman I kept at Mogul Serai when I was a platelayer?" says I. "A fat lot o' good she was to me. She taught me the lingo and one or two other things; but what happened? She ran away with the Station-master's servant and half my month's pay. Then she turned up at Dadur Junction in tow of a half-caste, and had the impudence to say I was her husband—all among the drivers in the running-shed too!"

'"We've done with that," says Dravot; "these women are whiter than you or me, and a Queen I will have for the winter months."

'"For the last time o' asking, Dan, do *not,*" I says. "It'll only bring us harm. The Bible says that Kings ain't to waste their strength on women, 'specially when they've got a raw new Kingdom to work over."

'"For the last time of answering, I will," said Dravot, and he went away through the pine-trees looking like a big red devil, the sun being on his crown and beard and all.

'But getting a wife was not as easy as Dan thought. He put it before the Council, and there was no answer till Billy Fish said that he'd better ask the girls. Dravot damned them all round. "What's wrong with me?" he shouts, standing by the idol Imbra. "Am I a dog or am I not enough of a man for your wenches? Haven't I put the shadow of my hand over this country? Who stopped the last Afghan raid?" It was me really, but Dravot was too angry to remember. "Who bought your guns? Who repaired the bridges? Who's the Grand-Master of the Sign cut in the stone?" says he, and he thumped his hand on the block that he used to sit on in Lodge, and at Council, which opened like Lodge always. Billy Fish said nothing and no more did the others. "Keep your hair on, Dan," said I; "and ask the girls. That's how it's done at Home, and these people are quite English."

'"The marriage of the King is a matter of State," says Dan, in a red-hot rage, for he could feel, I hope, that he was going against his better mind. He walked out of the Council-room, and the others sat still, looking at the ground.

'"Billy Fish," says I to the Chief of Bashkai, "what's the difficulty here? A straight answer to a true friend."

'"You know," says Billy Fish. "How should a man tell you who knows everything? How can daughters of men marry Gods or Devils? It's not proper."

'I remembered something like that in the Bible; but if, after seeing us as long as they had, they still believed we were Gods, 'twasn't for me to undeceive them.

'"A God can do anything," says I. "If the King is fond of a girl he'll not let her die."—"She'll have to," says Billy Fish. "There are all sorts of Gods and Devils in these mountains, and now and again a girl marries one of them and isn't seen any more. Besides, you two know the Mark cut in the stone. Only the Gods know that. We thought you were men till you showed the Sign of the Master."

'I wished then that we had explained about the loss of the genuine secrets of a Master-Mason at the first go-off; but I said nothing. All that night there was a blowing of horns in a little dark temple half-way down the hill, and I heard a girl crying fit to die. One of the priests told us that she was being prepared to marry the King.

'"I'll have no nonsense of that kind," says Dan. "I don't want to interfere with your customs, but I'll take my own wife."—"The girl's a little bit afraid," says the priest. "She thinks she's going to die, and they are a-heartening of her up down in the temple."

'"Hearten her very tender, then," says Dravot, "or I'll hearten you with the butt of a gun so you'll never want to be heartened again." He licked his lips, did Dan, and stayed up walking about more than half the night, thinking of the wife that he was going to get in the morning. I wasn't any means comfortable, for I knew that dealings with a woman in foreign parts, though you was a crowned King twenty times over, could not but be risky. I got up very early in the morning, while Dravot was asleep, and I saw the priests talking together in whispers, and the Chiefs talking together too, and they looked at me out of the corners of their eyes.

'"What is up, Fish?" I says to the Bashkai man, who was wrapped up in his furs and looking splendid to behold.

'"I can't rightly say," says he; "but if you can make the King drop all this nonsense about marriage, you'll be doing him and me and yourself a great service."

'"That I do believe," says I. "But sure, you know, Billy, as well as me, having fought against and for us, that the King and me are nothing more than two of the finest men that God Almighty ever made. Nothing more, I do assure you."

'"That may be," says Billy Fish, "and yet I should be sorry if it was." He sinks his head upon his great fur cloak for a minute and thinks. "King," says he, "be you man or God or Devil, I'll stick by you to-day. I have twenty of my men with me, and they will follow me. We'll go to Bashkai until the storm blows over."

'A little snow had fallen in the night, and everything was white except them greasy fat clouds that blew down and down from the north. Dravot came out with his crown on his head, swinging his arms and stamping his feet, and looking more pleased than Punch.

'"For the last time, drop it, Dan," says I in a whisper. "Billy Fish here says that there will be a row."

'"A row among my people!" says Dravot. "Not much. Peachey, you're a fool not to get a wife too. Where's the girl?" says he with a voice as loud as the braying of a jackass. "Call up all the Chiefs and priests, and let the Emperor see if his wife suits him."

'There was no need to call any one. They were all there leaning on their guns and spears round the clearing in the centre of the pine-wood. A lot of priests went down to the little temple to bring up the girl, and the horns blew fit to wake the dead. Billy Fish saunters round and gets as close to Daniel as he could, and behind him stood his twenty men with matchlocks. Not a man of them under six feet. I was next to Dravot, and behind me was twenty men of the regular Army. Up comes the girl, and a strapping wench she was, covered with silver and turquoises, but white as death, and looking back every minute at the priests.

'"She'll do," said Dan, looking her over. "What's to be afraid of, lass? Come and kiss me." He puts his arm round her. She shuts her eyes, gives a bit of a squeak, and down goes her face in the side of Dan's flaming red beard.

'"The slut's bitten me!" says he, clapping his hand to his neck, and, sure enough, his hand was red with blood. Billy Fish and two of his matchlock-men catches hold of Dan by the shoulders and drags him into the Bashkai lot, while the priests howls in their lingo: "Neither God nor Devil but a man!" I was all taken aback, for a priest cut at me in front, and the Army behind began firing into the Bashkai men.

' "God A'mighty!" says Dan. "What is the meaning o' this?"

' "Come back! Come away!" says Billy Fish. "Ruin and Mutiny's the matter. We'll break for Bashkai if we can."

'I tried to give some sort of orders to my men—the men o' the regular Army—but it was no use, so I fired into the brown of 'em with an English Martini and drilled three beggars in a line. The valley was full of shouting, howling people, and every soul was shrieking, "Not a God nor a Devil but only a man!" The Bashkai troops stuck to Billy Fish all they were worth, but their matchlocks wasn't half as good as the Kabul breech-loaders, and four of them dropped. Dan was bellowing like a bull, for he was very wrathy; and Billy Fish had a hard job to prevent him running out at the crowd.

' "We can't stand," says Billy Fish. "Make a run for it down the valley! The whole place is against us." The matchlock-men ran, and we went down the valley in spite of Dravot. He was swearing horrible and crying out he was a King. The priests rolled great stones on us, and the regular Army fired hard, and there wasn't more than six men, not counting Dan, Billy Fish, and me, that came down to the bottom of the valley alive.

'Then they stopped firing and the horns in the temple blew again. "Come away—for God's sake come away!" says Billy Fish. "They'll send runners out to all the villages before ever we get to Bashkai. I can protect you there, but I can't do anything now."

'My own notion is that Dan began to go mad in his head from that hour. He stared up and down like a stuck pig. Then he was all for walking back alone and killing the priests with his bare hands; which he could have done. "An Emperor am I," says Daniel, "and next year I shall be a Knight of the Queen."

' "All right, Dan," says I; "but come along now while there's time."

' "It's your fault," says he, "for not looking after your Army better. There was mutiny in the midst, and you didn't know—you damned engine-driving, plate-laying, missionary's-pass-hunting hound!" He sat upon a rock and called me every name he could lay tongue to. I was too heart-sick to care, though it was all his foolishness that brought the smash.

' "I'm sorry, Dan," says I, "but there's no accounting for natives. This business is our 'Fifty-Seven. Maybe we'll make something out of it yet, when we've got to Bashkai."

' "Let's get to Bashkai, then," says Dan, "and, by God, when I come back here again I'll sweep the valley so there isn't a bug in a blanket left!"

'We walked all that day, and all that night Dan was stumping up and down on the snow, chewing his beard and muttering to himself.

' "There's no hope o' getting clear," said Billy Fish. "The priests will have sent runners to the villages to say that you are only men. Why didn't you stick on as Gods till things was more settled? I'm a dead man," says Billy Fish, and he throws himself down on the snow and begins to pray to his Gods.

'Next morning we was in a cruel bad country—all up and down, no level ground at all, and no food either. The six Bashkai men looked at Billy Fish hungry-ways as if they wanted to ask something, but they said never a word. At noon we came to the top of a flat mountain all covered with snow, and when we climbed up into it, behold, there was an Army in position waiting in the middle!

' "The runners have been very quick," says Billy Fish, with a little bit of a laugh. "They are waiting for us."

'Three or four men began to fire from the enemy's side, and a chance shot took Daniel in the calf of the leg. That brought him to his senses. He looks across the snow at the Army, and sees the rifles that we had brought into the country.

' "We're done for," says he. "They are Englishmen, these people,—and it's my blasted nonsense that has brought you to this. Get back, Billy Fish, and take your men away. You've done what you could, and now cut for it. Carnehan," says he, "shake hands with me and go along with Billy. Maybe they won't kill you. I'll go and meet 'em alone. It's me that did it. Me, the King!"

' "Go!" says I. "Go to Hell, Dan! I'm with you here. Billy Fish, you clear out, and we two will meet those folk."

' "I'm a Chief," says Billy Fish, quite quiet. "I stay with you. My men can go."

'The Bashkai fellows didn't wait for a second word, but ran off, and Dan and me and Billy Fish walked across to where the drums were drumming and the horns were horning. It was cold—awful cold. I've got that cold in the back of my head now. There's a lump of it there.'

The punkah-coolies had gone to sleep. Two kerosene lamps were blazing in the office, and the perspiration poured down my face and splashed on the blotter as I leaned forward. Carnehan was shivering, and I feared that his mind might go. I wiped my face, took a fresh grip of the piteously mangled hands, and said: 'What happened after that?'

The momentary shift of my eyes had broken the clear current.

'What was you pleased to say?' whined Carnehan. 'They took them without any sound. Not a little whisper all along the snow, not though the King knocked down the first man that set hand on him—not though old Peachey fired his last cartridge into the brown of 'em. Not a single solitary sound did those swines make. They just closed up tight, and I tell you their furs stunk. There was a man called Billy Fish, a good friend of us all, and they cut his throat, sir, then and there, like a pig; and the King kicks up the bloody snow and says: "We've had a dashed fine run for our money. What's coming next?" But Peachey, Peachey Taliaferro, I tell you, sir, in confidence as betwixt two friends, he lost his head, sir. No, he didn't neither. The King lost his head, so he did, all along o' one of those cunning rope-bridges. Kindly let me have the paper-cutter, sir. It tilted this way. They marched him a mile across that snow to a rope-bridge over a ravine with a river at the bottom. You may have seen such. They prodded him behind like an ox. "Damn your eyes!" says the King. "D'you suppose I can't die like a gentleman?" He turns to Peachey—Peachey that was crying like a child. "I've brought you to this, Peachey," says he. "Brought you out of your happy life to be killed in Kafiristan, where you was late Commander-in-Chief of the Emperor's forces. Say you forgive me, Peachey."—"I do," says Peachey. "Fully and freely do I forgive you, Dan."—"Shake hands, Peachey," says he. "I'm going now." Out he goes, looking neither right nor left, and when he was plumb in the middle of those dizzy dancing ropes—"Cut, you beggars," he shouts; and they cut, and old Dan fell, turning round and round and round, twenty thousand miles, for he took half an hour to fall till he struck the water, and I could see his body caught on a rock with the gold crown close beside.

'But do you know what they did to Peachey, between two pine-trees? They crucified him, sir, as Peachey's hands will show. They used wooden pegs for his hands and his feet; and he didn't die. He hung there and screamed, and they took him down next day, and said it was a miracle that he wasn't dead. They took him down—poor old Peachey that hadn't done them any harm—that hadn't done them any——"

He rocked to and fro and wept bitterly, wiping his eyes with the back of his scarred hands and moaning like a child for some ten minutes.

'They was cruel enough to feed him up in the temple, because they said he was more of a God than old Daniel that was a man. Then they turned him out on the snow, and told him to go home, and Peachey came home in about a year, begging along the roads quite safe; for Daniel Dravot he walked before and said: "Come along, Peachey. It's a big thing we're doing." The mountains they danced at night, and the mountains they tried to fall on Peachey's head, but Dan he held up his hand, and Peachey came along bent double. He never let go of Dan's hand, and he never let go of Dan's head. They gave it to him as a present in the temple, to remind him not to come again, and though the crown was pure gold, and Peachy was starving, never would Peachey sell the same. You knew Dravot, sir! You knew Right Worshipful Brother Dravot! Look at him now!'

He fumbled in the mass of rags round his bent waist; brought out a black horsehair bag embroidered with silver thread, and shook therefrom on to my table—the dried, withered head of Daniel Dravot! The morning sun that had long been paling the lamps struck the red beard and blind sunken eyes; struck, too, a heavy circlet of gold studded with raw turquoises, that Carnehan placed tenderly on the battered temples.

'You behold now,' said Carnehan, 'the Emperor in his habit as he lived—the King of Kafiristan with his crown upon his head. Poor old Daniel that was a monarch once!'

I shuddered, for, in spite of defacements manifold, I recognised the head of the man of Marwar Junction. Carnehan rose to go. I attempted to stop him. He was not fit to walk abroad. 'Let me take away the whisky, and give me a little money,' he gasped. 'I was a King once. I'll go to the Deputy-Commissioner and ask to set in the Poorhouse till I get my health. No, thank you, I can't wait till you get a carriage for me. I've urgent private affairs—in the South—at Marwar.'

He shambled out of the office and departed in the direction of the Deputy-Commissioner's house. That day at noon I had occasion to go down the blinding hot Mall, and I saw a crooked man crawling along the white dust of the roadside, his hat in his hand, quavering dolorously after the fashion of street-singers at Home. There was not a soul in sight, and he was out of all possible earshot of the houses. And he sang through his nose, turning his head from right to left:—

'The Son of God goes forth to war,
A kingly crown to gain;
His blood-red banner streams afar!
Who follows in his train?'

I waited to hear no more, but put the poor wretch into my carriage and drove him to the nearest missionary for eventual transfer to the Asylum. He repeated the hymn twice while he was with me, whom he did not in the least recognise, and I left him singing it to the missionary.

Two days later I inquired after his welfare of the Superintendent of the Asylum.

'He was admitted suffering from sunstroke. He died early yesterday morning,' said the Superintendent. 'Is it true that he was half an hour bare-headed in the sun at mid-day?'

'Yes,' said I, 'but do you happen to know if he had anything upon him by any chance when he died?'

'Not to my knowledge,' said the Superintendent.

And there the matter rests.

WILLIAM THE CONQUEROR

PART I

I have done one braver thing
Than all the Worthies did;
And yet a braver thence doth spring,
Which is, to keep that hid.
The Undertaking.

'Is it officially declared yet?'

'They've gone as far as to admit extreme local scarcity, and they've started relief-works in one or two districts, the paper says.'

'That means it will be declared as soon as they can make sure of the men and the rolling-stock. Shouldn't wonder if it were as bad as the Big Famine.'

'Can't be,' said Scott, turning a little in the long cane chair. 'We've had fifteen-anna crops in the north, and Bombay and Bengal report more than they know what to do with. They'll be able to check it before it gets out of hand. It will only be local.'

Martyn picked up the *Pioneer* from the table, read through the telegrams once more, and put up his feet on the chair-rests. It was a hot, dark, breathless evening, heavy with the smell of the newly-watered Mall. The flowers in the Club gardens were dead and black on their stalks, the little lotus-pond was a circle of caked mud, and the tamarisk-trees were white with the dust of days. Most of the men were at the band-stand in the public gardens—from the Club verandah you could hear the native Police band hammering stale waltzes—or on the polo-ground or in the high-walled fives-court, hotter than a Dutch oven. Half-a-dozen grooms, squatted at the heads of their ponies, waited their masters' return. From time to time a man would ride at a foot-pace into the Club compound, and listlessly loaf over to the whitewashed barracks beside the main building. These were supposed to be chambers. Men lived in them, meeting the same faces night after night at dinner, and drawing out their office-work till the latest possible hour, that they might escape that doleful company.

'What are you going to do?' said Martyn, with a yawn. 'Let's have a swim before dinner.'

'Water's hot,' said Scott. 'I was at the bath to-day.'

'Play you game o' billiards—fifty up.'

'It's a hundred and five in the hall now. Sit still and don't be so abominably energetic.'

A grunting camel swung up to the porch, his badged and belted rider fumbling a leather pouch.

'Kubber-kargaz—ki—yektraaa,' the man whined, handing down the newspaper extra—a slip printed on one side only, and damp from the press. It was pinned on the green-baize board, between notices of ponies for sale and fox-terriers missing.

Martyn rose lazily, read it, and whistled. 'It's declared!' he cried. 'One, two, three—eight districts go under the operations of the Famine Code *ek dum*. They've put Jimmy Hawkins in charge.'

'Good business!' said Scott, with the first sign of interest he had shown. 'When in doubt hire a Punjabi. I worked under Jimmy when I first came out and he belonged to the Punjab. He has more *bundobust* than most men.'

'Jimmy's a Jubilee Knight now,' said Martyn. 'He was a good chap, even though he is a thrice-born civilian and went to the Benighted Presidency. What unholy names these Madras districts rejoice in—all *ungas* or *rungas* or *pillays* or *polliums*.'

A dog-cart drove up, and a man entered, mopping his head. He was editor of the one daily paper at the capital of a province of twenty-five million natives and a few hundred white men, and as his staff was limited to himself and one assistant, his office hours ran variously from ten to twenty a day.

'Hi, Raines; you're supposed to know everything,' said Martyn, stopping him. 'How's this Madras "scarcity" going to turn out?'

'No one knows as yet. There's a message as long as your arm coming in on the telephone. I've left my cub to fill it out. Madras has owned she can't manage it alone, and Jimmy seems to have a free hand in getting all the men he needs. Arbuthnot's warned to hold himself in readiness.'

' "Badger" Arbuthnot?'

'The Peshawur chap. Yes, and the *Pi* wires that Ellis and Clay have been moved from the North-West already, and they've taken half-a-dozen Bombay men, too. It's *pukka* famine, by the looks of it.'

'They're nearer the scene of action than we are; but if it comes to indenting on the Punjab this early, there's more in this than meets the eye,' said Martyn.

'Here to-day and gone to-morrow. Didn't come to stay for ever,' said Scott, dropping one of Marryat's novels, and rising to his feet. 'Martyn, your sister's waiting for you.'

A rough grey horse was backing and shifting at the edge of the verandah, where the light of a kerosene lamp fell on a brown calico habit and a white face under a grey felt hat.

'Right-oh,' said Martyn. 'I'm ready. Better come and dine with us if you've nothing to do, Scott. William, is there any dinner in the house?'

'I'll go home first and see,' was the rider's answer. 'You can drive him over—at eight, remember.'

Scott moved leisurely to his room, and changed into the evening-dress of the season and the country: spotless white linen from head to foot, with a broad silk cummerbund. Dinner at the Martyns' was a decided improvement on the goat-mutton, twiney-tough fowl, and tinned entrées of the Club. But it was a great pity Martyn could not afford to send his sister to the Hills for the hot weather. As an Acting District Superintendent of Police, Martyn drew the magnificent pay of six hundred depreciated silver rupees a month, and his little four-roomed bungalow said just as much. There were the usual blue-and-white striped jail-made rugs on the uneven floor; the usual glass-studded Amritsar *phulkaris* draped to nails driven into the flaking whitewash of the walls; the usual half-dozen chairs that did not match, picked up at sales of dead men's effects; and the usual streaks of black grease where the leather punkah-thong ran through the wall. It was as though everything had been unpacked the night before to be repacked next morning. Not a door in the house was true on its hinges. The little windows, fifteen feet up, were darkened with wasp-nests, and lizards hunted flies between the beams of the wood-ceiled roof. But all this was part of Scott's life. Thus did people live who had such an income; and in a land where each man's pay, age, and position are printed in a book, that all may read, it is hardly worth while to play at pretences in word or deed. Scott counted eight years' service in the Irrigation Department, and drew eight hundred rupees a month, on the understanding that if he served the State faithfully for another twenty-two years he could retire on a pension of some four hundred rupees a month. His working life, which had been spent chiefly under canvas or in temporary shelters where a man could sleep, eat, and write letters, was bound up with the opening and guarding of irrigation canals, the handling of two or three thousand workmen of all castes and creeds, and the payment of vast sums of coined silver. He had finished that spring, not without credit, the last section of the great Mosuhl Canal, and—much against his will, for he hated office work—had been sent in to serve during the hot weather on the accounts and supply side of the Department, with sole charge of the sweltering sub-office at the capital of the Province. Martyn knew this; William, his sister, knew it; and everybody knew it.

Scott knew, too, as well as the rest of the world, that Miss Martyn had come out to India four years before, to keep house for her brother, who, as every one, again, knew, had borrowed the money to pay for her passage, and that she ought, as all the world said, to have married long ago. Instead of this, she had refused some half-a-dozen subalterns, a civilian twenty years her senior, one major, and a man in the Indian Medical Department. This, too, was common property. She had 'stayed down three hot weathers, as the saying is, because her brother was in debt and could not afford the expense of her keep at even a cheap hill-station. Therefore her face was white as bone, and in the centre of her forehead was a big silvery scar about the size of a shilling —the mark of a Delhi sore, which is the same as a 'Bagdad date.' This comes from drinking bad water, and slowly eats into the flesh till it is ripe enough to be burned out with acids.

None the less William had enjoyed herself hugely in her four years. Twice she had been nearly drowned while fording a river on horse-back; once she had been run away with on a camel; had witnessed a midnight attack of thieves on her brother's camp; had seen justice administered, with long sticks, in the open under trees; could speak Urdu and even rough Punjabi with a fluency that was envied by her seniors; had altogether fallen out of the habit of writing to her aunts in England, or cutting the pages of the English magazines; had been through a very bad cholera year, seeing sights unfit to be told; and had wound up her experiences by six weeks of typhoid fever, during which her head had been shaved; and hoped to keep her twenty-third birthday that September. It is conceivable that her aunts would not have approved of a girl who never set foot on the ground if a horse were within hail; who rode to dances with a shawl thrown over her skirt; who wore her hair cropped and curling all over her head; who answered indifferently to the name of William or Bill; whose speech was heavy with the flowers of the vernacular; who could act in amateur theatricals, play on the banjo, rule eight servants and two horses, their accounts and their diseases, and look men slowly and deliberately between the eyes—yea, after they had proposed to her and been rejected.

'I like men who do things,' she had confided to a man in the Educational Department, who was teaching the sons of cloth merchants and dyers the beauty of Wordsworth's 'Excursion' in annotated cram-books; and when he grew poetical, William explained that she 'didn't understand poetry very much; it made her head ache,' and another broken heart took refuge at the Club. But it was all William's fault. She delighted in hearing men talk of their own work, and that is the most fatal way of bringing a man to your feet.

Scott had known her more or less for some three years, meeting her, as a rule, under canvas when his camp and her brother's joined for a day on the edge of the Indian Desert. He had danced with her several times at the big Christmas gatherings, when as many as five hundred white people came into the station; and he had always a great respect for her housekeeping and her dinners.

She looked more like a boy than ever when, after their meal, she sat, one foot tucked under her, on the leather camp-sofa, rolling cigarettes for her brother, her low forehead puckered beneath the dark curls as she twiddled the papers. She stuck out her rounded chin when the tobacco stayed in place, and, with a gesture as true as a school-boy's throwing a stone, tossed the finished article across the room to Martyn, who caught it with one hand and continued his talk with Scott. It was all 'shop,'—canals and the policing of canals; the sins of villagers who stole more water than they had paid for, and the grosser sin of native constables who connived at the thefts; of the transplanting bodily of villages to newly-irrigated ground, and of the coming fight with the desert in the south when the Provincial funds should warrant the opening of the long-surveyed Luni Protective Canal System. And Scott spoke openly of his great desire to be put on one particular section of the work where he knew the land and the people, and Martyn sighed for a billet in the Himalayan foot-hills, and spoke his mind of his superiors, and William rolled cigarettes and said nothing, but smiled gravely on her brother because he was happy.

At ten Scott's horse came to the door, and the evening was ended.

The lights of the two low bungalows in which the daily paper was printed showed bright across the road. It was too early to try to find sleep, and Scott drifted over to the editor. Raines, stripped to the waist like a sailor at a gun, lay in a long chair, waiting for night telegrams.

He had a theory that if a man did not stay by his work all day and most of the night he laid himself open to fever; so he ate and slept among his files.

'Can you do it?' he said drowsily. 'I didn't mean to bring you over.'

'About what? I've been dining at the Martyns'.'

'The famine, of course. Martyn's warned for it, too. They're taking men where they can find 'em. I sent a note to you at the Club just now, asking if you could do us a letter once a week from the south—between two and three columns, say. Nothing sensational, of course, but just plain facts about who is doing what, and so forth. Our regular rates—ten rupees a column.'

'Sorry, but it's out of my line,' Scott answered, staring absently at the map of India on the wall. 'It's rough on Martyn—very. Wonder what he'll do with his sister. Wonder what the deuce they'll do with me? I've no famine experience. This is the first I've heard of it. *Am* I ordered?'

'Oh, yes. Here's the wire. They'll put you on relief-works,' Raines went on, 'with a horde of Madrassis dying like flies; one native apothecary and half a pint of cholera-mixture among the ten thousand of you. It comes of your being idle for the moment. Every man who isn't doing two men's work seems to have been called upon. Hawkins evidently believes in Punjabis. It's going to be quite as bad as anything they have had in the last ten years.'

'It's all in a day's work, worse luck. I suppose I shall get my orders officially some time to-morrow. I'm glad I happened to drop in. Better go and pack my kit now. Who relieves me here—do you know?'

Raines turned over a sheaf of telegrams. 'McEuan,' said he, 'from Murree.'

Scott chuckled. 'He thought he was going to be cool all summer. He'll be very sick about this. Well, no good talking. 'Night.'

Two hours later, Scott, with a clear conscience, laid himself down to rest on a string cot in a bare room. Two worn bullock-trunks, a leather water-bottle, a tin ice-box, and his pet saddle sewed up in sacking were piled at the door, and the Club secretary's receipt for last month's bill was under his pillow. His orders came next morning, and with them an unofficial telegram from Sir James Hawkins, who did not forget good men, bidding him report himself with all speed at some unpronounceable place fifteen hundred miles to the south, for the famine was sore in the land, and white men were needed.

A pink and fattish youth arrived in the red-hot noonday whimpering a little at fate and famines, which never allowed any one three months' peace. He was Scott's successor—another cog in the machinery, moved forward behind his fellow, whose services, as the official announcement ran, 'were placed at the disposal of the Madras Government for famine duty until further orders.' Scott handed over the funds in his charge, showed him the coolest corner in the office, warned him against excess of zeal, and, as twilight fell, departed from the Club in a hired carriage with his faithful body-servant, Faiz Ullah, and a mound of disordered baggage atop, to catch the Southern Mail at the loopholed and bastioned railway-station. The heat from the thick brick walls struck him across the face as if it had been a hot towel, and he reflected that there were at least five nights and four days of travel before him. Faiz Ullah, used to the chances of service, plunged into the crowd on the stone platform, while Scott, a black cheroot between his teeth, waited till his compartment should be set away. A dozen native policemen, with their rifles and bundles, shouldered into the press of Punjabi farmers, Sikh craftsmen, and greasy-locked Afreedee pedlars, escorting with all pomp Martyn's uniform-case, water-bottles, ice-box, and bedding-roll. They saw Faiz Ullah's lifted hand, and steered for it.

'My Sahib and your Sahib,' said Faiz Ullah to Martyn's man, 'will travel together. Thou and I, O brother, will thus secure the servants' places close by, and because of our masters' authority none will dare to disturb us.'

When Faiz Ullah reported all things ready, Scott settled down coatless and bootless on the broad leather-covered bunk. The heat under the iron-arched roof of the station might have been anything over a hundred degrees. At the last moment Martyn entered, hot and dripping.

'Don't swear,' said Scott, lazily; 'it's too late to change your carriage; and we'll divide the ice.'

'What are you doing here?' said the policeman.

'Lent to the Madras Government, same as you. By Jove, it's a bender of a night! Are you taking any of your men down?'

'A dozen. Suppose I'll have to superintend relief distributions. Didn't know you were under orders too.'

'I didn't till after I left you last night. Raines had the news first. My orders came this morning. McEuan relieved me at four, and I got off at once. Shouldn't wonder if it wouldn't be a good thing—this famine—if we come through it alive.'

'Jimmy ought to put you and me to work together,' said Martyn; and then, after a pause: 'My sister's here.'

'Good business,' said Scott, heartily. 'Going to get off at Umballa, I suppose, and go up to Simla. Who'll she stay with there?'

'No-o; that's just the trouble of it. She's going down with me.'

Scott sat bolt upright under the oil lamp as the train jolted past Tarn-Taran station. 'What! You don't mean you couldn't afford——'

'Oh, I'd have scraped up the money somehow.'

'You might have come to me, to begin with,' said Scott stiffly; 'we aren't altogether strangers.'

'Well, you needn't be stuffy about it. I might, but—you don't know my sister. I've been explaining and exhorting and entreating and commanding and all the rest of it all day—lost my temper since seven this morning, and haven't got it back yet—but she wouldn't hear of any compromise. A woman's entitled to travel with her husband if she wants to, and William says she's on the same footing. You see, we've been together all our lives, more or less, since my people died. It isn't as if she were an ordinary sister.'

'All the sisters I've ever heard of would have stayed where they were well off.'

'She's as clever as a man, confound her,' Martyn went on. 'She broke up the bungalow over my head while I was talking at her. 'Settled the whole *subchiz* in three hours—servants, horses, and all. I didn't get my orders till nine.'

'Jimmy Hawkins won't be pleased,' said Scott. 'A famine's no place for a woman.'

'Mrs. Jim—I mean Lady Jim's in camp with him. At any rate, she says she will look after my sister. William wired down to her on her own responsibility, asking if she could come, and knocked the ground from under me by showing me her answer.'

Scott laughed aloud. 'If she can do that she can take care of herself, and Mrs. Jim won't let her run into any mischief. There aren't many women, sisters or wives, who would walk into a famine with their eyes open. It isn't as if she didn't know what these things mean. She was through the Jaloo cholera last year.'

The train stopped at Amritsar, and Scott went back to the ladies' compartment, immediately behind their carriage. William, a cloth riding-cap on her curls, nodded affably.

'Come in and have some tea,' she said. 'Best thing in the world for heat-apoplexy.'

'Do I look as if I were going to have heat-apoplexy?'

'Never can tell,' said William, wisely. 'It's always best to be ready.'

She had arranged her belongings with the knowledge of an old campaigner. A felt-covered water-bottle hung in the draught of one of the shuttered windows; a tea-set of Russian china, packed in a wadded basket, stood ready on the seat; and a travelling spirit-lamp was clamped against the woodwork above it.

William served them generously, in large cups, hot tea, which saves the veins of the neck from swelling inopportunely on a hot night. It was characteristic of the girl that, her plan of action once settled, she asked for no comments on it. Life with men who had a great deal of work to do, and very little time to do it in, had taught her the wisdom of effacing as well as of fending for herself. She did not by word or deed suggest that she would be useful, comforting, or beautiful in their travels, but continued about her business serenely: put the cups back without clatter when tea was ended, and made cigarettes for her guests.

'This time last night,' said Scott, 'we didn't expect—er—this kind of thing, did we?'

'I've learned to expect anything,' said William. 'You know, in our service, we live at the end of the telegraph; but, of course, this ought to be a good thing for us all, departmentally—if we live.'

'It knocks us out of the running in our own Province,' Scott replied, with equal gravity. 'I hoped to be put on the Luni Protective Works this cold weather; but there's no saying how long the famine may keep us.'

'Hardly beyond October, I should think,' said Martyn. 'It will be ended, one way or the other, then.'

'And we've nearly a week of this,' said William. 'Shan't we be dusty when it's over?'

For a night and a day they knew their surroundings; and for a night and a day, skirting the edge of the great Indian Desert on a narrow-gauge line, they remembered how in the days of their apprenticeship they had come by that road from Bombay. Then the languages in which the names of the stations were written changed, and they launched south into a foreign land, where the very smells were new. Many long and heavily-laden grain trains were in front of them, and they could feel the hand of Jimmy Hawkins from far off. They waited in extemporised sidings blocked by processions of empty trucks returning to the north, and were coupled on to slow, crawling trains, and dropped at midnight, Heaven knew where; but it was furiously hot; and they walked to and fro among sacks, and dogs howled.

Then they came to an India more strange to them than to the untravelled Englishman—the flat, red India of palm-tree, palmyra-palm, and rice, the India of the picture-books, of *Little Henry and His Bearer*—all dead and dry in the baking heat. They had left the incessant passenger-traffic of the north and west far and far behind them. Here the people crawled to the side of the train, holding their little ones in their arms; and a loaded truck would be left behind, men and women clustering round and above it like ants by spilled honey. Once in the twilight they saw on a dusty plain a regiment of little brown men, each bearing a body over his shoulder; and when the train stopped to leave yet another truck, they perceived that the burdens were not corpses, but only foodless folk picked up beside their dead oxen by a corps of Irregular troops. Now they met more white men, here one and there two, whose tents stood close to the line, and who came armed with written authorities and angry words to cut off a truck. They were too busy to do more than nod at Scott and Martyn, and stare curiously at William, who could do nothing except make tea, and watch how her men staved off the rush of wailing, walking skeletons, putting them down three at a time in heaps, with their own hands uncoupling the marked trucks, or taking receipts from the hollow-eyed, weary white men, who spoke another argot than theirs.

They ran out of ice, out of soda-water, and out of tea; for they were six days and seven nights on the road, and it seemed to them like seven times seven years.

At last, in a dry, hot dawn, in a land of death, lit by long red fires of railway sleepers, where they were burning the dead, they came to their destination, and were met by Jim Hawkins, the Head of the Famine, unshaven, unwashed, but cheery, and entirely in command of affairs.

Martyn, he decreed, then and there, was to live on trains till further orders; was to go back with empty trucks, filling them with starving people as he found them, and dropping them at a Famine-camp on the edge of the Eight Districts. He would pick up supplies and return, and his constables would guard the loaded grain-cars, also picking up people, and would drop them at a camp a hundred miles south. Scott—Hawkins was very glad to see Scott again—would, that same hour, take charge of a convoy of bullock-carts, and would go south, feeding as he went, to yet another famine-camp, far from the rail, where he would leave his starving—there would be no lack of starving on the route—and wait for orders by telegraph. Generally, Scott was in all small things to do what he thought best.

William bit her underlip. There was no one in the wide world like her one brother, but Martyn's orders gave him no discretion. She came out, masked with dust from head to foot, a horse-shoe wrinkle on her forehead, put there by much thinking during the past week, but as self-possessed as ever. Mrs. Jim—who should have been Lady Jim, but that no one remembered to call her aright—took possession of her with a little gasp.

'Oh, I'm so glad you're here,' she almost sobbed. 'You oughtn't to, of course, but there—there isn't another woman in the place, and we must help each other, you know; and we've all the wretched people and the little babies they are selling.'

'I've seen some,' said William.

'Isn't it ghastly? I've bought twenty; they're in our camp; but won't you have something to eat first? We've more than ten people can do here; and I've got a horse for you. Oh, I'm so glad you've come! You're a Punjabi too, you know.'

'Steady, Lizzie,' said Hawkins, over his shoulder. 'We'll look after you, Miss Martyn. Sorry I can't ask you to breakfast, Martyn. You'll have to eat as you go. Leave two of your men to help Scott. These poor devils can't stand up to load carts. Saunders' (this to the engine-driver, half asleep in the cab), 'back down and get those empties away. You've "line clear" to Anundrapillay; they'll give you orders north of that. Scott, load up your carts from that B. P. P. truck, and be off as soon as you can. The Eurasian in the pink shirt is your interpreter and guide. You'll find an apothecary of sorts tied to the yoke of the second waggon. He's been trying to bolt; you'll have to look after him. Lizzie, drive Miss Martyn to camp, and tell them to send the red horse down here for me.'

Scott, with Faiz Ullah and two policemen, was already busy on the carts, backing them up to the truck and unbolting the sideboards quietly, while the others pitched in the bags of millet and wheat. Hawkins watched him for as long as it took to fill one cart.

'That's a good man,' he said. 'If all goes well I shall work him—hard.' This was Jim Hawkins's notion of the highest compliment one human being could pay another.

An hour later Scott was under way; the apothecary threatening him with the penalties of the law for that he, a member of the Subordinate Medical Department, had been coerced and bound against his will and all laws governing the liberty of the subject; the pink-shirted Eurasian begging leave to see his mother, who happened to be dying some three miles away: 'Only verree, verree short leave of absence, and will presently return, sar——'; the two constables, armed with staves, bringing up the rear; and Faiz Ullah, a Mohammedan's contempt for all Hindus and foreigners in every line of his face, explaining to the drivers that though Scott Sahib was a man to be feared on all fours, he, Faiz Ullah, was Authority itself.

The procession creaked past Hawkins's camp—three stained tents under a clump of dead trees; behind them the famine-shed where a crowd of hopeless ones tossed their arms around the cooking-kettles.

'Wish to Heaven William had kept out of it,' said Scott to himself, after a glance. 'We'll have cholera, sure as a gun, when the Rains come.'

But William seemed to have taken kindly to the operations of the Famine Code, which, when famine is declared, supersede the workings of the ordinary law. Scott saw her, the centre of a mob of weeping women, in a calico riding-habit and a blue-grey felt hat with a gold pugaree.

'I want fifty rupees, please. I forgot to ask Jack before he went away. Can you lend it me? It's for condensed milk for the babies,' said she.

Scott took the money from his belt, and handed it over without a word. 'For goodness' sake take care of yourself,' he said.

'Oh, I shall be all right. We ought to get the milk in two days. By the way, the orders are, I was to tell you, that you're to take one of Sir Jim's horses. There's a grey Cabuli here that I thought would be just your style, so I've said you'd take him. Was that right?'

'That's awfully good of you. We can't either of us talk much about style, I'm afraid.'

Scott was in a weather-stained drill shooting-kit, very white at the seams and a little frayed at the wrists. William regarded him thoughtfully, from his pith helmet to his greased ankle-boots. 'You look very nice, I think. Are you sure you've everything you'll need—quinine, chlorodyne, and so on?'

'Think so,' said Scott, patting three or four of his shooting-pockets as the horse was led up, and he mounted and rode alongside his convoy.

'Good-bye,' he cried.

'Good-bye, and good luck,' said William. 'I'm awfully obliged for the money.' She turned on a spurred heel and disappeared into the tent, while the carts pushed on past the famine-sheds, past the roaring lines of the thick, fat fires, down to the baked Gehenna of the south.

PART II

So let us melt and make no noise,
 No tear-floods nor sigh-tempests move;
'Twere profanation of our joys
 To tell the laity our love.
 A Valediction.

It was punishing work, even though he travelled by night and camped by day; but within the limits of his vision there was no man whom Scott could call master. He was as free as Jimmy Hawkins—freer, in fact, for the Government held the Head of the Famine tied neatly to a telegraph wire, and if Jimmy had ever regarded telegrams seriously, the death-rate of that famine would have been much higher than it was.

At the end of a few days' crawling Scott learned something of the size of the India which he served; and it astonished him. His carts, as you know, were loaded with wheat, millet, and barley, good food-grains needing only a little grinding. But the people to whom he brought the life-giving stuffs were rice-eaters. They knew how to hull rice in their mortars, but they knew nothing of the heavy stone querns of the North, and less of the material that the white man conveyed so laboriously. They clamoured for rice—unhusked paddy, such as they were accustomed to—and, when they found that there was none, broke away weeping from the sides of the cart. What was the use of these strange hard grains that choked their throats? They would die. And then and there were many of them kept their word. Others took their allowance, and bartered enough millet to feed a man through a week for a few handfuls of rotten rice saved by some less unfortunate. A few put their shares into the rice-mortars, pounded it, and made a paste with foul water; but they were very few. Scott understood dimly that many people in the India of the South ate rice, as a rule, but he had spent his service in a grain Province, had seldom seen rice in the blade or the ear, and least of all would have believed that, in time of deadly need, men would die at arm's length of plenty, sooner than touch food they did not know. In vain the interpreters interpreted; in vain his two policemen showed by vigorous pantomime what should be done. The starving crept away to their bark and weeds, grubs, leaves, and clay, and left the open sacks untouched. But sometimes the women laid their phantoms of children at Scott's feet, looking back as they staggered away.

Faiz Ullah opined it was the will of God that these foreigners should die, and therefore it remained only to give orders to burn the dead. None the less there was no reason why the Sahib should lack his comforts, and Faiz Ullah, a campaigner of experience, had picked up a few lean goats and had added them to the procession. That they might give milk for the morning meal, he was feeding them on the good grain that these imbeciles rejected. 'Yes,' said Faiz Ullah; 'if the Sahib thought fit, a little milk might be given to some of the babies'; but, as the Sahib well knew, babies were cheap, and, for his own part, Faiz Ullah held that there was no Government order as to babies. Scott spoke forcefully to Faiz Ullah and the two policemen, and bade them capture goats where they could find them. This they most joyfully did, for it was a recreation, and many ownerless goats were driven in. Once fed, the poor brutes were willing enough to follow the carts, and a few days' good food–food such as human beings died for lack of–set them in milk again.

'But I am no goatherd,' said Faiz Ullah. 'It is against my *izzat* [my honour].'

'When we cross the Bias River again we will talk of *izzat,*' Scott replied. 'Till that day thou and the policemen shall be sweepers to the camp, if I give the order.'

'Thus, then, it is done,' grunted Faiz Ullah, 'if the Sahib will have it so'; and he showed how a goat should be milked, while Scott stood over him.

'Now we will feed them,' said Scott; 'thrice a day we will feed them'; and he bowed his back to the milking, and took a horrible cramp.

When you have to keep connection unbroken between a restless mother of kids and a baby who is at the point of death, you suffer in all your system. But the babies were fed. Morning, noon and evening Scott would solemnly lift them out one by one from their nest of gunny-bags under the cart-tilts. There were always many who could do no more than breathe, and the milk was dropped into their toothless mouths drop by drop, with due pauses when they choked. Each morning, too, the goats were fed; and since they would straggle without a leader, and since the natives were hirelings, Scott was forced to give up riding, and pace slowly at the head of his flocks, accommodating his step to their weaknesses. All this was sufficiently absurd, and he felt the absurdity keenly; but at least he was saving life, and when the women saw that their children did not die, they made shift to eat a little of the strange foods, and crawled after the carts, blessing the master of the goats.

'Give the women something to live for,' said Scott to himself, as he sneezed in the dust of a hundred little feet, 'and they'll hang on somehow. But this beats William's condensed-milk trick all to pieces. I shall never live it down, though.'

He reached his destination very slowly, found that a rice-ship had come in from Burma, and that stores of paddy were available; found also an overworked Englishman in charge of the shed, and, loading the carts, set back to cover the ground he had already passed. He left some of the children and half his goats at the famine-shed. For this he was not thanked by the Englishman, who had already more stray babies than he knew what to do with. Scott's back was suppled to stooping now, and he went on with his wayside ministrations in addition to distributing the paddy. More babies and more goats were added unto him; but now some of the babies wore rags, and beads round their wrists or necks. '*That,*' said the interpreter, as though Scott did not know, 'signifies that their mothers hope in eventual contingency to resume them offeecially.'

'The sooner the better,' said Scott; but at the same time he marked, with the pride of ownership, how this or that little Ramaswamy was putting on flesh like a bantam. As the paddy-carts were emptied he headed for Hawkins's camp by the railway, timing his arrival to fit in with the dinner-hour, for it was long since he had eaten at a cloth. He had no desire to make any dramatic entry, but an accident of the sunset ordered it that, when he had taken off his helmet to get the evening breeze, the low light should fall across his forehead, and he could not see what was before him; while one waiting at the tent door beheld, with new eyes, a young man, beautiful as Paris, a god in a halo of golden dust, walking slowly at the head of his flocks, while at his knee ran small naked Cupids. But she laughed—William in a slate-coloured blouse, laughed consumedly till Scott, putting the best face he could upon the matter, halted his armies and bade her admire the kindergarten. It was an unseemly sight, but the proprieties had been left ages ago, with the tea-party at Amritsar Station, fifteen hundred miles to the northward.

'They are coming on nicely,' said William. 'We've only five-and-twenty here now. The women are beginning to take them away again.'

'Are you in charge of the babies, then?'

'Yes—Mrs. Jim and I. We didn't think of goats, though. We've been trying condensed milk and water.'

'Any losses?'

'More than I care to think of,' said William, with a shudder. 'And you?'

Scott said nothing. There had been many little burials along his route—many mothers who had wept when they did not find again the children they had trusted to the care of the Government.

Then Hawkins came out carrying a razor, at which Scott looked hungrily, for he had a beard that he did not love. And when they sat down to dinner in the tent he told his tale in few words, as it might have been an official report. Mrs. Jim snuffled from time to time, and Jim bowed his head judicially; but William's grey eyes were on the clean-shaven face, and it was to her that Scott seemed to speak.

'Good for the Pauper Province!' said William, her chin in her hand, as she leaned forward among the wine-glasses. Her cheeks had fallen in, and the scar on her forehead was more prominent than ever, but the well-turned neck rose roundly as a column from the ruffle of the blouse which was the accepted evening-dress in camp.

'It was awfully absurd at times,' said Scott. 'You see, I don't know much about milking or babies. They'll chaff my head off, if the tale goes north.'

'Let 'em,' said William, haughtily. 'We've all done coolie-work since we came. I know Jack has.' This was to Hawkins's address, and the big man smiled blandly.

'Your brother's a highly efficient officer, William,' said he, 'and I've done him the honour of treating him as he deserves. Remember, I write the confidential reports.'

'Then you must say that William's worth her weight in gold,' said Mrs. Jim. 'I don't know what we should have done without her. She has been everything to us.' She dropped her hand upon William's, which was rough with much handling of reins, and William patted it softly. Jim beamed on the company. Things were going well with his world. Three of his more grossly incompetent men had died, and their places had been filled by their betters. Every day brought the Rains nearer. They had put out the famine in five of the Eight Districts, and, after all, the death-rate had not been too heavy—things considered. He looked Scott over carefully, as an ogre looks over a man, and rejoiced in his thews and iron-hard condition.

'He's just the least bit in the world tucked up,' said Jim to himself, 'but he can do two men's work yet.' Then he was aware that Mrs. Jim was telegraphing to him, and according to the domestic code the message ran: 'A clear case. Look at them!'

He looked and listened. All that William was saying was: 'What can you expect of a country where they call a *bhistee* [a water-carrier] a *tunni-cutch?*' and all that Scott answered was: 'I shall be precious glad to get back to the Club. Save me a dance at the Christmas ball, won't you?'

'It's a far cry from here to the Lawrence Hall,' said Jim. 'Better turn in early, Scott. It's paddy-carts to-morrow; you'll begin loading at five.'

'Aren't you going to give Mr. Scott one day's rest?'

'Wish I could, Lizzie. 'Fraid I can't. As long as he can stand up we must use him.'

'Well, I've had one Europe evening at least. . . . By Jove, I'd nearly forgotten! What do I do about those babies of mine?'

'Leave them here,' said William,—'we are in charge of that—and as many goats as you can spare. I must learn how to milk now.'

'If you care to get up early enough to-morrow I'll show you. I have to milk, you see; and, by the way, half of 'em have beads and things round their necks. You must be careful not to take 'em off, in case the mothers turn up.'

'You forget I've had some experience here.'

'I hope to goodness you won't overdo it.' Scott's voice was unguarded.

'I'll take care of her,' said Mrs. Jim, telegraphing hundred-word messages as she carried William off, while Jim gave Scott his orders for the coming campaign. It was very late—nearly nine o'clock.

'Jim, you're a brute,' said his wife, that night; and the Head of the Famine chuckled.

'Not a bit of it, dear. I remember doing the first Jandiala Settlement for the sake of a girl in a crinoline; and she was slender, Lizzie. I've never done as good a piece of work since. *He*'ll work like a demon.'

'But you might have given him one day.'

'And let things come to a head now? No, dear; it's their happiest time.'

'I don't believe either of the dears know what's the matter with them. Isn't it beautiful? Isn't it lovely?'

'Getting up at three to learn to milk, bless her heart! Ye gods, why must we grow old and fat?'

'She's a darling. She has done more work under me——'

'Under *you!* The day after she came she was in charge and you were her subordinate, and you've stayed there ever since. She manages you almost as well as you manage me.'

'She doesn't, and that's why I love her. She's as direct as a man—as her brother.'

'Her brother's weaker than she is. He's always coming to me for orders; but he's honest and a glutton for work. I confess I'm rather fond of William, and if I had a daughter——'

The talk ended there. Far away in the Derajat was a child's grave more than twenty years old, and neither Jim nor his wife spoke of it any more.

'All the same, you're responsible,' Jim added, after a moment's silence.

'Bless 'em!' said Mrs. Jim sleepily.

Before the stars paled, Scott, who slept in an empty cart, waked and went about his work in silence; it seemed at that hour unkind to rouse Faiz Ullah and the interpreter. His head being close to the ground, he did not hear William till she stood over him in the dingy old riding-habit, her eyes still heavy with sleep, a cup of tea and a piece of toast in her hands. There was a baby on the ground, squirming on a piece of blanket, and a six-year-old child peered over Scott's shoulder.

'Hai, you little rip,' said Scott, 'how the deuce do you expect to get your rations if you aren't quiet?'

A cool white hand steadied the brat, who forthwith choked as the milk gurgled into his mouth.

'Mornin',' said the milker. 'You've no notion how these little fellows can wriggle.'

'Oh yes, I have.' She whispered, because the world was asleep. 'Only I feed them with a spoon or a rag. Yours are fatter than mine. . . . And you've been doing this day after day, twice a day?' The voice was almost lost.

'Yes; it was absurd. Now you try,' he said, giving place to the girl. 'Look out! A goat's not a cow.'

The goat protested against the amateur, and there was a scuffle, in which Scott snatched up the baby. Then it was all to do over again, and William laughed softly and merrily. She managed, however, to feed two babies, and a third.

'Don't the little beggars take it well!' said Scott. 'I trained 'em.'

They were very busy and interested, when, lo! it was broad daylight, and before they knew, the camp was awake, and they kneeled among the goats, surprised by the day, both flushed to the temples. Yet all the round world rolling up out of the darkness might have heard and seen all that had passed between them.

'Oh,' said William, unsteadily, snatching up the tea and toast. 'I had this made for you. It's stone-cold now. I thought you mightn't have anything ready so early. Better not drink it. It's—it's stone-cold.'

'That's awfully kind of you. It's just right. It's awfully good of you, really. I'll leave my kids and goats with you and Mrs. Jim; and, of course, any one in camp can show you about the milking.'

'Of course,' said William; and she grew pinker and pinker and statelier and more stately, as she strode back to her tent, fanning herself vigorously with the saucer.

There were shrill lamentations through the camp when the elder children saw their nurse move off without them. Faiz Ullah unbent so far as to jest with the policemen, and Scott turned purple with shame because Hawkins, already in the saddle, roared.

A child escaped from the care of Mrs. Jim, and, running like a rabbit, clung to Scott's boot, William pursuing with long, easy strides.

'I will not go—I will not go!' shrieked the child, twining his feet round Scott's ankle. 'They will kill me here. I do not know these people.'

'I say,' said Scott, in broken Tamil, 'I say, she will do you no harm. Go with her and be well fed.'

'Come!' said William, panting, with a wrathful glance at Scott, who stood helpless and, as it were, hamstrung.

'Go back,' said Scott quickly to William. 'I'll send the little chap over in a minute.'

The tone of authority had its effect, but in a way Scott did not exactly intend. The boy loosened his grasp, and said with gravity, 'I did not know the woman was thine. I will go.' Then he cried to his companions, a mob of three-, four-, and five-year-olds waiting on the success of his venture ere they stampeded: 'Go back and eat. It is our man's woman. She will obey his orders.'

Jim collapsed where he sat; Faiz Ullah and the two policemen grinned; and Scott's orders to the cartmen flew like hail.

'That is the custom of the Sahibs when truth is told in their presence,' said Faiz Ullah. 'The time comes that I must seek new service. Young wives, especially such as speak our language and have knowledge of the ways of the Police, make great trouble for honest butlers in the matter of weekly accounts.'

What William thought of it all she did not say, but when her brother, ten days later, came to camp for orders, and heard of Scott's performances, he said, laughing: 'Well, that settles it. He'll be *Bakri* Scott to the end of his days' [*Bakri,* in the northern vernacular, means a goat]. 'What a lark! I'd have given a month's pay to have seen him nursing famine babies. I fed some with *conjee* [rice-water], but that was all right.'

'It's perfectly disgusting,' said his sister, with blazing eyes. 'A man does something like—like that—and all you other men think of is to give him an absurd nickname, and then you laugh and think it's funny.'

'Ah,' said Mrs. Jim, sympathetically.

'Well, *you* can't talk, William. You christened little Miss Demby the Button-quail last cold weather; you know you did. India's the land of nicknames.'

'That's different,' William replied. 'She was only a girl, and she hadn't done anything except walk like a quail, and she *does.* But it isn't fair to make fun of a man.'

'Scott won't care,' said Martyn. 'You can't get a rise out of old Scotty. I've been trying for eight years, and you've only known him for three. How does he look?'

'He looks very well,' said William, and went away with a flushed cheek. '*Bakri* Scott, indeed!' Then she laughed to herself, for she knew the country of her service. 'But it will be *Bakri* all the same'; and she repeated it under her breath several times slowly, whispering it into favour.

When he returned to his duties on the railway, Martyn spread the name far and wide among his associates, so that Scott met it as he led his paddy-carts to war. The natives believed it to be some English title of honour, and the cart-drivers used it in all simplicity till Faiz Ullah, who did not approve of foreign japes, broke their heads. There was very little time for milking now, except at the big camps, where Jim had extended Scott's idea, and was feeding large flocks on the useless northern grains. Enough paddy had come into the Eight Districts to hold the people safe, if it were only distributed quickly; and for that purpose no one was better than the big Canal officer, who never lost his temper, never gave an unnecessary order, and never questioned an order given. Scott pressed on, saving his cattle, washing their galled necks daily, so that no time should be lost on the road; reported himself with his rice at the minor famine-sheds, unloaded, and went back light by forced night-march to the next distributing centre, to find Hawkins's unvarying telegram: 'Do it again.' And he did it again and again, and yet again, while Jim Hawkins, fifty miles away, marked off on a big map the tracks of his wheels gridironing the stricken lands. Others did well—Hawkins reported at the end that they all did well—but Scott was the most excellent, for he kept good coined rupees by him, and paid for his own cart-repairs on the spot, and ran to meet all sorts of unconsidered extras, trusting to be recouped later. Theoretically, the Government should have paid for every shoe and linchpin, for every hand employed in the loading; but Government vouchers cash themselves slowly, and intelligent and efficient clerks write at great length, contesting unauthorised expenditures of eight annas. The man who wishes to make his work a success must draw on his own bank-account of money or other things as he goes.

'I told you he'd work,' said Jimmy to his wife at the end of six weeks. 'He's been in sole charge of a couple of thousand men up north on the Mosuhl Canal for a year, and he gives one less trouble than young Martyn with his ten constables; and I'm morally certain—only Government doesn't recognise moral obligations—that he's spent about half his pay to grease his wheels. Look at this, Lizzie, for one week's work! Forty miles in two days with twelve carts; two days' halt building a famine-shed for young Rogers (Rogers ought to have built it himself, the idiot!). Then forty miles back again, loading six carts on the way, and distributing all Sunday. Then in the evening he pitches in a twenty-page demi-official to me, saying that the people where he is might be "advantageously employed on relief-work," and suggesting that he put 'em to work on some broken-down old reservoir he's discovered, so as to have a good water-supply when the Rains come. He thinks he can caulk the dam in a fortnight. Look at his marginal sketches—aren't they clear and good? I knew he was *pukka,* but I didn't know he was as *pukka* as this!'

'I must show these to William,' said Mrs. Jim. 'The child's wearing herself out among the babies.'

'Not more than you are, dear. Well, another two months ought to see us out of the wood. I'm sorry it's not in my power to recommend you for a V.C.'

William sat late in her tent that night, reading through page after page of the square handwriting, patting the sketches of proposed repairs to the reservoir, and wrinkling her eyebrows over the columns of figures of estimated water-supply.

'And he finds time to do all this,' she cried to herself, 'and . . . well, I also was present. I've saved one or two babies.'

She dreamed for the twentieth time of the god in the golden dust, and woke refreshed to feed loathsome black children, scores of them, wastrels picked up by the wayside, their bones almost breaking their skin, terrible and covered with sores.

Scott was not allowed to leave his cart-work, but his letter was duly forwarded to the Government, and he had the consolation, not rare in India, of knowing that another man was reaping where he had sown. That also was discipline profitable to the soul.

'He's much too good to waste on canals,' said Jimmy. 'Any one can oversee coolies. You needn't be angry, William: he can—but I need my pearl among bullock-drivers, and I've transferred him to the Khanda district, where he'll have it all to do over again. He should be marching now.'

'He's *not* a coolie,' said William, furiously. 'He ought to be doing his regulation work.'

'He's the best man in his service, and that's saying a good deal; but if you *must* use razors to cut grindstones, why, I prefer the best cutlery.'

'Isn't it almost time we saw him again?' said Mrs. Jim. 'I'm sure the poor boy hasn't had a respectable meal for a month. He probably sits on a cart and eats sardines with his fingers.'

'All in good time, dear. Duty before decency—wasn't it Mr. Chucks said that?'

'No; it was Midshipman Easy,' William laughed. 'I sometimes wonder how it will feel to dance or listen to a band again, or sit under a roof. I can't believe that I ever wore a ball-frock in my life.'

'One minute,' said Mrs. Jim, who was thinking. 'If he goes to Khanda, he passes within five miles of us. Of course he'll ride in.'

'Oh no, he won't,' said William.

'How do you know, dear?'

'It'll take him off his work. He won't have time.'

'He'll make it,' said Mrs. Jim, with a twinkle.

'It depends on his own judgment. There's absolutely no reason why he shouldn't, if he thinks fit,' said Jim.

'He won't see fit,' William replied, without sorrow or emotion. 'It wouldn't be him if he did.'

'One certainly gets to know people rather well in times like these,' said Jim, drily; but William's face was serene as ever, and, as she prophesied, Scott did not appear.

The Rains fell at last, late, but heavily; and the dry, gashed earth was red mud, and servants killed snakes in the camp, where everyone was weather-bound for a fortnight—all except Hawkins, who took horse and splashed about in the wet, rejoicing. Now the Government decreed that seed-grain should be distributed to the people as well as advances of money for the purchase of new oxen; and the white men were doubly worked for this new duty, while William skipped from brick to brick laid down on the trampled mud, and dosed her charges with warming medicines that made them rub their little round stomachs; and the milch-goats throve on the rank grass. There was never a word from Scott in the Khanda district, away to the south-east, except the regular telegraphic report to Hawkins. The rude country roads had disappeared; his drivers were half mutinous; one of Martyn's loaned policemen had died of cholera; and Scott was taking thirty grains of quinine a day to fight the fever that comes if one works hard in heavy rain; but those were things he did not consider necessary to report. He was, as usual, working from a base of supplies on a railway line, to cover a circle of fifteen miles radius, and since full loads were impossible, he took quarter-loads, and toiled four times as hard by consequence; for he did not choose to risk an epidemic which might have grown uncontrollable by assembling villagers in thousands at the relief-sheds. It was cheaper to take Government bullocks, work them to death, and leave them to the crows in the wayside sloughs.

That was the time when eight years of clean living and hard condition told, though a man's head were ringing like a bell from the cinchona, and the earth swayed under his feet when he stood and under his bed when he slept. If Hawkins had seen fit to make him a bullock-driver, that, he thought, was entirely Hawkins's own affair. There were men in the North who would know what he had done; men of thirty years' service in his own Department who would say that it was 'not half bad'; and above, immeasurably above all men of all grades, there was William in the thick of the fight, who would approve because she understood. He had so trained his mind that it would hold fast to the mechanical routine of the day, though his own voice sounded strange in his own ears, and his hands, when he wrote, grew large as pillows or small as peas at the end of his wrists. That steadfastness bore his body to the telegraph-office at the railway-station, and dictated a telegram to Hawkins, saying that the Khanda district was, in his judgment, now safe, and he 'waited further orders.'

The Madrassee telegraph-clerk did not approve of a large, gaunt man falling over him in a dead faint, not so much because of the weight, as because of the names and blows that Faiz Ullah dealt him when he found the body rolled under a bench. Then Faiz Ullah took blankets and quilts and coverlets where he found them, and lay down under them at his master's side, and bound his arms with a tent-rope, and filled him with a horrible stew of herbs, and set the policeman to fight him when he wished to escape from the intolerable heat of his coverings, and shut the door of the telegraph-office to keep out the curious for two nights and one day; and when a light engine came down the line, and Hawkins kicked in the door, Scott hailed him weakly, but in a natural voice, and Faiz Ullah stood back and took all the credit.

'For two nights, Heaven-born, he was *pagal,*' said Faiz Ullah. 'Look at my nose, and consider the eye of the policeman. He beat us with his bound hands; but we sat upon him, Heaven-born, and though his words were *tez,* we sweated him. Heaven-born, never has been such a sweat! He is weaker now than a child; but the fever has gone out of him, by the grace of God. There remains only my nose and the eye of the constabeel. Sahib, shall I ask for my dismissal because my Sahib has beaten me?' And Faiz Ullah laid his long thin hand carefully on Scott's chest to be sure that the fever was all gone, ere he went out to open tinned soups and discourage such as laughed at his swelled nose.

'The district's all right,' Scott whispered. 'It doesn't make any difference. You got my wire? I shall be fit in a week. 'Can't understand how it happened. I shall be fit in a few days.'

'You're coming into camp with us,' said Hawkins.

'But look here—but——'

'It's all over except the shouting. We shan't need you Punjabis any more. On my honour, we shan't. Martyn goes back in a few weeks; Arbuthnot's returned already; Ellis and Clay are putting the last touches to a new feeder-line the Government's built as relief-work. Morten's dead—he was a Bengal man, though; you wouldn't know him. 'Pon my word, you and Will—Miss Martyn—seem to have come through it as well as anybody.'

'Oh, how is she?' The voice went up and down as he spoke.

'She was in great form when I left her. The Roman Catholic Missions are adopting the unclaimed babies to turn them into little priests; the Basel Mission is taking some, and the mothers are taking the rest. You should hear the little beggars howl when they're sent away from William. She's pulled down a bit, but so are we all. Now, when do you suppose you'll be able to move?'

'I can't come into camp in this state. I won't,' he replied pettishly.

'Well, you *are* rather a sight, but from what I gathered there it seemed to me they'd be glad to see you under any conditions. I'll look over your work here, if you like, for a couple of days, and you can pull yourself together while Faiz Ullah feeds you up.'

Scott could walk dizzily by the time Hawkins's inspection was ended, and he flushed all over when Jim said of his work in the district that it was 'not half bad,' and volunteered, further, that he had considered Scott his right-hand man through the famine, and would feel it his duty to say as much officially.

So they came back by rail to the old camp; but there were no crowds near it, the long fires in the trenches were dead and black, and the famine-sheds stood almost empty.

'You see!' said Jim. 'There isn't much more for us to do. Better ride up and see the wife. They've pitched a tent for you. Dinner's at seven. I'll see you then.'

Riding at a foot-pace, Faiz Ullah by his stirrup, Scott came to William in the brown-calico riding-habit, sitting at the dining-tent door, her hands in her lap, white as ashes, thin and worn, with no lustre in her hair. There did not seem to be any Mrs. Jim on the horizon, and all that William could say was: 'My word, how pulled down you look!'

'I've had a touch of fever. You don't look very well yourself.'

'Oh, I'm fit enough. We've stamped it out. I suppose you know?'

Scott nodded. 'We shall all be returned in a few weeks. Hawkins told me.'

'Before Christmas, Mrs. Jim says. Shan't you be glad to go back? I can smell the wood-smoke already'; William sniffed. 'We shall be in time for all the Christmas doings. I don't suppose even the Punjab Government would be base enough to transfer Jack till the new year?'

'It seems hundreds of years ago—the Punjab and all that—doesn't it? Are you glad you came?'

'Now it's all over, yes. It has been ghastly here. You knew we had to sit still and do nothing, and Sir Jim was away so much.'

'Do nothing! How did you get on with the milking?'

'I managed it somehow—after you taught me.'

Then the talk stopped with an almost audible jar. Still no Mrs. Jim.

'That reminds me I owe you fifty rupees for the condensed milk. I thought perhaps you'd be coming here when you were transferred to the Khanda district, and I could pay you then; but you didn't.'

'I passed within five miles of the camp. It was in the middle of a march, you see, and the carts were breaking down every few minutes and I couldn't get 'em over the ground till ten o'clock that night. But I wanted to come awfully. You knew I did, didn't you?'

'I—believe—I—did,' said William, facing him with level eyes. She was no longer white.

'Did you understand?'

'Why you didn't ride in? Of course I did.'

'Why?'

'Because you couldn't, of course. I knew that.'

'Did you care?'

'If you had come in—but I knew you wouldn't—but if you *had,* I should have cared a great deal. You know I should.'

'Thank God I didn't! Oh, but I wanted to! I couldn't trust myself to ride in front of the carts, because I kept edging 'em over here, don't you know?'

'I knew you wouldn't,' said William, contentedly. 'Here's your fifty.'

Scott bent forward and kissed the hand that held the greasy notes. Its fellow patted him awkwardly but very tenderly on the head.

'And *you* knew, too, didn't you?' said William, in a new voice.

'No, on my honour, I didn't. I hadn't the—the cheek to expect anything of the kind, except . . . I say, were you out riding anywhere the day I passed by to Khanda?'

William nodded, and smiled after the manner of an angel surprised in a good deed.

'Then it was just a speck I saw of your habit in the——'

'Palm-grove on the Southern cart-road. I saw your helmet when you came up from the nullah by the temple—just enough to be sure that you were all right. D'you care?'

This time Scott did not kiss her hand, for they were in the dusk of the dining-tent, and, because William's knees were trembling under her, she had to sit down in the nearest chair, where she wept long and happily, her head on her arms; and when Scott imagined that it would be well to comfort her, she needing nothing of the kind, she ran to her own tent; and Scott went out into the world, and smiled upon it largely and idiotically. But when Faiz Ullah brought him a drink, he found it necessary to support one hand with the other, or the good whisky and soda would have been spilled abroad. There are fevers and fevers.

But it was worse—much worse—the strained, eye-shirking talk at dinner till the servants had withdrawn, and worst of all when Mrs. Jim, who had been on the edge of weeping from the soup down, kissed Scott and William, and they drank one whole bottle of champagne, hot, because there was no ice, and Scott and William sat outside the tent in the starlight till Mrs. Jim drove them in for fear of more fever.

Apropos of these things and some others William said: 'Being engaged is abominable, because, you see, one has no official position. We must be thankful that we've lots of things to do.'

'Things to do!' said Jim, when that was reported to him. 'They're neither of them any good any more. I can't get five hours' work a day out of Scott. He's in the clouds half the time.'

'Oh, but they're so beautiful to watch, Jimmy. It will break my heart when they go. Can't you do anything for him?'

'I've given the Government the impression—at least, I hope I have—that he personally conducted the entire famine. But all he wants is to get on to the Luni Canal Works, and William's just as bad. Have you ever heard 'em talking of barrage and aprons and waste water? It's their style of spooning, I suppose.'

Mrs. Jim smiled tenderly. 'Ah, that's in the intervals—bless 'em.'

And so Love ran about the camp unrebuked in broad daylight, while men picked up the pieces and put them neatly away of the Famine in the Eight Districts.

Morning brought the penetrating chill of the Northern December, the layers of wood-smoke, the dusty grey-blue of the tamarisks, the domes of ruined tombs, and all the smell of the white Northern plains, as the mail-train ran on to the mile-long Sutlej Bridge. William, wrapped in a *poshteen*—silk-embroidered sheepskin jacket trimmed with rough astrakhan—looked out with moist eyes and nostrils that dilated joyously. The South of pagodas and palm-trees, the over-populated Hindu South, was done with. Here was the land she knew and loved, and before her lay the good life she understood, among folk of her own caste and mind.

They were picking them up at almost every station now—men and women coming in for the Christmas Week, with racquets, with bundles of polo-sticks, with dear and bruised cricket-bats, with fox-terriers and saddles. The greater part of them wore jackets like William's, for the Northern cold is as little to be trifled with as the Northern heat. And William was among them and of them, her hands deep in her pockets, her collar turned up over her ears, stamping her feet on the platforms as she walked up and down to get warm, visiting from carriage to carriage, and everywhere being congratulated. Scott was with bachelors at the far end of the train, where they chaffed him mercilessly about feeding babies and milking goats; but from time to time he would stroll up to William's window, and murmur: 'Good enough, isn't it?' and William would answer with sighs of pure delight: 'Good enough, indeed.' The large open names of the home towns were good to listen to. Umballa, Ludhiana, Phillour, Jullundur, they rang like the coming marriage-bells in her ears, and William felt deeply and truly sorry for all strangers and outsiders—visitors, tourists, and those fresh-caught for the service of the country.

It was a glorious return, and when the bachelors gave the Christmas ball, William was, unofficially, you might say, the chief and honoured guest among the stewards, who could make things very pleasant for their friends. She and Scott danced nearly all the dances together, and sat out the rest in the big dark gallery overlooking the superb teak floor, where the uniforms blazed, and the spurs clinked, and the new frocks and four hundred dancers went round and round till the draped flags on the pillars flapped and bellied to the whirl of it.

About midnight half-a-dozen men who did not care for dancing came over from the Club to play 'Waits,' and—that was a surprise the stewards had arranged—before any one knew what had happened, the band stopped, and hidden voices broke into 'Good King Wenceslaus,' and William in the gallery hummed and beat time with her foot:

> Mark my footsteps well, my page,
> Tread thou in them boldly,
> Thou shalt find the winter's rage
> Freeze thy blood less coldly!

'Oh, I hope they are going to give us another! Isn't it pretty, coming out of the dark in that way? Look—look down. There's Mrs. Gregory wiping her eyes!'

'It's like home, rather,' said Scott. 'I remember——'

'H'sh! Listen!—dear.' And it began again:

> When shepherds watched their flocks by night—

'A-h-h!' said William, drawing closer to Scott.

> All seated on the ground,
> The Angel of the Lord came down,
> And glory shone around.
>
> 'Fear not,' said he (for mighty dread
> Had seized their troubled mind);
> 'Glad tidings of great joy I bring
> To you and all mankind.'

This time it was William that wiped her eyes.

'THEY'

ONE VIEW called me to another; one hill-top to its fellow, half across the county, and since I could answer at no more trouble than the snapping forward of a lever, I let the county flow under my wheels. The orchid-studded flats of the East gave way to the thyme, ilex, and grey grass of the Downs; these again to the rich cornland and fig-trees of the lower coast, where you carry the beat of the tide on your left hand for fifteen level miles; and when at last I turned inland through a huddle of rounded hills and woods I had run myself clean out of my known marks. Beyond that precise hamlet which stands godmother to the capital of the United States, I found hidden villages where bees, the only things awake, boomed in eighty-foot lindens that overhung grey Norman churches; miraculous brooks diving under stone bridges built for heavier traffic than would ever vex them again; tithe-barns larger than their churches, and an old smithy that cried out aloud how it had once been a hall of the Knights of the Temple. Gipsies I found on a common where the gorse, bracken, and heath fought it out together up a mile of Roman road; and a little farther on I disturbed a red fox rolling dog-fashion in the naked sunlight.

As the wooded hills closed about me I stood up in the car to take the bearings of that great Down whose ringed head is a landmark for fifty miles across the low countries. I judged that the lie of the country would bring me across some westward-running road that went to his feet, but I did not allow for the confusing veils of the woods. A quick turn plunged me first into a green cutting brim-full of liquid sunshine, next into a gloomy tunnel where last year's dead leaves whispered and scuffled about my tyres. The strong hazel stuff meeting overhead had not been cut for a couple of generations at least, nor had any axe helped the moss-cankered oak and beech to spring above them. Here the road changed frankly into a carpeted ride on whose brown velvet spent primrose-clumps showed like jade, and a few sickly, white-stalked bluebells nodded together. As the slope favoured I shut off the power and slid over the whirled leaves, expecting every moment to meet a keeper; but I only heard a jay, far off, arguing against the silence under the twilight of the trees.

Still the track descended. I was on the point of reversing and working my way back on the second speed ere I ended in some swamp, when I saw sunshine through the tangle ahead and lifted the brake.

It was down again at once. As the light beat across my face my fore-wheels took the turf of a great still lawn from which sprang horsemen ten feet high with levelled lances, monstrous peacocks, and sleek round-headed maids of honour—blue, black, and glistening—all of clipped yew. Across the lawn—the marshalled woods besieged it on three sides—stood an ancient house of lichened and weather-worn stone, with mullioned windows and roofs of rose-red tile. It was flanked by semi-circular walls, also rose-red, that closed the lawn on the fourth side, and at their feet a box hedge grew man-high. There were doves on the roof about the slim brick chimneys, and I caught a glimpse of an octagonal dove-house behind the screening wall.

Here, then, I stayed; a horseman's green spear laid at my breast; held by the exceeding beauty of that jewel in that setting.

'If I am not packed off for a trespasser, or if this knight does not ride a wallop at me,' thought I, 'Shakespeare and Queen Elizabeth at least must come out of that half-open garden door and ask me to tea.'

A child appeared at an upper window, and I thought the little thing waved a friendly hand. But it was to call a companion, for presently another bright head showed. Then I heard a laugh among the yew-peacocks, and turning to make sure (till then I had been watching the house only) I saw the silver of a fountain behind a hedge thrown up against the sun. The doves on the roof cooed to the cooing water; but between the two notes I caught the utterly happy chuckle of a child absorbed in some light mischief.

The garden door—heavy oak sunk deep in the thickness of the wall—opened further: a woman in a big garden hat set her foot slowly on the time-hollowed stone step and as slowly walked across the turf. I was forming some apology when she lifted up her head and I saw that she was blind.

'I heard you,' she said. 'Isn't that a motor car?'

'I'm afraid I've made a mistake in my road. I should have turned off up above—I never dreamed——' I began.

'But I'm very glad. Fancy a motor car coming into the garden! It will be such a treat——' She turned and made as though looking about her. 'You—you haven't seen any one, have you—perhaps?'

'No one to speak to, but the children seemed interested at a distance.'

'Which?'

'I saw a couple up at the window just now, and I think I heard a little chap in the grounds.'

'Oh, lucky you!' she cried, and her face brightened. 'I hear them, of course, but that's all. You've seen them and heard them?'

'Yes,' I answered. 'And if I know anything of children, one of them's having a beautiful time by the fountain yonder. Escaped, I should imagine.'

'You're fond of children?'

I gave her one or two reasons why I did not altogether hate them.

'Of course, of course,' she said. 'Then you understand. Then you won't think it foolish if I ask you to take your car through the gardens, once or twice—quite slowly. I'm sure they'd like to see it. They see so little, poor things. One tries to make their life pleasant, but——' she threw out her hands towards the woods. 'We're so out of the world here.'

'That will be splendid,' I said. 'But I can't cut up your grass.'

She faced to the right. 'Wait a minute,' she said. 'We're at the South gate, aren't we? Behind those peacocks there's a flagged path. We call it the Peacocks' Walk. You can't see it from here, they tell me, but if you squeeze along by the edge of the wood you can turn at the first peacock and get on to the flags.'

It was sacrilege to wake that dreaming house-front with the clatter of machinery, but I swung the car to clear the turf, brushed along the edge of the wood and turned in on the broad stone path where the fountain-basin lay like one star-sapphire.

'May I come too?' she cried. 'No, please don't help me. They'll like it better if they see me.'

She felt her way lightly to the front of the car, and with one foot on the step she called: 'Children, oh, children! Look and see what's going to happen!'

The voice would have drawn lost souls from the Pit, for the yearning that underlay its sweetness, and I was not surprised to hear an answering shout behind the yews. It must have been the child by the fountain, but he fled at our approach, leaving a little toy boat in the water. I saw the glint of his blue blouse among the still horsemen.

Very disposedly we paraded the length of the walk and at her request backed again. This time the child had got the better of his panic, but stood far off and doubting.

'The little fellow's watching us,' I said. 'I wonder if he'd like a ride.'

'They're very shy still. Very shy. But, oh, lucky you to be able to see them! Let's listen.'

I stopped the machine at once, and the humid stillness, heavy with the scent of box, cloaked us deep. Shears I could hear where some gardener was clipping; a mumble of bees and broken voices that might have been the doves.

'Oh, unkind!' she said weariedly.

'Perhaps they're only shy of the motor. The little maid at the window looks tremendously interested.'

'Yes?' She raised her head. 'It was wrong of me to say that. They are really fond of me. It's the only thing that makes life worth living—when they're fond of you, isn't it? I daren't think what the place would be without them. By the way, is it beautiful?'

'I think it is the most beautiful place I have ever seen.'

'So they all tell me. I can feel it, of course, but that isn't quite the same thing.'

'Then have you never——?' I began, but stopped abashed.

'Not since I can remember. It happened when I was only a few months old, they tell me. And yet I must remember something, else how could I dream about colours? I see light in my dreams, and colours, but I never see *them*. I only hear them just as I do when I'm awake.'

'It's difficult to see faces in dreams. Some people can, but most of us haven't the gift,' I went on, looking up at the window where the child stood all but hidden.

'I've heard that too,' she said. 'And they tell me that one never sees a dead person's face in a dream. Is that true?'

'I believe it is—now I come to think of it.'

'But how is it with yourself—yourself?' The blind eyes turned towards me.

'I have never seen the faces of my dead in any dream,' I answered.

'Then it must be as bad as being blind.'

The sun had dipped behind the woods and the long shades were possessing the insolent horsemen one by one. I saw the light die from off the top of a glossy-leafed lance and all the brave hard green turn to soft black. The house, accepting another day at end, as it had accepted an hundred thousand gone, seemed to settle deeper into its rest among the shadows.

'Have you ever wanted to?' she said after the silence.

'Very much sometimes,' I replied. The child had left the window as the shadows closed upon it.

'Ah! So've I, but I don't suppose it's allowed. . . . Where d'you live?'

'Quite the other side of the county—sixty miles and more, and I must be going back. I've come without my big lamps.'

'But it's not dark yet. I can feel it.'

'I'm afraid it will be by the time I get home. Could you lend me someone to set me on my road at first? I've utterly lost myself.'

'I'll send Madden with you to the cross-roads. We are so out of the world, I don't wonder you were lost! I'll guide you round to the front of the house; but you will go slowly, won't you, till you're out of the grounds? It isn't foolish, do you think?'

'I promise you I'll go like this,' I said, and let the car start herself down the flagged path.

We skirted the left wing of the house, whose elaborately cast lead guttering alone was worth a day's journey; passed under a great rose-grown gate in the red wall, and so round to the high front of the house, which in beauty and stateliness as much excelled the back as that all others I had seen.

'Is it so very beautiful?' she said wistfully when she heard my raptures. 'And you like the lead figures too? There's the old azalea garden behind. They say that this place must have been made for children. Will you help me out, please? I should like to come with you as far as the cross-roads, but I mustn't leave them. Is that you, Madden? I want you to show this gentleman the way to the cross-roads. He has lost his way, but —he has seen them.

A butler appeared noiselessly at the miracle of old oak that must be called the front door, and slipped aside to put on his hat. She stood looking at me with open blue eyes in which no sight lay, and I saw for the first time that she was beautiful.

'Remember,' she said quietly, 'if you are fond of them you will come again, and disappeared within the house.

The butler in the car said nothing till we were nearly at the lodge gates, where catching a glimpse of a blue blouse in a shrubbery I swerved amply lest the devil that leads little boys to play should drag me into child-murder.

'Excuse me, he asked of a sudden, 'but why did you do that, sir?'

'The child yonder.'

'Our young gentleman in blue?'

'Of course.

'He runs about a good deal. Did you see him by the fountain, sir?'

'Oh, yes, several times. Do we turn here?'

'Yes, sir. And did you 'appen to see them upstairs too?'

'At the upper window? Yes.'

'Was that before the mistress come out to speak to you, sir?'

'A little before that. Why d'you want to know?'

He paused a little. 'Only to make sure that—that they had seen the car, sir, because with children running about, though I'm sure you're driving particularly careful, there might be an accident. That was all, sir. Here are the cross-roads. You can't miss your way from now on. Thank you, sir, but that isn't *our* custom, not with——'

'I beg your pardon,' I said, and thrust away the British silver.

'Oh, it's quite right with the rest of 'em as a rule. Good-bye, sir.'

He retired into the armour-plated conning-tower of his caste and walked away. Evidently a butler solicitous for the honour of his house, and interested, probably through a maid, in the nursery.

Once beyond the signposts at the cross-roads I looked back, but the crumpled hills interlaced so jealously that I could not see where the house had lain. When I asked its name at a cottage along the road, the fat woman who sold sweetmeats there gave me to understand that people with motor cars had small right to live—much less to 'go about talking like carriage folk.' They were not a pleasant-mannered community.

When I retraced my route on the map that evening I was little wiser. Hawkin's Old Farm appeared to be the Survey title of the place, and the old County Gazetteer, generally so ample, did not allude to it. The big house of those parts was Hodnington Hall, Georgian with early Victorian embellishments, as an atrocious steel engraving attested. I carried my difficulty to a neighbour—a deep-rooted tree of that soil—and he gave me a name of a family which conveyed no meaning.

A month or so later—I went again, or it may have been that my car took the road of her own volition. She over-ran the fruitless Downs, threaded every turn of the maze of lanes below the hills, drew through the high-walled woods, impenetrable in their full leaf, came out at the cross-roads where the butler had left me, and a little farther on developed an internal trouble which forced me to turn her in on a grass way-waste that cut into a summer-silent hazel wood. So far as I could make sure by the sun and a six-inch Ordnance map, this should be the road flank of that wood which I had first explored from the heights above. I made a mighty serious business of my repairs and a glittering shop of my repair kit, spanners, pump, and the like, which I spread out orderly upon a rug. It was a trap to catch all childhood, for on such a day, I argued, the children would not be far off. When I paused in my work I listened, but the wood was so full of the noises of summer (though the birds had mated) that I could not at first distinguish these from the tread of small cautious feet stealing across the dead leaves. I rang my bell in an alluring manner, but the feet fled, and I repented, for to a child a sudden noise is very real terror. I must have been at work half an hour when I heard in the wood the voice of the blind woman crying: 'Children, oh, children! Where are you?' and the stillness made slow to close on the perfection of that cry. She came towards me, half feeling her way between the tree boles, and though a child, it seemed, clung to her skirt, it swerved into the leafage like a rabbit as she drew nearer.

'Is that you?' she said, 'from the other side of the county?'

'Yes, it's me from the other side of the county.'

'Then why didn't you come through the upper woods? They were there just now.'

'They were here a few minutes ago. I expect they knew my car had broken down, and came to see the fun.'

'Nothing serious, I hope? How do cars break down?'

'In fifty different ways. Only mine has chosen the fifty-first.'

She laughed merrily at the tiny joke, cooed with delicious laughter, and pushed her hat back.

'Let me hear,' she said.

'Wait a moment,' I cried, 'and I'll get you a cushion.'

She set her foot on the rug all covered with spare parts, and stooped above it eagerly. 'What delightful things!' The hands through which she saw glanced in the chequered sunlight. 'A box here—another box! Why, you've arranged them like playing shop!'

'I confess now that I put it out to attract them. I don't need half those things really.'

'How nice of you! I heard your bell in the upper wood. You say they were here before that?'

'I'm sure of it. Why are they so shy? That little fellow in blue who was with you just now ought to have got over his fright. He's been watching me like a Red Indian.'

'It must have been your bell,' she said. 'I heard one of them go past me in trouble when I was coming down. They're shy—so shy even with me.' She turned her face over her shoulder and cried again: 'Children, oh, children! Look and see!'

'They must have gone off together on their own affairs,' I suggested, for there was a murmur behind us of lowered voices broken by the sudden squeaking giggles of childhood. I returned to my tinkerings and she leaned forward, her chin on her hand, listening interestedly.

'How many are they?' I said at last. The work was finished, but I saw no reason to go.

Her forehead puckered a little in thought. 'I don't quite know,' she said simply. 'Sometimes more–sometimes less. They come and stay with me because I love them, you see.'

'That must be very jolly,' I said, replacing a drawer, and as I spoke I heard the inanity of my answer.

'You–you aren't laughing at me?' she cried. 'I–I haven't any of my own. I never married. People laugh at me sometimes about them because –because—'

'Because they're savages,' I returned. 'It's nothing to fret for. That sort laugh at everything that isn't in their own fat lives.'

'I don't know. How should I? I only don't like being laughed at about *them*. It hurts; and when one can't see. . . . I don't want to seem silly,' her chin quivered like a child's as she spoke, 'but we blindies have only one skin, I think. Everything outside hits straight at our souls. It's different with you. You've such good defences in your eyes–looking out–before anyone can really pain you in your soul. People forget that with us.'

I was silent, reviewing that inexhaustible matter–the more than inherited (since it is also carefully taught) brutality of the Christian peoples, beside which the mere heathendom of the West Coast nigger is clean and restrained. It led me a long distance into myself.

'Don't do that!' she said of a sudden, putting her hands before her eyes.

'What?'

She made a gesture with her hand.

'That! It's–it's all purple and black. Don't! That colour hurts.'

'But how in the world do you know about colours?' I exclaimed, for here was a revelation indeed.

'Colours as colours?' she asked.

'No. *Those* Colours which you saw just now.'

'You know as well as I do,' she laughed, 'else you wouldn't have asked that question. They aren't in the world at all. They're in *you*–when you went so angry.'

'D'you mean a dull purplish patch, like port wine mixed with ink?' I said.

'I've never seen ink or port wine, but the colours aren't mixed. They are separate–all separate.'

'Do you mean black streaks and jags across the purple?'

She nodded. 'Yes–if they are like this,' and zig-zagged her finger again, 'but it's more red than purple–that bad colour.'

'And what are the colours at the top of the–whatever you see?'

Slowly she leaned forward and traced on the rug the figure of the Egg itself.

'I see them so,' she said, pointing with a grass stem, 'white, green, yellow, red, purple, and when people are angry or bad, black across the red–as you were just now.'

'Who told you anything about it–in the beginning?' I demanded.

'About the Colours? No one. I used to ask what Colours were when I was little–in table-covers and curtains and carpets, you see–because some colours hurt me and some made me happy. People told me; and when I got older that was how I saw people.' Again she traced the outline of the Egg which it is given to very few of us to see.

'All by yourself?' I repeated.

'All by myself. There wasn't anyone else. I only found out afterwards that other people did not see the Colours.'

She leaned against the tree-bole plaiting and unplaiting chance-plucked grass stems. The children in the wood had drawn nearer. I could see them with the tail of my eye frolicking like squirrels.

'Now I am sure you will never laugh at me,' she went on after a long silence. 'Nor at *them.*'

'Goodness! No!' I cried, jolted out of my train of thought. 'A man who laughs at a child–unless the child is laughing too–is a heathen!'

'I didn't mean that, of course. You'd never laugh *at* children, but I thought–I used to think–that perhaps you might laugh about *them.* So now I beg your pardon. . . . What are you going to laugh at?'

I had made no sound, but she knew.

'At the notion of your begging my pardon. If you had done your duty as a pillar of the State and a landed proprietress you ought to have summoned me for trespass when I barged through your woods the other day. It was disgraceful of me–inexcusable.'

She looked at me, her head against the tree-trunk–long and steadfastly–this woman who could see the naked soul.

'How curious,' she half whispered. 'How very curious.'

'Why, what have I done?'

'You don't understand . . . and yet you understood about the Colours. Don't you understand?'

She spoke with a passion that nothing had justified, and I faced her bewilderedly as she rose. The children had gathered themselves in a roundel behind a bramble bush. One sleek head bent over something smaller, and the set of the little shoulders told me that fingers were on lips. They, too, had some child's tremendous secret. I alone was hopelessly astray there in the broad sunlight.

'No,' I said, and shook my head as though the dead eyes could note. 'Whatever it is, I don't understand yet. Perhaps I shall later—if you'll let me come again.'

'You will come again,' she answered. 'You will surely come again and walk in the wood.'

'Perhaps the children will know me well enough by that time to let me play with them—as a favour. You know what children are like.'

'It isn't a matter of favour but of right,' she replied, and while I wondered what she meant, a dishevelled woman plunged round the bend of the road, loose-haired, purple, almost lowing with agony as she ran. It was my rude, fat friend of the sweetmeat shop. The blind woman heard and stepped forward. 'What is it, Mrs. Madehurst?' she asked.

The woman flung her apron over her head and literally grovelled in the dust, crying that her grandchild was sick to death, that the local doctor was away fishing, that Jenny the mother was at her wits' end, and so forth, with repetitions and bellowings.

'Where's the next nearest doctor?' I asked between paroxysms.

'Madden will tell you. Go round to the house and take him with you. I'll attend to this. Be quick!' She half supported the fat woman into the shade. In two minutes I was blowing all the horns of Jericho under the front of the House Beautiful, and Madden, in the pantry, rose to the crisis like a butler and a man.

A quarter of an hour at illegal speeds caught us a doctor five miles away. Within the half-hour we had decanted him, much interested in motors, at the door of the sweetmeat shop, and drew up the road to await the verdict.

'Useful things cars,' said Madden, all man and no butler. 'If I'd had one when mine took sick she wouldn't have died.'

'How was it?' I asked.

'Croup. Mrs. Madden was away. No one knew what to do. I drove eight miles in a tax-cart for the doctor. She was choked when we came back. This car 'd ha' saved her. She'd have been close on ten now.'

'I'm sorry,' I said. 'I thought you were rather fond of children from what you told me going to the cross-roads the other day.'

'Have you seen 'em again, sir—this mornin'?'

'Yes, but they're well broke to cars. I couldn't get any of them within twenty yards of it.'

He looked at me carefully as a scout considers a stranger—not as a menial should lift his eyes to his divinely appointed superior.

'I wonder why,' he said just above the breath that he drew.

We waited on. A light wind from the sea wandered up and down the long lines of the woods, and the wayside grasses, whitened already with summer dust, rose and bowed in sallow waves.

A woman, wiping the suds off her arms, came out of the cottage next the sweetmeat shop.

'I've be'n listenin' in de back-yard,' she said cheerily. 'He says Arthur's unaccountable bad. Did ye hear him shruck just now? Unaccountable bad. I reckon t'will come Jenny's turn to walk in de wood nex' week along, Mr. Madden.'

'Excuse me, sir, but your lap-robe is slipping,' said Madden deferentially. The woman started, dropped a curtsey, and hurried away.

'What does she mean by "walking in the wood"?' I asked.

'It must be some saying they use hereabouts. I'm from Norfolk myself,' said Madden. 'They're an independent lot in this county. She took you for a chauffeur, sir.'

I saw the Doctor come out of the cottage followed by a draggle-tailed wench who clung to his arm as though he could make treaty for her with Death. 'Dat sort,' she wailed—'dey're just as much to us dat has 'em as if dey was lawful born. Just as much—just as much! An' God, He'd be just as pleased if you saved 'un, Doctor. Don't take it from me. Miss Florence will tell ye de very same. Don't leave 'im, Doctor!'

'I know, I know,' said the man; 'but he'll be quiet for a while now. We'll get the nurse and the medicine as fast as we can.' He signalled me to come forward with the car, and I strove not to be privy to what followed; but I saw the girl's face, blotched and frozen with grief, and I felt the hand without a ring clutching at my knees when we moved away.

The Doctor was a man of some humour, for I remember he claimed my car under the Oath of Æsculapius, and used it and me without mercy. First we convoyed Mrs. Madehurst and the blind woman to wait by the sick-bed till the nurse should come. Next we invaded a neat county town for prescriptions (the Doctor said the trouble was cerebrospinal meningitis), and when the County Institute, banked and flanked with scared market cattle, reported itself out of nurses for the moment we literally flung ourselves loose upon the county. We conferred with the owners of great houses—magnates at the ends of overarching avenues whose big-boned womenfolk strode away from their tea-tables to listen to the imperious Doctor. At last a white-haired lady sitting under a cedar of Lebanon and surrounded by a court of magnificent Borzois—all hostile to motors—gave the Doctor, who received them as from a princess, written orders which we bore many miles at top speed, through a park, to a French nunnery, where we took over in exchange a pallid-faced and trembling Sister. She knelt at the bottom of the tonneau telling her beads without pause till, by short cuts of the Doctor's invention, we had her to the sweetmeat shop once more. It was a long afternoon crowded with mad episodes that rose and dissolved like the dust of our wheels; cross-sections of remote and incomprehensible lives through which we raced at right angles; and I went home in the dusk, wearied out, to dream of the clashing horns of cattle; round-eyed nuns walking in a garden of graves; pleasant tea-parties beneath shady trees; the carbolic-scented, grey-painted corridors of the County Institute; the steps of shy children in the wood, and the hands that clung to my knees as the motor began to move.

I had intended to return in a day or two, but it pleased Fate to hold me from that side of the county, on many pretexts, till the elder and the wild rose had fruited. There came at last a brilliant day, swept clear from the south-west, that brought the hills within hand's reach—a day of unstable airs and high filmy clouds. Through no merit of my own I was free, and set the car for the third time on that known road. As I reached the crest of the Downs I felt the soft air change, saw it glaze under the sun; and, looking down at the sea, in that instant beheld the blue of the Channel turn through polished silver and dulled steel to dingy pewter. A laden collier hugging the coast steered outward for deeper water, and, across copper-coloured haze, I saw sails rise one by one on the anchored fishing-fleet. In a deep dene behind me an eddy of sudden wind drummed through sheltered oaks, and spun aloft the first dry sample of autumn leaves. When I reached the beach road the sea-fog fumed over the brickfields, and the tide was telling all the groynes of the gale beyond Ushant. In less than an hour summer England vanished in chill grey. We were again the shut island of the North, all the ships of the world bellowing at our perilous gates; and between their outcries ran the piping of bewildered gulls. My cap dripped moisture, the folds of the rug held it in pools or sluiced it away in runnels, and the salt-rime stuck to my lips.

Inland the smell of autumn loaded the thickened fog among the trees, and the drip became a continuous shower. Yet the late flowers—mallow of the wayside, scabious of the field, and dahlia of the garden—showed gay in the mist, and beyond the sea's breath there was little sign of decay in the leaf. Yet in the villages the house doors were all open, and bare-legged, bare-headed children sat at ease on the damp doorsteps to shout 'pip-pip' at the stranger.

I made bold to call at the sweetmeat shop, where Mrs. Madehurst met me with a fat woman's hospitable tears. Jenny's child, she said, had died two days after the nun had come. It was, she felt, best out of the way, even though insurance offices, for reasons which she did not pretend to follow, would not willingly insure such stray lives. 'Not but what Jenny didn't tend to Arthur as though he'd come all proper at de end of de first year—like Jenny herself.' Thanks to Miss Florence, the child had been buried with a pomp which, in Mrs. Madehurst's opinion, more than covered the small irregularity of its birth. She described the coffin, within and without, the glass hearse, and the evergreen lining of the grave.

'But how's the mother?' I asked.

'Jenny? Oh, she'll get over it. I've felt dat way with one or two o' my own. She'll get over. She's walkin' in de wood now.'

'In this weather?'

Mrs. Madehurst looked at me with narrowed eyes across the counter.

'I dunno but it opens de 'eart like. Yes, it opens de 'eart. Dat's where losin' and bearin' comes so alike in de long run, we do say.'

Now the wisdom of the old wives is greater than that of all the Fathers, and this last oracle sent me thinking so extendedly as I went up the road, that I nearly ran over a woman and a child at the wooded corner by the lodge gates of the House Beautiful.

'Awful weather!' I cried, as I slowed dead for the turn.

'Not so bad,' she answered placidly out of the fog. 'Mine's used to 'un. You'll find yours indoors, I reckon.'

Indoors, Madden received me with professional courtesy, and kind inquiries for the health of the motor, which he would put under cover.

I waited in a still, nut-brown hall, pleasant with late flowers and warmed with a delicious wood fire—a place of good influence and great peace. (Men and women may sometimes, after great effort, achieve a creditable lie; but the house, which is their temple, cannot say anything save the truth of those who have lived in it.) A child's cart and a doll lay on the black-and-white floor, where a rug had been kicked back. I felt that the children had only just hurried away—to hide themselves, most like—in the many turns of the great adzed staircase that climbed statelily out of the hall, or to crouch at gaze behind the lions and roses of the carven gallery above. Then I heard her voice above me, singing as the blind sing—from the soul:—

'In the pleasant orchard-closes.'

And all my early summer came back at the call.

'In the pleasant orchard-closes,
God bless all our gains, say we—
But may God bless all our losses,
Better suits with our degree.'

She dropped the marring fifth line, and repeated—

'Better suits with our degree!'

I saw her lean over the gallery, her linked hands white as pearl against the oak.

'Is that you—from the other side of the county?' she called.

'Yes, me—from the other side of the county,' I answered, laughing.

'What a long time before you had to come here again.' She ran down the stairs, one hand lightly touching the broad rail. 'It's two months and four days. Summer's gone!'

'I meant to come before, but Fate prevented.'

'I knew it. Please do something to that fire. They won't let me play with it, but I can feel it's behaving badly. Hit it!'

I looked on either side of the deep fireplace, and found but a half-charred hedge-stake with which I punched a black log into flame.

'It never goes out, day or night,' she said, as though explaining. 'In case any one comes in with cold toes, you see.'

'It's even lovelier inside than it was out,' I murmured. The red light poured itself along the age-polished dusky panels till the Tudor roses and lions of the gallery took colour and motion. An old eagle-topped convex mirror gathered the picture into its mysterious heart, distorting afresh the distorted shadows, and curving the gallery lines into the curves of a ship. The day was shutting down in half a gale as the fog turned to stringy scud. Through the uncurtained mullions of the broad window

I could see the valiant horsemen of the lawn rear and recover against the wind that taunted them with legions of dead leaves.

'Yes, it must be beautiful,' she said. 'Would you like to go over it? There's still light enough upstairs.'

I followed her up the unflinching, wagon-wide staircase to the gallery whence opened the thin fluted Elizabethan doors.

'Feel how they put the latch low down for the sake of the children.' She swung a light door inward.

'By the way, where are they?' I asked. 'I haven't even heard them to-day.'

She did not answer at once. Then, 'I can only hear them,' she replied softly. 'This is one of their rooms—everything ready, you see.'

She pointed into a heavily-timbered room. There were little low gate tables and children's chairs. A dolls' house, its hooked front half open, faced a great dappled rocking-horse, from whose padded saddle it was but a child's scramble to the broad window-seat overlooking the lawn. A toy gun lay in a corner beside a gilt wooden cannon.

'Surely they've only just gone,' I whispered. In the failing light a door creaked cautiously. I heard the rustle of a frock and the patter of feet—quick feet through a room beyond.

'I heard that,' she cried triumphantly. 'Did you? Children, oh, children! Where are you?'

The voice filled the walls that held it lovingly to the last perfect note, but there came no answering shout such as I had heard in the garden. We hurried on from room to oak-floored room; up a step here, down three steps there; among a maze of passages; always mocked by our quarry. One might as well have tried to work an unstopped warren with a single ferret. There were bolt-holes innumerable—recesses in walls, embrasures of deep-slitted windows now darkened, whence they could start up behind us; and abandoned fireplaces, six feet deep in the masonry, as well as the tangle of communicating doors. Above all, they had the twilight for their helper in our game. I had caught one or two joyous chuckles of evasion, and once or twice had seen the silhouette of a child's frock against some darkening window at the end of a passage; but we returned empty-handed to the gallery, just as a middle-aged woman was setting a lamp in its niche.

'No, I haven't seen her either this evening, Miss Florence,' I heard her say, 'but that Turpin he says he wants to see you about his shed.'

'Oh, Mr. Turpin must want to see me very badly. Tell him to come to the hall, Mrs. Madden.'

I looked down into the hall whose only light was the dulled fire, and deep in the shadow I saw them at last. They must have slipped down while we were in the passages, and now thought themselves perfectly hidden behind an old gilt leather screen. By child's law, my fruitless chase was as good as an introduction, but since I had taken so much trouble I resolved to force them to come forward later by the simple trick, which children detest, of pretending not to notice them. They lay close, in a little huddle, no more than shadows except when a quick flame betrayed an outline.

'And now we'll have some tea,' she said. 'I believe I ought to have offered it you at first, but one doesn't arrive at manners somehow when one lives alone and is considered–h'm–peculiar.' Then with very pretty scorn, 'Would you like a lamp to see to eat by?'

'The firelight's much pleasanter, I think.' We descended into that delicious gloom and Madden brought tea.

I took my chair in the direction of the screen ready to surprise or be surprised as the game should go, and at her permission, since a hearth is always sacred, bent forward to play with the fire.

'Where do you get these beautiful short faggots from?' I asked idly. 'Why, they are tallies!'

'Of course,' she said. 'As I can't read or write I'm driven back on the early English tally for my accounts. Give me one and I'll tell you what it meant.'

I passed her an unburned hazel-tally, about a foot long, and she ran her thumb down the nicks.

'This is the milk-record for the home farm for the month of April last year, in gallons,' said she. 'I don't know what I should have done without tallies. An old forester of mine taught me the system. It's out of date now for every one else; but my tenants respect it. One of them's coming now to see me. Oh, it doesn't matter. He has no business here out of office hours. He's a greedy, ignorant man–very greedy, or–he wouldn't come here after dark.'

'Have you much land then?'

'Only a couple of hundred acres in hand, thank goodness. The other six hundred are nearly all let to folk who knew my folk before me, but this Turpin is quite a new man–and a highway robber.'

'But are you sure I shan't be——?'

'Certainly not. You have the right. He hasn't any children.'

'Ah, the children!' I said, and slid my low chair back till it nearly touched the screen that hid them. 'I wonder whether they'll come out for me.'

There was a murmur of voices—Madden's and a deeper note—at the low, dark side door, and a ginger-headed, canvas-gaitered giant of the unmistakable tenant-farmer type stumbled or was pushed in.

'Come to the fire, Mr. Turpin,' she said.

'If—if you please, Miss, I'll—I'll be quite as well by the door.' He clung to the latch as he spoke like a frightened child. Of a sudden I realised that he was in the grip of some almost overpowering fear.

'Well?'

'About that new shed for the young stock—that was all. These first autumn storms settin' in . . . but I'll come again, Miss.' His teeth did not chatter much more than the door-latch.

'I think not,' she answered levelly. 'The new shed—m'm. What did my agent write you on the 15th?'

'I—fancied p'raps that if I came to see you—ma—man to man like, Miss. But——'

His eyes rolled into every corner of the room wide with horror. He half opened the door through which he had entered, but I noticed it shut again—from without and firmly.

'He wrote what I told him,' she went on. 'You are overstocked already. Dunnett's Farm never carried more than fifty bullocks—even in Mr. Wright's time. And *he* used cake. You've sixty-seven and you don't cake. You've broken the lease in that respect. You're dragging the heart out of the farm.'

'I'm—I'm getting some minerals—superphosphates—next week. I've as good as ordered a truck-load already. I'll go down to the station tomorrow about 'em. Then I can come and see you man to man like, Miss, in the daylight. . . . That gentleman's not going away, is he?' He almost shrieked.

I had only slid the chair a little farther back, reaching behind me to tap on the leather of the screen, but he jumped like a rat.

'No. Please attend to me, Mr. Turpin.' She turned in her chair and faced him with his back to the door. It was an old and sordid little piece of scheming that she forced from him—his plea for the new cow-shed at his landlady's expense, that he might with the covered manure pay his next year's rent out of the valuation after, as she made clear, he had bled the enriched pastures to the bone. I could not but admire the intensity of his greed, when I saw him outfacing for its sake whatever terror it was that ran wet on his forehead.

I ceased to tap the leather—was, indeed, calculating the cost of the shed—when I felt my relaxed hand taken and turned softly between the soft hands of a child. So at last I had triumphed. In a moment I would turn and acquaint myself with those quick-footed wanderers. . . .

The little brushing kiss fell in the centre of my palm—as a gift on which the fingers were, once, expected, to close: as the all-faithful, half-reproachful signal of a waiting child not used to neglect even when grown-ups were busiest—a fragment of the mute code devised very long ago.

Then I knew. And it was as though I had known from the first day when I looked across the lawn at the high window.

I heard the door shut. The woman turned to me in silence, and I felt that she knew.

What time passed after this I cannot say. I was roused by the fall of a log, and mechanically rose to put it back. Then I returned to my place in the chair very close to the screen.

'Now you understand,' she whispered, across the packed shadows.

'Yes, I understand—now. Thank you.'

'I—I only hear them.' She bowed her head in her hands. 'I have no right, you know—no other right. I have neither borne nor lost—neither borne nor lost!'

'Be very glad then,' said I, for my soul was torn open within me.

'Forgive me!'

She was still, and I went back to my sorrow and my joy.

'It was because I loved them so,' she said at last, brokenly. '*That* was why it was, even from the first—even before I knew that they—they were all I should ever have. And I loved them so!'

She stretched out her arms to the shadows and the shadows within the shadow.

'They came because I loved them—because I needed them. I—I must have made them come. Was that wrong, think you?'

'No—no.'

'I—I grant you that the toys and—and all that sort of thing were nonsense, but—but I used to so hate empty rooms myself when I was little.' She pointed to the gallery. 'And the passages all empty. . . . And how could I ever bear the garden door shut? Suppose——'

'Don't! For pity's sake, don't!' I cried. The twilight had brought a cold rain with gusty squalls that plucked at the leaded windows.

'And the same thing with keeping the fire in all night. *I* don't think it so foolish—do you?'

I looked at the broad brick hearth, saw, through tears, I believe, that there was no unpassable iron on or near it, and bowed my head.

'I did all that and lots of other things—just to make believe. Then they came. I heard them, but I didn't know that they were not mine by right till Mrs. Madden told me——'

'The butler's wife? What?'

'One of them—I heard—she saw. And knew Hers! *Not* for me. I didn't know at first. Perhaps I was jealous. Afterwards, I began to understand that it was only because I loved them, not because—— . . . Oh, you *must* bear or lose,' she said piteously. 'There is no other way—and yet they love me. They must! Don't they?'

There was no sound in the room except the lapping voices of the fire, but we two listened intently, and she at least took comfort from what she heard. She recovered herself and half rose. I sat still in my chair by the screen.

'Don't think me a wretch to whine about myself like this, but—but I'm all in the dark, you know, and *you* can see.'

In truth I could see, and my vision confirmed me in my resolve, though that was like the very parting of spirit and flesh. Yet a little longer I would stay since it was the last time.

'You think it is wrong, then?' she cried sharply, though I had said nothing.

'Not for you. A thousand times no. For you it is right. . . . I am grateful to you beyond words. For me it would be wrong. For me only. . . .'

'Why?' she said, but passed her hand before her face as she had done at our second meeting in the wood. 'Oh, I see,' she went on simply as a child. 'For you it would be wrong.' Then with a little indrawn laugh, 'And, d'you remember, I called you lucky—once—at first. You who must never come here again!'

She left me to sit a little longer by the screen, and I heard the sound of her feet die out along the gallery above.

TODS' AMENDMENT

The World hath set its heavy yoke
Upon the old white-bearded folk
  Who strive to please the King.
God's mercy is upon the young,
God's wisdom in the baby tongue
  That fears not anything.
The Parable of Chajju Bhagat

Now TODS' Mamma was a singularly charming woman, and every one in Simla knew Tods. Most men had saved him from death on occasions. He was beyond his *ayah's* control altogether, and perilled his life daily to find out what would happen if you pulled a Mountain Battery mule's tail. He was an utterly fearless young pagan, about six years old, and the only baby who ever broke the holy calm of the Supreme Legislative Council.

It happened this way: Tods' pet kid got loose, and fled up the hill, off the Boileaugunge Road, Tods after it, until it burst in to the Viceregal Lodge lawn, then attached to 'Peterhof.' The Council were sitting at the time, and the windows were open because it was warm. The Red Lancer in the porch told Tods to go away; but Tods knew the Red Lancer and most of the Members of Council personally. Moreover, he had firm hold of the kid's collar, and was being dragged all across the flower-beds. 'Give my *salaam* to the long Councillor Sahib, and ask him to help me take Moti back!' gasped Tods. The Council heard the noise through the open windows; and, after an interval, was seen the shocking spectacle of a Legal Member and a Lieutenant-Governor helping, under the direct patronage of a Commander-in-Chief and a Viceroy, one small and very dirty boy, in a sailor's suit and a tangle of brown hair, to coerce a lively and rebellious kid. They headed it off down the path to the Mall, and Tods went home in triumph and told his Mamma that *all* the Councillor Sahibs had been helping him to catch Moti. Whereat his Mamma smacked Tods for interfering with the administration of the Empire; but Tods met the Legal Member the next day, and told him in confidence that if the Legal Member ever wanted to catch a goat, he, Tods, would give him all the help in his power. 'Thank you, Tods,' said the Legal Member.

Tods was the idol of some eighty *jhampanis,* and half as many *saises.* He saluted them all as 'O Brother.' It never entered his head that any living human being could disobey his orders; and he was the buffer between the servants and his Mamma's wrath. The working of that household turned on Tods, who was adored by every one from the *dhobi* to the dog-boy. Even Futteh Khan, the villainous loafer *khit* from Mussoorie, shirked risking Tods' displeasure for fear his co-mates should look down on him.

So Tods had honour in the land from Boileaugunge to Chota Simla, and ruled justly according to his lights. Of course, he spoke Urdu, but he had also mastered many queer side-speeches like the *chotee bolee* of the women, and held grave converse with shopkeepers and Hill-coolies alike. He was precocious for his age, and his mixing with natives had taught him some of the more bitter truths of life: the meanness and the sordidness of it. He used, over his bread and milk, to deliver solemn and serious aphorisms, translated from the vernacular into the English, that made his Mamma jump and vow that Tods *must* go Home next hot weather.

Just when Tods was in the bloom of his power, the Supreme Legislature were hacking out a Bill for the Sub-Montane Tracts, a revision of the then Act, smaller than the Punjab Land Bill, but affecting a few hundred thousand people none the less. The Legal Member had built, and bolstered, and embroidered, and amended that Bill till it looked beautiful on paper. Then the Council began to settle what they called the 'minor details.' As if any Englishman legislating for natives knows enough to know which are the minor and which are the major points, from the native point of view, of any measure! That Bill was a triumph of 'safeguarding the interests of the tenant.' One clause provided that land should not be leased on longer terms than five years at a stretch; because, if the landlord had a tenant bound down for, say, twenty years, he would squeeze the very life out of him. The notion was to keep up a stream of independent cultivators in the Sub-Montane Tracts; and ethnologically and politically the notion was correct. The only drawback was that it was altogether wrong. A native's life in India implies the life of his son. Wherefore, you cannot legislate for one generation at a time. You must consider the next from the native point of view. Curiously enough, the native now and then, and in Northern India more particularly, hates being over-protected against himself. There was a Naga village once, where they lived on dead *and* buried Commissariat mules. . . . But that is another story.

For many reasons, to be explained later, the people concerned objected to the Bill. The Native Member of Council knew as much about Punjabis as he knew about Charing Cross. He had said in Calcutta that 'the Bill was entirely in accord with the desires of that large and important class, the cultivators'; and so on, and so on. The Legal Member's knowledge of natives was limited to English-speaking Durbaris, and his own red *chaprassis,* the Sub-Montane Tracts concerned no one in particular, the Deputy Commissioners were a good deal too driven to make representations, and the measure was one which dealt with small landholders only. Nevertheless, the Legal Member prayed that it might be correct, for he was a nervously conscientious man. He did not know that no man can tell what natives think unless he mixes with them with the varnish off. And not always then. But he did the best he knew. And the measure came up to the Supreme Council for the final touches, while Tods patrolled the Burra Simla Bazar in his morning rides, and played with the monkey belonging to Ditta Mull, the *bunnia,* and listened, as a child listens, to all the stray talk about this new freak of the Lord Sahib's.

One day there was a dinner-party at the house of Tods' Mamma, and the Legal Member came. Tods was in bed, but he kept awake till he heard the bursts of laughter from the men over the coffee. Then he paddled out in his little red flannel dressing-gown and his night-suit, and took refuge by the side of his father, knowing that he would not be sent back. 'See the miseries of having a family!' said Tods' father, giving Tods three prunes, some water in a glass that had been used for claret, and telling him to sit still. Tods sucked the prunes slowly, knowing that he would have to go when they were finished, and sipped the pink water like a man of the world, as he listened to the conversation. Presently, the Legal Member, talking 'shop' to the Head of a Department, mentioned his Bill by its full name—'The Sub-Montane Tracts *Ryotwary* Revised Enactment.' Tods caught the one native word, and lifting up his small voice said—

'Oh, I know *all* about that! Has it been *murramutted* yet, Councillor Sahib?'

'How much?' said the Legal Member.

'*Murramutted*—mended.—Put *theek,* you know—made nice to please Ditta Mull!'

The Legal Member left his place and moved up next to Tods.

'What do you know about *ryotwari,* little man?' he said.

'I'm not a little man, I'm Tods, and I know *all* about it. Ditta Mull, and Choga Lall, and Amir Nath, and–oh, *lakhs* of my friends tell me about it in the bazaars when I talk to them.'

'Oh, they do–do they? What do they say, Tods?'

Tods tucked his feet under his red flannel dressing-gown and said–'I must *fink.*'

The Legal Member waited patiently. Then Tods, with infinite compassion–

'You don't speak my talk, do you, Councillor Sahib?'

'No; I am sorry to say I do not,' said the Legal Member.

'Very well,' said Tods, 'I must *fink* in English.'

He spent a minute putting his ideas in order, and began very slowly, translating in his mind from the vernacular to English, as many Anglo-Indian children do. You must remember that the Legal Member helped him on by questions when he halted, for Tods was not equal to the sustained flight of oratory that follows.

'Ditta Mull says, "This thing is the talk of a child, and was made up by fools." But *I* don't think you are a fool, Councillor Sahib,' said Tods hastily. 'You caught my goat. This is what Ditta Mull says–"I am not a fool, and why should the Sirkar say I am a child? I can see if the land is good and if the landlord is good. If I am a fool, the sin is upon my own head. For five years I take my ground for which I have saved money, and a wife I take too, and a little son is born." Ditta Mull has one daughter now, but he *says* he will have a son, soon. And he says, "At the end of five years, by this new *bundobust,* I must go. If I do not go, I must get fresh seals and *takkus*-stamps on the papers, perhaps in the middle of the harvest, and to go to the law-courts once is wisdom, but to go twice is *Jehannum.*" That is *quite* true,' explained Tods gravely. 'All my friends say so. And Ditta Mull says, "Always fresh *takkus* and paying money to *vakils* and *chaprassis* and law-courts every five years, or else the landlord makes me go. Why do I want to go? Am I a fool? If I am a fool and do not know, after forty years, good land when I see it, let me die! But if the new *bundobust* says for *fifteen* years, that is good and wise. My little son is a man, and I am burnt, and he takes the ground or another ground, paying only once for the *takkus*-stamps on the papers, and his little son is born, and at the end of fifteen years is a man too. But what profit is there in five years and fresh papers? Nothing but *dikh,* trouble, *dikh.* We are not young men who take these lands, but old ones–not farmers, but tradesmen with a little money—and for fifteen years we shall have peace. Nor are we children that the Sirkar should treat us so." '

Here Tods stopped short, for the whole table were listening. The Legal Member said to Tods, 'Is that all?'

'All I can remember,' said Tods. 'But you should see Ditta Mull's big monkey. It's just like a Councillor Sahib.'

'Tods! Go to bed,' said his father.

Tods gathered up his dressing-gown tail and departed.

The Legal Member brought his hand down on the table with a crash. 'By Jove!' said the Legal Member, 'I believe the boy is right. The short tenure *is* the weak point.'

He left early, thinking over what Tods had said. Now, it was obviously impossible for the Legal Member to play with a *bunnia's* monkey, by way of getting understanding; but he did better. He made inquiries, always bearing in mind the fact that the real native—not the hybrid, University-trained mule—is as timid as a colt, and, little by little, he coaxed some of the men whom the measure concerned most intimately to give in their views, which squared very closely with Tods' evidence.

So the Bill was amended in that clause; and the Legal Member was filled with an uneasy suspicion that Native Members represent very little except the Orders they carry on their bosoms. But he put the thought from him as illiberal. He was a most Liberal man.

After a time the news spread through the bazaars that Tods had got the Bill recast in the tenure-clause, and if Tods' Mamma had not interfered, Tods would have made himself sick on the baskets of fruit and pistachio nuts and Cabuli grapes and almonds that crowded the verandah. Till he went Home, Tods ranked some few degrees before the Viceroy in popular estimation. But for the little life of him Tods could not understand why.

In the Legal Member's private-paper-box still lies the rough draft of the Sub-Montane Tracts *Ryotwary* Revised Enactment; and, opposite the twenty-second clause, pencilled in blue chalk, and signed by the Legal Member, are the words *'Tods' Amendment.'*

MOWGLI'S BROTHERS

Now Chil the Kite brings home the night
  That Mang the Bat sets free—
The herds are shut in byre and hut,
  For loosed till dawn are we.
This is the hour of pride and power,
  Talon and tush and claw.
Oh, hear the call!—Good hunting all
  That keep the Jungle Law!
Night-Song in the Jungle.

IT WAS seven o'clock of a very warm evening in the Seeonee hills when Father Wolf woke up from his day's rest, scratched himself, yawned, and spread out his paws one after the other to get rid of the sleepy feeling in their tips. Mother Wolf lay with her big grey nose dropped across her four tumbling, squealing cubs, and the moon shone into the mouth of the cave where they all lived. 'Augrh!' said Father Wolf, 'it is time to hunt again'; and he was going to spring down-hill when a little shadow with a bushy tail crossed the threshold and whined: 'Good luck go with you, O Chief of the Wolves; and good luck and strong white teeth go with the noble children, that they may never forget the hungry in this world.'

It was the jackal—Tabaqui, the Dish-licker—and the wolves of India despise Tabaqui because he runs about making mischief, and telling tales, and eating rags and pieces of leather from the village rubbish-heaps. But they are afraid of him too, because Tabaqui, more than any one else in the Jungle, is apt to go mad, and then he forgets that he was ever afraid of any one, and runs through the forest biting everything in his way. Even the tiger runs and hides when little Tabaqui goes mad, for madness is the most disgraceful thing that can overtake a wild creature. We call it hydrophobia, but they call it *dewanee*—the madness—and run.

'Enter, then, and look,' said Father Wolf stiffly; 'but there is no food here.'

'For a wolf, no,' said Tabaqui; 'but for so mean a person as myself a dry bone is a good feast. Who are we, the *Gidur-log* [the Jackal-People], to pick and choose?' He scuttled to the back of the cave, where he found the bone of a buck with some meat on it, and sat cracking the end merrily.

'All thanks for this good meal,' he said, licking his lips. 'How beautiful are the noble children! How large are their eyes! And so young too! Indeed, indeed, I might have remembered that the children of Kings are men from the beginning.'

Now, Tabaqui knew as well as any one else that there is nothing so unlucky as to compliment children to their faces; and it pleased him to see Mother and Father Wolf look uncomfortable.

Tabaqui sat still, rejoicing in the mischief that he had made: then he said spitefully:

'Shere Khan, the Big One, has shifted his hunting-grounds. He will hunt among these hills for the next moon, so he has told me.'

Shere Khan was the tiger who lived near the Waingunga River, twenty miles away.

'He has no right!' Father Wolf began angrily—'By the Law of the Jungle he has no right to change his quarters without due warning. He will frighten every head of game within ten miles, and I—I have to kill for two, these days.'

'His mother did not call him Lungri [the Lame One] for nothing,' said Mother Wolf quietly. 'He has been lame in one foot from his birth. That is why he has only killed cattle. Now the villagers of the Waingunga are angry with him, and he has come here to make *our* villagers angry. They will scour the Jungle for him when he is far away, and we and our children must run when the grass is set alight. Indeed, we are very grateful to Shere Khan!'

'Shall I tell him of your gratitude?' said Tabaqui.

'Out!' snapped Father Wolf. 'Out and hunt with thy master. Thou hast done harm enough for one night.'

'I go,' said Tabaqui quietly. 'Ye can hear Shere Khan below in the thickets. I might have saved myself the message.'

Father Wolf listened, and below in the valley that ran down to a little river, he heard the dry, angry, snarly, singsong whine of a tiger who has caught nothing and does not care if all the Jungle knows it.

'The fool!' said Father Wolf. 'To begin a night's work with that noise! Does he think that our buck are like his fat Waingunga bullocks?'

'H'sh! It is neither bullock nor buck he hunts to-night,' said Mother

Wolf. 'It is Man.' The whine had changed to a sort of humming purr that seemed to come from every quarter of the compass. It was the noise that bewilders wood-cutters and gipsies sleeping in the open, and makes them run sometimes into the very mouth of the tiger.

'Man!' said Father Wolf, showing all his white teeth. 'Faugh! Are there not enough beetles and frogs in the tanks that he must eat Man, and on our ground too?'

The Law of the Jungle, which never orders anything without a reason, forbids every beast to eat Man except when he is killing to show his children how to kill, and then he must hunt outside the hunting-grounds of his pack or tribe. The real reason for this is that man-killing means, sooner or later, the arrival of white men on elephants, with guns, and hundreds of brown men with gongs and rockets and torches. Then everybody in the Jungle suffers. The reason the beasts give among themselves is that Man is the weakest and most defenceless of all living things, and it is unsportsmanlike to touch him. They say too—and it is true—that man-eaters become mangy, and lose their teeth.

The purr grew louder, and ended in the full-throated 'Aaarh!' of the tiger's charge.

Then there was a howl—an untigerish howl—from Shere Khan. 'He has missed,' said Mother Wolf. 'What is it?'

Father Wolf ran out a few paces and heard Shere Khan muttering and mumbling savagely, as he tumbled about in the scrub.

'The fool has had no more sense than to jump at a woodcutter's camp-fire, and has burned his feet,' said Father Wolf, with a grunt. 'Tabaqui is with him.'

'Something is coming uphill,' said Mother Wolf, twitching one ear. 'Get ready.'

The bushes rustled a little in the thicket, and Father Wolf dropped with his haunches under him, ready for his leap. Then, if you had been watching, you would have seen the most wonderful thing in the world—the wolf checked in mid-spring. He made his bound before he saw what it was he was jumping at, and then he tried to stop himself. The result was that he shot up straight into the air for four or five feet, landing almost where he left ground.

'Man!' he snapped. 'A man's cub. Look!'

Directly in front of him, holding on by a low branch, stood a naked brown baby who could just walk—as soft and as dimpled a little atom as ever came to a wolf's cave at night. He looked up into Father Wolf's face, and laughed.

'Is that a man's cub?' said Mother Wolf. 'I have never seen one. Bring it here.'

A wolf accustomed to moving his own cubs can, if necessary, mouth an egg without breaking it, and though Father Wolf's jaws closed right on the child's back not a tooth even scratched the skin, as he laid it down among the cubs.

'How little! How naked, and—how bold!' said Mother Wolf softly. The baby was pushing his way between the cubs to get close to the warm hide. '*Ahai!* He is taking his meal with the others. And so this is a man's cub. Now, was there ever a wolf that could boast of a man's cub among her children?'

'I have heard now and again of such a thing, but never in our Pack or in my time,' said Father Wolf. 'He is altogether without hair, and I could kill him with a touch of my foot. But see, he looks up and is not afraid.'

The moonlight was blocked out of the mouth of the cave, for Shere Khan's great square head and shoulders were thrust into the entrance. Tabaqui, behind him, was squeaking: 'My lord, my lord, it went in here!'

'Shere Khan does us great honour,' said Father Wolf, but his eyes were very angry. 'What does Shere Khan need?'

'My quarry. A man's cub went this way,' said Shere Khan. 'Its parents have run off. Give it to me.'

Shere Khan had jumped at a woodcutter's camp-fire, as Father Wolf had said, and was furious from the pain of his burned feet. But Father Wolf knew that the mouth of the cave was too narrow for a tiger to come in by. Even where he was, Shere Khan's shoulders and forepaws were cramped for want of room, as a man's would be if he tried to fight in a barrel.

'The Wolves are a free people,' said Father Wolf. 'They take orders from the Head of the Pack, and not from any striped cattle-killer. The man's cub is ours—to kill if we choose.'

'Ye choose and ye do not choose! What talk is this of choosing? By the bull that I killed, am I to stand nosing into your dog's den for my fair dues? It is I, Shere Khan, who speak!'

The tiger's roar filled the cave with thunder. Mother Wolf shook herself clear of the cubs and sprang forward, her eyes, like two green moons in the darkness, facing the blazing eyes of Shere Khan.

'And it is I, Raksha [The Demon], who answer. The man's cub is mine, Lungri—mine to me! He shall not be killed. He shall live to run with the Pack and to hunt with the Pack; and in the end, look you, hunter of little naked cubs—frog-eater—fish-killer—he shall hunt *thee!* Now get hence, or by the Sambhur that I killed (*I* eat no starved cattle), back thou goest to thy mother, burned beast of the jungle, lamer than ever thou camest into the world! Go!'

Father Wolf looked on amazed. He had almost forgotten the days when he won Mother Wolf in fair fight from five other wolves, when she ran in the Pack and was not called The Demon for compliment's sake. Shere Khan might have faced Father Wolf, but he could not stand up against Mother Wolf, for he knew that where he was she had all the advantage of the ground, and would fight to the death. So he backed out of the cave-mouth growling, and when he was clear he shouted:—

'Each dog barks in his own yard! We will see what the Pack will say to this fostering of man-cubs. The cub is mine, and to my teeth he will come in the end, O bush-tailed thieves!'

Mother Wolf threw herself down panting among the cubs, and Father Wolf said to her gravely:—

'Shere Khan speaks this much truth. The cub must be shown to the Pack. Wilt thou still keep him, Mother?'

'Keep him!' she gasped. 'He came naked, by night, alone and very hungry; yet he was not afraid! Look, he has pushed one of my babes to one side already. And that lame butcher would have killed him and would have run off to the Waingunga while the villagers here hunted through all our lairs in revenge! Keep him? Assuredly I will keep him. Lie still, little frog. O thou Mowgli—for Mowgli the Frog I will call thee—the time will come when thou wilt hunt Shere Khan as he has hunted thee.'

'But what will our Pack say?' said Father Wolf.

The Law of the Jungle lays down very clearly that any wolf may, when he marries, withdraw from the Pack he belongs to; but as soon as his cubs are old enough to stand on their feet he must bring them to the Pack Council, which is generally held once a month at full moon, in order that the other wolves may identify them. After that inspection the cubs are free to run where they please, and until they have killed their first buck no excuse is accepted if a grown wolf of the Pack kills one of them. The punishment is death where the murderer can be found; and if you think for a minute you will see that this must be so.

Father Wolf waited till his cubs could run a little, and then on the night of the Pack Meeting took them and Mowgli and Mother Wolf to the Council Rock—a hilltop covered with stones and boulders where a hundred wolves could hide. Akela, the great grey Lone Wolf, who led all the Pack by strength and cunning, lay out at full length on his rock, and below him sat forty or more wolves of every size and colour, from badger-coloured veterans who could handle a buck alone, to young black three-year-olds who thought they could. The Lone Wolf had led them for a year now. He had fallen twice into a wolf-trap in his youth, and once he had been beaten and left for dead; so he knew the manners and customs of men. There was very little talking at the Rock. The cubs tumbled over each other in the centre of the circle where their mothers and fathers sat, and now and again a senior wolf would go quietly up to a cub, look at him carefully, and return to his place on noiseless feet. Sometimes a mother would push her cub far out into the moonlight, to be sure that he had not been overlooked. Akela from his rock would cry: 'Ye know the Law—ye know the Law. Look well, O Wolves!' and the anxious mothers would take up the call: 'Look—look well, O Wolves!'

At last—and Mother Wolf's neck-bristles lifted as the time came—Father Wolf pushed 'Mowgli the Frog,' as they called him, into the centre, where he sat laughing and playing with some pebbles that glistened in the moonlight.

Akela never raised his head from his paws, but went on with the monotonous cry: 'Look well!' A muffled roar came up from behind the rocks—the voice of Shere Khan crying: 'The cub is mine. Give him to me. What have the Free People to do with a man's cub?' Akela never even twitched his ears: all he said was: 'Look well, O Wolves! What have the Free People to do with the orders of any save the Free People? Look well!'

There was a chorus of deep growls, and a young wolf in his fourth year flung back Shere Khan's question to Akela: 'What have the Free People to do with a man's cub?' Now, the Law of the Jungle lays down that if there is any dispute as to the right of a cub to be accepted by the Pack, he must be spoken for by at least two members of the Pack who are not his father and mother.

'Who speaks for this cub?' said Akela. 'Among the Free People who speaks?' There was no answer, and Mother Wolf got ready for what she knew would be her last fight, if things came to fighting.

Then the only other creature who is allowed at the Pack Council—Baloo, the sleepy brown bear who teaches the wolf-cubs the Law of the Jungle: old Baloo, who can come and go where he pleases because he eats only nuts and roots and honey—rose up on his hindquarters and grunted.

'The man's cub—the man's cub?' he said. '*I* speak for the man's cub. There is no harm in a man's cub. I have no gift of words, but I speak the truth. Let him run with the Pack, and be entered with the others. I myself will teach him.'

'We need yet another,' said Akela. 'Baloo has spoken, and he is our teacher for the young cubs. Who speaks besides Baloo?'

A black shadow dropped down into the circle. It was Bagheera the Black Panther, inky black all over, but with the panther markings showing up in certain lights like the pattern of watered silk. Everybody knew Bagheera, and nobody cared to cross his path; for he was as cunning as Tabaqui, as bold as the wild buffalo, and as reckless as the wounded elephant. But he had a voice as soft as wild honey dripping from a tree, and a skin softer than down.

'O Akela, and ye the Free People,' he purred, 'I have no right in your assembly; but the Law of the Jungle says that if there is a doubt which is not a killing matter in regard to a new cub, the life of that cub may be bought at a price. And the Law does not say who may or may not pay that price. Am I right?'

'Good! good!' said the young wolves, who are always hungry. 'Listen to Bagheera. The cub can be bought for a price. It is the Law.'

'Knowing that I have no right to speak here, I ask your leave.'

'Speak then,' cried twenty voices.

'To kill a naked cub is shame. Besides, he may make better sport for you when he is grown. Baloo has spoken in his behalf. Now to Baloo's word I will add one bull, and a fat one, newly killed, not half a mile from here, if ye will accept the man's cub according to the Law. Is it difficult?'

There was a clamour of scores of voices, saying: 'What matter? He will die in the winter rains. He will scorch in the sun. What harm can a naked frog do us? Let him run with the Pack. Where is the bull, Bagheera? Let him be accepted.' And then came Akela's deep bay, crying: 'Look well—look well, O Wolves!'

Mowgli was still deeply interested in the pebbles and he did not notice when the wolves came and looked at him one by one. At last they all went down the hill for the dead bull, and only Akela, Bagheera, Baloo, and Mowgli's own wolves were left. Shere Khan roared still in the night, for he was very angry that Mowgli had not been handed over to him.

'Ay, roar well,' said Bagheera, under his whiskers; 'for the time comes when this naked thing will make thee roar to another tune, or I know nothing of Man.'

'It was well done,' said Akela. 'Men and their cubs are very wise. He may be a help in time.'

'Truly, a help in time of need; for none can hope to lead the Pack for ever,' said Bagheera.

Akela said nothing. He was thinking of the time that comes to every leader of every pack when his strength goes from him and he gets feebler and feebler, till at last he is killed by the wolves and a new leader comes up–to be killed in his turn.

'Take him away,' he said to Father Wolf, 'and train him as befits one of the Free People.'

And that is how Mowgli was entered into the Seeonee Wolf-Pack at the price of a bull and on Baloo's good word.

Now you must be content to skip ten or eleven whole years, and only guess at all the wonderful life that Mowgli led among the wolves, because if it were written out it would fill ever so many books. He grew up with the cubs, though they, of course, were grown wolves almost before he was a child, and Father Wolf taught him his business, and the meaning of things in the Jungle, till every rustle in the grass, every breath of the warm night air, every note of the owls above his head, every scratch of a bat's claws as it roosted for a while in a tree, and every splash of every little fish jumping in a pool, meant just as much to him as the work of his office means to a business man. When he was not learning, he sat out in the sun and slept, and ate and went to sleep again; when he felt dirty or hot he swam in the forest pools; and when he wanted honey (Baloo told him that honey and nuts were just as pleasant to eat as raw meat) he climbed up for it, and that Bagheera showed him how to do. Bagheera would lie out on a branch and call, 'Come along, Little Brother,' and at first Mowgli would cling like the sloth, but afterwards he would fling himself through the branches almost as boldly as the grey ape. He took his place at the Council Rock, too, when the Pack met, and there he discovered that if he stared hard at any wolf, the wolf would be forced to drop his eyes, and so he used to stare for fun. At other times he would pick the long thorns out of the pads of his friends, for wolves suffer terribly from thorns and burrs in their coats. He would go down the hillside into the cultivated lands by night, and look very curiously at the villagers in their huts, but he had a mistrust of men because Bagheera showed him a square box with a drop-gate so cunningly hidden in the Jungle that he nearly walked into it, and told him that it was a trap. He loved better than anything else to go with Bagheera into the dark warm heart of the forest, to sleep all through the drowsy day, and at night to see how Bagheera did his killing. Bagheera killed right and left as he felt hungry, and so did Mowgli—with one exception. As soon as he was old enough to understand things, Bagheera told him that he must never touch cattle because he had been bought into the Pack at the price of a bull's life. 'All the Jungle is thine,' said Bagheera, 'and thou canst kill everything that thou art strong enough to kill; but for the sake of the bull that bought thee thou must never kill or eat any cattle young or old. That is the Law of the Jungle.' Mowgli obeyed faithfully.

And he grew and grew strong as a boy must grow who does not know that he is learning any lessons, and who has nothing in the world to think of except things to eat.

Mother Wolf told him once or twice that Shere Khan was not a creature to be trusted, and that some day he must kill Shere Khan; but though a young wolf would have remembered that advice every hour, Mowgli forgot it because he was only a boy—though he would have called himself a wolf if he had been able to speak in any human tongue.

Shere Khan was always crossing his path in the Jungle, for as Akela grew older and feebler the lame tiger had come to be great friends with the younger wolves of the Pack, who followed him for scraps, a thing that Akela would never have allowed if he had dared to push his authority to the proper bounds. Then Shere Khan would flatter them and wonder that such fine young hunters were content to be led by a dying wolf and a man's cub. 'They tell me,' Shere Khan would say, 'that at Council ye dare not look him between the eyes'; and the young wolves would growl and bristle.

Bagheera, who had eyes and ears everywhere, knew something of this, and once or twice he told Mowgli in so many words that Shere Khan would kill him some day; and Mowgli would laugh and answer: 'I have the Pack and I have thee; and Baloo, though he is so lazy, might strike a blow or two for my sake. Why should I be afraid?'

It was one very warm day that a new notion came to Bagheera—born of something that he had heard. Perhaps Ikki the Porcupine had told him; but he said to Mowgli when they were deep in the Jungle, as the boy lay with his head on Bagheera's beautiful black skin: 'Little

Brother, how often have I told thee that Shere Khan is thy enemy?'

'As many times as there are nuts on that palm,' said Mowgli, who, naturally, could not count. 'What of it? I am sleepy, Bagheera, and Shere Khan is all long tail and loud talk—like Mao, the Peacock.'

'But this is no time for sleeping. Baloo knows it; I know it; the Pack know it; and even the foolish, foolish deer know. Tabaqui has told thee, too.'

'Ho! ho!' said Mowgli. 'Tabaqui came to me not long ago with some rude talk that I was a naked man's cub and not fit to dig pig-nuts; but I caught Tabaqui by the tail and swung him twice against a palm-tree to teach him better manners.'

'That was foolishness; for though Tabaqui is a mischief-maker, he would have told thee of something that concerned thee closely. Open those eyes, Little Brother. Shere Khan dare not kill thee in the Jungle; but remember, Akela is very old, and soon the day comes when he cannot kill his buck, and then he will be leader no more. Many of the wolves that looked thee over when thou wast brought to the Council first are old too, and the young wolves believe, as Shere Khan has taught them, that a man-cub has no place with the Pack. In a little time thou wilt be a man.'

'And what is a man that he should not run with his brothers?' said Mowgli. 'I was born in the Jungle. I have obeyed the Law of the Jungle and there is no wolf of ours from whose paws I have not pulled a thorn. Surely they are my brothers!'

Bagheera stretched himself at full length and half shut his eyes. 'Little Brother,' said he, 'feel under my jaw.'

Mowgli put up his strong brown hand, and just under Bagheera's silky chin, where the giant rolling muscles were all hid by the glossy hair, he came upon a little bald spot.

'There is no one in the Jungle that knows that I, Bagheera, carry that mark—the mark of the collar; and yet, Little Brother, I was born among men, and it was among men that my mother died—in the cages of the King's Palace at Oodeypore. It was because of this that I paid the price for thee at the Council when thou wast a little naked cub. Yes, I too was born among men. I had never seen the Jungle. They fed me behind bars from an iron pan till one night I felt that I was Bagheera—the Panther—and no man's plaything, and I broke the silly lock with one blow of my paw and came away; and because I had learned the ways of men, I became more terrible in the Jungle than Shere Khan. Is it not so?'

'Yes,' said Mowgli; 'all the Jungle fear Bagheera—all except Mowgli.'

'Oh, *thou* art a man's cub,' said the Black Panther, very tenderly; 'and even as I returned to my Jungle, so thou must go back to men at last,—to the men who are thy brothers,—if thou art not killed in the Council.'

'But why—but why should any wish to kill me?' said Mowgli.

'Look at me,' said Bagheera; and Mowgli looked at him steadily between the eyes. The big panther turned his head away in half a minute.

'*That* is why,' he said, shifting his paw on the leaves. 'Not even I can look thee between the eyes, and I was born among men, and I love thee, Little Brother. The others they hate thee because their eyes cannot meet thine—because thou art wise—because thou hast pulled out thorns from their feet—because thou art a man.'

'I did not know these things,' said Mowgli sullenly; and he frowned under his heavy black eyebrows.

'What is the Law of the Jungle? Strike first and then give tongue. By thy very carelessness they know that thou art a man. But be wise. It is in my heart that when Akela misses his next kill,—and at each hunt it costs him more to pin the buck,—the Pack will turn against him and against thee. They will hold a Jungle Council at the Rock, and then —and then—I have it!' said Bagheera, leaping up. 'Go thou down quickly to the men's huts in the valley, and take some of the Red Flower which they grow there, so that when the time comes thou mayest have even a stronger friend than I or Baloo or those of the Pack that love thee. Get the Red Flower.'

By Red Flower Bagheera meant fire, only no creature in the Jungle will call fire by its proper name. Every beast lives in deadly fear of it, and invents a hundred ways of describing it.

'The Red Flower?' said Mowgli. 'That grows outside their huts in the twilight. I will get some.'

'There speaks the man's cub,' said Bagheera proudly. 'Remember that it grows in little pots. Get one swiftly, and keep it by thee for time of need.'

'Good!' said Mowgli. 'I go. But art thou sure, O my Bagheera'—he slipped his arm round the splendid neck, and looked deep into the big eyes—'art thou sure that all this is Shere Khan's doing?'

'By the Broken Lock that freed me, I am sure, Little Brother.'

'Then, by the Bull that bought me, I will pay Shere Khan full tale for this, and it may be a little over,' said Mowgli; and he bounded away.

'That is a man. That is all a man,' said Bagheera to himself, lying down again. 'Oh, Shere Khan, never was a blacker hunting than that frog-hunt of thine ten years ago!'

Mowgli was far and far through the forest, running hard, and his heart was hot in him. He came to the cave as the evening mist rose, and drew breath, and looked down the valley. The cubs were out, but Mother Wolf, at the back of the cave, knew by his breathing that something was troubling her frog.

'What is it, Son?' she said.

'Some bat's chatter of Shere Khan,' he called back. 'I hunt among the ploughed fields to-night,' and he plunged downward through the bushes, to the stream at the bottom of the valley. There he checked, for he heard the yell of the Pack hunting, heard the bellow of a hunted sambhur, and the snort as the buck turned at bay. Then there were wicked, bitter howls from the young wolves: 'Akela! Akela! Let the Lone Wolf show his strength. Room for the leader of the Pack! Spring, Akela!'

The Lone Wolf must have sprung and missed his hold, for Mowgli heard the snap of his teeth and then a yelp as the sambhur knocked him over with his fore-foot.

He did not wait for anything more, but dashed on; and the yells grew fainter behind him as he ran into the crop-lands where the villagers lived.

'Bagheera spoke truth,' he panted, as he nestled down in some cattle-fodder by the window of a hut. 'To-morrow is one day both for Akela and for me.'

Then he pressed his face close to the window and watched the fire on the hearth. He saw the husbandman's wife get up and feed it in the night with black lumps; and when the morning came and the mists were all white and cold, he saw the man's child pick up a wicker pot plastered inside with earth, fill it with lumps of red-hot charcoal, put it under his blanket, and go out to tend the cows in the byre.

'Is that all?' said Mowgli. 'If a cub can do it, there is nothing to fear'; so he strode round the corner and met the boy, took the pot from his hand, and disappeared into the mist while the boy howled with fear.

'They are very like me,' said Mowgli, blowing into the pot, as he had seen the woman do. 'This thing will die if I do not give it things to eat'; and he dropped twigs and dried bark on the red stuff. Half-way up the hill he met Bagheera with the morning dew shining like moonstones on his coat.

'Akela has missed,' said the Panther. 'They would have killed him last night, but they needed thee also. They were looking for thee on the hill.'

'I was among the ploughed lands. I am ready. See!' Mowgli held up the fire-pot.

'Good! Now, I have seen men thrust a dry branch into that stuff, and presently the Red Flower blossomed at the end of it. Art thou not afraid?'

'No. Why should I fear? I remember now–if it is not a dream–how, before I was a Wolf, I lay beside the Red Flower, and it was warm and pleasant.'

All that day Mowgli sat in the cave tending his fire-pot and dipping dry branches into it to see how they looked. He found a branch that satisfied him, and in the evening when Tabaqui came to the cave and told him rudely enough that he was wanted at the Council Rock, he laughed till Tabaqui ran away. Then Mowgli went to the Council, still laughing.

Akela the Lone Wolf lay by the side of his rock as a sign that the leadership of the Pack was open, and Shere Khan with his following of scrap-fed wolves walked to and fro openly, being flattered. Bagheera lay close to Mowgli, and the fire-pot was between Mowgli's knees. When they were all gathered together, Shere Khan began to speak–a thing he would never have dared to do when Akela was in his prime.

'He has no right,' whispered Bagheera. 'Say so. He is a dog's son. He will be frightened.'

Mowgli sprang to his feet. 'Free People,' he cried, 'does Shere Khan lead the Pack? What has a tiger to do with our leadership?'

'Seeing that the leadership is yet open, and being asked to speak——' Shere Khan began.

'By whom?' said Mowgli. 'Are we *all* jackals, to fawn on this cattle-butcher? The leadership of the Pack is with the Pack alone.'

There were yells of 'Silence, thou man's cub!' 'Let him speak. He has kept our Law'; and at last the seniors of the Pack thundered: 'Let the Dead Wolf speak.' When a leader of the Pack has missed his kill, he is called the Dead Wolf as long as he lives, which is not long, as a rule.

Akela raised his old head wearily:–

'Free People, and ye too, jackals of Shere Khan, for many seasons I have led ye to and from the kill, and in all my time not one has been trapped or maimed. Now I have missed my kill. Ye know how that plot was made. Ye know how ye brought me up to an untried buck to make my weakness known. It was cleverly done. Your right is to kill me here on the Council Rock now. Therefore, I ask, who comes to make an end of the Lone Wolf? For it is my right, by the Law of the Jungle, that ye come one by one.'

There was a long hush, for no single wolf cared to fight Akela to the death. Then Shere Khan roared: 'Bah! what have we to do with this toothless fool? He is doomed to die! It is the man-cub who has lived too long. Free People, he was my meat from the first. Give him to me. I am weary of this man-wolf folly. He has troubled the Jungle for ten seasons. Give me the man-cub, or I will hunt here always, and not give you one bone. He is a man, a man's child, and from the marrow of my bones I hate him!'

Then more than half the Pack yelled: 'A man! a man! What has a man to do with us? Let him go to his own place.'

'And turn all the people of the villages against us?' clamoured Shere Khan. 'No; give him to me. He is a man, and none of us can look him between the eyes.'

Akela lifted his head again, and said: 'He has eaten our food. He has slept with us. He has driven game for us. He has broken no word of the Law of the Jungle.'

'Also, I paid for him with a bull when he was accepted. The worth of a bull is little, but Bagheera's honour is something that he will perhaps fight for,' said Bagheera, in his gentlest voice.

'A bull paid ten years ago!' the Pack snarled. 'What do we care for bones ten years old?'

'Or for a pledge?' said Bagheera, his white teeth bared under his lip. 'Well are ye called the Free People!'

'No man's cub can run with the people of the Jungle,' howled Shere Khan. 'Give him to me!'

'He is our brother in all but blood,' Akela went on; 'and ye would kill him here! In truth, I have lived too long. Some of ye are eaters of cattle, and of others I have heard that, under Shere Khan's teaching, ye go by dark night and snatch children from the villager's doorstep. Therefore I know ye to be cowards, and it is to cowards I speak. It is certain that I must die, and my life is of no worth, or I would offer that in the Man-cub's place. But for the sake of the Honour of the Pack,—a little matter that by being without a leader ye have forgotten,—I promise that if ye let the Man-cub go to his own place, I will not, when my time comes to die, bare one tooth against ye. I will die without fighting. That will at least save the Pack three lives. More I cannot do; but if ye will, I can save ye the shame that comes of killing a brother against whom there is no fault,—a brother spoken for and bought into the Pack according to the Law of the Jungle.'

'He is a man—a man—a man!' snarled the Pack; and most of the wolves began to gather round Shere Khan, whose tail was beginning to switch.

'Now the business is in thy hands,' said Bagherra to Mowgli. '*We* can do no more except fight.'

Mowgli stood upright—the fire-pot in his hands. Then he stretched out his arms, and yawned in the face of the Council; but he was furious with rage and sorrow, for, wolf-like, the wolves had never told him how they hated him. 'Listen, you!' he cried. 'There is no need for this dog's jabber. Ye have told me so often to-night that I am a man (and indeed I would have been a wolf with you to my life's end), that I feel your words are true. So I do not call ye my brothers any more, but *sag* [dogs], as a man should. What ye will do, and what ye will not do, is not yours to say. That matter is with *me;* and that we may see the matter more plainly, I, the man, have brought here a little of the Red Flower which ye, dogs, fear.'

He flung the fire-pot on the ground, and some of the red coals lit a tuft of dried moss that flared up, as all the Council drew back in terror before the leaping flames.

Mowgli thrust his dead branch into the fire till the twigs lit and crackled, and whirled it above his head among the cowering wolves.

'Thou art the master,' said Bagheera, in an undertone. 'Save Akela from the death. He was ever thy friend.'

Akela, the grim old wolf who had never asked for mercy in his life, gave one piteous look at Mowgli as the boy stood all naked, his long black hair tossing over his shoulders in the light of the blazing branch that made the shadows jump and quiver.

'Good!' said Mowgli, staring round slowly. 'I see that ye are dogs. I go from you to my own people—if they be my own people. The Jungle is shut to me, and I must forget your talk and your companionship; but I will be more merciful than ye are. Because I was all but your brother in blood, I promise that when I am a man among men I will not betray ye to men as you have betrayed me.' He kicked the fire with his foot, and the sparks flew up. 'There shall be no war between any of us and the Pack. But there is a debt to pay before I go.' He strode forward to where Shere Khan sat blinking stupidly at the flames, and caught him by the tuft on his chin. Bagheera followed in case of accidents. 'Up, dog!' Mowgli cried. 'Up, when a man speaks, or I will set that coat ablaze!'

Shere Khan's ears lay flat back on his head, and he shut his eyes, for the blazing branch was very near.

'This cattle-killer said he would kill me in the Council because he had not killed me when I was a cub. Thus and thus, then, do we beat dogs when we are men. Stir a whisker, Lungri, and I ram the Red Flower down thy gullet!' He beat Shere Khan over the head with the branch, and the tiger whimpered and whined in an agony of fear.

'Pah! Singed jungle-cat–go now! But remember when next I come to the Council Rock, as a man should come, it will be with Shere Khan's hide on my head. For the rest, Akela goes free to live as he pleases. Ye will *not* kill him, because that is not my will. Nor do I think that ye will sit here any longer, lolling out your tongues as though ye were somebodies, instead of dogs whom I drive out–thus! Go!' The fire was burning furiously at the end of the branch, and Mowgli struck right and left round the circle, and the wolves ran howling with the sparks burning their fur. At last there were only Akela, Bagheera, and perhaps ten wolves that had taken Mowgli's part. Then something began to hurt Mowgli inside him, as he had never been hurt in his life before, and he caught his breath and sobbed, and the tears ran down his face.

'What is it? What is it?' he said. 'I do not wish to leave the Jungle, and I do not know what this is. Am I dying, Bagheera?'

'No, Little Brother. Those are only tears such as men use,' said Bagheera. 'Now I know thou art a man, and a man's cub no longer. The Jungle is shut indeed to thee henceforward. Let them fall, Mowgli. They are only tears.' So Mowgli sat and cried as though his heart would break; and he had never cried in all his life before.

'Now,' he said, 'I will go to men. But first I must say farewell to my mother'; and he went to the cave where she lived with Father Wolf, and he cried on her coat, while the four cubs howled miserably.

'Ye will not forget me?' said Mowgli.

'Never while we can follow a trail,' said the cubs. 'Come to the foot of the hill when thou art a man, and we will talk to thee; and we will come into the crop-lands to play with thee by night.'

'Come soon!' said Father Wolf. 'Oh, wise little frog, come again soon; for we be old, thy mother and I.'

'Come soon,' said Mother Wolf, 'little naked son of mine; for, listen, child of man, I loved thee more than ever I loved my cubs.'

'I will surely come,' said Mowgli; 'and when I come it will be to lay out Shere Khan's hide upon the Council Rock. Do not forget me! Tell them in the Jungle never to forget me!'

The dawn was beginning to break when Mowgli went down the hillside alone, to meet those mysterious things that are called men.

THE MIRACLE OF PURUN BHAGAT

The night we felt the earth would move
  We stole and plucked him by the hand,
Because we loved him with the love
  That knows but cannot understand.

And when the roaring hillside broke,
  And all our world fell down in rain,
We saved him, we the Little Folk;
  But lo! he does not come again!

Mourn now, we saved him for the sake
  Of such poor love as wild ones may.
Mourn ye! Our brother will not wake,
  And his own kind drive us away!

Dirge of the Langurs.

THERE was once a man in India who was Prime Minister of one of the semi-independent native States in the north-western part of the country. He was a Brahmin, so high-caste that caste ceased to have any particular meaning for him; and his father had been an important official in the gay-coloured tag-rag and bobtail of an old-fashioned Hindu Court. But as Purun Dass grew up he felt that the old order of things was changing, and that if any one wished to get on in the world he must stand well with the English, and imitate all that the English believed to be good. At the same time a native official must keep his own master's favour. This was a difficult game, but the quiet, close-mouthed young Brahmin, helped by a good English education at a Bombay University, played it coolly, and rose, step by step, to be Prime Minister of the kingdom. That is to say, he held more real power than his master the Maharajah.

When the old king—who was suspicious of the English, their railways and telegraphs—died, Purun Dass stood high with his young successor, who had been tutored by an Englishman; and between them, though he always took care that his master should have the credit, they established schools for little girls, made roads, and started State dispensaries and shows of agricultural implements, and published a yearly blue-book on the 'Moral and Material Progress of the State,' and the Foreign Office and the Government of India were delighted. Very few native States take up English progress altogether, for they will not believe, as Purun Dass showed he did, that what was good for the Englishman must be twice as good for the Asiatic. The Prime Minister became the honoured friend of Viceroys, and Governors, and Lieutenant-Governors, and medical missionaries, and common missionaries, and hard-riding English officers who came to shoot in the State preserves, as well as of whole hosts of tourists who travelled up and down India in the cold weather, showing how things ought to be managed. In his spare time he would endow scholarships for the study of medicine and manufactures on strictly English lines, and write letters to the *Pioneer,* the greatest Indian daily paper, explaining his master's aims and objects.

At last he went to England on a visit, and had to pay enormous sums to the priests when he came back; for even so high-caste a Brahmin as Purun Dass lost caste by crossing the black sea. In London he met and talked with every one worth knowing—men whose names go all over the world—and saw a great deal more than he said. He was given honorary degrees by learned universities, and he made speeches and talked of Hindu social reform to English ladies in evening dress, till all London cried, 'This is the most fascinating man we have ever met at dinner since cloths were first laid.'

When he returned to India there was a blaze of glory, for the Viceroy himself made a special visit to confer upon the Maharajah the Grand Cross of the Star of India—all diamonds and ribbons and enamel; and at the same ceremony, while the cannon boomed, Purun Dass was made a Knight Commander of the Order of the Indian Empire; so that his name stood Sir Purun Dass, K.C.I.E.

That evening, at dinner in the big Viceregal tent, he stood up with the badge and the collar of the Order on his breast, and replying to the toast of his master's health, made a speech few Englishmen could have bettered.

Next month, when the city had returned to its sun-baked quiet, he did a thing no Englishman would have dreamed of doing; for, so far as the world's affairs went, he died. The jewelled order of his knighthood went back to the Indian Government, and a new Prime Minister was appointed to the charge of affairs, and a great game of General Post began in all the subordinate appointments. The priests knew what had happened, and the people guessed; but India is the one place in the world where a man can do as he pleases and nobody asks why; and the fact that Dewan Sir Purun Dass, K.C.I.E., had resigned position, palace, and power, and taken up the begging-bowl and ochre-coloured dress of a Sunnyasi, or holy man, was considered nothing extraordinary. He had been, as the Old Law recommends, twenty years a youth, twenty years a fighter,—though he had never carried a weapon in his life,—and twenty years head of a household. He had used his wealth and his power for what he knew both to be worth; he had taken honour when it came his way; he had seen men and cities far and near, and men and cities had stood up and honoured him. Now he would let those things go, as a man drops the cloak he no longer needs.

Behind him, as he walked through the city gates, an antelope skin and brass-handled crutch under his arm, and a begging-bowl of polished brown *coco-de-mer* in his hand, barefoot, alone, with eyes cast on the ground—behind him they were firing salutes from the bastions in honour of his happy successor. Purun Dass nodded. All that life was ended; and he bore it no more ill-will or good-will than a man bears to a colourless dream of the night. He was a Sunnyasi—a houseless, wandering mendicant, depending on his neighbours for his daily bread; and so long as there is a morsel to divide in India, neither priest nor beggar starves. He had never in his life tasted meat, and very seldom eaten even fish. A five-pound note would have covered his personal expenses for food through any one of the many years in which he had been absolute master of millions of money. Even when he was being lionised in London he had held before him his dream of peace and quiet—the long, white, dusty Indian road, printed all over with bare feet, the incessant, slow-moving traffic, and the sharp-smelling wood smoke curling up under the fig-trees in the twilight, where the wayfarers sit at their evening meal.

When the time came to make that dream true the Prime Minister took the proper steps, and in three days you might more easily have found a bubble in the trough of the long Atlantic seas than Purun Dass among the roving, gathering, separating millions of India.

At night his antelope skin was spread where the darkness overtook him—sometimes in a Sunnyasi monastery by the roadside; sometimes by a mud-pillar shrine of Kala Pir, where the Yogis, who are another misty division of holy men, would receive him as they do those who know what castes and divisions are worth; sometimes on the outskirts of a little Hindu village, where the children would steal up with the food their parents had prepared; and sometimes on the pitch of the bare grazing-grounds, where the flame of his stick fire waked the drowsy camels. It was all one to Purun Dass—or Purun Bhagat, as he called himself now. Earth, people, and food were all one. But unconsciously his feet drew him away northward and eastward; from the south to Rohtak; from Rohtak to Kurnool; from Kurnool to ruined Samanah, and then up-stream along the dried bed of the Gugger river that fills only when the rain falls in the hills, till one day he saw the far line of the great Himalayas.

Then Purun Bhagat smiled, for he remembered that his mother was of Rajput Brahmin birth, from Kulu way—a Hill-woman, always homesick for the snows—and that the least touch of Hill blood draws a man in the end back to where he belongs.

'Yonder,' said Purun Bhagat, breasting the lower slopes of the Sewaliks, where the cacti stand up like seven-branched candlesticks—'yonder I shall sit down and get knowledge'; and the cool wind of the Himalayas whistled about his ears as he trod the road that led to Simla.

The last time he had come that way it had been in state, with a clattering cavalry escort, to visit the gentlest and most affable of Viceroys; and the two had talked for an hour together about mutual friends in London, and what the Indian common folk really thought of things. This time Purun Bhagat paid no calls, but leaned on the rail of the Mall, watching that glorious view of the Plains spread out forty miles below, till a native Mohammedan policeman told him he was obstructing traffic; and Purun Bhagat salaamed reverently to the Law, because he knew the value of it, and was seeking for a Law of his own. Then he moved on, and slept that night in an empty hut at Chota Simla, which looks like the very last end of the earth, but it was only the beginning of his journey.

He followed the Himalaya-Tibet road, the little ten-foot track that is blasted out of solid rock, or strutted out on timbers over gulfs a thousand feet deep; that dips into warm, wet, shut-in valleys, and climbs out across bare, grassy hill-shoulders where the sun strikes like a burning-glass; or turns through dripping, dark forests where the tree-ferns dress the trunks from head to heel, and the pheasant calls to his mate. And he met Tibetan herdsmen with their dogs and flocks of sheep, each sheep with a little bag of borax on his back, and wandering wood-cutters, and cloaked and blanketed Lamas from Tibet, coming into India on pilgrimage, and envoys of little solitary Hill-states, posting furiously on ring-streaked and piebald ponies, or the cavalcade of a Rajah paying a visit; or else for a long, clear day he would see nothing more than a black bear grunting and rooting below in the valley. When he first started, the roar of the world he had left still rang in his ears, as the roar of a tunnel rings long after the train has passed through; but when he had put the Mutteeanee Pass behind him that was all done, and Purun Bhagat was alone with himself, walking, wondering, and thinking, his eyes on the ground, and his thoughts with the clouds.

One evening he crossed the highest pass he had met till then—it had been a two-days' climb—and came out on a line of snow-peaks that banded all the horizon—mountains from fifteen to twenty thousand feet high, looking almost near enough to hit with a stone, though they were fifty or sixty miles away. The pass was crowned with dense, dark forest—deodar, walnut, wild cherry, wild olive, and wild pear, but mostly deodar, which is the Himalayan cedar; and under the shadow of the deodars stood a deserted shrine to Kali—who is Durga, who is Sitala, who is sometimes worshipped against the smallpox.

Purun Bhagat swept the stone floor clean, smiled at the grinning statue, made himself a little mud fireplace at the back of the shrine, spread his antelope skin on a bed of fresh pine-needles, tucked his *bairagi*—his brass-handled crutch—under his armpit, and sat down to rest.

Immediately below him the hillside fell away, clean and cleared for fifteen hundred feet, where a little village of stone-walled houses, with roofs of beaten earth, clung to the steep tilt. All round it the tiny terraced fields lay out like aprons of patchwork on the knees of the mountain, and cows no bigger than beetles grazed between the smooth stone circles of the threshing-floors. Looking across the valley, the eye was deceived by the size of things, and could not at first realise that what seemed to be low scrub, on the opposite mountain-flank, was in truth a forest of hundred-foot pines. Purun Bhagat saw an eagle swoop across the gigantic hollow, but the great bird dwindled to a dot ere it was half-way over. A few bands of scattered clouds strung up and down the valley, catching on a shoulder of the hills, or rising up and dying out when they were level with the head of the pass. And 'Here shall I find peace,' said Purun Bhagat.

Now, a Hill-man makes nothing of a few hundred feet up or down, and as soon as the villagers saw the smoke in the deserted shrine, the village priest climbed up the terraced hillside to welcome the stranger.

When he met Purun Bhagat's eyes—the eyes of a man used to control thousands—he bowed to the earth, took the begging-bowl without a word, and returned to the village, saying, 'We have at last a holy man. Never have I seen such a man. He is of the Plains—but pale-coloured—a Brahmin of the Brahmins.' Then all the housewives of the village said, 'Think you he will stay with us?' and each did her best to cook the most savoury meal for the Bhagat. Hill-food is very simple, but with buckwheat and Indian corn, and rice and red pepper, and little fish out of the stream in the valley, and honey from the flue-like hives built in the stone walls, and dried apricots, and turmeric, and wild ginger, and bannocks of flour, a devout woman can make good things, and it was a full bowl that the priest carried to the Bhagat. Was he going to stay? asked the priest. Would he need a *chela*—a disciple—to beg for him? Had he a blanket against the cold weather? Was the food good?

Purun Bhagat ate, and thanked the giver. It was in his mind to stay. That was sufficient, said the priest. Let the begging-bowl be placed outside the shrine, in the hollow made by those two twisted roots, and daily should the Bhagat be fed; for the village felt honoured that such a man—he looked timidly into the Bhagat's face—should tarry among them.

That day saw the end of Purun Bhagat's wanderings. He had come to the place appointed for him—the silence and the space. After this, time stopped, and he, sitting at the mouth of the shrine, could not tell whether he were alive or dead; a man with control of his limbs, or a part of the hills, and the clouds, and the shifting rain and sunlight. He would repeat a Name softly to himself a hundred hundred times, till, at each repetition, he seemed to move more and more out of his body, sweeping up to the doors of some tremendous discovery; but, just as the door was opening, his body would drag him back, and, with grief, he felt he was locked up again in the flesh and bones of Purun Bhagat.

Every morning the filled begging-bowl was laid silently in the crutch of the roots outside the shrine. Sometimes the priest brought it; sometimes a Ladakhi trader, lodging in the village, and anxious to get merit, trudged up the path; but, more often, it was the woman who had cooked the meal overnight; and she would murmur, hardly above her breath: 'Speak for me before the gods, Bhagat. Speak for such a one, the wife of so-and-so!' Now and then some bold child would be allowed the honour, and Purun Bhagat would hear him drop the bowl and run as fast as his little legs could carry him, but the Bhagat never came down to the village. It was laid out like a map at his feet. He could see the evening gatherings, held on the circle of the threshing-floors, because that was the only level ground; could see the wonderful unnamed green of the young rice, the indigo blues of the Indian corn, the dock-like patches of buckwheat, and, in its season, the red bloom of the amaranth, whose tiny seeds, being neither grain nor pulse, make a food that can be lawfully eaten by Hindus in time of fasts.

When the year turned, the roofs of the huts were all little squares of purest gold, for it was on the roofs that they laid out their cobs of the corn to dry. Hiving and harvest, rice-sowing and husking, passed before his eyes, all embroidered down there on the many-sided plots of fields, and he thought of them all, and wondered what they all led to at the long last.

Even in populated India a man cannot a day sit still before the wild things run over him as though he were a rock; and in that wilderness very soon the wild things, who knew Kali's Shrine well, came back to look at the intruder. The *langurs,* the big grey-whiskered monkeys of the Himalayas, were, naturally, the first, for they are alive with curiosity; and when they had upset the begging-bowl, and rolled it round the floor, and tried their teeth on the brass-handled crutch, and made faces at the antelope skin, they decided that the human being who sat so still was harmless. At evening, they would leap down from the pines, and beg with their hands for things to eat, and then swing off in graceful curves. They liked the warmth of the fire, too, and huddled round it till Purun Bhagat had to push them aside to throw on more fuel; and in the morning, as often as not, he would find a furry ape sharing his blanket. All day long, one or other of the tribe would sit by his side, staring out at the snows, crooning and looking unspeakably wise and sorrowful.

After the monkeys came the *barasingh,* that big deer which is like our red deer, but stronger. He wished to rub off the velvet of his horns against the cold stones of Kali's statue, and stamped his feet when he saw the man at the shrine. But Purun Bhagat never moved, and, little by little, the royal stag edged up and nuzzled his shoulder. Purun Bhagat slid one cool hand along the hot antlers, and the touch soothed the fretted beast, who bowed his head, and Purun Bhagat very softly rubbed and ravelled off the velvet. Afterward, the *barasingh* brought his doe and fawn—gentle things that mumbled on the holy man's blanket—or would come alone at night, his eyes green in the fire-flicker, to take his share of fresh walnuts. At last, the musk-deer, the shyest and almost the smallest of the deerlets, came, too, her big rabbity ears erect; even brindled, silent *mushicknabha* must needs find out what the light in the shrine meant, and drop out her moose-like nose into Purun Bhagat's lap, coming and going with the shadows of the fire. Purun Bhagat called them all 'my brothers,' and his low call of *'Bhai! Bhai!'* would draw them from the forest at noon if they were within earshot. The Himalayan black bear, moody and suspicious—Sona, who has the V-shaped white mark under his chin—passed that way more than once; and since the Bhagat showed no fear, Sona showed no anger, but watched him, and came closer, and begged a share of the caresses, and a dole of bread or wild berries. Often, in the still dawns, when the Bhagat would climb to the very crest of the pass to watch the red day walking along the peaks of the snows, he would find Sona shuffling and grunting at his heels, thrusting a curious fore-paw under fallen trunks, and bringing it away with a *whoof* of impatience; or his early steps would wake Sona where he lay curled up, and the great brute, rising erect, would think to fight, till he heard the Bhagat's voice and knew his best friend.

Nearly all hermits and holy men who live apart from the big cities have the reputation of being able to work miracles with the wild things, but all the miracle lies in keeping still, in never making a hasty movement, and, for a long time, at least, in never looking directly at a visitor. The villagers saw the outline of the *barasingh* stalking like a shadow through the dark forest behind the shrine; saw the *minaul,* the Himalayan pheasant, blazing in her best colours before Kali's statue; and the *langurs* on their haunches, inside, playing with the walnut shells. Some of the children, too, had heard Sona singing to himself, bear-fashion, behind the fallen rocks, and the Bhagat's reputation as miracle-worker stood firm.

Yet nothing was farther from his mind than miracles. He believed that all things were one big Miracle, and when a man knows that much he knows something to go upon. He knew for a certainty that there was nothing great and nothing little in this world: and day and night he strove to think out his way into the heart of things, back to the place whence his soul had come.

So thinking, his untrimmed hair fell down about his shoulders, the stone slab at the side of the antelope skin was dented into a little hole by the foot of his brass-handled crutch, and the place between the tree-trunks, where the begging-bowl rested day after day, sunk and wore into a hollow almost as smooth as the brown shell itself; and each beast knew his exact place at the fire. The fields changed their colours with the seasons; the threshing-floors filled and emptied, and filled again and again; and again and again, when winter came, the *langurs* frisked among the branches feathered with light snow, till the mother-monkeys brought their sad-eyed little babies up from the warmer valleys with the spring. There were few changes in the village. The priest was older, and many of the little children who used to come with the begging-dish sent their own children now; and when you asked of the villagers how long their holy man had lived in Kali's Shrine at the head of the pass, they answered, 'Always.'

Then came such summer rains as had not been known in the Hills for many seasons. Through three good months the valley was wrapped in cloud and soaking mist—steady, unrelenting downfall, breaking off into thunder-shower after thunder-shower. Kali's Shrine stood above the clouds, for the most part, and there was a whole month in which the Bhagat never caught a glimpse of his village. It was packed away under a white floor of cloud that swayed and shifted and rolled on itself and bulged upward, but never broke from its piers—the streaming flanks of the valley.

All that time he heard nothing but the sound of a million little waters, overhead from the trees, and underfoot along the ground, soaking through the pine-needles, dripping from the tongues of draggled fern, and spouting in newly-torn muddy channels down the slopes. Then the sun came out, and drew forth the good incense of the deodars and the rhododendrons, and that far-off, clean smell which the Hill people call 'the smell of the snows.' The hot sunshine lasted for a week, and then the rains gathered together for their last downpour, and the water fell in sheets that flayed off the skin of the ground and leaped back in mud. Purun Bhagat heaped his fire high that night, for he was sure his brothers would need warmth; but never a beast came to the shrine, though he called and called till he dropped asleep, wondering what had happened in the woods.

It was in the black heart of the night, the rain drumming like a thousand drums, that he was roused by a plucking at his blanket, and, stretching out, felt the little hand of a *langur*. 'It is better here than in the trees,' he said sleepily, loosening a fold of blanket; 'take it and be warm.' The monkey caught his hand and pulled hard. 'Is it food, then?' said Purun Bhagat. 'Wait awhile, and I will prepare some.' As he kneeled to throw fuel on the fire the *langur* ran to the door of the shrine, crooned and ran back again, plucking at the man's knee.

"What is it? What is thy trouble, Brother?' said Purun Bhagat, for the *langur's* eyes were full of things that he could not tell. 'Unless one of thy caste be in a trap—and none set traps here—I will not go into that weather. Look, Brother, even the *barasingh* comes for shelter!'

The deer's antlers clashed as he strode into the shrine, clashed against the grinning statue of Kali. He lowered them in Purun Bhagat's direction and stamped uneasily, hissing through his half-shut nostrils.

'Hai! Hai! Hai!' said the Bhagat, snapping his fingers. 'Is *this* payment for a night's lodging?' But the deer pushed him toward the door, and as he did so Purun Bhagat heard the sound of something opening with a sigh, and saw two slabs of the floor draw away from each other, while the sticky earth below smacked its lips.

'Now I see,' said Purun Bhagat. 'No blame to my brothers that they did not sit by the fire to-night. The mountain is falling. And yet—why should I go?' His eye fell on the empty begging-bowl, and his face changed. 'They have given me good food daily since—since I came, and, if I am not swift, to-morrow there will not be one mouth in the valley. Indeed, I must go and warn them below. Back there, Brother! Let me get to the fire.'

The *barasingh* backed unwillingly as Purun Bhagat drove a pine torch deep into the flame, twirling it till it was well lit. 'Ah! ye came to warn me,' he said, rising. 'Better than that we shall do; better than that. Out, now, and lend me thy neck, Brother, for I have but two feet.'

He clutched the bristling withers of the *barasingh* with his right hand, held the torch away with his left, and stepped out of the shrine into the desperate night. There was no breath of wind, but the rain nearly drowned the flare as the great deer hurried down the slope, sliding on his haunches. As soon as they were clear of the forest more of the Bhagat's brothers joined them. He heard, though he could not see, the *langurs* pressing about him, and behind them the *uhh! uhh!* of Sona. The rain matted his long white hair into ropes; the water splashed beneath his bare feet, and his yellow robe clung to his frail old body, but he stepped down steadily, leaning against the *barasingh*. He was no longer a holy man, but Sir Purun Dass, K.C.I.E., Prime Minister of no small State, a man accustomed to command, going out to save life. Down the steep, plashy path they poured all together, the Bhagat and his brothers, down and down till the deer's feet clicked and stumbled on the wall of a threshing-floor, and he snorted because he smelt Man. Now they were at the head of the one crooked village street, and the Bhagat beat with his crutch on the barred windows of the blacksmith's house, as his torch blazed up in the shelter of the eaves. 'Up and out!' cried Purun Bhagat; and he did not know his own voice, for it was years since he had spoken aloud to a man. 'The hill falls! The hill is falling! Up and out, oh, you within!'

'It is our Bhagat,' said the blacksmith's wife. 'He stands among his beasts. Gather the little ones and give the call.'

It ran from house to house, while the beasts, cramped in the narrow way, surged and huddled round the Bhagat, and Sona puffed impatiently.

The people hurried into the street—they were no more than seventy souls all told—and in the glare of the torches they saw their Bhagat holding back the terrified *barasingh,* while the monkeys plucked piteously at his skirts, and Sona sat on his haunches and roared.

'Across the valley and up the next hill!' shouted Purun Bhagat. 'Leave none behind! We follow!'

Then the people ran as only Hill folk can run, for they knew that in a landslip you must climb for the highest ground across the valley. They fled, splashing through the little river at the bottom, and panted up the terraced fields on the far side, while the Bhagat and his brethren followed. Up and up the opposite mountain they climbed, calling to each other by name—the roll-call of the village—and at their heels toiled the big *barasingh,* weighted by the failing strength of Purun Bhagat. At last the deer stopped in the shadow of a deep pine-wood, five hundred feet up the hillside. His instinct, that had warned him of the coming slide, told him he would be safe here.

Purun Bhagat dropped fainting by his side, for the chill of the rain and that fierce climb were killing him; but first he called to the scattered torches ahead, 'Stay and count your numbers'; then, whispering to the deer as he saw the lights gather in a cluster: 'Stay with me, Brother. Stay—till—I—go!'

There was a sigh in the air that grew to a mutter, and a mutter that grew to a roar, and a roar that passed all sense of hearing, and the hillside on which the villagers stood was hit in the darkness, and rocked to the blow. Then a note as steady, deep, and true as the deep C of the organ drowned everything for perhaps five minutes, while the very roots of the pines quivered to it. It died away, and the sound of the rain falling on miles of hard ground and grass changed to the muffled drum of water on soft earth. That told its own tale.

Never a villager—not even the priest—was bold enough to speak to the Bhagat who had saved their lives. They crouched under the pines and waited till the day. When it came they looked across the valley and saw that what had been forest, and terraced field, and track-threaded grazing-ground was one raw, red, fan-shaped smear, with a few trees flung head-down on the scarp. That red ran high up the hill of their refuge, damming back the little river, which had begun to spread into a brick-coloured lake. Of the village, of the road to the shrine, of the shrine itself, and the forest behind, there was no trace. For one mile in width and two thousand feet in sheer depth the mountain-side had come away bodily, planed clean from head to heel.

And the villagers, one by one, crept through the wood to pray before their Bhagat. They saw the *barasingh* standing over him, who fled when they came near, and they heard the *langurs* wailing in the branches, and Sona moaning up the hill; but their Bhagat was dead, sitting cross-legged, his back against a tree, his crutch under his armpit, and his face turned to the north-east.

The priest said: 'Behold a miracle after a miracle, for in this very attitude must all Sunnyasis be buried! Therefore where he now is we will build the temple to our holy man.'

They built the temple before a year was ended—a little stone-and-earth shrine—and they called the hill the Bhagat's hill, and they worship there with lights and flowers and offerings to this day. But they do not know that the saint of their worship is the late Sir Purun Dass, K.C.I.E., D.C.L., Ph.D., etc., once Prime Minister of the progressive and enlightened State of Mohiniwala, and honorary or corresponding member of more learned and scientific societies than will ever do any good in this world or the next.

WITHOUT BENEFIT OF CLERGY

Before my Spring I garnered Autumn's gain,
Out of her time my field was white with grain,
The year gave up her secrets to my woe.
Forced and deflowered each sick season lay,
In mystery of increase and decay;
I saw the sunset ere men saw the day,
Who am too wise in that I should not know.

Bitter Waters.

I

But if it be a girl?'

'Lord of my life, it cannot be. I have prayed for so many nights, and sent gifts to Sheikh Badl's shrine so often, that I know God will give us a son—a man-child that shall grow into a man. Think of this and be glad. My mother shall be his mother till I can take him again, and the mullah of the Pattan mosque shall cast his nativity—God send he be born in an auspicious hour!—and then, and then thou wilt never weary of me, thy slave.'

'Since when hast thou been a slave, my queen?'

'Since the beginning—till this mercy came to me. How could I be sure of thy love when I knew that I had been bought with silver?'

'Nay, that was the dowry. I paid it to thy mother.'

'And she has buried it, and sits upon it all day long like a hen. What talk is yours of dower! I was bought as though I had been a Lucknow dancing-girl instead of a child.'

'Art thou sorry for the sale?'

'I have sorrowed; but to-day I am glad. Thou wilt never cease to love me now?—answer, my king.'

'Never—never. No.'

'Not even though the *mem-log*—the white women of thy own blood—love thee? And remember, I have watched them driving in the evening; they are very fair.'

'I have seen fire-balloons by the hundred. I have seen the moon, and —then I saw no more fire-balloons.'

Ameera clapped her hands and laughed. 'Very good talk,' she said. Then with an assumption of great stateliness, 'It is enough. Thou hast my permission to depart,—if thou wilt.'

The man did not move. He was sitting on a low red-lacquered couch in a room furnished only with a blue and white floor-cloth, some rugs, and a very complete collection of native cushions. At his feet sat a woman of sixteen, and she was all but all the world in his eyes. By every rule and law she should have been otherwise, for he was an Englishman, and she a Mussulman's daughter bought two years before from her mother, who, being left without money, would have sold Ameera shrieking to the Prince of Darkness if the price had been sufficient.

It was a contract entered into with a light heart; but even before the girl had reached her bloom she came to fill the greater portion of John Holden's life. For her, and the withered hag her mother, he had taken a little house overlooking the great red-walled city and found,—when the marigolds had sprung up by the well in the courtyard, and Ameera had established herself according to her own ideas of comfort, and her mother had ceased grumbling at the inadequacy of the cooking-places, the distance from the daily market, and at matters of house-keeping in general,—that the house was to him his home. Any one could enter his bachelor's bungalow by day or night, and the life that he led there was an unlovely one. In the house in the city his feet only could pass beyond the outer courtyard to the women's rooms; and when the big wooden gate was bolted behind him he was king in his own territory, with Ameera for queen. And there was going to be added to this kingdom a third person whose arrival Holden felt inclined to resent. It interfered with his perfect happiness. It disarranged the orderly peace of the house that was his own. But Ameera was wild with delight at the thought of it, and her mother not less so. The love of a man, and particularly a white man, was at the best an inconstant affair, but it might, both women argued, be held fast by a baby's hands. 'And then,' Ameera would always say, 'then he will never care for the white *mem-log*. I hate them all—I hate them all.'

'He will go back to his own people in time,' said the mother; 'but by the blessing of God that time is yet afar off.'

Holden sat silent on the couch thinking of the future, and his thoughts were not pleasant. The drawbacks of a double life are manifold. The Government, with singular care, had ordered him out of the station for a fortnight on special duty in the place of a man who was watching by the bedside of a sick wife. The verbal notification of the transfer had been edged by a cheerful remark that Holden ought to think himself lucky in being a bachelor and a free man. He came to break the news to Ameera.

'It is not good,' she said slowly, 'but it is not all bad. There is my mother here, and no harm will come to him—unless indeed I die of pure joy. Go thou to thy work and think no troublesome thoughts. When the days are done I believe . . . nay, I am sure. And—and then I shall lay *him* in thy arms, and thou wilt love me for ever. The train goes to-night, at midnight, is it not? Go now, and do not let thy heart be heavy by cause of me. But thou wilt not delay in returning? Thou wilt not stay on the road to talk to the bold white *mem-log*. Come back to me swiftly, my life.'

As he left the courtyard to reach his horse that was tethered to the gate-post, Holden spoke to the white-haired old watchman who guarded the house, and bade him under certain contingencies despatch the filled-up telegraph-form that Holden gave him. It was all that could be done, and with the sensations of a man who has attended his own funeral Holden went away by the night mail to his exile. Every hour of the day he dreaded the arrival of the telegram, and every hour of the night he pictured to himself the death of Ameera. In consequence his work for the State was not of first-rate quality, nor was his temper towards his colleagues of the most amiable. The fortnight ended without a sign from his home, and, torn to pieces by his anxieties, Holden returned to be swallowed up for two precious hours by a dinner at the club, wherein he heard, as a man hears in a swoon, voices telling him how execrably he had performed the other man's duties, and how he had endeared himself to all his associates. Then he fled on horseback through the night with his heart in his mouth. There was no answer at first to his blow on the gate, and he had just wheeled his horse round to kick it in when Pir Khan appeared with a lantern and held his stirrup.

'Has aught occurred?' said Holden.

'The news does not come from my mouth, Protector of the Poor, but——' He held out his shaking hand as befitted the bearer of good news who is entitled to a reward.

Holden hurried through the courtyard. A light burned in the upper room. His horse neighed in the gateway, and he heard a shrill little wail that sent all the blood into the apple of his throat. It was a new voice, but it did not prove that Ameera was alive.

'Who is there?' he called up the narrow brick staircase.

There was a cry of delight from Ameera, and then the voice of the mother, tremulous with old age and pride—'We be two women and—the —man—thy—son.'

On the threshold of the room Holden stepped on a naked dagger, that was laid there to avert ill-luck, and it broke at the hilt under his impatient heel.

'God is great!' cooed Ameera in the half-light. 'Thou hast taken his misfortunes on thy head.'

'Ay, but how is it with thee, life of my life? Old woman, how is it with her?'

'She has forgotten her sufferings for joy that the child is born. There is no harm; but speak softly,' said the mother.

'It only needed thy presence to make me all well,' said Ameera. 'My king, thou hast been very long away. What gifts hast thou for me? Ah, ah! It is I that bring gifts this time. Look, my life, look. Was there ever such a babe? Nay, I am too weak even to clear my arm from him.'

'Rest then, and do not talk. I am here, *bachari* [little woman].'

'Well said, for there is a bond and a heel-rope [*peecharee*] between us now that nothing can break. Look—canst thou see in this light? He is without spot or blemish. Never was such a man-child. *Ya illah!* he shall be a pundit—no, a trooper of the Queen. And, my life, dost thou love me as well as ever, though I am faint and sick and worn? Answer truly.'

'Yea. I love as I have loved, with all my soul. Lie still, pearl, and rest.'

'Then do not go. Sit by my side here—so. Mother, the lord of this house needs a cushion. Bring it.' There was an almost imperceptible movement on the part of the new life that lay in the hollow of Ameera's arm. 'Aho!' she said, her voice breaking with love. 'The babe is a champion from his birth. He is kicking me in the side with mighty kicks. Was there ever such a babe! And he is ours to us—thine and mine. Put thy hand on his head, but carefully, for he is very young, and men are unskilled in such matters.'

Very cautiously Holden touched with the tips of his fingers the downy head.

'He is of the Faith,' said Ameera; 'for lying here in the night-watches I whispered the call to prayer and the profession of faith into his ears. And it is most marvellous that he was born upon a Friday, as I was born. Be careful of him, my life; but he can almost grip with his hands.'

Holden found one helpless little hand that closed feebly on his finger. And the clutch ran through his body till it settled about his heart. Till then his sole thought had been for Ameera. He began to realise that there was some one else in the world, but he could not feel that it was a veritable son with a soul. He sat down to think, and Ameera dozed lightly.

'Get hence, Sahib,' said her mother under her breath. 'It is not good that she should find you here on waking. She must be still.'

'I go,' said Holden submissively. 'Here be rupees. See that my *baba* gets fat and finds all that he needs.'

The chink of the silver roused Ameera. 'I am his mother, and no hireling,' she said weakly. 'Shall I look to him more or less for the sake of money? Mother, give it back. I have borne my lord a son.'

The deep sleep of weakness came upon her almost before the sentence was completed. Holden went down to the courtyard very softly with his heart at ease. Pir Khan, the old watchman, was chuckling with delight. 'This house is now complete,' he said, and without further comment thrust into Holden's hands the hilt of a sabre worn many years ago when he, Pir Khan, served the Queen in the police. The bleat of a tethered goat came from the well-kerb.

'There be two,' said Pir Khan, 'two goats of the best. I bought them, and they cost much money; and since there is no birth-party assembled their flesh will be all mine. Strike craftily, Sahib! 'Tis an ill-balanced sabre at the best. Wait till they raise their heads from cropping the marigolds.'

'And why?' said Holden, bewildered.

'For the birth-sacrifice. What else? Otherwise the child being unguarded from fate may die. The Protector of the Poor knows the fitting words to be said.'

Holden had learned them once with little thought that he would ever speak them in earnest. The touch of the cold sabre-hilt in his palm turned suddenly to the clinging grip of the child upstairs—the child that was his own son—and a dread of loss filled him.

'Strike!' said Pir Khan. 'Never life came into the world but life was paid for it. See, the goats have raised their heads. Now! With a drawing cut!'

Hardly knowing what he did, Holden cut twice as he muttered the Mohammedan prayer that runs: 'Almighty! In place of this my son I offer life for life, blood for blood, head for head, bone for bone, hair for hair, skin for skin.' The waiting horse snorted and bounded in his pickets at the smell of the raw blood that spirted over Holden's riding-boots.

'Well smitten!' said Pir Khan wiping the sabre. 'A swordsman was lost in thee. Go with a light heart, Heaven-born. I am thy servant, and the servant of thy son. May the Presence live a thousand years and . . . the flesh of the goats is all mine?' Pir Khan drew back richer by a month's pay. Holden swung himself into the saddle and rode off through the low-hanging wood-smoke of the evening. He was full of riotous exultation, alternating with a vast vague tenderness directed towards no particular object, that made him choke as he bent over the neck of his uneasy horse. 'I never felt like this in my life,' he thought. 'I'll go to the club and pull myself together.'

A game of pool was beginning, and the room was full of men. Holden entered, eager to get to the light and the company of his fellows, singing at the top of his voice—

'In Baltimore a-walking, a lady I did meet!'

'Did you?' said the club-secretary from his corner. 'Did she happen to tell you that your boots were wringing wet? Great goodness, man, it's blood!'

'Bosh!' said Holden, picking his cue from the rack. 'May I cut in? It's dew. I've been riding through high crops. My faith! my boots are in a mess though!

'And if it be a girl she shall wear a wedding-ring,
And if it be a boy he shall fight for his king,
With his dirk, and his cap, and his little jacket blue,
He shall walk the quarter-deck——'

'Yellow on blue—green next player,' said the marker monotonously.

'*He shall walk the quarter-deck,*—Am I green, marker? *He shall walk the quarter-deck,*—Eh! that's a bad shot,—*As his daddy used to do!*'

'I don't see that you have anything to crow about,' said a zealous junior civilian acidly. 'The Government is not exactly pleased with your work when you relieved Sanders.'

'Does that mean a wigging from headquarters?' said Holden with an abstracted smile. 'I think I can stand it.'

The talk beat up round the ever-fresh subject of each man's work and steadied Holden till it was time to go to his dark empty bungalow, where his butler received him as one who knew all his affairs. Holden remained awake for the greater part of the night, and his dreams were pleasant ones.

II

'How old is he now?'

'*Ya illah!* What a man's question! He is all but six weeks old; and on this night I go up to the house-top with thee, my life, to count the stars. For that is auspicious. And he was born on a Friday under the sign of the Sun, and it has been told to me that he will outlive us both and get wealth. Can we wish for aught better, beloved?'

'There is nothing better. Let us go up to the roof, and thou shalt count the stars—but a few only, for the sky is heavy with cloud.'

'The winter rains are late, and maybe they come out of season. Come, before all the stars are hid. I have put on my richest jewels.'

'Thou hast forgotten the best of all.'

'*Ai!* Ours. He comes also. He has never yet seen the skies.'

Ameera climbed the narrow staircase that led to the flat roof. The child, placid and unwinking, lay in the hollow of her right arm, gorgeous in silver-fringed muslin with a small skull-cap on his head. Ameera wore all that she valued most. The diamond nose-stud that takes the place of the Western patch in drawing attention to the curve of the nostril, the gold ornament in the centre of the forehead studded with tallow-drop emeralds and flawed rubies, the heavy circlet of beaten gold that was fastened round her neck by the softness of the pure metal, and the chinking curb-patterned silver anklets hanging low over the rosy ankle-bone. She was dressed in jade-green muslin as befitted a daughter of the Faith, and from shoulder to elbow and elbow to wrist ran bracelets of silver tied with floss silk, frail glass bangles slipped over the wrist in proof of the slenderness of the hand, and certain heavy gold bracelets that had no part in her country's ornaments, but since they were Holden's gift and fastened with a cunning European snap, delighted her immensely.

They sat down by the low white parapet of the roof, overlooking the city and its lights.

'They are happy down there,' said Ameera. 'But I do not think that they are as happy as we. Nor do I think the white *mem-log* are as happy. And thou?'

'I know they are not.'

'How dost thou know?'

'They give their children over to the nurses.'

'I have never seen that,' said Ameera with a sigh, 'nor do I wish to see.

Ahi!'—she dropped her head on Holden's shoulder,—'I have counted forty stars, and I am tired. Look at the child, love of my life, he is counting too.'

The baby was staring with round eyes at the dark of the heavens. Ameera placed him in Holden's arms, and he lay there without a cry.

'What shall we call him among ourselves?' she said. 'Look! Art thou ever tired of looking? He carries thy very eyes. But the mouth——'

'Is thine, most dear. Who should know better than I?'

' 'Tis such a feeble mouth. Oh, so small! And yet it holds my heart between its lips. Give him to me now. He has been too long away.'

'Nay, let him lie; he has not yet begun to cry.'

'When he cries thou wilt give him back—eh? What a man of mankind thou art! if he cried he were only the dearer to me. But, my life, what little name shall we give him?'

The small body lay close to Holden's heart. It was utterly helpless and very soft. He scarcely dared to breathe for fear of crushing it. The caged green parrot that is regarded as a sort of guardian-spirit in most native households moved on its perch and fluttered a drowsy wing.

'There is the answer,' said Holden. 'Mian Mittu has spoken. He shall be the parrot. When he is ready he will talk mightily and run about. Mian Mittu is the parrot in thy—in the Mussulman tongue, is it not?'

'Why put me so far off?' said Ameera fretfully. 'Let it be like unto some English name—but not wholly. For he is mine.'

'Then call him Tota, for that is likest English.'

'Ay, Tota, and that is still the parrot. Forgive me, my lord, for a minute ago, but in truth he is too little to wear all the weight of Mian Mittu for name. He shall be Tota—our Tota to us. Hearest thou, oh, small one? Littlest, thou art Tota.' She touched the child's cheek, and he waking wailed, and it was necessary to return him to his mother, who soothed him with the wonderful rhyme of *Aré koko, Jaré koko!* which says—

> 'Oh, crow! Go, crow! Baby's sleeping sound,
> And the wild plums grow in the jungle, only a penny a pound.
> Only a penny a pound, *baba,* only a penny a pound.'

Reassured many times as to the price of those plums, Tota cuddled himself down to sleep. The two sleek, white well-bullocks in the courtyard were steadily chewing the cud of their evening meal; old Pir Khan squatted at the head of Holden's horse, his police sabre across his knees, pulling drowsily at a big water-pipe that croaked like a bull-frog in a pond. Ameera's mother sat spinning in the lower verandah, and the wooden gate was shut and barred. The music of a marriage-procession came to the roof above the gentle hum of the city, and a string of flying-foxes crossed the face of the low moon.

'I have prayed,' said Ameera, after a long pause, 'I have prayed for two things. First that I may die in thy stead if thy death is demanded, and in the second, that I may die in the place of the child. I have prayed to the Prophet and to Beebee Miriam [the Virgin Mary]. Thinkest thou either will hear?'

'From thy lips who would not hear the lightest word?'

'I asked for straight talk, and thou hast given me sweet talk. Will my prayers be heard?'

'How can I say? God is very good.'

'Of that I am not sure. Listen now. When I die, or the child dies, what is thy fate? Living, thou wilt return to the bold white *mem-log*, for kind calls to kind.'

'Not always.'

'With a woman, no; with a man it is otherwise. Thou wilt in this life, later on, go back to thine own folk. That I could almost endure, for I should be dead. But in thy very death thou wilt be taken away to a strange place and a paradise that I do not know.'

'Will it be paradise?'

'Surely, for who would harm thee? But we two—I and the child—shall be elsewhere, and we cannot come to thee, nor canst thou come to us. In the old days, before the child was born, I did not think of these things; but now I think of them always. It is very hard talk.'

'It will fall as it will fall. To-morrow we do not know, but to-day and love we know well. Surely we are happy now.'

'So happy that it were well to make our happiness assured. And thy Beebee Miriam should listen to me; for she is also a woman. But then she would envy me! It is not seemly for men to worship a woman.'

Holden laughed aloud at Ameera's little spasm of jealousy.

'Is it not seemly? Why didst thou not turn me from worship of thee, then?'

'Thou a worshipper! And of me? My king, for all thy sweet words, well I know that I am thy servant and thy slave, and the dust under thy feet. And I would not have it otherwise. See!'

Before Holden could prevent her she stooped forward and touched his feet; recovering herself with a little laugh she hugged Tota closer to her bosom. Then, almost savagely—

'Is it true that the bold white *mem-log* live for three times the length of my life? Is it true that they make their marriages not before they are old women?'

'They marry as do others—when they are women.'

'That I know, but they wed when they are twenty-five. Is that true?'

'That is true.'

'*Ya illah!* At twenty-five! Who would of his own will take a wife even of eighteen? She is a woman—ageing every hour. Twenty-five! I shall be an old woman at that age, and—— Those *mem-log* remain young for ever. How I hate them!'

'What have they to do with us?'

'I cannot tell. I know only that there may now be alive on this earth a woman ten years older than I who may come to thee and take thy love ten years after I am an old woman, grey-headed, and the nurse of Tota's son. That is unjust and evil. They should die too.'

'Now, for all thy years thou art a child, and shalt be picked up and carried down the staircase.'

'Tota! Have a care for Tota, my lord! Thou at least art as foolish as any babe!' Ameera tucked Tota out of harm's way in the hollow of her neck, and was carried downstairs laughing in Holden's arms, while Tota opened his eyes and smiled after the manner of the lesser angels.

He was a silent infant, and, almost before Holden could realise that he was in the world, developed into a small gold-coloured little god and unquestioned despot of the house overlooking the city. Those were months of absolute happiness to Holden and Ameera—happiness withdrawn from the world, shut in behind the wooden gate that Pir Khan guarded. By day Holden did his work with an immense pity for such as were not so fortunate as himself, and a sympathy for small children that amazed and amused many mothers at the little station-gatherings. At nightfall he returned to Ameera,—Ameera, full of the wondrous doings of Tota; how he had been seen to clap his hands together and move his fingers with intention and purpose—which was manifestly a miracle—how later, he had of his own initiative crawled out of his low bedstead on to the floor and swayed on both feet for the space of three breaths.

'And they were long breaths, for my heart stood still with delight,' said Ameera.

Then Tota took the beasts into his councils—the well-bullocks, the little grey squirrels, the mongoose that lived in a hole near the well, and especially Mian Mittu, the parrot, whose tail he grievously pulled, and Mian Mittu screamed till Ameera and Holden arrived.

'Oh, villain! Child of strength! This to thy brother on the house-top!

Tobah, tobah! Fie! Fie! But I know a charm to make him wise as Suleiman and Aflatoun [Solomon and Plato]. Now look,' said Ameera. She drew from an embroidered bag a handful of almonds. 'See! we count seven. In the name of God!'

She placed Mian Mittu, very angry and rumpled, on the top of his cage, and seating herself between the babe and the bird she cracked and peeled an almond less white than her teeth. 'This is a true charm, my life, and do not laugh. See! I give the parrot one-half and Tota the other.' Mian Mittu with careful beak took his share from between Ameera's lips, and she kissed the other half into the mouth of the child, who ate it slowly with wondering eyes. 'This I will do each day of seven, and without doubt he who is ours will be a bold speaker and wise. Eh, Tota, what wilt thou be when thou art a man and I am grey-headed?' Tota tucked his fat legs into adorable creases. He could crawl, but he was not going to waste the spring of his youth in idle speech. He wanted Mian Mittu's tail to tweak.

When he was advanced to the dignity of a silver belt—which, with a magic square engraved on silver and hung round his neck, made up the greater part of his clothing—he staggered on a perilous journey down the garden to Pir Khan, and proffered him all his jewels in exchange for one little ride on Holden's horse, having seen his mother's mother chaffering with pedlars in the verandah. Pir Khan wept and set the untried feet on his own grey head in sign of fealty, and brought the bold adventurer to his mother's arms, vowing that Tota would be a leader of men ere his beard was grown.

One hot evening, while he sat on the roof between his father and mother watching the never-ending warfare of the kites that the city boys flew, he demanded a kite of his own with Pir Khan to fly it, because he had a fear of dealing with anything larger than himself, and when Holden called him a 'spark,' he rose to his feet and answered slowly in defence of his new-found individuality, '*Hum 'park nahin hai. Hum admi hai* [I am no spark, but a man.]'

The protest made Holden choke and devote himself very seriously to a consideration of Tota's future. He need hardly have taken the trouble. The delight of that life was too perfect to endure. Therefore it was taken away as many things are taken away in India—suddenly and without warning. The little lord of the house, as Pir Khan called him, grew sorrowful and complained of pains who had never known the meaning of pain. Ameera, wild with terror, watched him through the night, and in the dawning of the second day the life was shaken out of him by fever

—the seasonal autumn fever. It seemed altogether impossible that he could die, and neither Ameera nor Holden at first believed the evidence of the little body on the bedstead. Ameera beat her head against the wall and would have flung herself down the well in the garden had Holden not restrained her by main force.

One mercy only was granted to Holden. He rode to his office in broad daylight and found waiting him an unusually heavy mail that demanded concentrated attention and hard work. He was not, however, alive to this kindness of the gods.

III

The first shock of a bullet is no more than a brisk pinch. The wrecked body does not send in its protest to the soul till ten or fifteen seconds later. Holden realised his pain slowly, exactly as he had realised his happiness, and with the same imperious necessity for hiding all trace of it. In the beginning he only felt that there had been a loss, and that Ameera needed comforting, where she sat with her head on her knees shivering as Mian Mittu from the house-top called, *Tota! Tota! Tota!* Later all his world and the daily life of it rose up to hurt him. It was an outrage that any one of the children at the band-stand in the evening should be alive and clamorous, when his own child lay dead. It was more than mere pain when one of them touched him, and stories told by over-fond fathers of their children's latest performances cut him to the quick. He could not declare his pain. He had neither help, comfort, nor sympathy; and Ameera at the end of each weary day would lead him through the hell of self-questioning reproach which is reserved for those who have lost a child, and believe that with a little—just a little more care—it might have been saved.

'Perhaps,' Ameera would say, 'I did not take sufficient heed. Did I, or did I not? The sun on the roof that day when he played so long alone and I was—*ahi!* braiding my hair—it may be that the sun then bred the fever. If I had warned him from the sun he might have lived. But, oh my life, say that I am guiltless! Thou knowest that I loved him, as I love thee. Say that there is no blame on me, or I shall die—I shall die!'

'There is no blame,—before God, none. It was written, and how could we do aught to save? What has been, has been. Let it go, beloved.'

'He was all my heart to me. How can I let the thought go when my arm tells me every night that he is not here? *Ahi! Ahi!* Oh, Tota, come back to me—come back again, and let us be all together as it was before!'

'Peace, peace! For thine own sake, and for mine also, if thou lovest me—rest.'

'By this I know thou dost not care; and how shouldst thou? The white men have hearts of stone and souls of iron. Oh, that I had married a man of mine own people—though he beat me—and had never eaten the bread of an alien!'

'Am I an alien—mother of my son?'

'What else—Sahib? . . . Oh, forgive me—forgive! The death has driven me mad. Thou art the life of my heart, and the light of my eyes, and the breath of my life, and—and I have put thee from me, though it was but for a moment. If thou goest away, to whom shall I look for help? Do not be angry. Indeed, it was the pain that spoke and not thy slave.'

'I know, I know. We be two who were three. The greater need therefore that we should be one.'

They were sitting on the roof as of custom. The night was a warm one in early spring, and sheet-lightning was dancing on the horizon to a broken tune played by far-off thunder. Ameera settled herself in Holden's arms.

'The dry earth is lowing like a cow for the rain, and I—I am afraid. It was not like this when we counted the stars. But thou lovest me as much as before, though a bond is taken away? Answer!'

'I love more because a new bond has come out of the sorrow that we have eaten together, and that thou knowest.'

'Yea, I knew,' said Ameera in a very small whisper. 'But it is good to hear thee say so, my life, who art so strong to help. I will be a child no more, but a woman and an aid to thee. Listen! Give me my *sitar* and I will sing bravely.'

She took the light silver-studded *sitar* and began a song of the great hero Rajah Rasalu. The hand failed on the strings, the tune halted, checked, and at a low note turned off to the poor little nursery-rhyme about the wicked crow—

> 'And the wild plums grow in the jungle, only a penny a pound.
> Only a penny a pound, *baba*—only . . .'

Then came the tears, and the piteous rebellion against fate till she slept, moaning a little in her sleep, with the right arm thrown clear of the body as though it protected something that was not there. It was after this night that life became a little easier for Holden. The ever-present pain of loss drove him into his work, and the work repaid him by filling up his mind for nine or ten hours a day. Ameera sat alone in the house and brooded, but grew happier when she understood that Holden was more at ease, according to the custom of women. They touched happiness again, but this time with caution.

'It was because we loved Tota that he died. The jealousy of God was upon us,' said Ameera. 'I have hung up a large black jar before our window to turn the evil eye from us, and we must make no protestations of delight, but go softly underneath the stars, lest God find us out. Is that not good talk, worthless one?'

She had shifted the accent on the word that means 'beloved,' in proof of the sincerity of her purpose. But the kiss that followed the new christening was a thing that any deity might have envied. They went about henceforward saying, 'It is naught, it is naught;' and hoping that all the Powers heard.

The Powers were busy on other things. They had allowed thirty million people four years of plenty, wherein men fed well and the crops were certain, and the birth-rate rose year by year; the districts reported a purely agricultural population varying from nine hundred to two thousand to the square mile of the overburdened earth; and the Member for Lower Tooting, wandering about India in top-hat and frock-coat, talked largely of the benefits of British rule, and suggested as the one thing needful the establishment of a duly qualified electoral system and a general bestowal of the franchise. His long-suffering hosts smiled and made him welcome, and when he paused to admire, with pretty picked words, the blossom of the blood-red *dhak*-tree that had flowered untimely for a sign of what was coming, they smiled more than ever.

It was the Deputy-Commissioner of Kot-Kumharsen, staying at the club for a day, who lightly told a tale that made Holden's blood run cold as he overheard the end.

'He won't bother any one any more. Never saw a man so astonished in my life. By Jove, I thought he meant to ask a question in the House about it. Fellow-passenger in his ship—dined next him—bowled over by cholera and died in eighteen hours. You needn't laugh, you fellows. The Member for Lower Tooting is awfully angry about it; but he's more scared. I think he's going to take his enlightened self out of India.'

'I'd give a good deal if he were knocked over. It might keep a few vestrymen of his kidney to their own parish. But what's this about cholera? It's full early for anything of that kind,' said the warden of an unprofitable salt-lick.

'Don't know,' said the Deputy-Commissioner reflectively. 'We've got locusts with us. There's sporadic cholera all along the north—at least we're calling it sporadic for decency's sake. The spring crops are short in five districts, and nobody seems to know where the Rains are. It's nearly March now. I don't want to scare anybody, but it seems to me that Nature's going to audit her accounts with a big red pencil this summer.'

'Just when I wanted to take leave, too!' said a voice across the room.

'There won't be much leave this year, but there ought to be a great deal of promotion. I've come in to persuade the Government to put my pet canal on the list of famine-relief works. It's an ill-wind that blows no good. I shall get that canal finished at last.'

'Is it the old programme then,' said Holden; 'famine, fever, and cholera?'

'Oh no. Only local scarcity and an unusual prevalence of seasonal sickness. You'll find it all in the reports if you live till next year. You're a lucky chap. *You* haven't got a wife to send out of harm's way. The hill-stations ought to be full of women this year.'

'I think you're inclined to exaggerate the talk in the bazaars,' said a young civilian in the Secretariat. 'Now I have observed——'

'I daresay you have,' said the Deputy Commissioner, 'but you've a great deal more to observe, my son. In the meantime, I wish to observe to you——' and he drew him aside to discuss the construction of the canal that was so dear to his heart. Holden went to his bungalow and began to understand that he was not alone in the world, and also that he was afraid for the sake of another,—which is the most soul-satisfying fear known to man.

Two months later, as the Deputy had foretold, Nature began to audit her accounts with a red pencil. On the heels of the spring-reapings came a cry for bread, and the Government, which had decreed that no man should die of want, sent wheat. Then came the cholera from all four quarters of the compass. It struck a pilgrim-gathering of half a million at a sacred shrine. Many died at the feet of their god; the others broke and ran over the face of the land carrying the pestilence with them. It smote a walled city and killed two hundred a day. The people crowded the trains, hanging on to the footboards and squatting on the roofs of the carriages, and the cholera followed them, for at each station they dragged out the dead and the dying. They died by the roadside, and the horses of the Englishmen shied at the corpses in the grass. The Rains did not come, and the earth turned to iron lest man should escape death by hiding in her. The English sent their wives away to the hills and went about their work, coming forward as they were bidden to fill the gaps in the fighting-line. Holden, sick with fear of losing his chiefest treasure on earth, had done his best to persuade Ameera to go away with her mother to the Himalayas.

'Why should I go?' said she one evening on the roof.

'There is sickness, and people are dying, and all the white *mem-log* have gone.'

'All of them?'

'All—unless perhaps there remain some old scald-head who vexes her husband's heart by running risk of death.'

'Nay; who stays is my sister, and thou must not abuse her, for I will be a scald-head too. I am glad all the bold *mem-log* are gone.'

'Do I speak to a woman or a babe? Go to the hills, and I will see to it that thou goest like a queen's daughter. Think, child. In a red-lacquered bullock cart, veiled and curtained, with brass peacocks upon the pole and red cloth hangings. I will send two orderlies for guard and——'

'Peace! Thou art the babe in speaking thus. What use are those toys to me? *He* would have patted the bullocks and played with the housings. For his sake, perhaps,—thou hast made me very English—I might have gone. Now, I will not. Let the *mem-log* run.'

'Their husbands are sending them, beloved.'

'Very good talk. Since when hast thou been my husband to tell me what to do? I have but borne thee a son. Thou art only all the desire of my soul to me. How shall I depart when I know that if evil befall thee by the breadth of so much as my littlest finger-nail—is that not small?—I should be aware of it though I were in paradise. And here, this summer thou mayest die—*ai, janee,* die! and in dying they might call to tend thee a white woman, and she would rob me in the last of thy love!'

'But love is not born in a moment or on a death-bed!'

'What dost thou know of love, stoneheart? She would take thy thanks at least and, by God and the Prophet and Beebee Miriam the mother of thy Prophet, that I will never endure. My lord and my love, let there be no more foolish talk of going away. Where thou art, I am. It is enough.' She put an arm round his neck and a hand on his mouth.

There are not many happinesses so complete as those that are snatched under the shadow of the sword. They sat together and laughed, calling each other openly by every pet name that could move the wrath of the gods. The city below them was locked up in its own torments. Sulphur fires blazed in the streets; the conches in the Hindu temples screamed and bellowed, for the gods were inattentive in those days. There was a service in the great Mohammedan shrine, and the call to prayer from the minarets was almost unceasing. They heard the wailing in the houses of the dead, and once the shriek of a mother who had lost a child and was calling for its return. In the grey dawn they saw the dead borne out through the city gates, each litter with its own little knot of mourners. Wherefore they kissed each other and shivered.

It was a red and heavy audit, for the land was very sick and needed a little breathing-space ere the torrent of cheap life should flood it anew. The children of immature fathers and undeveloped mothers made no resistance. They were cowed and sat still, waiting till the sword should be sheathed in November if it were so willed. There were gaps among the English, but the gaps were filled. The work of superintending famine-relief, cholera-sheds, medicine-distribution, and what little sanitation was possible, went forward because it was so ordered.

Holden had been told to keep himself in readiness to move to replace the next man who should fall. There were twelve hours in each day when he could not see Ameera, and she might die in three. He was considering what his pain would be if he could not see her for three months, or if she died out of his sight. He was absolutely certain that her death would be demanded—so certain, that when he looked up from the telegram and saw Pir Khan breathless in the doorway, he laughed aloud. 'And?' said he,——

'When there is a cry in the night and the spirit flutters into the throat, who has a charm that will restore? Come swiftly, Heaven-born! It is the black cholera.'

Holden galloped to his home. The sky was heavy with clouds, for the long-deferred Rains were near and the heat was stifling. Ameera's mother met him in the courtyard, whimpering, 'She is dying. She is nursing herself into death. She is all but dead. What shall I do, Sahib?'

Ameera was lying in the room in which Tota had been born. She made no sign when Holden entered, because the human soul is a very lonely thing and, when it is getting ready to go away, hides itself in a misty borderland where the living may not follow. The black cholera does its work quietly and without explanation. Ameera was being thrust out of life as though the Angel of Death had himself put his hand upon her. The quick breathing seemed to show that she was either afraid or in pain, but neither eyes nor mouth gave any answer to Holden's kisses. There was nothing to be said or done. Holden could only wait and suffer. The first drops of the rain began to fall on the roof and he could hear the shouts of joy in the parched city.

The soul came back a little and the lips moved. Holden bent down to listen. 'Keep nothing of mine,' said Ameera. 'Take no hair from my head. *She* would make thee burn it later on. That flame I should feel. Lower! Stoop lower! Remember only that I was thine and bore thee a son. Though thou wed a white woman to-morrow, the pleasure of receiving in thy arms thy first son is taken from thee for ever. Remember me when thy son is born—the one that shall carry thy name before all men. His misfortunes be on my head. I bear witness—I bear witness'—the lips were forming the words on his ear—'that there is no God but—thee, beloved!'

Then she died. Holden sat still, and all thought was taken from him,—till he heard Ameera's mother lift the curtain.

'Is she dead, Sahib?'

'She is dead.'

'Then I will mourn, and afterwards take an inventory of the furniture in this house. For that will be mine. The Sahib does not mean to resume it? It is so little, so very little, Sahib, and I am an old woman. I would like to lie softly.'

'For the mercy of God be silent a while. Go out and mourn where I cannot hear.'

'Sahib she will be buried in four hours.'

'I know the custom. I shall go ere she is taken away. That matter is in thy hands. Look to it, that the bed on which—on which she lies——'

'Aha! That beautiful red-lacquered bed. I have long desired——'

'That the bed is left here untouched for my disposal. All else in the house is thine. Hire a cart, take everything, go hence, and before sunrise let there be nothing in this house but that which I have ordered thee to respect.'

'I am an old woman. I would stay at least for the days of mourning, and the Rains have just broken. Whither shall I go?'

'What is that to me? My order is that there is a going. The house gear is worth a thousand rupees and my orderly shall bring thee a hundred rupees to-night.'

'That is very little. Think of the cart-hire.'

'It shall be nothing unless thou goest, and with speed. O woman, get hence and leave me with my dead!'

The mother shuffled down the staircase, and in her anxiety to take stock of the house-fittings forgot to mourn. Holden stayed by Ameera's side and the rain roared on the roof. He could not think connectedly by reason of the noise, though he made many attempts to do so. Then four sheeted ghosts glided dripping into the room and stared at him through their veils. They were the washers of the dead. Holden left the room and went out to his horse. He had come in a dead, stifling calm through ankle-deep dust. He found the courtyard a rain-lashed pond alive with frogs; a torrent of yellow water ran under the gate, and a roaring wind drove the bolts of the rain like buckshot against the mud walls. Pir Khan was shivering in his little hut by the gate, and the horse was stamping uneasily in the water.

'I have been told the Sahib's order,' said Pir Khan. 'It is well. This house is now desolate. I go also, for my monkey-face would be a reminder of that which has been. Concerning the bed, I will bring that to thy house yonder in the morning; but remember, Sahib, it will be to thee a knife turning in a green wound. I go upon a pilgrimage, and I will take no money. I have grown fat in the protection of the Presence whose sorrow is my sorrow. For the last time I hold his stirrup.'

He touched Holden's foot with both hands and the horse sprang out into the road, where the creaking bamboos were whipping the sky and all the frogs were chuckling. Holden could not see for the rain in his face. He put his hands before his eyes and muttered—

'Oh, you brute! You utter brute!'

The news of his trouble was already in his bungalow. He read the knowledge in his butler's eyes when Ahmed Khan brought in food, and for the first and last time in his life laid a hand upon his master's shoulder, saying, 'Eat, Sahib, eat. Meat is good against sorrow. I also have known. Moreover the shadows come and go, Sahib; the shadows come and go. These be curried eggs.'

Holden could neither eat nor sleep. The heavens sent down eight inches of rain in that night and washed the earth clean. The waters tore down walls, broke roads, and scoured open the shallow graves on the Mohammedan burying-ground. All next day it rained, and Holden sat still in his house considering his sorrow. On the morning of the third day he received a telegram which said only, 'Ricketts, Myndonie. Dying. Holden relieve. Immediate.' Then he thought that before he departed he would look at the house wherein he had been master and lord. There was a break in the weather, and the rank earth steamed with vapour.

He found that the rains had torn down the mud pillars of the gateway, and the heavy wooden gate that had guarded his life hung lazily from one hinge. There was grass three inches high in the courtyard; Pir Khan's lodge was empty, and the sodden thatch sagged between the beams. A grey squirrel was in possession of the verandah, as if the house had been untenanted for thirty years instead of three days. Ameera's mother had removed everything except some mildewed matting. The *tick-tick* of the little scorpions as they hurried across the floor was the only sound in the house. Ameera's room and the other one where Tota had lived were heavy with mildew; and the narrow staircase leading to the roof was streaked and stained with rain-borne mud. Holden saw all these things and came out again to meet in the road Durga Dass, his landlord,—portly, affable, clothed in white muslin, and driving a Cee-spring buggy. He was overlooking his property to see how the roofs stood the stress of the first rains.

'I have heard,' said he, 'you will not take this place any more, Sahib?'

'What are you going to do with it?'

'Perhaps I shall let it again.'

'Then I will keep it on while I am away.'

Durga Dass was silent for some time. 'You shall not take it on, Sahib,' he said. 'When I was a young man I also——, but to-day I am a member of the Municipality. Ho! Ho! No. When the birds have gone what need to keep the nest? I will have it pulled down—the timber will sell for something always. It shall be pulled down, and the Municipality shall make a road across, as they desire, from the burning-ghaut to the city wall, so that no man may say where this house stood.

THE VILLAGE THAT VOTED THE EARTH WAS FLAT

OUR DRIVE till then had been quite a success. The other men in the car were my friend Woodhouse, young Ollyett, a distant connection of his, and Pallant, the M.P. Woodhouse's business was the treatment and cure of sick journals. He knew by instinct the precise moment in a newspaper's life when the impetus of past good management is exhausted and it fetches up on the dead-centre between slow and expensive collapse and the new start which can be given by gold injections—and genius. He was wisely ignorant of journalism; but when he stooped on a carcase there was sure to be meat. He had that week added a half-dead, halfpenny evening paper to his collection, which consisted of a prosperous London daily, one provincial ditto, and a limp-bodied weekly of commercial leanings. He had also, that very hour, planted me with a large block of the evening paper's common shares, and was explaining the whole art of editorship to Ollyett, a young man three years from Oxford, with coir-matting-coloured hair and a face harshly modelled by harsh experiences, who, I understood, was assisting in the new venture. Pallant, the long, wrinkled M.P., whose voice is more like a crane's than a peacock's, took no shares, but gave us all advice.

'You'll find it rather a knacker's yard.' Woodhouse was saying. 'Yes, I know they call me The Knacker; but it will pay inside a year. All my papers do. I've only one motto: Back your luck and back your staff. It'll come out all right.'

Then the car stopped, and a policeman asked our names and addresses for exceeding the speed-limit. We pointed out that the road ran absolutely straight for half a mile ahead without even a side-lane. 'That's just what we depend on,' said the policeman unpleasantly.

'The usual swindle,' said Woodhouse under his breath. 'What's the name of this place?'

'Huckley,' said the policeman. 'H-u-c-k-l-e-y,' and wrote something in his note-book at which young Ollyett protested. A large red man on a grey horse who had been watching us from the other side of the hedge shouted an order we could not catch. The policeman laid his hand on the rim of the right driving-door (Woodhouse carries his spare tyre aft), and it closed on the button of the electric horn. The grey horse at once bolted, and we could hear the rider swearing all across the landscape.

'Damn it, man, you've got your silly fist on it! Take it off!' Woodhouse shouted.

'Ho!' said the constable, looking carefully at his fingers as though we had trapped them. 'That won't do you any good either,' and he wrote once more in his note-book before he allowed us to go.

This was Woodhouse's first brush with motor law, and since I expected no ill consequences to myself, I pointed out that it was very serious. I took the same view myself when in due time I found that I, too, was summoned on charges ranging from the use of obscene language to endangering traffic.

Judgment was done in a little pale-yellow market-town with a small Jubilee clock-tower and a large corn-exchange. Woodhouse drove us there in his car. Pallant, who had not been included in the summons, came with us as moral support. While we waited outside, the fat man on the grey horse rode up and entered into loud talk with his brother magistrates. He said to one of them—for I took the trouble to note it down—'It falls away from my lodge-gates, dead straight, three-quarters of a mile. I'd defy any one to resist it. We rooked seventy pounds out of 'em last month. No car can resist the temptation. You ought to have one your side the county, Mike. They simply can't resist it.'

'Whew!' said Woodhouse. 'We're in for trouble. Don't you say a word —or Ollyett either! I'll pay the fines and we'll get it over as soon as possible. Where's Pallant?'

'At the back of the court somewhere,' said Ollyett. 'I saw him slip in just now.'

The fat man then took his seat on the Bench, of which he was chairman, and I gathered from a bystander that his name was Sir Thomas Ingell, Bart., M.P., of Ingell Park, Huckley. He began with an allocution pitched in a tone that would have justified revolt throughout empires. Evidence, when the crowded little court did not drown it with applause, was given in the pauses of the address. They were all very proud of their Sir Thomas, and looked from him to us, wondering why we did not applaud too.

Taking its time from the chairman, the Bench rollicked with us for seventeen minutes. Sir Thomas explained that he was sick and tired of processions of cads of our type, who would be better employed breaking stones on the road than in frightening horses worth more than themselves or their ancestors. This was after it had been proved that Woodhouse's man had turned on the horn purposely to annoy Sir Thomas, who 'happened to be riding by'! There were other remarks too—primitive enough,—but it was the unspeakable brutality of the tone, even more than the quality of the justice, or the laughter of the audience that stung our souls out of all reason. When we were dismissed—to the tune of twenty-three pounds, twelve shillings and sixpence—we waited for Pallant to join us, while we listened to the next case—one of driving without a licence. Ollyett, with an eye to his evening paper, had already taken very full notes of our own, but we did not wish to seem prejudiced.

'It's all right,' said the reporter of the local paper soothingly. 'We never report Sir Thomas *in extenso*. Only the fines and charges.'

'Oh, thank you,' Ollyett replied, and I heard him ask who every one in court might be. The local reporter was very communicative.

The new victim, a large, flaxen-haired man in somewhat striking clothes, to which Sir Thomas, now thoroughly warmed, drew public attention, said that he had left his licence at home. Sir Thomas asked him if he expected the police to go to his home address at Jerusalem to find it for him; and the court roared. Nor did Sir Thomas approve of the man's name, but insisted on calling him 'Mr. Masquerader,' and every time he did so, all his people shouted. Evidently this was their established *auto-da-fé*.

'He didn't summons me—because I'm in the House, I suppose. I think I shall have to ask a Question,' said Pallant, reappearing at the close of the case.

'I think *I* shall have to give it a little publicity too,' said Woodhouse. 'We can't have this kind of thing going on, you know.' His face was set and quite white. Pallant's, on the other hand, was black, and I know that my very stomach had turned with rage. Ollyett was dumb.

'Well, let's have lunch,' Woodhouse said at last. 'Then we can get away before the show breaks up.'

We drew Ollyett from the arms of the local reporter, crossed the Market Square to the Red Lion and found Sir Thomas's 'Mr. Masquerader' just sitting down to beer, beef and pickles.

'Ah!' said he, in a large voice. 'Companions in misfortune. Won't you gentlemen join me?'

'Delighted,' said Woodhouse. 'What did you get?'

'I haven't decided. It might make a good turn, but—the public aren't educated up to it yet. It's beyond 'em. If it wasn't, that red dub on the Bench would be worth fifty a week.'

'Where?' said Woodhouse. The man looked at him with unaffected surprise.

'At any one of My places,' he replied. 'But perhaps you live here?'

'Good heavens!' cried young Ollyett suddenly. 'You *are* Masquerier, then? I thought you were!'

'Bat Masquerier.' He let the words fall with the weight of an international ultimatum. 'Yes, that's all I am. But you have the advantage of me, gentlemen.'

For the moment, while we were introducing ourselves, I was puzzled. Then I recalled prismatic music-hall posters—of enormous acreage—that had been the unnoticed background of my visits to London for years past. Posters of men and women, singers, jongleurs, impersonators and audacities of every draped and undraped brand, all moved on and off in London and the Provinces by Bat Masquerier—with the long wedge-tailed flourish following the final 'r'.

'*I* knew you at once,' said Pallant, the trained M.P., and I promptly backed the lie. Woodhouse mumbled excuses. Bat Masquerier was not moved for or against us any more than the frontage of one of his own palaces.

'I always tell My people there's a limit to the size of the lettering,' he said. 'Overdo that and the ret'na doesn't take it in. Advertisin' is the most delicate of all the sciences.'

'There's one man in the world who is going to get a little of it if I live for the next twenty-four hours,' said Woodhouse, and explained how this would come about.

Masquerier stared at him lengthily with gun-metal-blue eyes.

'You mean it?' he drawled; the voice was as magnetic as the look.

'I *do,*' said Ollyett. 'That business of the horn alone ought to have him off the Bench in three months.' Masquerier looked at him even longer than he had looked at Woodhouse.

'He told *me,*' he said suddenly, 'that my home-address was Jerusalem. You heard that?'

'But it was the tone—the tone,' Ollyett cried.

'You noticed that, too, did you?' said Masquerier. 'That's the artistic temperament. You can do a lot with it. And I'm Bat Masquerier,' he went on. He dropped his chin in his fists and scowled straight in front of him. . . . 'I made the Silhouettes—I made the Trefoil and the Jocunda. I made 'Dal Benzaguen.' Here Ollyett sat straight up, for in common with the youth of that year he worshipped Miss Vidal Benzaguen of the Trefoil immensely and unreservedly. '"*Is* that a dressing-gown or an ulster you're supposed to be wearing?" You heard *that?* . . . "And I suppose you hadn't time to brush your hair either?" You heard *that?* . . . Now, you hear *me!*' His voice filled the coffee-room, then dropped to a whisper as dreadful as a surgeon's before an operation. He spoke for several minutes. Pallant muttered 'Hear! hear!' I saw Ollyett's eye flash—it was to Ollyett that Masquerier addressed himself chiefly,—and Woodhouse leaned forward with joined hands.

'Are you *with* me?' he went on, gathering us all up in one sweep of the arm. 'When I begin a thing I see it through, gentlemen. What Bat can't break, breaks him! But I haven't struck that thing yet. This is no one-turn turn-it-down show. This is business to the dead finish. Are you with me, gentlemen? Good! Now, we'll pool our assets. One London morning, and one provincial daily, didn't you say? One weekly commercial ditto and one M.P.'

'Not much use, I'm afraid,' Pallant smirked.

'But privileged. *But* privileged,' he returned. 'And we have also my little team—London, Blackburn, Liverpool, Leeds—I'll tell you about Manchester later—and Me! Bat Masquerier.' He breathed the name reverently into his tankard. 'Gentlemen, when our combination has finished with Sir Thomas Ingell, Bart., M.P., and everything else that is his, Sodom and Gomorrah will be a winsome bit of Merrie England beside 'em. I must go back to town now, but I trust you gentlemen will give me the pleasure of your company at dinner to-night at the Chop Suey—the Red Amber Room—and we'll block out the scenario.' He laid his hand on young Ollyett's shoulder and added: 'It's your brains I want.' Then he left, in a good deal of astrakhan collar and nickel-plated limousine, and the place felt less crowded.

We ordered our car a few minutes later. As Woodhouse, Ollyett and I were getting in, Sir Thomas Ingell, Bart., M.P., came out of the Hall of Justice across the square and mounted his horse. I have sometimes thought that if he had gone in silence he might even then have been saved, but as he settled himself in the saddle he caught sight of us and must needs shout: 'Not off yet? You'd better get away and you'd better be careful.' At that moment Pallant, who had been buying picture-postcards, came out of the inn, took Sir Thomas's eye and very leisurely entered the car. It seemed to me that for one instant there was a shade of uneasiness on the baronet's grey-whiskered face.

'I hope,' said Woodhouse after several miles, 'I hope he's a widower.'

'Yes,' said Pallant. 'For his poor, dear wife's sake I hope that, very much indeed. I suppose he didn't see me in Court. Oh, here's the parish history of Huckley written by the Rector and here's your share of the picture-postcards. Are we all dining with this Mr. Masquerier to-night?'

'Yes!' said we all.

If Woodhouse knew nothing of journalism, young Ollyett, who had graduated in a hard school, knew a good deal. Our halfpenny evening paper, which we will call *The Bun* to distinguish her from her prosperous morning sister, *The Cake,* was not only diseased but corrupt. We found this out when a man brought us the prospectus of a new oil-field and demanded sub-leaders on its prosperity. Ollyett talked pure Brasenose to him for three minutes. Otherwise he spoke and wrote trade-English—a toothsome amalgam of Americanisms and epigrams. But though the slang changes, the game never alters, and Ollyett and I and, in the end, some others enjoyed it immensely. It was weeks ere we could see the wood for the trees, but so soon as the staff realised that they had proprietors who backed them right or wrong, and specially when they were wrong (which is the sole secret of journalism), and that their fate did not hang on any passing owner's passing mood, they did miracles.

But we did not neglect Huckley. As Ollyett said our first care was to create an 'arresting atmosphere' round it. He used to visit the village of week-ends, on a motor-bicycle with a side-car; for which reason I left the actual place alone and dealt with it in the abstract. Yet it was I who drew first blood. Two inhabitants of Huckley wrote to contradict a small, quite solid paragraph in *The Bun* that a hoopoe had been seen at Huckley and had, 'of course, been shot by the local sportsmen.' There was some heat in their letters, both of which we published. Our version of how the hoopoe got his crest from King Solomon was, I grieve to say, so inaccurate that the Rector himself—no sportsman, as he pointed out, but a lover of accuracy—wrote to us to correct it. We gave his letter good space and thanked him.

'This priest is going to be useful,' said Ollyett. 'He has the impartial mind. I shall vitalise him.'

Forthwith he created M. L. Sigden, a recluse of refined tastes who in *The Bun* demanded to know whether this Huckley-of-the-Hoopoe was the Hugly of his boyhood and whether, by any chance, the fell change of name had been wrought by collusion between a local magnate and the railway, in the mistaken interests of spurious refinement. 'For I knew it and loved it with the maidens of my day—*eheu ab angulo!*—as Hugly,' wrote M. L. Sigden from Oxford.

Though other papers scoffed, *The Bun* was gravely sympathetic. Several people wrote to deny that Huckley had been changed at birth. Only the Rector—no philosopher, as he pointed out, but a lover of accuracy—had his doubts, which he laid publicly before Mr. M. L. Sigden, who suggested, through *The Bun,* that the little place might have begun life in Anglo-Saxon days as 'Hogslea' or among the Normans as 'Argilé,' on account of its much clay. The Rector had his own ideas too (he said it was mostly gravel), and M. L. Sigden had a fund of reminiscences. Oddly enough—which is seldom the case with free reading-matter—our subscribers rather relished the correspondence, and contemporaries quoted freely.

'The secret of power,' said Ollyett, 'is not the big stick. It's the liftable stick.' (This means the 'arresting' quotation of six or seven lines.) 'Did you see the *Spec.* had a middle on "Rural Tenacities" last week? That was all Huckley. I'm doing a "Mobiquity" on Huckley next week.'

Our 'Mobiquities' were Friday evening accounts of easy motor-bike-*cum*-side-car trips round London, illustrated (we could never get that machine to work properly) by smudgy maps. Ollyett wrote the stuff with a fervour and a delicacy which I always ascribed to the side-car. His account of Epping Forest, for instance, was simply young love with its soul at its lips. But his Huckley 'Mobiquity' would have sickened a soap-boiler. It chemically combined loathsome familiarity, leering suggestion, slimy piety and rancid 'social service' in one fuming compost that fairly lifted me off my feet.

'Yes,' said he, after compliments. 'It's the most vital, arresting and dynamic bit of tump I've done up to date. *Non nobis gloria!* I met Sir Thomas Ingell in his own park. He talked to me again. He inspired most of it.'

'Which? The "glutinous native drawl," or "the neglected adenoids of the village children"?' I demanded.

'Oh, no! That's only to bring in the panel doctor. It's the last flight we—I'm proudest of.'

This dealt with 'the crepuscular penumbra spreading her dim limbs over the boskage'; with 'jolly rabbits'; with a herd of 'gravid polled Angus'; and with the 'arresting, gipsy-like face of their swart, scholarly owner—as well known at the Royal Agricultural Shows as that of our late King-Emperor.'

'"Swart" is good and so's "gravid,"' said I, 'but the panel doctor will be annoyed about the adenoids.'

'Not half as much as Sir Thomas will about his face,' said Ollyett. 'And if you only knew what I've left out!'

He was right. The panel doctor spent his week-end (this is the advantage of Friday articles) in overwhelming us with a professional counterblast of no interest whatever to our subscribers. We told him so, and he, then and there, battered his way with it into the *Lancet* where they are keen on glands, and forgot us altogther. But Sir Thomas Ingell was of sterner stuff. He must have spent a happy week-end too. The letter which we received from him on Monday proved him to be a kinless loon of upright life, for no woman, however remotely interested in a man, would have let it pass the home wastepaper-basket. He objected to our references to his own herd, to his own labours in his own village, which he said was a Model Village, and to our infernal insolence; but he objected most to our invoice of his features. We wrote him courteously to ask whether the letter was meant for publication. He, remembering, I presume, the Duke of Wellington, wrote back, 'Publish and be damned.'

'Oh! This is too easy,' Ollyett said as he began heading the letter.

'Stop a minute,' I said. 'The game is getting a little beyond us. To-night's the Bat dinner.' (I may have forgotten to tell you that our dinner with Bat Masquerier in the Red Amber Room of the Chop Suey had come to be a weekly affair.) 'Hold it over till they've all seen it.'

'Perhaps you're right,' he said. 'You might waste it.'

At dinner, then, Sir Thomas's letter was handed round. Bat seemed to be thinking of other matters, but Pallant was very interested.

'I've got an idea,' he said presently. 'Could you put something into *The Bun* to-morrow about foot-and-mouth disease in that fellow's herd?'

'Oh, plague if you like,' Ollyett replied. 'They're only five measly Shorthorns. I saw one lying down in the park. She'll serve as a substratum of fact.'

'Then, do that; and hold the letter over meanwhile. I think *I* come in here,' said Pallant.

'Why?' said I.

'Because there's something coming up in the House about foot-and-mouth, and because he wrote me a letter after that little affair when he fined you. 'Took ten days to think it over. Here you are,' said Pallant. 'House of Commons paper, you see.'

We read:

DEAR PALLANT—Although in the past our paths have not lain much together, I am sure you will agree with me that on the floor of the House all members are on a footing of equality. I make bold, therefore, to approach you in a matter which I think capable of a very different interpretation from that which perhaps was put upon it by your friends. Will you let them know that that was the case and that I was in no way swayed by animus in the exercise of my magisterial duties, which as you, as a brother magistrate, can imagine are frequently very distasteful to—Yours very sincerely,

T. INGELL.

P.S.—I have seen to it that the motor vigilance to which your friends took exception has been considerably relaxed in my district.

'What did you answer?' said Ollyett, when all our opinions had been expressed.

'I told him I couldn't do anything in the matter. And I couldn't—then. But you'll remember to put in that foot-and-mouth paragraph. I want something to work upon.'

'It seems to me *The Bun* has done all the work up to date,' I suggested. 'When does *The Cake* come in?'

'The Cake,' said Woodhouse, and I remembered afterwards that he spoke like a Cabinet Minister on the eve of a Budget, 'reserves to itself the fullest right to deal with situations as they arise.'

'Ye-eh!' Bat Masquerier shook himself out of his thoughts. ' "Situations as they arise." I ain't idle either. But there's no use fishing till the swim's baited. You'—he turned to Ollyett—'manufacture very good ground-bait. . . . I always tell My people—— What the deuce is that?'

There was a burst of song from another private dining-room across the landing. 'It ees some ladies from the Trefoil,' the waiter began.

'Oh, I know that. What are they singing, though?'

He rose and went out, to be greeted by shouts of applause from that merry company. Then there was silence, such as one hears in the form-room after a master's entry. Then a voice that we loved began again: 'Here we go gathering nuts in May—nuts in May—nuts in May!'

'It's only 'Dal—and some nuts,' he explained when he returned. 'She says she's coming in to dessert.' He sat down, humming the old tune to himself, and till Miss Vidal Benzaguen entered, he held us speechless with tales of the artistic temperament.

We obeyed Pallant to the extent of slipping into *The Bun* a wary paragraph about cows lying down and dripping at the mouth, which might be read either as an unkind libel or, in the hands of a capable lawyer, as a piece of faithful nature-study.

'And besides,' said Ollyett, 'we allude to "gravid polled Angus." I am advised that no action can lie in respect of virgin Shorthorns. Pallant wants us to come to the House to-night. He's got us places for the Strangers' Gallery. I'm beginning to like Pallant.'

'Masquerier seems to like you,' I said.

'Yes, but I'm afraid of him,' Ollyett answered with perfect sincerity. 'I am. He's the Absolutely Amoral Soul. I've never met one yet.'

We went to the House together. It happened to be an Irish afternoon, and as soon as I had got the cries and the faces a little sorted out, I gathered there were grievances in the air, but how many of them was beyond me.

'It's all right,' said Ollyett of the trained ear. 'They've shut their ports against—oh yes—export of Irish cattle! Foot-and-mouth disease at Ballyhellion. *I* see Pallant's idea!'

The House was certainly all mouth for the moment, but, as I could feel, quite in earnest. A Minister with a piece of typewritten paper seemed to be fending off volleys of insults. He reminded me somehow of a nervous huntsman breaking up a fox in the face of rabid hounds.

'It's question-time. They're asking questions,' said Ollyett. 'Look! Pallant's up.'

There was no mistaking it. His voice, which his enemies said was his one parliamentary asset, silenced the hubbub as toothache silences mere singing in the ears. He said:

'Arising out of that, may I ask if any special consideration has recently been shown in regard to any suspected outbreak of this disease on *this* side of the Channel?'

He raised his hand; it held a noon edition of *The Bun*. We had thought it best to drop the paragraph out of the later ones. He would have continued, but something in a grey frock-coat roared and bounded on a bench opposite, and waved another *Bun*. It was Sir Thomas Ingell.

'As the owner of the herd so dastardly implicated——' His voice was drowned in shouts of 'Order!'—the Irish leading.

'What's wrong?' I asked Ollyett. 'He's got his hat on his head, hasn't he?'

'Yes, but his wrath should have been put as a question.'

'Arising out of that, Mr. Speaker, Sirrr!' Sir Thomas bellowed through a lull, 'are you aware that—that all this is a conspiracy—part of a dastardly conspiracy to make Huckley ridiculous—to make *us* ridiculous? Part of a deep-laid plot to make *me* ridiculous, Mr. Speaker, Sir!'

The man's face showed almost black against his white whiskers, and he struck out swimmingly with his arms. His vehemence puzzled and held the House for an instant, and the Speaker took advantage of it to lift his pack from Ireland to a new scent. He addressed Sir Thomas Ingell in tones of measured rebuke, meant also, I imagine, for the whole House, which lowered its hackles at the word. Then Pallant, shocked and pained: 'I can only express my profound surprise that in response to my simple question the honourable member should have thought fit to indulge in a personal attack. If I have in any way offended——'

Again the Speaker intervened, for it appeared that he regulated these matters.

He, too, expressed surprise, and Sir Thomas sat back in a hush of reprobation that seemed to have the chill of the centuries behind it. The Empire's work was resumed.

'Beautiful!' said I, and I felt hot and cold up my back.

'And now we'll publish his letter,' said Ollyett.

We did—on the heels of his carefully reported outburst. We made no comment. With that rare instinct for grasping the heart of a situation which is the mark of the Anglo-Saxon, all our contemporaries and, I should say, two-thirds of our correspondents demanded how such a person could be made more ridiculous than he had already proved himself to be. But beyond spelling his name 'Injle,' we alone refused to hit a man when he was down.

'There's no need,' said Ollyett. 'The whole Press is on the huckle from end to end.'

Even Woodhouse was a little astonished at the ease with which it had come about, and said as much.

'Rot!' said Ollyett. 'We haven't really begun. Huckley isn't news yet.'

'What do you mean?' said Woodhouse, who had grown to have great respect for his young but by no means distant connection.

'Mean? By the grace of God, Master Ridley, I mean to have it so that when Huckley turns over in its sleep, Reuters and the Press Association jump out of bed to cable.' Then he went off at score about certain restorations in Huckley Church which, he said—and he seemed to spend his every week-end there—had been perpetrated by the Rector's predecessor, who had abolished a 'leper-window' or a 'squinch-hole' (whatever these may be) to institute a lavatory in the vestry. It did not strike me as stuff for which Reuters or the Press Association would lose much sleep, and I left him declaiming to Woodhouse about a fourteenth-century font which, he said, he had unearthed in the sexton's tool-shed.

My methods were more on the lines of peaceful penetration. An odd copy, in *The Bun's* rag-and-bone library, of Hone's *Every-Day Book* had revealed to me the existence of a village dance founded, like all village dances, on Druidical mysteries connected with the Solar Solstice (which is always unchallengeable) and Midsummer Morning, which is dewy and refreshing to the London eye. For this I take no credit—Hone being a mine any one can work—but that I rechristened that dance, after I had revised it, 'The Gubby' is my title to immortal fame. It was still to be witnessed, I wrote, 'in all its poignant purity at Huckley, that last home of significant mediæval survivals'; and I fell so in love with my creation that I kept it back for days, enamelling and burnishing.

'You'd better put it in,' said Ollyett at last. 'It's time we asserted ourselves again. The other fellows are beginning to poach. You saw that thing in the *Pinnacle* about Sir Thomas's Model Village? He must have got one of their chaps down to do it.'

' 'Nothing like the wounds of a friend,' I said. 'That account of the non-alcoholic pub alone was——'

'I liked the bit best about the white-tiled laundry and the Fallen Virgins who wash Sir Thomas's dress shirts. Our side couldn't come within a mile of that, you know. We haven't the proper flair for sexual slobber.'

'That's what I'm always saying,' I retorted. 'Leave 'em alone. The other fellows are doing our work for us now. Besides I want to touch up my "Gubby Dance" a little more.'

'No. You'll spoil it. Let's shove it in to-day. For one thing it's Literature. I don't go in for compliments as you know, but, etc. etc.'

I had a healthy suspicion of young Ollyett in every aspect, but though I knew that I should have to pay for it, I fell to his flattery, and my priceless article on the 'Gubby Dance' appeared. Next Saturday he asked me to bring out *The Bun* in his absence, which I naturally assumed would be connected with the little maroon side-car. I was wrong.

On the following Monday I glanced at *The Cake* at breakfast-time to make sure, as usual, of her inferiority to my beloved but unremunerative *Bun*. I opened on a heading: 'The Village that Voted the Earth was Flat.' I read . . . I read that the Geoplanarian Society—a society devoted to the proposition that the earth is flat—had held its Annual

Banquet and Exercises at Huckley on Saturday, when after convincing addresses, amid scenes of the greatest enthusiasm, Huckley village had decided by an unanimous vote of 438 that the earth was flat. I do not remember that I breathed again till I had finished the two columns of description that followed. Only one man could have written them. They were flawless—crisp, nervous, austere yet human, poignant, vital, arresting—most distinctly arresting—dynamic enough to shift a city—and quotable by whole sticks at a time. And there was a leader, a grave and poised leader, which tore me in two with mirth, until I remembered that I had been left out—infamously and unjustifiably dropped. I went to Ollyett's rooms. He was breakfasting, and, to do him justice, looked conscience-stricken.

'It wasn't my fault,' he began. 'It was Bat Masquerier. I swear *I* would have asked you to come if——'

'Never mind that,' I said. 'It's the best bit of work you've ever done or will do. Did any of it happen?'

'Happen? Heavens! D'you think even *I* could have invented it?'

'Is it exclusive to *The Cake?*' I cried.

'It cost Bat Masquerier two thousand,' Ollyett replied. 'D'you think he'd let any one else in on that? But I give you my sacred word I knew nothing about it till he asked me to come down and cover it. He had Huckley posted in three colours, "The Geoplanarians' Annual Banquet and Exercises." Yes, he invented "Geoplanarians." He wanted Huckley to think it meant aeroplanes. Yes, I know that there is a real Society that thinks the world's flat—they ought to be grateful for the lift—but Bat made his own. He did! He created the whole show, I tell you. He swept out half his Halls for the job. Think of that—on a Saturday! They—we went down in motor char-à-bancs—three of 'em—one pink, one primrose, and one forget-me-not blue—twenty people in each one and "The Earth *is* Flat" on each side and across the back. I went with Teddy Rickets and Lafone from the Trefoil, and both the Silhouette Sisters, and—wait a minute!—the Crossleigh Trio. You know the Every-Day Dramas Trio at the Jocunda—Ada Crossleigh, "Bunt" Crossleigh, and little Victorine? Them. And there was Hoke Ramsden, the lightning-change chap in *Morgiana and Drexel*—and there was Billy Turpeen. Yes, you know him! The North London Star. "I'm the Referee that got himself disliked at Blackheath." *That* chap! And there was Mackaye—that one-eyed Scotch fellow that all Glasgow is crazy about. Talk of subordinating yourself for Art's sake! Mackaye was the earnest inquirer who got converted at the end of the meeting. And there was quite a lot of girls I didn't know, and—oh, yes—there was 'Dal! 'Dal Benzaguen herself! We sat together, going and coming. She's all the darling there ever was. She sent you her love, and she told me to tell you that she won't forget about Nellie Farren. She says you've given her an ideal to work for. She? Oh, she was the Lady Secretary to the Geoplanarians, of course. I forget who were in the other brakes—provincial stars mostly—but they played up gorgeously. The art of the music-hall's changed since your day. They didn't overdo it a bit. You see, people who believe the earth is flat don't dress quite like other people. You may have noticed that I hinted at that in my account. It's a rather flat-fronted Ionic style—neo-Victorian, except for the bustles, 'Dal told me,—but 'Dal looked heavenly in it! So did little Victorine. And there was a girl in the blue brake—she's a provincial—but she's coming to town this winter and she'll knock 'em—Winnie Deans. Remember that! She told Huckley how she had suffered for the Cause as a governess in a rich family where they believed that the world is round, and how she threw up her job sooner than teach immoral geography. That was at the overflow meeting outside the Baptist chapel. She knocked 'em to sawdust! We must look out for Winnie. . . . But Lafone! Lafone was beyond everything. Impact, personality—conviction—the whole bag o' tricks! He sweated conviction. Gad, he convinced *me* while he was speaking! (Him? He was President of the Geoplanarians, of course. Haven't you read my account?) It *is* an infernally plausible theory. After all, no one has actually proved the earth is round, have they?'

'Never mind the earth. What about Huckley?'

'Oh, Huckley got tight. That's the worst of these model villages if you let 'em smell fire-water. There's one alcoholic pub in the place that Sir Thomas can't get rid of. Bat made it his base. He sent down the banquet in two motor lorries—dinner for five hundred and drinks for ten thousand. Huckley voted all right. Don't you make any mistake about that. No vote, no dinner. A unanimous vote—exactly as I've said. At least, the Rector and the Doctor were the only dissentients. We didn't count them. Oh yes, Sir Thomas was there. He came and grinned at us through his park gates. He'll grin worse to-day. There's an aniline dye that you rub through a stencil-plate that eats about a foot into any stone and wears good to the last. Bat had both the lodge-gates stencilled "The Earth *is* flat!" and all the barns and walls they could get at. . . . Oh Lord, but Huckley was drunk! We had to fill 'em up to make 'em forgive us for not being aeroplanes. Unthankful yokels! D'you realise that Emperors couldn't have commanded the talent Bat decanted on 'em? Why, 'Dal alone was. . . . And by eight o'clock not even a bit of paper left! The whole show packed up and gone, and Huckley hoo-raying for the earth being flat.'

'Very good, I began. 'I am, as you know, a one-third proprietor of *The Bun.*'

'I didn't forget that,' Ollyett interrupted. 'That was uppermost in my mind all the time. I've got a special account for *The Bun* to-day—it's an idyll—and just to show how I thought of you, I told 'Dal, coming home, about your Gubby Dance, and she told Winnie. Winnie came back in our char-à-banc. After a bit we had to get out and dance it in a field. It's quite a dance the way we did it—and Lafone invented a sort of gorilla lockstep procession at the end. Bat had sent down a film-chap on the chance of getting something. He was the son of a clergyman—most dynamic personality. He said there isn't anything for the cinema in meetings *qua* meetings—they lack action. Films are a branch of art by themselves. But he went wild over the Gubby. He said it was like Peter's vision at Joppa. He took about a million feet of it. Then I photoed it exclusive for *The Bun*. I've sent 'em in already, only remember we must eliminate Winnie's left leg in the first figure. It's too arresting. . . . And there you are! But I tell you I'm afraid of Bat. That man's the Personal Devil. He did it all. He didn't even come down himself. He said he'd distract his people.'

'Why didn't he ask me to come?' I persisted.

'Because he said you'd distract me. He said he wanted my brains on ice. He got 'em. I believe it's the best thing I've ever done.' He reached for *The Cake* and re-read it luxuriously. 'Yes, out and away the best—supremely quotable,' he concluded, and—after another survey—'By God, what a genius I was yesterday!'

I would have been angry, but I had not the time. That morning, Press agencies grovelled to me in *The Bun* office for leave to use certain photos, which, they understood, I controlled, of a certain village dance. When I had sent the fifth man away on the edge of tears, my self-respect came back a little. Then there was *The Bun's* poster to get out. Art being elimination, I fined it down to two words (one too many, as it proved)—'The Gubby!' in red, at which our manager protested; but by five o'clock he told me that I was *the* Napoleon of Fleet Street. Ollyett's account in *The Bun* of the Geoplanarians' Exercises and Love Feast lacked the supreme shock of his version in *The Cake* but it bruised more; while the photos of 'The Gubby' (which, with Winnie's left leg, was why I had set the doubtful press to work so early) were beyond praise and next day, beyond price. But even then I did not understand.

A week later, I think it was, Bat Masquerier telephoned to me to come to the Trefoil.

'It's your turn now,' he said. 'I'm not asking Ollyett. Come to the stage-box.'

I went, and, as Bat's guest, was received as Royalty is not. We sat well back and looked out on the packed thousands. It was *Morgiana and Drexel,* that fluid and electric review which Bat—though he gave Lafone the credit—really created.

'Ye-es,' said Bat dreamily, after Morgiana had given 'the nasty jar' to the Forty Thieves in their forty oil 'combinations.' 'As you say, I've got 'em and I can hold 'em. What a man does doesn't matter much; and how he does it don't matter either. It's the *when*—the psychological moment. 'Press can't make up for it; money can't; brains can't. A lot's luck, but all the rest is genius. I'm not speaking about My people now. I'm talking of Myself.'

Then 'Dal—she was the only one who dared—knocked at the door and stood behind us all alive and panting as Morgiana. Lafone was carrying the police-court scene, and the house was ripped up crossways with laughter.

'Ah! Tell a fellow now,' she asked me for the twentieth time, 'did you love Nellie Farren when you were young?'

'Did we love her?' I answered. '"If the earth and the sky and the sea"—There were three million of us, 'Dal, and we worshipped her.'

'How did she get it across?' 'Dal went on.

'She was Nellie. The houses used to coo over her when she came on.'

'I've had a good deal, but I've never been cooed over yet,' said 'Dal wistfully.

'It isn't the how, it's the when,' Bat repeated. 'Ah!'

He leaned forward as the house began to rock and peal full-throatedly. 'Dal fled. A sinuous and silent procession was filing into the police-court to a scarcely audible accompaniment. It was dressed—but the world and all its picture-palaces know how it was dressed. It danced and it danced, and it danced the dance which bit all humanity in the leg for half a year, and it wound up with the lockstep finale that mowed the house down in swathes, sobbing and aching. Somebody in the gallery moaned, 'Oh Gord, the Gubby!' and we heard the word run like a shudder, for they had not a full breath left among them. Then

'Dal came on, an electric star in her dark hair, the diamonds flashing in her three-inch heels—a vision that made no sign for thirty counted seconds while the police-court scene dissolved behind her into Morgiana's Manicure Palace, and they recovered themselves. The star on her forehead went out, and a soft light bathed her as she took—slowly, slowly to the croon of adoring strings—the eighteen paces forward. We saw her first as a queen alone; next as a queen for the first time conscious of her subjects, and at the end, when her hands fluttered, as a woman delighted, awed not a little, but transfigured and illuminated with sheer, compelling affection and goodwill. I caught the broken mutter of welcome—the coo which is more than tornadoes of applause. It died and rose and died again lovingly.

'She's got it across,' Bat whispered. 'I've never seen her like this. I told her to light up the star, but I was wrong, and she knew it. She's an artist.'

' 'Dal, you darling!' some one spoke, not loudly but it carried through the house.

'Thank *you!*' 'Dal answered, and in that broken tone one heard the last fetter riveted. 'Good evening, boys! I've just come from—now—where the dooce was it I have come from?' She turned to the impassive files of the Gubby dancers, and went on: 'Ah, so good of you to remind me, you dear, bun-faced things. I've just come from the village—The Village that Voted the Earth was Flat.'

She swept into that song with the full orchestra. It devastated the habitable earth for the next six months. Imagine, then, what its rage and pulse must have been at the incandescent hour of its birth! She only gave the chorus once. At the end of the second verse, 'Are you *with* me, boys?' she cried, and the house tore it clean away from her—'*Earth* was flat—*Earth* was flat. Flat as my hat—Flatter than that'—drowning all but the bassoons and double-basses that marked the word.

'Wonderful,' I said to Bat. 'And it's only "Nuts in May" with variations.'

'Yes—but *I* did the variations,' he replied.

At the last verse she gestured to Carlini the conductor, who threw her up his baton. She caught it with a boy's ease. 'Are you *with* me?' she cried once more, and—the maddened house behind her—abolished all the instruments except the guttural belch of the double-basses on '*Earth*'—'*The* Village that voted the *Earth* was flat—*Earth* was flat!' It was delirium. Then she picked up the Gubby dancers and led them in a clattering improvised lockstep thrice round the stage till her last kick sent her diamond-hilted shoe catherine-wheeling to the electrolier.

I saw the forest of hands raised to catch it, heard the roaring and stamping pass through hurricanes to full typhoon; heard the song, pinned down by the faithful double-basses as the bull-dog pins down the bellowing bull, overbear even those; till at last the curtain fell and Bat took me round to her dressing-room, where she lay spent after her seventh call. Still the song, through all those white-washed walls, shook the reinforced concrete of the Trefoil as steam pile-drivers shake the flanks of a dock.

'I'm all out—first time in my life. Ah! Tell a fellow now, did I get it across?' she whispered huskily.

'You know you did,' I replied as she dipped her nose deep in a beaker of barley-water. 'They cooed over you.'

Bat nodded. 'And poor Nellie's dead—in Africa, ain't it?'

'I hope I'll die before they stop cooing,' said 'Dal.

' "*Earth* was flat—*Earth* was flat!" ' Now it was more like mine-pumps in flood.

'They'll have the house down if you don't take another,' some one called.

'Bless 'em!' said 'Dal, and went out for her eighth, when in the face of that cataract she said yawning, 'I don't know how *you* feel, children, but *I'm* dead. You be quiet.'

'Hold a minute,' said Bat to me. 'I've got to hear how it went in the provinces. Winnie Deans had it in Manchester, and Ramsden at Glasgow—and there are all the films too. I had rather a heavy week-end.'

The telephones presently reassured him.

'It'll do,' said he. 'And *he* said my home address was Jerusalem.' He left me humming the refrain of 'The Holy City.' Like Ollyett I found myself afraid of that man.

When I got out into the street and met the disgorging picture-palaces capering on the pavements and humming it (for he had put the gramophones on with the films), and when I saw far to the south the red electrics flash 'Gubby' across the Thames, I feared more than ever.

A few days passed which were like nothing except, perhaps, a suspense of fever in which the sick man perceives the searchlights of the world's assembled navies in act to converge on one minute fragment of wreckage—one only in all the black and agony-strewn sea. Then those beams focused themselves. Earth as we knew it—the full circuit of our orb—laid the weight of its impersonal and searing curiosity on this Huckley which had voted that it was flat. It asked for news about Huckley—where and what it might be, and how it talked—it knew how it danced—and how it thought in its wonderful soul. And then, in all the zealous, merciless press, Huckley was laid out for it to look at, as a drop of pond water is exposed on the sheet of a magic-lantern show. But Huckley's sheet was only coterminous with the use of type among mankind. For the precise moment that was necessary, Fate ruled it that there should be nothing of first importance in the world's idle eye. One atrocious murder, a political crisis, an incautious or heady continental statesman, the mere catarrh of a king, would have wiped out the significance of our message, as a passing cloud annuls the urgent helio. But it was halcyon weather in every respect. Ollyett and I did not need to lift our little fingers any more than the Alpine climber whose last sentence has unkeyed the arch of the avalanche. The thing roared and pulverised and swept beyond eyesight all by itself—all by itself. And once well away, the fall of kingdoms could not have diverted it.

Ours is, after all, a kindly earth. While The Song ran and raped it with the cataleptic kick of 'Ta-ra-ra-boom-de-ay,' multiplied by the West African significance of 'Everybody's doing it,' plus twice the infernal elementality of a certain tune in *Dona et Gamma;* when for all practical purposes, literary, dramatic, artistic, social, municipal, political, commercial, and administrative, the Earth *was* flat, the Rector of Huckley wrote to us—again as a lover of accuracy—to point out that the Huckley vote on 'the alleged flatness of this scene of our labours here below' was *not* unanimous; he and the doctor having voted against it. And the great Baron Reuter himself (I am sure it could have been none other) flashed that letter in full to the front, back, and both wings of this scene of our labours. For Huckley was News. *The Bun* also contributed a photograph which cost me some trouble to fake.

'We are a vital nation,' said Ollyet while we were discussing affairs at a Bat dinner. 'Only an Englishman could have written that letter at this present juncture.'

'It reminded me of a tourist in the Cave of the Winds under Niagara. Just one figure in a mackintosh. But perhaps you saw our photo?' I said proudly.

'Yes,' Bat replied. 'I've been to Niagara, too. And how's Huckley taking it?'

'They don't quite understand, of course,' said Ollyett. 'But it's bringing pots of money into the place. Ever since the motor-bus excursions were started——'

'I didn't know they had been,' said Pallant.

'Oh yes. Motor char-à-bancs—uniformed guides and key-bugles included. They're getting a bit fed up with the tune there nowadays,' Ollyett added.

'They play it under his windows, don't they?' Bat asked. 'He can't stop the right of way across his park.'

'He cannot,' Ollyett answered. 'By the way, Woodhouse, I've bought that font for you from the sexton. I paid fifteen pounds for it.'

'What am I supposed to do with it?' asked Woodhouse.

'You give it to the Victoria and Albert Museum. It is fourteenth-century work all right. You can trust me.'

'Is it worth it—now?' said Pallant. 'Not that I'm weakening, but merely as a matter of tactics?'

'But this is true,' said Ollyett. 'Besides, it is my hobby, I always wanted to be an architect. I'll attend to it myself. It's too serious for *The Bun* and miles too good for *The Cake*.'

He broke ground in a ponderous architectural weekly, which had never heard of Huckley. There was no passion in his statement, but mere fact backed by a wide range of authorities. He established beyond doubt that the old font at Huckley had been thrown out, on Sir Thomas's instigation, twenty years ago, to make room for a new one of Bath stone adorned with Limoges enamels; and that it had lain ever since in a corner of the sexton's shed. He proved, with learned men to support him, that there was only one other font in all England to compare with it. So Woodhouse bought it and presented it to a grateful South Kensington which said it would see the earth still flatter before it returned the treasure to purblind Huckley. Bishops by the benchful and most of the Royal Academy, not to mention 'Margaritas ante Porcos,' wrote fervently to the papers. *Punch* based a political cartoon on it; the *Times* a third leader, 'The Lust of Newness'; and the *Spectator* a scholarly and delightful middle, 'Village Hausmania.' The vast amused outside world said in all its tongues and types: 'Of course! This is just what Huckley would do!' And neither Sir Thomas nor the Rector nor the sexton nor any one else wrote to deny it.

'You see,' said Ollyett, 'this is much more of a blow to Huckley than it looks—because every word of it's true. Your Gubby Dance was inspiration, I admit, but it hadn't its roots in——'

'Two hemispheres and four continents so far,' I pointed out.

'Its roots in the hearts of Huckley was what I was going to say. Why don't you ever come down and look at the place? You've never seen it since we were stopped there.'

'I've only my week-ends free,' I said, 'and you seem to spend yours there pretty regularly—with the side-car. I was afraid——'

'Oh, *that's* all right,' he said cheerily. 'We're quite an old engaged couple now. As a matter of fact, it happened after the "gravid polled Angus" business. Come along this Saturday. Woodhouse says he'll run us down after lunch. He wants to see Huckley too.'

Pallant could not accompany us, but Bat took his place.

'It's odd,' said Bat, 'that none of us except Ollyett has ever set eyes on Huckley since that time. That's what I always tell My people. Local colour is all right after you've got your idea. Before that, it's a mere nuisance.' He regaled us on the way down with panoramic views of the success—geographical and financial—of 'The Gubby' and The Song.

'By the way,' said he, 'I've assigned 'Dal all the gramophone rights of "The Earth." She's a born artist. Hadn't sense enough to hit me for triple-dubs the morning after. She'd have taken it out in coos.'

'Bless her! And what'll she make out of the gramophone rights?' I asked.

'Lord knows!' he replied. 'I've made fifty-four thousand my little end of the business, and it's only just beginning. Hear *that!*'

A shell-pink motor-brake roared up behind us to the music on a key-bugle of 'The Village that Voted the Earth was Flat.' In a few minutes we overtook another, in natural wood, whose occupants were singing it through their noses.

'I don't know that agency. It must be Cook's,' said Ollyett. 'They *do* suffer.' We were never out of earshot of the tune the rest of the way to Huckley.

Though I knew it would be so, I was disappointed with the actual aspect of the spot we had—it is not too much to say—created in the face of the nations. The alcoholic pub; the village green; the Baptist chapel; the church; the sexton's shed; the Rectory whence the so-wonderful letters had come; Sir Thomas's park gate-pillars still violently declaring 'The Earth *is* flat,' were as mean, as average, as ordinary as the photograph of a room where a murder has been committed. Ollyett, who, of course, knew the place specially well, made the most of it to us. Bat, who had employed it as a back-cloth to one of his own dramas, dismissed it as a thing used and emptied, but Woodhouse expressed my feelings when he said: 'Is that all—after all we've done?'

'*I* know,' said Ollyett soothingly. ' "Like that strange song I heard

Apollo sing: When Ilion like a mist rose into towers." I've felt the same sometimes, though it has been Paradise for me. But they *do* suffer.'

The fourth brake in thirty minutes had just turned into Sir Thomas's park to tell the Hall that 'The *Earth* was flat'; a knot of obviously American tourists were kodaking his lodge gates; while the tea-shop opposite the lych-gate was full of people buying postcards of the old font as it had lain twenty years in the sexton's shed. We went to the alcoholic pub and congratulated the proprietor.

'It's bringin' money to the place,' said he. 'But in a sense you can buy money too dear. It isn't doin' us any good. People are laughin' at us. That's what they're doing. . . . Now, with regard to that Vote of ours you may have heard talk about. . . .'

'For Gorze sake, chuck that votin' business,' cried an elderly man at the door. 'Money-gettin' or no money-gettin', we're fed up with it.'

'Well, I do think,' said the publican, shifting his ground, 'I do think Sir Thomas might ha' managed better in some things.'

'He tole me,'—the elderly man shouldered his way to the bar—'he tole me twenty years ago to take an' lay that font in my tool-shed. He *tole* me so himself. An' now, after twenty years, me own wife makin' me out little better than the common 'angman!'

'That's the sexton,' the publican explained. 'His good lady sells the postcards—if you 'aven't got some. But we feel Sir Thomas might ha' done better.'

'What's he got to do with it?' said Woodhouse.

'There's nothin' we can trace 'ome to 'im in so many words, but we think he might 'ave saved us the font business. Now, in regard to that votin' business——'

'Chuck it! Oh, chuck it!' the sexton roared, 'or you'll 'ave me cuttin' my throat at cock-crow. 'Ere's another parcel of fun-makers!'

A motor-brake had pulled up at the door and a multitude of men and women immediately descended. We went out to look. They bore rolled banners, a reading-desk in three pieces, and, I specially noticed, a collapsible harmonium, such as is used on ships at sea.

'Salvation Army?' I said, though I saw no uniforms.

Two of them unfurled a banner between poles which bore the legend: 'The Earth *is* flat.' Woodhouse and I turned to Bat. He shook his head. 'No, no! Not me. . . . If I had only seen their costumes in advance!'

'Good Lord!' said Ollyett. 'It's the genuine Society!'

The company advanced on the green with the precision of people well broke to these movements. Scene-shifters could not have been quicker with the three-piece rostrum, nor stewards with the harmonium. Almost before its cross-legs had been kicked into their catches, certainly before the tourists by the lodge-gates had begun to move over, a woman sat down to it and struck up a hymn:

'Hear ther truth our tongues are telling,
  Spread ther light from shore to shore,
God hath given man a dwelling
  Flat and flat for evermore.

'When ther Primal Dark retreated,
  When ther deeps were undesigned,
He with rule and level meted
  Habitation for mankind!'

I saw sick envy on Bat's face. 'Curse Nature,' he muttered. 'She gets ahead of you every time. To think *I* forgot hymns and a harmonium!'

Then came the chorus:

'Hear ther truth our tongues are telling,
  Spread ther light from shore to shore—
Oh, be faithful! Oh, be truthful!
  Earth is flat for evermore.'

They sang several verses with the fervour of Christians awaiting their lions. Then there were growlings in the air. The sexton, embraced by the landlord, two-stepped out of the pub-door. Each was trying to outroar the other. 'Apologising in advarnce for what he says,' the landlord shouted, 'you'd better go away' (here the sexton began to speak words). 'This isn't the time nor yet the place for—for any more o' this chat.'

The crowd thickened. I saw the village police-sergeant come out of his cottage buckling his belt.

'But surely,' said the woman at the harmonium, 'there must be some mistake. We are not suffragettes.'

'Damn it! They'd be a change,' cried the sexton. 'You get out of this! Don't talk! *I* can't stand it for one! Get right out, or we'll font you!'

The crowd which was being recruited from every house in sight echoed the invitation. The sergeant pushed forward. A man beside the reading-desk said: 'But surely we are among dear friends and sympathisers. Listen to me for a moment.'

It was the moment that a passing char-à-banc chose to strike into The Song. The effect was instantaneous. Bat, Ollyett, and I, who by divers roads have learned the psychology of crowds, retreated towards the tavern door. Woodhouse, the newspaper proprietor, anxious, I presume, to keep touch with the public, dived into the thick of it. Every one else told the Society to go away at once. When the lady at the harmonium (I began to understand why it is sometimes necessary to kill women) pointed at the stencilled park pillars and called them 'the cromlechs of our common faith,' there was a snarl and a rush. The police-sergeant checked it, but advised the Society to keep on going. The Society withdrew into the brake fighting, as it were, a rearguard action of oratory up each step. The collapsed harmonium was hauled in last, and with the perfect unreason of crowds, they cheered it loudly till the chauffeur slipped in his clutch and sped away. Then the crowd broke up, congratulating all concerned except the sexton, who was held to have disgraced his office by having sworn at ladies. We strolled across the green towards Woodhouse, who was talking to the police-sergeant near the park-gates. We were not twenty yards from him when we saw Sir Thomas Ingell emerge from the lodge and rush furiously at Woodhouse with an uplifted stick, at the same time shrieking: 'I'll teach you to laugh, you——' but Ollyett has the record of the language. By the time we reached them, Sir Thomas was on the ground; Woodhouse, very white, held the walking-stick and was saying to the sergeant:

'I give this person in charge for assault.'

'But, good Lord!' said the sergeant, whiter than Woodhouse. 'It's Sir Thomas.'

'Whoever it is, it isn't fit to be at large,' said Woodhouse. The crowd suspecting something wrong began to reassemble, and all the English horror of a row in public moved us, headed by the sergeant, inside the lodge. We shut both park-gates and lodge-door.

'You saw the assault, sergeant,' Woodhouse went on. 'You can testify I used no more force than was necessary to protect myself. You can testify that I have not even damaged this person's property. (Here! take your stick, you!) You heard the filthy language he used.'

'I–I can't say I did,' the sergeant stammered.

'Oh, but *we* did!' said Ollyett, and repeated it, to the apron-veiled horror of the lodge-keeper's wife.

Sir Thomas on a hard kitchen chair began to talk. He said he had 'stood enough of being photographed like a wild beast,' and expressed loud regret that he had not killed 'that man,' who was 'conspiring with the sergeant to laugh at him.'

''Ad you ever seen 'im before, Sir Thomas?' the sergeant asked.

'No! But it's time an example was made here. I've never seen the sweep in my life.'

I think it was Bat Masquerier's magnetic eye that recalled the past to him, for his face changed and his jaw dropped. 'But I have!' he groaned. 'I remember now.'

Here a writhing man entered by the back door. He was, he said, the village solicitor. I do not assert that he licked Woodhouse's boots, but we should have respected him more if he had and been done with it. His notion was that the matter could be accommodated, arranged and compromised for gold, and yet more gold. The sergeant thought so too. Woodhouse undeceived them both. To the sergeant he said, 'Will you or will you not enter the charge?' To the village solicitor he gave the name of his lawyers, at which the man wrung his hands and cried, 'Oh, Sir T., Sir T.!' in a miserable falsetto, for it was a Bat Masquerier of a firm. They conferred together in tragic whispers.

'I don't dive after Dickens,' said Ollyett to Bat and me by the window, 'but every time *I* get into a row I notice the police-court always fills up with his characters.'

'I've noticed that too,' said Bat. 'But the odd thing is you mustn't give the public straight Dickens—not in My business. I wonder why that is.'

Then Sir Thomas got his second wind and cursed the day that he, or it may have been we, were born. I feared that though he was a Radical he might apologise and, since he was an M.P., might lie his way out of the difficulty. But he was utterly and truthfully beside himself. He asked foolish questions—such as what we were doing in the village at all, and how much blackmail Woodhouse expected to make out of him. But neither Woodhouse nor the sergeant nor the writhing solicitor listened. The upshot of their talk, in the chimney-corner, was that Sir Thomas stood engaged to appear next Monday before his brother magistrates on charges of assault, disorderly conduct, and language calculated, etc. Ollyett was specially careful about the language.

Then we left. The village looked very pretty in the late light—pretty and tuneful as a nest of nightingales.

'You'll turn up on Monday, I hope,' said Woodhouse, when we reached town. That was his only allusion to the affair.

So we turned up—through a world still singing that the Earth was flat—at the little clay-coloured market-town with the large Corn Exchange and the small Jubilee memorial. We had some difficulty in getting seats in the court. Woodhouse's imported London lawyer was a man of commanding personality, with a voice trained to convey blasting imputations by tone. When the case was called, he rose and stated his client's intention not to proceed with the charge. His client, he went on to say, had not entertained, and, of course, in the circumstances could not have entertained, any suggestion of accepting on behalf of public charities any moneys that might have been offered to him on the part of Sir Thomas's estate. At the same time, no one acknowledged more sincerely than his client the spirit in which those offers had been made by those entitled to make them. But, as a matter of fact—here he became the man of the world colloguing with his equals—certain—er—details had come to his client's knowledge *since* the lamentable outburst, which . . . He shrugged his shoulders. Nothing was served by going into them, but he ventured to say that, had those painful circumstances only been known earlier, his client would—again 'of course'—never have dreamed—— A gesture concluded the sentence, and the ensnared Bench looked at Sir Thomas with new and withdrawing eyes. Frankly, as they could see, it would be nothing less than cruelty to proceed further with this—er—unfortunate affair. He asked leave, therefore, to withdraw the charge *in toto,* and at the same time to express his client's deepest sympathy with all who had been in any way distressed, as his client had been, by the fact and the publicity of proceedings which he could, of course, again assure them that his client would never have dreamed of instituting if, as he hoped he had made plain, certain facts had been before his client at the time when . . . But he had said enough. For his fee it seemed to me that he had.

Heaven inspired Sir Thomas's lawyer—all of a sweat lest his client's language should come out—to rise up and thank him. Then, Sir Thomas —not yet aware what leprosy had been laid upon him, but grateful to escape on any terms—followed suit. He was heard in interested silence, and people drew back a pace as Gehazi passed forth.

'You hit hard,' said Bat to Woodhouse afterwards. 'His own people think he's mad.'

'You don't say so? I'll show you some of his letters to-night at dinner,' he replied.

He brought them to the Red Amber Room of the Chop Suey. We forgot to be amazed, as till then we had been amazed, over the Song or 'The Gubby,' or the full tide of Fate that seemed to run only for our sakes. It did not even interest Ollyett that the verb 'to huckle' had passed into the English leader-writers' language. We were studying the interior of a soul, flash-lighted to its grimiest corners by the dread of 'losing its position.'

'And then it thanked you, didn't it, for dropping the case?' said Pallant.

'Yes, and it sent me a telegram to confirm.' Woodhouse turned to Bat. 'Now d'you think I hit too hard?' he asked.

'No–o!' said Bat. 'After all–I'm talking of every one's business now–one can't ever do anything in Art that comes up to Nature in any game in life. Just think how this thing has——'

'Just let me run through that little case of yours again,' said Pallant, and picked up *The Bun* which had it set out in full.

'Any chance of 'Dal looking in on us to-night?' Ollyett began.

'She's occupied with her Art too,' Bat answered bitterly. 'What's the use of Art? Tell me, some one!' A barrel-organ outside promptly pointed out that the *Earth* was flat. 'The gramophone's killing street organs, but I let loose a hundred-and-seventy-four of those hurdygurdys twelve hours after The Song,' said Bat. 'Not counting the Provinces.' His face brightened a little.

'Look here!' said Pallant over the paper. 'I don't suppose you or those asinine J.P.'s knew it–but your lawyer ought to have known that you've all put your foot in it most confoundedly over this assault case.'

'What's the matter?' said Woodhouse.

'It's ludicrous. It's insane. There isn't two penn'orth of legality in the whole thing. Of course, you could have withdrawn the charge, but the way you went about it is childish–besides being illegal. What on earth was the Chief Constable thinking of?'

'Oh, he was a friend of Sir Thomas's. They all were for that matter,' I replied.

'He ought to be hanged. So ought the Chairman of the Bench. I'm talking as a lawyer now.'

'Why, what have we been guilty of? Misprision of treason or compounding a felony–or what?' said Ollyett.

'I'll tell you later.' Pallant went back to the paper with knitted brows, smiling unpleasantly from time to time. At last he laughed.

'Thank you!' he said to Woodhouse. 'It ought to be pretty useful–for us.'

'What d'you mean?' said Ollyett.

'For our side. They are all Rads who are mixed up in this–from the Chief Constable down. There must be a Question. There must be a Question.'

'Yes, but I wanted the charge withdrawn in my own way,' Woodhouse insisted.

'That's nothing to do with the case. It's the legality of your silly methods. You wouldn't understand if I talked till morning.' He began to pace the room, his hands behind him. 'I wonder if I can get it through our Whip's thick head that it's a chance. . . . That comes of stuffing the Bench with Radical tinkers,' he muttered.

'Oh, sit down!' said Woodhouse.

'Where's your lawyer to be found now?' he jerked out.

'At the Trefoil,' said Bat promptly. 'I gave him the stage-box for to-night. He's an artist too.'

'Then I'm going to see him,' said Pallant. 'Properly handled this ought to be a godsend for our side.' He withdrew without apology.

'Certainly, this thing keeps on opening up, and up,' I remarked inanely.

'It's beyond me!' said Bat. 'I don't think if I'd known I'd have ever . . . Yes, I would, though. He said my home address was——'

'It was his tone—his tone!' Ollyett almost shouted. Woodhouse said nothing, but his face whitened as he brooded.

'Well, anyway,' Bat went on, 'I'm glad I always believed in God and Providence and all those things. Else I should lose my nerve. We've put it over the whole world—the full extent of the geographical globe. We couldn't stop it if we wanted to now. It's got to burn itself out. I'm not in charge any more. What'd you expect'll happen next. Angels?'

I expected nothing. Nothing that I expected approached what I got. Politics are not my concern, but, for the moment, since it seemed that they were going to 'huckle' with the rest, I took an interest in them. They impressed me as a dog's life without a dog's decencies, and I was confirmed in this when an unshaven and unwashen Pallant called on me at ten o'clock one morning, begging for a bath and a couch.

'Bail too?' I asked. He was in evening dress and his eyes were sunk feet in his head.

'No,' he said hoarsely. 'All night sitting. Fifteen divisions. 'Nother to-night. Your place was nearer than mine, so——' He began to undress in the hall.

When he awoke at one o'clock he gave me lurid accounts of what he said was history, but which was obviously collective hysteria. There had been a political crisis. He and his fellow M.P.'s had 'done things'—I never quite got at the things—for eighteen hours on end, and the pitiless Whips were even then at the telephones to herd 'em up to another dog-fight. So he snorted and grew hot all over again while he might have been resting.

'I'm going to pitch in my question about that miscarriage of justice at Huckley this afternoon, if you care to listen to it,' he said. 'It'll be absolutely thrown away—in our present state. I told 'em so; but it's my only chance for weeks. P'raps Woodhouse would like to come.'

'I'm sure he would. Anything to do with Huckley interests us,' I said.

'It'll miss fire, I'm afraid. Both sides are absolutely cooked. The present situation has been working up for some time. You see, the row was bound to come, etc. etc.,' and he flew off the handle once more.

I telephoned to Woodhouse, and we went to the House together. It was a dull, sticky afternoon with thunder in the air. For some reason or other, each side was determined to prove its virtue and endurance to the utmost. I heard men snarling about it all round me. 'If they won't spare us, we'll show 'em no mercy.' 'Break the brutes up from the start. They can't stand late hours.' 'Come on! No shirking! I know *you*'ve had a Turkish bath,' were some of the sentences I caught on our way. The House was packed already, and one could feel the negative electricity of a jaded crowd wrenching at one's own nerves, and depressing the afternoon soul.

'This is bad!' Woodhouse whispered. 'There'll be a row before they've finished. Look at the Front Benches!' And he pointed out little personal signs by which I was to know that each man was on edge. He might have spared himself. The House was ready to snap before a bone had been thrown. A sullen Minister rose to reply to a staccato question. His supporters cheered defiantly. 'None o' that! None o' that!' came from the Back Benches. I saw the Speaker's face stiffen like the face of a helmsman as he humours a hard-mouthed yacht after a sudden following sea. The trouble was barely met in time. There came a fresh, apparently causeless gust a few minutes later—savage, threatening, but futile. It died out—one could hear the sigh—in sudden wrathful realisation of the dreary hours ahead, and the ship of state drifted on.

Then Pallant—and the raw House winced at the torture of his voice—rose. It was a twenty-line question, studded with legal technicalities. The gist of it was that he wished to know whether the appropriate Minister was aware that there had been a grave miscarriage of justice on such and such a date, at such and such a place, before such and such justices of the peace, in regard to a case which arose——

I heard one desperate, weary 'damn!' float up from the pit of that torment. Pallant sawed on—'out of certain events which occurred at the village of Huckley.'

The House came to attention with a parting of the lips like a hiccough, and it flashed through my mind. . . . Pallant repeated, 'Huckley. The village——'

'That voted the *Earth* was flat.' A single voice from a back bench sang it once like a lone frog in a far pool.

'*Earth* was flat,' croaked another voice opposite.

'*Earth* was flat.' There were several. Then several more.

It was, you understand, the collective, over-strained nerve of the House, snapping, strand by strand, to various notes, as the hawser parts from its moorings.

'The Village that voted the *Earth* was flat.' The tune was beginning to shape itself. More voices were raised and feet began to beat time. Even so it did not occur to me that the thing would——

'The Village that voted the *Earth* was flat!' It was easier now to see who were not singing. There were still a few. Of a sudden (and this proves the fundamental instability of the cross-bench mind) a cross-bencher leaped on his seat and there played an imaginary double-bass with tremendous maestro-like wagglings of the elbow.

The last strand parted. The ship of state drifted out helpless on the rocking tide of melody.

'The Village that voted the *Earth* was flat!
The Village that voted the *Earth* was flat!'

The Irish first conceived the idea of using their order-papers as funnels wherewith to reach the correct '*vroom–vroom*' on '*Earth.*' Labour, always conservative and respectable at a crisis, stood out longer than any other section, but when it came in it was howling syndicalism. Then, without distinction of Party, fear of constituents, desire for office, or hope of emolument, the House sang at the tops and at the bottoms of their voices, swaying their stale bodies and epileptically beating with their swelled feet. They sang 'The Village that voted the *Earth* was flat': first, because they wanted to, and secondly–which is the terror of that song–because they could not stop. For no consideration could they stop.

Pallant was still standing up. Some one pointed at him and they laughed. Others began to point, lunging, as it were, in time with the tune. At this moment two persons came in practically abreast from behind the Speaker's chair, and halted appalled. One happened to be the Prime Minister and the other a messenger. The House, with tears running down their cheeks, transferred their attention to the paralysed couple. They pointed six hundred forefingers at them. They rocked, they waved, and they rolled while they pointed, but still they sang. When they weakened for an instant, Ireland would yell: 'Are ye *with* me, bhoys?' and they all renewed their strength like Antaeus. No man could say afterwards what happened to the Press or the Strangers' Gallery. It was the House, the hysterical and abandoned House of Commons, that held all eyes, as it deafened all ears. I saw both Front Benches bend forward, some with their foreheads on their dispatch-boxes, the rest with their faces in their hands; and their moving shoulders jolted the House out of its last rag of decency. Only the Speaker remained unmoved. The entire Press of Great Britain bore witness next day that he had not even bowed his head. The Angel of the Constitution, for vain was the help of man, foretold him the exact moment at which the House would have broken into 'The Gubby.' He is reported to have said: 'I heard the Irish beginning to shuffle it. So I adjourned.' Pallant's version is that he added: 'And I was never so grateful to a private member in all my life as I was to Mr. Pallant.'

He made no explanation. He did not refer to orders or disorders. He simply adjourned the House till six that evening. And the House adjourned—some of it nearly on all fours.

I was not correct when I said that the Speaker was the only man who did not laugh. Woodhouse was beside me all the time. His face was set and quite white—as white, they told me, as Sir Thomas Ingell's when he went, by request, to a private interview with his Chief Whip.